I0580859

PRAISE FOR *THE HERO GENE*

"What a ride! Very enjoyable. Congratulations on creating a likeable climate change superhero."
Tom Flood, Miles Franklin award-winning author

"This is an important book for these challenging times, especially for young people. We all need to activate our Hero Gene to create a world where we are living in harmony with each other and our environment."
Sue Lennox, 2020 NSW Senior Australian of the year and OzGREEN Co-Founder

"Action, adventure, and real danger chase Sam, the young hero of this fast-paced thriller, across continents, oceans, and even undersea as he tries to stop an alien force from warming Earth's oceans and destroying the planet. But there is so much more. Take a deep breath, dive in, and you'll see!"
Lesley Dahl, editor @ Zizzle Literary and author of *The Problem with Paradise*

"I wasn't expecting to enjoy it, but I must admit The Hero Gene had me hooked from the start. The futuristic setting, action and adventure, and a deep connection to nature make for a fantastic experience. A brilliant read."
Mali Doyle, 15-year-old student (My son and harshest critic)

"This page-turner will take your mind from reality into a world full of new possibilities.
Reader's Favourite Review

THE HERO GENE

STEVEN J DOYLE

For those who answer the call to adventure, especially our young heroes, fighting to create a brighter future for nature and humanity.

1

CLIMATE CHANGE HASN'T KILLED ME YET

The year 2032 – Planet Earth

As I aimed from behind a rocky rift, I had no idea that this was to be the last day of life as I knew it. Two drones rocketed across the sky toward me. My finger quivered on the trigger. White light burst from my assault blaster. Blinding explosions engulfed the drones. Blue sky turned red with fury. I ducked as flaming debris slammed into the rocks around me.

"Watch my back," I called.

Behind me, the tak-tak-tak of rapid blast fire masked end-of-life groans.

"Blitzed them!" Tom shouted.

"Ground troops ahead!" I took shelter against a jagged boulder, ignited an energy blade, and ran.

Rocky sand crunched with each footfall. Blast fire streaked toward me and flared against my blade as I blocked the blasts and scurried into a canyon.

"Damn." Tom limped into the towering formation behind me. "I've taken a hit, Sam. I can't run. I'll cover you."

"Above!" I warned.

Troopers with dark red helmets leapt from the rim. Tom fired high. Dust flew as two troopers thudded into the ground.

I readied my blade and sighted my blaster at the entrance. A squad of troopers rushed the jagged canyon. I deflected blasts with my blade, sliced an attacker, and blasted three others.

"Almost there," Tom called.

A rectangular patch of light appeared in the floor as the loft hatch opened. I spun around. Swathi emerged from the hatch, a holographic rock projecting over her white smile and curly black hair.

"Get out you idiot!" Tom shouted.

Swathi's smile turned into a frown.

"Take it easy on Swathi, Tom," I said.

An enemy blade sliced me. A blast ended Tom, and he threw his blaster on the sofa.

Swathi shook her head and glared at me. "Your dad said it's time to leave and you should save your energy for football."

TERMINATED flashed red and black across the holographic sky.

"Continue Hero-G Challenge or Start New Mission?" Repeated the controller.

Swathi left the hatch open. I listened to her climb down the steps as I removed my mask and stepped over to the H-Verse controller.

"Let's fight through this section," Tom said. "Hero-G day is next week. We need to practice for the tournament."

I wanted to continue playing, but I pressed the button and the rugged desert landscape evaporated into shabby carpet and the spider webs that hung from the loft's grey timber rafters.

"We're playing Hawks. Everyone thinks they'll win the Sunday League, but we have a good team, Bridge can beat them," I said.

The drab loft drained my energy. Craving the sun, I trudged to the shuttered window.

"Swathi's so annoying," Tom moaned. "Everyone thinks she's your girlfriend. You should lose her, Sam."

"You know she's like my little sister." I knew Tom was still angry at Swathi for interrupting the game. "She just dropped around to get a lift to the football." Swathi was fourteen, two years younger than me. Although we weren't related, Swathi and her mum were like family. My mum had died giving birth to me. Apart from my dad, I have no other family.

Swathi's mass of curly dark hair and vibrant emerald eyes are striking. She's tall for her age and does Taekwondo. Tom has a smaller, slim frame. If he ever pushed Swathi too far and she lashed out, I don't think Tom would stand a chance.

I hoisted the shutter. True to the forecast, the sky was grey and gloomy. I absorbed the weak solar radiation filtering through the window and cursed the weird affliction that left me dependent on the sun for strength. Holographic light sustained me for an hour's gaming, but more than sleep and food combined, it was the sun that gave me energy. Today was an important match. Half my school would be there. With no sun, I'd struggle to run, and if the clouds darkened, I wouldn't be able to play.

"Better go." I removed my body armour. I was wearing a t-shirt and jeans underneath and descended the ladder into the upstairs hall. Once Tom was down, I folded the ladder back into the ceiling and entered my bedroom. After checking that my shorts, boots, and shin guards were in my bag, I put my football socks on and plodded downstairs.

"We almost reached our highest score," Tom grumbled, glaring at Swathi, as we donned jackets in the alcove by the stairs. It annoyed me the way Tom spoke down to Swathi, but I didn't want to start an argument right then.

Dr Russell Edwards, my dad and England's most outspoken climate scientist, strode out of his study with his phone to his ear. Tom, Swathi, and I made way as he marched past, gesturing for us to follow him through the kitchen to the rear courtyard.

Neighboring terrace houses pressed in above our tiny yard. Dad's vertical vegetable garden was crammed with weeds and smelled of wet soil. Drizzle pricked a shallow puddle covering the mossy pavers, and mist rose from our breath as we paraded into the weather-beaten garage.

Shelves crammed with diving gear and plastic tubs full of books, files, and scientific equipment occupied one wall. There was barely enough room for Dad's sports car.

"Don't scrape the doors," Dad said as he uncoupled the charger of his carbon-composite 1964 Aston Martin replica. Tom and I squeezed into the rear. Swathi sat in front.

"*Mazu,* take us to Bridge Football Park," Dad said.

"Autopilot engaged. Confirm destination, Bridge Football Park," replied the car.

"Confirmed. Let's go, *Mazu.*" The car reversed into the alley, drove forward into the lane and turned right past our corner terrace. When my dad finished his phone call, he made another, speaking loudly. Tom mimicked him.

I shook my head, wishing Tom would stop, and stared out the window as my dad glanced into the rear vision mirror. I was interested in Dad's work and focused my hearing to listen to both sides of his conversation about undersea eruptions superheating the ocean and the urgency to secure more research funding. Dad's voice dominated the drive until we neared the football field.

"Sorry," Dad said. "Undersea eruptions have triggered another dramatic warming event in the Tonga Trench. The eruptions keep spreading along the Trench in a strange but predictable pattern. Intense heat is gushing into the ocean through multitudes of newly formed hydrothermal vents. If it doesn't stop spreading, life as we know it is in grave danger."

Tom flicked back his messy brown hair. His sparkling hazel eyes and cheeky grin put me on edge. "Dr Edwards, England is so cold. We could benefit from some global warming," he said.

I cringed. My dad shook his head, and Swathi swallowed the bait.

"You're pathetic, Tom," Swathi said. "We need to support Dr Edwards. And if us kids didn't make adults reduce carbon emissions, we'd be gripped by catastrophic climate change. All around the world, fires and storms have been so severe, but if us kids didn't act, countless more animals, homes, and ecosystems would have perished."

Tom gave Swathi a cheesy look and was about to hit back, but I nudged him, pleading with him to stop.

Swathi shook her head and turned to my dad. "Dr Edwards, did I tell you I won a scholarship to work with Youth Leading the World in Australia next year?"

"Sam told me. Congratulations, Swathi. And you're right, if you kids don't continue to pressure adults to reduce carbon emissions, the planet will get hotter, sea levels will rise quicker, and storms and wildfires will be more frequent and destructive. Let me know if there's anything I can do to help, Swathi."

My dad took the wheel and turned into the car park, but instead of parking, he pulled up at the admission gate and turned to me with a thin smile. "I have to go to the university to check the data from Tonga and make a few calls. I'll be back for kick-off."

Feeling cast adrift, I watched him drive away from the car park. Gravel popped and crunched under the tyres. *What a load of bollocks. Kick-off was in forty minutes.* Both Dad and I knew he would be lucky to make it back for the end of the match.

When I turned toward the gate, my heart leapt. Sonia Williams strolled towards the entrance—with Striker, my teammate and nemesis, right beside her. Sonia was sweet and beautiful, and I didn't like seeing her anywhere near that grub.

"Hi, Sam," Sonia said.

Her blonde hair and warm smile dazzled me. "Hi … Sonia." Along with every other boy in my year, I had a crush on Sonia. There was so much I wanted to say, but I just stood there like an idiot.

Striker smirked. "The weather is crap, Edwards. You should've stayed home."

Tom was waiting near the gate. "Well, Striker, you better pull your finger out and score a goal for a change."

The space around Sonia glowed pure and bright. Striker was a dark blemish beside her. I hoped she wasn't going out with him. Maybe she'd just bumped into him on the way...

Sonia smiled at Swathi. I remembered what Tom had said about everyone thinking Swathi was my girlfriend. Heat rushed to my face.

"Are you coming to the after-match party, Sam?" Sonia asked.

My eyes lit up. Everyone stared at me. I felt my face turning bright red. Was Sonia hoping to see me at the party? Although we'd never spoken much, I was pretty sure she liked me. While I was thinking of something to say, Striker cut in.

"Ha-ha!" Striker laughed. "No need to blush, Sam. We all know your daddy will tuck you into bed as soon as it gets dark."

Desolation pounded inside my chest. Soon after the sun goes down, I fall asleep, and my dad often has to carry me to bed. It would be dark by the time the party started. I was desperate to hit back with some clever words, but the power of speech deserted me.

2

THE GAME

The grass was soggy beneath my boots and icy drafts tugged my umbrella as I sat on a plastic seat. My coach and our subs stood either side of me. Supporters wearing red, grey, or black coats crammed the touchline to either side of us. It was the under sixteen's local derby. Hawks always beat us. With five minutes to go and the score nil each, I begged for the sun to pierce the drizzle and mist.

A bearded kid, Hawks' biggest player, barged forward, dwarfing my team. He was like a grown man and didn't look right playing schoolboy football. Coach Elkins stomped his feet and called out to our team, "Take him on, Bridge. Ball. Get the ball!"

Desperate shouts rang from the crowd. I clenched my teeth as Tom charged the bearded giant. At the last second the bearded kid swerved left, colliding into Tom.

Crunch! The bearded kid's shoulder smashed into Tom's nose. Blood spurted and mud sprayed as Tom crashed to the ground. The bearded kid stepped right and struck the ball, spraying it wide of our keeper, stretching the net.

"Penalty!" yelled our supporters.

Clutching my nose as though I'd been the one to take the hit, I stood up from my chair, hoping Tom was okay. Old Harry, our coach's assistant, grabbed the water and ran to Tom.

The ref put the whistle to his mouth and blew for a goal.

"Penalty! No way he's sixteen!" bellowed our supporters. My team rushed the referee, shouting protests. Coach Elkins stormed onto the pitch; the linesman demanded he step back. Coach Elkins threw his hands in the air. "It's not a goal! It's a penalty!" he shouted.

Out on the pitch, Tom had regained his feet and fronted the ref. Old Harry tried to hold Tom back. The ref held up a yellow card, threatening anyone who didn't move away.

With the score 1-0, I hunched back under my umbrella. The other subs were still shouting at the ref. I could feel my blue eyes fading to grey. Solar narcolepsy. That's what the doctors called my weird affliction. Whatever it was, it sucked. I ached to get out there and help my team.

Devastated by the goal, our team trudged back into position. One of our subs warmed up while he waited to replace Tom. Old Harry did his best to lead Tom from the field, but Tom kept pulling away, insisting that he could still play.

"You have time, Bridge. Control the ball. Work it downfield. Control the ball!" Coach Elkins bellowed. The crowd and everyone shouted and yelled all around me.

I put my hands over my ears. If only the sun would burst through the cloud, I could get out there and help my team. The rain and the mist and the grey sky crumpled me. I closed my eyes and visualised brilliant sun-rays bursting onto the pitch. Vivid thoughts of sunshine lifted my spirits. When I opened my eyes, the sky had brightened a touch.

Roger Stipple, our only player with clean shorts, ran to his position on the near wing.

"Come on, Roger. Get in the game, lad." Coach shouted.

Poor Roger. He hated football and getting dirty. I wondered why Roger's dad made him play. I peeped from beneath the brolly. Icy drops prickled my face, but as I searched for my own dad in the crowd, the drizzle slowed. It was cool having a world-renowned climate scientist for a father, but he always managed to find some excuse to work, even on Sundays.

A patch of grey cloud whitened. The drizzle became irregular. I lowered the umbrella as the faintest hint of sunlight fought through cloud and mist. The drizzle stopped. Filtered rays strengthened. My whole body tingled, and a smile broke across my face as I stood.

I slipped the parka from my shoulders, pulled the front of my jersey over my head, and spread my arms, absorbing energy from the sun.

Bemused murmurs spread through the crowd.

Coach Elkins' eyes widened. "Are you right, lad? Can you play?"

My stomach fluttered. I worried the clouds would close over again, but nodded.

Still protesting, Tom neared the sideline where our sub waited to replace him.

"Wait! Sam is going on." Coach Elkins quivered with excitement. "Shoot a goal! Two minutes to go. It's all up to you, Sam."

Energy tingled through my body. Goosebumps broke out all over my skin. I could feel my eyes brighten.

"Go Sam!" shouted our subs.

Amongst the away team's bench to my right, I noticed Hawks' coach watch me limber up then turn to his assistant. I focussed my acute hearing and heard him say, "Tell them Narco is on. Slow the game. Keep the ball from Narco. If he gets near it … take him out!"

Not very sportsman like, but at least I knew what to expect. When Tom saw that I was waiting to replace him, he stopped protesting, and Old Harry shuffled him over the touchline. The linesmen flagged me on. My heart thumped, and brilliant sunrays streamed through an impossible hole in the cloud as I ran onto the pitch. Mud squelched underfoot. The smell of wet turf thickened the air. Steam floated from the muddy players contesting the kick off.

I took the kick off, passed forward to Striker, and ran into space. Striker passed the ball back quicker than I expected. Two Hawks players smothered me, and a third stole the ball. I bustled to challenge, but as I broke free, a Hawks boot clipped my heel, sending me ploughing chest-first into the mud.

"Penalty!" yelled my team. I couldn't believe the ref missed it.

"You're a disgrace ref," rang out over the protests from our supporters.

With only a minute to go, I sprang to my feet and focused on stealing the ball. Spray splashed from my footfalls as I dashed over the pitch.

The bearded kid fielded the ball in our territory. With the game all but lost, our defenders hung off. The bearded kid dribbled the ball over the penalty box, sighted the goal, and raised his left arm, ready to shoot.

I charged in fast. I'm one of the tallest in my team, but I felt small as I challenged at speed for the ball. The bearded kid kicked for goal and thrust his forearm into my face. A sickening crack preceded the blood-curdling cry. The ball ricocheted between us.

My head jolted. My feet lifted off the ground. A stabbing screech jarred my ears. I saw sky, then landed with the ball at my feet. Beside me, the bearded kid splattered into the mud, clutching his arm.

The ref put the whistle to his mouth, then waved to play-on.

I felt as if I were emerging from underwater as I pushed the ball with my outstep and ran. An opponent charged with his shoulder. The impact made me stumble, but I regained balance, tapped the ball ahead, and bolted. Another defender slid, crashing his studs into my ankle.

I chipped the ball and jumped with the impact. My eyes zoomed in on the scoreboard clock: twelve seconds to go, seventy metres to cover. I skirted an attacker and stepped inside another.

"Go, lad! Go, Sam!" yelled our supporters. Glancing over my shoulder I saw some of my team running with their arms in the air as though we'd already won it.

"Help him! Help him!" Coach Elkins yelled himself dizzy.

Hawks defenders challenged, but I streaked through them. The sun was shining and I scorched into Hawks territory with only the keeper to beat, a heroic dream in reach. I wondered if my dad had made it back, then pictured Sonia cheering me and overstepped the ball.

NO! I couldn't believe I'd lost concentration.

"Get him!" screamed Hawks supporters. Even the most reserved supporters bellowed.

Using my left boot, I dragged the ball forward and stumbled. Trying to regain balance, my arms swung as though I were swimming. Screams from the crowd jumped an octave. I sensed new energy materialise in the Hawks chasers' legs. The clouds closed. Sunrays vanished. Footfalls splattered towards me. My rhythm returned. I poked the ball ahead and gaped over my shoulder.

A wall of Hawks players stampeded. The pitch sunk into grey darkness. I kicked the ball over the penalty box. My legs felt heavy. Sound blurred. Dark clouds dumped icy rain.

I looked into the keeper's eyes, took another pace, propped, and readied my right boot.

Two Hawks defenders slid feet-first.

The keeper braced—swayed left—swayed right.

I struck the ball an instant before Hawks defenders toppled me.

Hawks' keeper stood motionless, then bent forward, and the ball trickled into his arms.

The ref blew full time.

I lay in the mud and all around me the Hawks players jumped for joy.

3

SLEEPY

Vapour rose from my breath and my runners scraped as I dragged my feet across the deserted car park, still shattered from missing the goal. Dad opened the door and I sank into the seat. The car was warm inside.

I stared at my dad. "When did you arrive?"

"*Mazu*, I'll take the wheel," Dad said.

"Manual drive engaged," replied the car.

Dad glanced over his shoulder and reversed the Aston. He drove through the car park, pulled into a gap in the traffic, and continued driving the car himself. Drizzle dotted the windscreen and the wipers juddered. I shook my head. He probably didn't even arrive in time to see me miss the goal. Red and white lights blurred into the distance. A wave of heaviness flowed over me.

"It's your birthday tomorrow, and I have some exciting news." Dad kept his eyes on the road as he spoke to me. My mind became fuzzy and my eyes blinked closed.

"We're going on an adventure," he continued, "and it's time I told you why you are different, and … about your mother."

At the mention of why I'm different and talk of my mother, my eyes blinked open, but my mind and body were so heavy that I drifted and the next sentence was like part of a dream.

"Sorry I've kept this a secret, but your mother told me to wait until you turned sixteen."

4

PLANET LUATU, THE ANDROMEDA GALAXY

The flicker of astral light could have been mistaken for a shooting star. But the momentary flicker was a clue, the only visible clue, that Coaliferos had materialised in the oxygen-rich atmosphere above planet Luatu. Moonlight glimmered on his black body armour. Charred lines marred his ashen face. The desire to reclaim his destiny smouldered inside him as he hovered and gazed through midnight-blue eyes at the remains of an ancient volcano.

Grasslands now covered the vast crater. A solitary farmhouse lay on a hillock at the northern end. Scattered rocky outcrops were all that remained of the volcanic rim, and dense jungle surrounded it.

Drifting with the breeze, Coaliferos closed his eyes and used his psionic vision to scan the grasslands and the farmhouse. The modest stone house was dark and deserted, as were the storage shed and silo beside it. Antilows grazed in the surrounding pasture.

Certain he'd arrived undetected, Coaliferos relaxed to freefall, chest-first. Wind buffeted his cheeks as he plunged until, just above the surface, he slowed and righted himself to land feet first on a flat section of the volcanic rim. Loose stones crunched underfoot as he strolled, investigating a rocky formation. He jumped from boulder to boulder to a position that afforded a view of the farmhouse, camouflage, and a comfortable rock to sit on. If all went to plan, he'd have plenty of time to set his trap and the rebels would arrive in the dead of night.

Satisfied that everything was in order, Coaliferos focused on the half-moon rising over the jungle. Using telepathy, he contacted the troop carrier hiding in the moon's shadow. "Captain, dispatch the troopers then return to position," Coaliferos communicated.

After scanning the rim and the crater a second time, Coaliferos sat on the rock he'd selected and rested his arm on a cool, smooth ledge. His excellent night vision zoomed in on the shadowy farmhouse 1500 metres away when an old memory came back to haunt him. In an ambush like the one he was setting now, his hesitation—just a fleeting moment—had allowed Princess Hila to escape with the Guardian's Ring and the Cintamani Pearl.

Time had pushed his catastrophic failure to the depths of his being, but now it surfaced to stab at his heart and torment him. Since the fall of the Mega Empire, his deeds for the Coaliferite Nation had made him a feared warrior throughout Andromeda, but the title of Lord was below his station. While he'd undergone the painful transformation to a carbon breathing entity, he retained his astral powers. His masters still saw him as an astral warrior and sought to smother his ambition. But if he kept performing, he had value, and when he found the ring, it would lead him to the pearl, and then everything would change.

A tingling sensation in the centre of his brow alerted him to the troop carrier's approach. He vacated his rocky perch, jumped over a boulder, and marched to the centre of a gravelly clearing. The carbon breathing Coaliferite troopers descended in groups of five, dust kicking up as they landed feet first and formed two lines in front of him. The squad of twenty troopers stood at attention while Coaliferos inspected them.

"The farmhouse is deserted. We don't know how long the rebels will be." Coaliferos turned and leapt up onto a boulder. "Take cover in this rock formation. Deactivate life support to conserve energy. The air is rich in oxygen, but you can breathe it. Maintain silence. Keep a sharp watch and stay alert." Reclaiming his perch, Coaliferos watched the troopers select positions and their blood-red battle suits blend into the nooks and shadows on either side of him.

Stars twinkled in an infinite sky. An antilow calf lowed in the crater below. A meteoroid burned bright then faded into oblivion. Coaliferos gazed at the heavens and visualised the success of this mission, but the memory of allowing Princess Hila to steal his destiny, to escape with Andromeda's most powerful treasures, kept repeating. He was a young buck then, sixteen annos had passed. If the ambush was a success, he could join the Milky Way invasion; and, he was sure that he'd find the ring and the pearl somewhere in the Milky Way. If this ambush failed, he'd be stuck here in Andromeda.

The shrill call of a curfeather pierced the darkness, and then silence —just the sound of the universe vibrating. Nights were long on Luatu, and as the hours passed the Coaliferite troopers became restless. The Coaliferite craved carbon and heat. Planet Luatu's cool, oxygen-rich air enraged them.

"When this mission is completed, we'll torch the forests on this vile, green planet," one of the troopers grumbled.

"Bathe in the heat and breathe sweet carbon," another trooper added. Muffled voices drifted. They shifted positions, and a boulder tumbled down the craggy rim.

"*TSS!*" Coaliferos hissed, jolting his troopers with a telepathic shock. The voices silenced. Movement ceased.

The oxygen-rich air and the lush forest surrounding the rim took Coaliferos back to Megasis, his home planet before the Coaliferite invasion. With two suns, nights were short on Megasis. Society depended on the sun for energy. Even the Mega citizens derived much of their personal energy from the sun. Coaliferos gazed into the heavens and remembered how he sat with his father at sunset on the rocks by the sea, and a vision of his father turning the Guardian's Ring around his finger to the left, then to the right, engrossed him. His eyes glazed with the memory.

A disc-wing spacecraft streaked over the far side of the rim. Coaliferos ducked behind his shelter. He cursed himself for allowing his mind to wander and signalled his troopers to hide and engage their battle suit's stealth function. The disc-wing circled the rim. He sensed the ship's scanners pass over them.

Thrusters blazed through the darkness, illuminating the farmhouse as the disc-wing descended to land beside it. Relieved they'd not been detected, Coaliferos spied through a gap in the rocks. Four warriors exited the disc-wing; their paramilitary uniforms confirmed they were part of the rebel militia. One warrior waited by the ship, three entered the farmhouse. A light switched on, glowed through the curtains, then one of the three came back outside to stand guard by the door.

A second lux-class ship cruised overhead. Coaliferos grinned. His intelligence had been correct. Diplomats and ministers used the lux-class ships. There was sure to be a government official aboard. The ship landed on the opposite side of the farmhouse. A central figure with guards on either side marched down the ship's ramp. The central figure entered the farmhouse with one guard and the second patrolled the exterior.

The Coaliferite troopers readied to attack. Coaliferos waved them back, ducked behind his shelter, and ordered them to wait for his signal.

Wind gusted, swept like waves over the jungle, and scattered dust from the crumbling volcanic rim. Subtle energy flickered above the farmhouse. Coaliferos froze. He sensed an astral warrior had arrived, projecting straight into the stone dwelling. Three rebels patrolled the exterior. Including the astral warrior, five rebels were inside.

Trembling with anticipation, Coaliferos repeated his plan. "Wait for the meeting to begin, signal the troopers to attack, then astral jump into the farmhouse; disable or kill the astral warrior before the troopers arrive." A simple plan, but he must time it to perfection. Taking an astral warrior by surprise was no easy task; they could fall into an astral jump and disappear in seconds. Heart pounding, he eased forward and spied through the gap in the rock.

Within the farmhouse's stone walls, the special minister for defence, two leaders from the rebel militia, and an astral warrior sat at a round wooden table in the centre of the single room dwelling. Stairs led to a loft at one end. A fireplace occupied the opposite wall. Armed with a blaster, the special minister's bodyguard stood at the door.

"It's true the Milky Way invasion will weaken the Coaliferite defences here in Andromeda," the astral warrior said, "but you are not strong enough for a direct confrontation."

"We need your help!" the special minister for defence said. "We need to show strength, pose a threat. Then others will join us."

The militia leaders nodded in agreement.

"The resistance is too fragile. A loose tongue or even a loose thought could bring the whole movement crashing down." The astral warrior narrowed his eyes. His brow furrowed, and he raised a hand to silence the meeting. His chair scraped over the timber floor as he stood and strode to a window. Lifting the curtain, he stared into the night.

A light in one of the farmhouse windows brightened. Coaliferos tensed. He sensed the astral warrior staring at the exact position where he hid. Long ago, a moment's hesitation had cost him the ring and the pearl. Fear of failure flashed through his mind, jolting him into action. He signalled the troopers, who leaped from the rocky rim and rocketed through the air toward the farmhouse.

Coaliferos visualised himself arriving inside the farmhouse and fell back, vanishing into a flash of astral light.

5

AMBUSH

Inside the farmhouse, the astral warrior turned from the window shouting, "Evacuate! We're compromised." Behind him, a faint flicker preceded a dazzling flash; the astral warrior spun around, and seeing Coaliferos materialising, he fell back to escape into an astral jump.

As Coaliferos emerged from the bright flash, white light arced around the astral warrior. In a fraction of a second the warrior would vanish. Using visualisation, Coaliferos ignited his astral blade. Midnight-blue astral energy glowed around it as he lunged at the falling warrior. His blade hummed when it struck, and light exploded from the astral warrior. The militia leaders reached for their blasters and the minister's body-guard opened fire on Coaliferos.

Coaliferos parried the blasts with unnatural speed. Four windows shattered as Coaliferite troopers burst into the room. The militia leaders and the bodyguard turned their fire on the troopers. The door exploded from its hinges, lifting the bodyguard from his feet and smashing him against the loft stairs.

Splinters and shattered glass hurtled through the farmhouse. Blasters blazing, troopers stormed in.

Within the confusion of crowding bodies and blast fire, Coaliferos saw one of his troopers take aim at the special minister. In desperation, Coaliferos leapt, deflecting the blast fire with his blade and, thrusting his free arm, launched a searing blast through the heel of his palm that cannoned into the trooper's chest and tore right through him.

"Take prisoners!" Coaliferos shouted as he gripped the special minister by the throat and slammed him into a corner. Still more troopers crowded in. Blast fire ceased, and through the haze of spent weaponry, Coaliferos searched for the astral warrior's body. Although sure he'd struck the warrior before he'd made the astral jump, he hadn't had time to confirm it, and he smiled when he located the body lying on the floor with a blade wound burnt through the heart.

The old farmhouse shook as an armed freighter landed beside it. The troopers ushered the two surviving prisoners outside to load them into the freighter.

"Leave the special minister here with me," Coaliferos said, gloating at his prisoner. The mission had been a success. It was unlikely that the special minister could tell him what he wanted to know, but he'd hand him over to the Coaliferites and they'd extract some useful information on the rebel militia.

"Special Minister, I've known of your rebel links, but it's taken a long time to catch you. And your presence here implicates the Governor," Coaliferos said.

"The Governor has nothing to do with this, Coaliferos." The minister glared in defiance.

"Lord Coaliferos to you, Minister." Coaliferos ignited an astral blade in his right hand.

"Many years ago, you and Princess Hila were friends. Tell me, where did she go when she escaped?'

A thin strip of midnight-blue astral energy glimmered on the edge of his blade as he levelled it at the minister's throat.

"Where are the Guardian's Ring and the Cintamani Pearl?"

The minister smirked, "you're famous for allowing Princess Hila to escape with the treasures. Why ask me? You know you'll never find them."

Coaliferos held his blade so close that blisters bubbled on the minister's neck. "Where is the ring and Cintamani Pearl, Minister?"

The minister grit his teeth. "You're a traitor, Coaliferos. You have no honour," he said, goading Coaliferos to kill him.

"Haha!" Coaliferos laughed and de-energised his blade. "Killing you would be too kind. Perhaps you'll be willing to talk to save your wife and children." Coaliferos turned to the captain of the guards and nodded.

The guard beamed a life-size holographic image of the minister's wife and teenage son and daughter chained to a wall. Two troopers stood guard over them.

"Nella! Surne! Lanu!" the minister called to his family. When they couldn't hear him, his face soured. "You scum, Coaliferos."

"Minister, I'm the reason your family isn't in a slave camp right now. Address me as Lord Coaliferos and answer all my questions or your wife and children will spend the rest of their days mining anthracite." Coaliferos smirked at the minister. "When she escaped, Princess Hila carried an unborn child and stole the Guardian's Ring and the Cintamani Pearl. Tell me where she fled, Minister."

The minister closed his eyes and swallowed. Slavery at the hands of the Coaliferite was far worse than death. "Lord Coaliferos, I've had no contact with the Princess since her departure, but I believe she absconded to the Milky Way galaxy with the ring and the pearl."

"Where is she now? Where is the child? Where are the ring and the pearl? And remember Minister, your family's future depends on how you answer."

Sweat beaded on the minister's brow and he inhaled several deep breaths. "As far as I know she was headed for planet Earth. Mother and child most probably died within days of crossing the Milky Way's convergence zone. I have no idea what she did with the ring and the pearl. Somewhere on planet Earth is my best guess."

"I asked for answers, not gossip, Minister." Coaliferos shook his head and turned to the captain of the guards. "Transport the minister's family to the slave camp on Rotan. Take the minister back to base and extract what you can from him."

6

BIRTHDAY SURPRISE

A truck labouring up the hill roused me from a deep sleep. I opened my eyes and stared at the curtains beside my bed. Headlights flashed against the window as a car crested the rise. Lifting a pillow, I wriggled into a sitting position and lifted the curtain.

Mist glowed around a streetlight, and across the road the slate roofs of two-storey terrace houses blended into the darkness. I couldn't remember going to bed. Light rain peppered the window, beading until drops combined and ran. My last recollection was trying to stay awake when Dad said something about my mother. He must have put me to bed. It was probably lucky that Dad was tall and strong, but I hated the idea of him carrying me upstairs and putting me to bed like a baby. Although revived by sleep, I'll be lethargic until I can absorb some energy from the sun.

I flopped back into my pillow and winked at my phone in the dock beside my bed. A holographic screen materialised above me, listing two new messages and a social media post. First, I left-winked at the Hero-G app. I was still number one in singles and Tom and I were second in doubles. Warmth flowed through my chest. I inhaled a deep breath, closed my eyes, and smiled. And then the memory of missing the goal came pressing in on me.

"Tom," I said, to check the first message. A strange holographic image opened before me. *What the heck was it?* I squinted, shook my head, then winced in horror: a pimply white butt with ginger hair sprouting from the crack polluted my space.

"Eww," I groaned and turned away from the image. It was so disgusting I could almost smell it. I swiped the image away.

Red butt hair—it couldn't be Tom, but the picture came from Tom's phone. It must have been at the party. Striker! Who else would be such a grub? Striker must have pinched Tom's phone at the party. I shook my head and stewed until I calmed down enough to blink open the second message.

A holographic image of Swathi materialised before me, "Happy birthday to you, happy birthday to you." Smiles and crazy excitement radiated as she sang.

Birthdays weren't something I looked forward to, but I smiled and laughed as Swathi finished with an animated jig.

"Thank you. That was awesome," I said and winked the reply back to Swathi.

I blinked at my social media feed. "Brrwhhhaargh," a hairy gorilla identified my home page. The first post was a photo of my team at the party, and Sonia with Striker by her side.

I raised my hands, crashed them into the duvet, then slapped the image away. Narcolepsy sucks. I miss the goal in front of half the school, then I get Striker's butt shoved in my face. Sonia was too nice. She couldn't be dating Striker. I stared at the stars and galaxies that I'd stuck on the ceiling when I was a kid, and pictured myself thumping Striker in the nose then grabbing him by an arm and a leg and throwing him out into space. The thought of Sonia going out with him was so disturbing, it kept circling around in my head. My heart thumped and my stomach knotted to the point I wanted to be sick. To try and get the thought out of my head, I turned to my phone.

"Books. Stellar astrophysics. Andromeda Galaxy," I said. A metre-by-metre hologram of my favourite spiral galaxy swirled before me; I gazed at the luminous arms swirling above me, then at the framed picture of my mother on the shelf. She had to be the reason for my weird affliction … and my special talents. I wished I could have met her. I wished she was here right now. Her emerald eyes calmed my mind and for a while I lay as though surrounded by an impenetrable cocoon and imagined myself a brave warrior soaring the galaxies.

Real life was often boring and brought up all kinds of worries, so I spent a lot of time in imaginary adventures. Sometimes I'd be saving cute, helpless creatures from evil aliens, but this morning, I decided to focus on an old favourite: I imagined I was in my Hero-G game, and I was just about to rescue Princess Zola when footsteps on the stairs surprised me. A floorboard creaked, a cup and saucer chinked, and my door swished open.

With a right blink, I closed the Andromeda hologram as my dad entered the room. Dad was usually asleep at this hour, and I wondered where he was going dressed in a tweed jacket and slacks.

"Good morning, Sam." Dad placed a cup of tea on the bedside table and sat on the swivel chair at my desk.

"Morning, Dad." I used both arms to push myself up, pulled the curtain, and reaffirmed another depressing, grey day was dawning.

Dad took an envelope from his jacket pocket, rolled forward in the chair, and handed it to me. "Happy birthday, Sam."

After looking around and not seeing a present, I pulled the card from the envelope. Two airborne dolphins graced the cover.

"Cool. Thanks, Dad," I said, and when I opened the card, a British Airways ticket fell out. I glanced at my dad, read the card, then opened the airline ticket: London, Heathrow to Los Angeles—tomorrow morning?

"From L.A. we fly to Tahiti, then Rangiroa," Dad said.

My heart thumped. Rangiroa was where my mum and dad had met, where I was born, and where just minutes after giving birth to me, my mother had died. Neither my dad nor I had ever been back.

"Then I want you to come to Tonga. I finally secured funding for my Tonga Trench program," Dad said.

Visions of sunshine, a blue lagoon, and a white-sand beach flooded my mind. I knew everything about Dad's research of the trench. The rapid ocean warming was undoing all of humanity's good work. I wanted to help, but now that I had the opportunity, I remembered the last time I went on a field trip; Dad had worked around the clock. There'd been no one of my age and I'd had to explain my narcolepsy to everyone. And the Wi-Fi was crap. Then I remembered that the Hero-G tournament was next weekend.

"It's Hero-G day next Sunday," I said.

Dad shook his head. "Hero-G has a day?"

"You know it does. I'm the reigning champion. Tom and I are second in doubles."

"This trip is an opportunity of a lifetime. I thought you'd be excited." Dad said.

This would devastate Tom. I stared out the window. Rain fell. Nerves fluttered in my chest. "How long will I be away?"

"Look," Dad said checking his watch, "my research could save the planet. If events in the Tonga Trench continue to superheat the ocean, it will accelerate global warming much faster than the sum of all carbon," he huffed. "You've been part of this research from the start; you're my assistant, you score one hundred percent on the submarine simulators. I secured the funding! You know how hard I fought for this, and Rangiroa is paradise. I booked two nights in an overwater bungalow. You'll get to see where you were born."

We'd been talking about this trip for years. Visiting Rangiroa was like a far-off dream. The idea that I could help save the planet inspired me. But all this global warming gloom and doom was like facing an invincible monster. Sometimes just thinking about it overwhelmed me.

"Can't we go after the tournament?" I said.

Dad shook his head. "I fly to New York to meet my new sponsor this morning. You stay with Swathi tonight. Aunt Jindhi will drop you at Heathrow tomorrow."

"Fly by myself?" I'd never done that before.

Dad glanced at his watch again. "I'll meet you at two o'clock in the afternoon, L.A. time. The flight is long, but all daylight. We can relax in a hotel for a few hours, then fly to Tahiti."

A daytime flight meant I wouldn't need to explain my narcolepsy to strangers. *But why tomorrow, why so suddenly?*

"Sorry to rush," Dad continued, "but my flight leaves in two hours. I have a present from your mother."

My jaw dropped. *Was this some sick joke? A present from my dead mother?* My mind spun as Dad took a small velvet box from his jacket.

"Take it." Dad smiled and nodded. "It belonged to your mother."

My eyes flicked from the box to my dad. *What the heck? Why had he kept this a secret until now?* My arm trembled as I reached for the box.

"Open it," he said.

The hinge resisted, then sprang open. Atop blue velvet sat a titanium-coloured ring. A tingle ran up my spine. Goosebumps broke out on my arms and neck.

"'Give him the ring on his sixteenth birthday. Tell him I love him. Tell him he must follow his heart and the ring will guide him. Those were your mother's last words." Dad bent over the bed and hugged me, trapping my arms in front. I was glad when his phone rang.

"Hold ten seconds, please," Dad said, walking to the bedroom door, then holding the phone against his chest. "Sam, there will be controversy about my new funding. Remember, humanity depends on this research. Sorry, I must dash. Aunt Jindhi is expecting you. There's so much I must tell you, but I'll explain everything in Los Angeles tomorrow. This trip will be the making of you, Sam."

Footsteps disappeared downstairs. I knew so little of my mother. No memories of course—just a few stories, a photo, and the knowledge that she died giving me life. It had never made sense that Dad knew so little of Mum's background. There was nothing about her on the net. Now her last words, *Tell him he must follow his heart* and, *the ring will guide him*, echoed in my head.

Intricate maze-like engravings covered the ring, and while it looked like titanium, it was too light to be metal. I held the mysterious gift near the tip of my finger. A spark jumped from it, and I jerked the ring away.

7

ATLO TRUDOCK AND RADLEY JONES

On the other side of the Atlantic, city lights blazed golden. So as not to ruffle his hair, Atlo Trudock waited for the rotor to slow and alighted on the roof of Trudock Tower. He took seven paces in the crisp night air, saluted the Statue of Liberty, and thanked the Great Lady for the privilege of being the only private citizen allowed to operate a chopper in New York City airspace since 9/11.

The city rumbled. A siren blared. His eyes took on a steely intensity as he strode across the rooftop like a quarterback emerging from the Super Bowl tunnel. On either side of the entry, vapour drifted from the guards' breath. They stood at attention and tilted their heads. "Good morning, Sir," they said.

"Ryan. Ethan," Atlo tilted his head in reply and marched through the portico. Water cascaded over the circular glass walls on either side giving the illusion that he was walking on water as he crossed over the limestone floor, then entered his private elevator and descended one floor.

"Good morning, Sir." The doorman tilted his head, smiled, and took Atlo's gloves and coat.

"Morning, Jacob, thanks for coming in early." Atlo continued along the hall and glanced through the doorways of his bedroom, lounge, and pool with gymnasium; the Great Lady sparkled through the windows of every room, and the doorman trailed, closing the doors.

Atlo limbered his shoulders, rolled his neck, and marched into his office. His secretary, dressed in a skirt suit and scarf, placed a mug of steaming coffee on his oak desk.

"Thanks for coming in early, Ellie. You're looking gorgeous and bright for two in the morning."

"A pleasure, Sir," Ellie said, backing out of the office.

The windows and flags behind his desk resembled those in the president's oval office. Except Atlo's windows were bigger, and Xcon Corporation's black X replaced the star section of one flag. Atlo sat at his desk, picked up his coffee, and swivelled his chair to see the Great Lady with her greenish tinge glowing in the distance.

A speaker blipped. "Yes?" Atlo said.

"Radley Jones has geared his European listeners for a shock and has gone to a commercial break."

Taking care not to wet more lip than necessary, Atlo sipped his coffee. The old shock jock had the highest-rated program in the solar system and presented a live hour-long morning show in Europe while preparing his U.S. breakfast gig.

"Put him on." Atlo took another sip and reclined.

"Radley's Galaxy beaming live from New York," announced a husky female voice.

"To my listeners in Europe, and throughout our wonderful system, I have dispiriting news ... daunting for humanity, daunting for our world."

Atlo's face soured. "Radley's dramatic voice is so annoying."

"In response to the Paris climate agreements, the nations of Planet Earth faltered. But the youth of our planet took to the streets, took to social media and made adults listen. Our children supported the scientists. Young people exposed the sceptics, exposed the vested interests. Kids demanded we tackle global warming, and humanity listened. We slowed the warming, slowed the melt. Peoples of Earth united. And yes, we succeeded!"

"So full of himself." Atlo shook his head.

"But, as my listeners on Earth know, as my listeners on Mars and throughout our magnificent system know, it's the year 2032, and the times they are a changing."

Atlo swallowed, sat upright, put the cup on the desk, and clasped his hands.

"Temperatures are up. The ice caps have resumed melting. In South America, Australia, and Asia, wildfires are consuming the forests. Hurricanes have smashed wind farms in the North Sea and Europe. Fires in Los Angeles and greater California have inflicted momentous human loss and halved the state's renewable capacity. In Texas, hail the size of baseballs smashed the largest solar farms in our country. Storms in China and India have crippled renewable production. Listeners around the system, it pains me to say … we have a climate crisis. We have an energy crisis and the renewable revolution has failed us!"

"Ha!" Atlo laughed out loud. Radley Jones was a moderate, a purveyor of truth, and the universe listened to his show through Atlo's broadcast empire.

"Ellie!" The intercom engaged as Atlo spoke. "Send Russell Edwards's statement about the Tonga Trench to Radley. Let Radley break the story. And turn the silly old fart off."

European and Asian stock markets projected in the centre of Atlo's office. News from Radley that renewable energy was failing sent Xcon coal and uranium stocks soaring.

8

SELL OUT

"Eight-thirty bus departs in ten minutes," my phone alerted me. I pocketed the ring and crammed mango jam toast into my mouth. Grabbing my bag and parka at the stairwell, I headed along the hall and halted at Dad's study.

The door was open. An aerial view of the Tonga Trench washed across the home computer screen. Dad's study gave me the creeps, and I always used my own mobile data because the house connection felt like someone was spying. But this morning the veil of blue sea on the screen drew me in, and I wondered why the computer hadn't hibernated. I double-blinked, but nothing happened. The wavering contours were hypnotic. I slouched in the chair and my eyes felt heavy. A faint burning odour drifted. Sounds like distant voices enticed me nearer the screen until a loud rap at the front door startled me.

I flinched, blinked the computer closed, but still nothing happened. I blinked Force Quit once, and then a second time, before the shutdown sequence began. The knocker rapped again, and a silhouette peeked through the frosted-glass panel.

Cold wind blasted me as I opened the door, and Swathi's bright smile and mass of curly dark hair greeted me. "Are you okay?" she asked.

I nodded, but Dad's computer had freaked me out.

"Happy birthday!" Swathi handed me a card, stood on tippy toes, and kissed me on the cheek.

"Thanks, Swathi. I blushed and glanced up the street before opening the card.

"A peregrine falcon, the fastest creature on Earth," Swathi said.

"Beautiful, thank you. And that was a cool message this morning."

We both admired the falcon, its talons reaching, ready to strike. I put the card on the shelf in Dad's office beside a portrait of the two us, and the front door shuddered as I closed it and stepped out into the grey morning. Traffic zoomed. Tyres sounded loud on the wet road. Lack of sunlight left me lethargic and I held the rail, descending one step at a time.

"Your trip sounds exciting," Swathi said.

I shrugged, annoyed that Swathi probably knew more about it than I did.

"Visiting Rangiroa and researching the Tonga Trench sounds awesome. You and your dad might save the world."

Horns blasted as a delivery van stopped. Saving the world sounded cool, but what could I really do about it? Missing the Hero-G tournament sucked and hanging out with my workaholic dad wasn't fun anymore.

"Well, are you going to say something?" Swathi asked. "I'm so jealous. It's so important that everyone does the little things like recycling and using renewable energy. But you have the chance be a hero. I know its cloudy, but you're going on an awesome adventure and you don't even look excited about it."

"You're right, I should be excited," I said. "Sorry to be such a drag. It's just the weather, and Dad only told me this morning as he rushed out, and I always think about my mother on my birthday."

The sound of heels clipping pavement approached. Swathi fell behind me, and a woman in a grey overcoat overtook us. It was weird, winning the Hero-G tournament seemed more important than saving the world. Bridge students crowded the bus stop. Farther up the street, Tom picked a gap in the traffic, ran across the road, then lumbered as though he were half asleep.

"Hey, Narco, bad luck about the game," called a Year 8 Bridge student; others sniggered. Swathi's nostrils flared.

"Just ignore them," I said, but Swathi glared until they turned away.

"Ay, Sam." Tom slouched in. His nose was swollen, and the corners of his eyes blackened. "Bad luck about yesterday. If the sun had stayed out a few more seconds, you'd have got the equaliser. At least you sorted that bearded kid out, yeah?"

I smiled and shrugged.

Swathi stared away, shook her head, and sidled up to me. "What were you thinking when you first stumbled … before the sun disappeared?"

Breath caught in my chest. Swathi was so sharp. Thinking about my dad and Sonia cheering me on had lost the match. I stood as though blinded by a spotlight.

"Shut up, Swathi. You know his condition. Don't listen, Sam." Tom pulled me away. "Shame you missed last night." He shouldered in tight, unfolded his phone, and showed me a selfie: Tom standing with his arm around Sonia's shoulders.

It was just a photo, but I experienced a stabbing emptiness. *Did Sonia have her picture taken with everyone?* I caught a whiff of Swathi's perfume and then her breasts pressed into my back as she leaned between our heads to look at the phone.

"Tom, did you pay Sonia for that picture?" Swathi asked.

"Sod off," Tom said. He shrugged Swathi away and looked at the photo again.

I took the phone from my wrist, unfolded the flat screen, and scrolled to the hairy butt photo. But then I glanced at Swathi. The image was so gross, and I didn't want her to see it. I decided to show Tom later and flicked the photo away.

Brakes squealed as the bus stopped. I climbed aboard and took a window seat three rows from the front. Tom sat beside me and bantered with two girls across the aisle while Swathi joined a girlfriend on the seat behind the driver. The bus laboured past the Indian takeaway and a charity shop. I zoned out, fidgeted with the ring in my pocket, and thought about my mother, about flying to Rangiroa and about the photo of Sonia and Striker.

"Hey, Sam," Tom said. "I spoke to Sonia last night. All she wanted to talk about was how cute you are with your blue eyes and dark hair. I said you were hot for her, and that Swathi's like your little sister."

My heart pounded. "There's nothing between her and Striker?"

"Striker! Hell, no. You're the one. Ask her to go ice skating or something."

Warmth spread through my chest. I pictured us skating together on an outdoor rink in the city.

The bus pulled over. Striker was at the stop, and he smirked at me as he boarded. "You missed an excellent party, Edwards. Pity you couldn't stay awake long enough to score that goal."

"Sod off, Striker," Tom said.

Now that I knew Sonia wasn't interested in him, I just smiled as he walked past. I turned to Tom. "Did you see the photo Striker sent from your phone?"

Tom screwed his face. "What?"

I showed him that the message had come from his phone before I opened the image.

"That's not me!" Tom said.

"I know. Must be Striker."

Tom looked like he was going to be sick. "Those pimples and that … oh, it's so disgusting. But Striker doesn't have ginger hair."

"A tinge," I said, and we craned our necks to get a good look at him.

Striker sat four rows behind on the opposite side of the bus. His hair was a rusty brown. He smiled, his lips covering his teeth, and gave us the finger.

"Hey, Striker, I didn't know you had ginger butt hair," Tom said.

Murder flashed in Striker's eyes. He smirked and gave us two fingers.

Several students laughed. I sank into my seat, and Tom acted as if he'd won the lottery.

"It's him." Tom trembled with excitement. "You got the H-Phone, beam it up."

I shook my head. "Not here."

Tom was beside himself and scrolled through his pictures.

"Striker must have deleted it after he sent. Send me the image, Sam," he knelt on the seat and grinned. "Hey, Striker, that picture of your butt is the most disgusting thing on Earth."

Laughter spread through the bus. Striker became the centre of attention. I shook my head and laughed and stared out the window.

"Seriously, Striker, you should have wiped your butt and squeezed those zits before taking the picture," Tom said.

The bus erupted with jeers and laughter. Striker blushed. All heads turned to stare at him.

Tom waved his hand in front of his nose. "How viral will Striker's stinking butt go?"

Brakes squeaked. Everyone leaned forward, then jerked back as the bus stopped at Bridge High. Everyone was laughing, checking their social media, and urging Tom to post.

"I don't know what you're talking about." Striker forced a smile through his teeth. "Fuck you, Narco," he said as he shuffled past my seat.

"Stinking ginger," announced Tom.

A wounded, toothy smile marred Striker's face as he exited the bus.

"Send that photo," Tom said.

I glanced at my wrist. "My phone is acting up. You go ahead. See you in maths."

"You okay?" Tom asked.

"Just another grey day," I sighed.

Tom hurried to exit the bus, pushed through the crowd, and walked backwards, fanning his face in front of his victim. Striker changed direction. Tom followed, waving his hand before his nose.

Thoughts of all the grief that I'd copped over my narcolepsy circled in my mind, and I glimpsed the pain that lay ahead for Striker. If he weren't such a tosser, it would have been an easy decision. I deleted the photo and exited the bus.

Swathi stood grim-faced on the kerb, looking up at me. "Have you seen the news about your dad?" she asked.

I shouldered up to Swathi and read *The Times* headline on her phone: ENGLAND'S LEADING CLIMATE SCIENTIST SELLS OUT.

9

COALIFEROS

In the darkness of deep space, a faint flicker folded through the astral dimension. Travelling as a circular disc of light, Coaliferos expected to journey from Andromeda to the edge of the Milky Way in seventy-four hours.

Full-body astral travel was usually a euphoric experience, with time to relax and arrive ready for action. But on this occasion, a thought, the very thought that instigated the journey, repeated: his catastrophic failure allowing Princess Hila to escape with the Guardian's Ring and the Cintamani Pearl … his destiny stolen.

Coaliferos traversed the vast gulf between the spiral galaxies at a speed limited only by the power of his mind. Negative thought had slowed the journey. Sensing the destination nearing after seventy-eight hours, he visualised arrival, and his transfer to a physical state commenced.

The circular disc of light expanded. A radiant point of light flashed. Shock waves rippled through the dark matter of space. Every molecule of his being vibrated as he materialised with his battle suit projecting a translucent shield to maintain bodily function.

There it was before him, the Milky Way. Immense spirals of countless stars mirrored in his midnight-blue eyes. The sound of a starry night rang in his ears, and the galactic tide swept him through the darkness of deep space.

The battle suit's black morganic material replenished astral force, and his wrist armour sucked in solar radiation while he floated.

He recollected his father talking of this mystical galaxy: the Milky Way, a symbol of youth and vitality, its trillions of worlds possessing the untold wealth of a pristine spiral galaxy. Soon, the convergence zone would synchronise, making the Milky Way accessible and attracting the ambitions of many tribes and nations.

Replenished energy tingled through his body. Coaliferos gazed into the Milky Way and sensed the Cintamani Pearl calling him. A smile creased his ashen face. Using visualisation, he engaged conventional flight, accelerated to the speed of sound, then half that of light. His internal scanners detected the Coaliferite base hitched to the galactic tide near the Orion arm and Earth.

With telescopic vision, Coaliferos searched and decelerated on approach. Stars disappeared. A dark patch grew, obscuring a whole section of the Milky Way. Soaring until a swirling black cloud consumed the sky, he slowed to hover before the gaseous giant and sent his telepathic signature.

Energetic pulses streaked like lightning through the cloud. It throbbed like a gargantuan heart, and a red glow guided him to an arterial portal. His shield reflected heat and the stench of sulphur, as he negotiated the swirling vortex to emerge in the clear zone around the Coaliferite base.

He drifted in the carbon-rich atmosphere and surveyed the ports and entrances that glowed like rubies and dotted the dark orb. The scale was impressive, and it turned like a small planet on a polar axis. Engaging forward propulsion, Coaliferos cruised. Two starship fighters came from behind, rumbled past, and freighters crisscrossed the base. Coaliferos sped up for the last part of the journey. The giant orb swallowed him, and he landed feet-first on the diplomatic platform.

Six troopers scrambled, sighting their blasters. Blue rays scanned him.

"Lord Coaliferos … sorry, Sir, we expected a ship. I'll escort you to your quarters," a trooper said.

Acclimatising and recouping was precisely what he should do. He lowered his shield, ready to follow the guard, when something in the ether triggered memories of the ring and the pearl.

"I need to see General Ignis," Coaliferos said.

The trooper avoided eye contact and spoke into a receiver.

"Immediately," Coaliferos demanded.

The trooper repeated the demand, waited, stared at the ground, then nodded.

"This way, Lord Coaliferos." The trooper led him through a dim hall to a stuffy lobby where he boarded a transport capsule. No windows and lighting by way of a red glow, the capsule shook as it rocketed through a duct.

The capsule rattled to a stop. Two troopers guarded the dark exit-corridor. Heat and carbon clotted the air. Coaliferos sensed he was in the heart of the orb. Blue rays scanned him again. A trooper moved aside, the other led him to a retracting door where he bent to enter a small room.

The low ceiling barely allowed him to straighten. A black desk and chairs occupied the far end of the room. Sweat beaded on his brow as he surveyed a wall of instruments and gauges.

Blast doors opened behind the desk, and the fiery glow of the magma core filled the room. Even by Coaliferite standards it was hot, the carbon levels extreme. General Ignis entered, and the door closed behind him.

"Lord Coaliferos. A welcome surprise."

"Thank you, General."

Ignis was a member of the oldest Coaliferite tribe, and exhibited their classic features: strong jaw, sunken yellow eyes, blue lips, black teeth, and pasty white skin. While Ignis enjoyed the rank of general, he was more scientist than warrior, and Coaliferos thought about how best to extract what he wanted.

"What brings you to the Milky Way?" Ignis asked.

"I sense an astral presence."

"I hear you've been effective in cleaning up the resistance in Andromeda, but you won't find any astral warriors or your fanciful Cintamani Pearl in the Milky Way. Too early. The convergence zone will synchronise when the galaxy reaches deeper into the Aquarian sector. Until then, only the Zorag can cross the convergence zone. You wouldn't survive a cycle." Ignis folded his arms. "Is that all? Our scheduled meeting is tomorrow."

General Ignis and the Coaliferite hierarchy wanted the Guardian's Ring and the Cintamani Pearl for their symbolic value and believed their power to be mystical nonsense. Once they were found, Coaliferos had no intention of surrendering the treasures, and if he could pinpoint the Guardian's Ring and immobilise a target he was confident he could survive a cycle in the Milky Way.

Coaliferos tried to spark a conversation. "General, I hear preparations for invasion are progressing well."

"We have Zorags incubating in the cores of a dozen blue planets. Carbon levels and temperatures are rising," General Ignis said.

"And Earth is first base for the invasion?"

"Yes. Humans will make good slaves. The Zorag on Earth has reached the size where it starts undersea eruptions and superheats the ocean. Earth's ice caps are melting."

"How does the planet react?" Coaliferos wasn't interested in the answer, but he'd seen the general's eyes sparkle when he talked about humans and Earth.

"Take a seat, Lord Coaliferos." Ignis sat on the chair behind the desk.

"The oceans and forests fight to keep the temperature at a level suitable for indigenous life. To reflect heat, the tropical forests seed clouds and make their foliage lighter, and the oceans absorb carbon and sink it to the floor via plankton."

"And the Zorag is overpowering this?"

"With the humans' help."

"Help?"

"Yes." Ignis was now quite animated. "Three hundred million years ago, organic material from immense forests were buried, capturing carbon on a spectacular scale. When the Earth experienced hot cycles, plankton absorbed vast quantities of carbon from the atmosphere and deposited it on the seafloor. Over millions of years, the forest deposits formed coal, and the plankton became oil. The humans are burning the coal and oil, releasing much-needed carbon back into the atmosphere and deforesting the planet at an impressive rate."

"Do humans benefit from the warming?"

"No. The warming magnifies storms and wildfires that makes life difficult for them. Humans have recognised their impact and for many years reduced emissions, but we changed all that." Ignis couldn't restrain a smile. "My telepaths have infiltrated the humans' primary communications, the Internet. We identified suitable human leaders, and stream viral thoughts that influence them.”

A shiver ran down Coaliferos's spine. Billions of humans inhabited Earth. How would he find a single astral warrior with the Guardian's Ring among them? This could be the key.

“Fascinating,” he said.

“Yes, a phenomenal success. One human has great influence, and we work the man like a puppet. The beauty is that we can exert influence and monitor our success over their Internet.”

“Magnificent work, General Ignis. My father always said that battle is won by the mind, and science is the key to victory.”

“We do our best, Lord Coaliferos.” The general's chest expanded. “Over the next hundred cycles, the convergence zone will synchronise. Earth will reach a tipping point. Volcanic eruptions and fires will ravage the planet, raising temperature and carbon levels – ready for our invasion.”

“Very impressive, General Ignis. Thank you for receiving me. Please accept my apologies for taking your valuable time. May I ask who's in charge of telepathic intelligence?”

“Captain Kexu,” Ignis said.

“Your preparations for Earth are fascinating. Would it be possible for Captain Kexu to demonstrate your systems?”

“Certainly,” Ignis said, visibly surprised that a warrior with such a brutal reputation would concern himself with intelligence. “Captain Kexu is at your disposal.”

Coaliferos stood, tilted his head, and left. Excitement tingled as he entered a capsule and torpedoed through the duct to the orb's outer edge. Doors were opening as though destiny guided him. He merged into another dark tunnel and followed the guard to a shadowy room.

Red backlight reflected on Captain Kexu's pale face as his beady, yellow eyes focused on Coaliferos.

“General Ignis told me of your invaluable work,” Coaliferos said.

“Thank you, Lord Coaliferos; please take a seat. My telepath to cyber connection is reaping extraordinary results.”

Coaliferos nodded as Captain Kexu continued to speak of his achievements, but Coaliferos concentrated on his own thoughts: If the pearl were on Earth, there would be an astral warrior guardian near. All he had to do was kill him and take the Guardian's Ring. By nature, an astral warrior would try to stop the Earth warming.

"Our telepaths are streaming viral thoughts to influence humans as we speak," Kexu said. "The humans have ramped up burning coal. And to counter the overwhelming evidence that it's destroying the climate they enjoy, we have powerful humans spreading disinformation and denying it."

Coaliferos cleared his throat. "I hear one man contributes greatly to the warming."

"Yes, our industrialist does much for our cause."

"Is anyone opposing him?" Coaliferos asked.

"Many, but our industrialist takes care of them."

"And the Zorag – Do the humans suspect anything?"

"Oblivious." Kexu scrunched his pale, wrinkled face, "perhaps one. A climate scientist has been poking around the Tonga Trench, the subduction zone that the Zorag inhabits, but the industrialist will dispose of him."

"Show me your data on the industrialist and the climate scientist," Coaliferos said.

10

GLOWING

'ENGLAND'S LEADING CLIMATE SCIENTIST SELLS OUT.'
I read the headline again. Under the headline was a photo of my dad. *What the heck?*

Swathi tapped the link. The article read,

"Ocean warming in the Tonga Trench is a greater threat to humanity than the sum of all carbon emissions," Russell Edwards said, in accepting multi-million-dollar funding from Atlo Trudock. Just last month, Dr Edwards famously dubbed the Xcon boss evil. Edwards asserted that Xcon scientists had understood the dire effects of carbon in the 1970s, but Trudock had fought emission cuts for obscene profits.

There was a picture of Atlo Trudock in a dark suit at the bottom and it looked as if they'd altered his eyes to make him look like a demon. Blood drained from my face. I slumped on Swathi's shoulder. This wasn't like Dad. Science and helping humanity motivated him. He was the most stubborn, opinionated person I knew. Another bus pulled up. With a rush of air the doors opened, and Sonia stepped out.

I slipped my hand from Swathi's shoulder.

"Are you okay, Sam?" Sonia asked.

Her soft eyes and tender smile were like bright sunshine and I just wanted to bathe in it for a moment.

"He just received some tough news," Swathi said.

"Yes, Sorry, Sonia … it's about my dad. I need to catch this bus home and call him."

The last of the passengers alighted. I boarded and watched Sonia fade into the throng of students. I'd made a fool of myself again. Lack of sun made everything feel ten times worse. I ignored a message from Tom and cursed my father.

"Call Dad," I said to my phone. The line answered. "Is it true?" I asked.

"Sam. Are you okay?" Dad said.

"Is it true about Xcon?" I asked.

"Sam, I told you there would be controversy."

"You accepted money from a man you said is evil?"

"Funding for research."

"The Xcon corporate army killed protesters at the Great Barrier Reef Coal Port last month. You told me Atlo Trudock is a madman."

"I'll explain everything tomorrow in Los Angeles," he said.

"I'm not coming." My voice trembled as I spoke.

"Sam—"

"I'm sixteen. Old enough to leave home."

"Listen. I could really use a little help right now," he said. "It's not about the money. Trust me on the funding! And we still need to talk about your mother."

I shook my head and reached for the ring in my pocket. "You said there was nothing else to tell."

"Well … there is … and you'll meet friends of your mother's in Rangiroa."

"Friends?" I couldn't believe what I was hearing.

"An old colleague named Oko, and Matahi, who skippered day trips," Dad said.

"Why tell me this now? Why keep the ring … everything … secret?"

"Sam, trust me. I must go. I'll call this evening and see you in L.A. tomorrow."

The line went dead. I folded the phone and slapped it on my wrist. My head throbbed. I hated the way Dad cut me off. *And why keep all this stuff about my mother secret?*

Three rows up, two girls talked and giggled. Another girl sat alone, her attention fixed on an eBook. I took the ring from my pocket, studied the etchings, and placed it in my palm. Drizzle speckled the bus window. Pedestrians opened umbrellas and sheltered under shop awnings.

As I ran my finger over the ring, my pulse slowed and my mind relaxed. I held the ring to the middle finger of my left hand. The etchings glowed as it slid over my nail. When I pulled the ring away, the etchings dulled.

I slid the ring over the tip of my finger again and the etchings glowed again, then intensified as I pushed it over my knuckle. The ring heated. I tried to pull it off, but it moulded behind my knuckle. Warmth spread up my arm, through my chest and head. My ears hummed. My whole body vibrated. I stared at my hands and arms thinking I might be going crazy. The vibration intensified until a translucent pulse burst from my heart.

"He's glowing!" shrieked the girl who'd been reading.

11

PULSE

This energetic pulse shot me out of my body. It was as if I was on the leading edge of an explosion going in every direction at once. I glimpsed a worker up a ladder washing windows; pigeons on the roof of the terrace house above him took to the sky in a flurry. Then the whole world opened.

I was rocketing over a dark ocean toward an intense light. From inside an office near the top of a tall tower, I saw the Statue of Liberty, and I was floating above a guy with dark hair that looked strangely familiar – he looked to the left and right, as though searching for my invisible presence, then resumed watching a table of holographic figures.

I had no control, and before I knew it, I was gone. I raced over a moon-licked ocean and somehow knew it was the South Pacific. Then I was right in the middle of a pod of dolphins, not the usual kind, but dolphins with white sides. They breached and chirped and whistled. An island loomed large in front of me. I plunged into the water, deeper and deeper; on the drop-off wall a brilliant light shone like a blue star in the blackness, and angelic tones hummed around me.

The light and the tones were so wonderful that I wanted to stay but found myself high in the sky with waves washing over the Tonga Trench below me. Next, I was in the water, in the depths of darkness. The sea floor trembled. Lava gushed from a vent. I sensed a terrible presence. I was terrified. With a sudden whoosh, I slammed back into my body.

12

COALIFEROS

The pulse folded past Saturn and Jupiter, beyond the Orion arm and the convergence zone. As it swept through the Coaliferite base in the galactic tide, Coaliferos jerked his head. His eyes opened wide.

"Are you all right, Lord Coaliferos?" Captain Kexu asked.

Coaliferos didn't answer. He stared at an image of Russell Edwards' son on the monitor and shivered. The boy had the Batavian Clan's electric-blue eyes, dark hair, and light brown skin. *Was this Hila's son? Surely it couldn't be this easy.* The pulse heralded a connection between the guardian and the pearl. Having just turned sixteen, the boy had reached the earliest age a guardian could be anointed.

Trembling with excitement, Coaliferos pictured the ring and the pearl—the power to influence thought and alter the force of nature at his discretion.

"Patch me into the telepathic link with the Internet," he said.

"This is most irregular, Lord Coaliferos. I'd need clearance and the connection would have to be made from our telepathic dish beyond the cloud. And using telepathy to navigate the human net is a specialised art."

"I'm a master telepath and well versed in cyber navigation, Captain. Please seek clearance immediately. And send your cyber brief to this station."

While Captain Kexu made enquiries, Coaliferos focussed on the image of the climate scientist's child on the monitor. Scrolling through the boy's social media, Coaliferos noted his primary interests were science, football, holographic warrior sports, and he was also a member of Youth Leading the World's climate change division. The profile was a perfect match for a guardian. Now he'd identified the new guardian, all he'd have to do was locate and immobilise him, then take the ring. Aroused by his success, Coaliferos opened the cyber brief and uploaded it to his augmented intelligence.

Captain Kexu waited for the process to finish before speaking. "You have clearance, Lord Coaliferos."

A guard led Coaliferos through a dim hallway to a compact dock with a shuttle parked in it. The shuttle powered through the clear zone surrounding the base, and Coaliferos looked back at the shadowy orb. For such a massive structure, everything was so cramped. He was glad to be out of it. A red arterial portal glowed in the dark cloud ahead.

The tiny shuttle negotiated the swirling vortex and burst through the black atmospheric cloud. The Milky Way lit the sky. Coaliferos breathed a sigh of relief – he'd joined the Coaliferites but he'd never get used the darkness, the carbon, the heat, and how they lived like ants in subterranean nests.

The spiralling arms of the Milky Way reached out before him. And to the side, where the dark cloud thinned, a white flower-like dish bathed in the galaxy's light. A stem-like chord hung from the underside of the dish, anchoring it to the cloud. The pilotless shuttle manoeuvred alongside the dock and shuddered as it coupled to the dish. With a sudden hiss the airlock opened.

A pale-faced Coaliferite with an all-white uniform draped over a feeble body stood before him. "Lord Coaliferos I'm the custodian. I'll take care of you during your stay." The custodian's serene tone and slow movements irritated Coaliferos as he followed him up a ramp. The air was humid and hot and carbon rich, but lighter and more energetic than inside the base. When Coaliferos arrived at the telepathic centre, he stood aghast at the spectacle.

Harnessed inside the dish were eleven telepaths. They were blind, with only empty sockets for eyes, and their arms and legs were withered. They lay on their backs in moulded chairs around a central clear dome filled with a thick bubbling liquid. Tubes extended from the central dome into their mouths and nostrils. Electrodes were clamped to their heads.

They lay in a trance-like state and, for all Coaliferos knew, they could be dead.

"All the telepaths are connected to the net on planet Earth," the custodian said. "Seven of them specialise in transmitting viral thoughts to influence humans in raising carbon levels and temperature for our invasion, while the others analyse data and collect intelligence."

The custodian pointed to the solitary spare seat. "I have cleared a space for you, Lord Coaliferos."

The translucent dome ceiling was focussed on the Milky Way's Orion Arm, and Coaliferos gazed at the wonderful spiralling galaxy, then screwed his face as he turned to the telepaths. There was no time to waste, and uncomfortable as he was with the closeness of the telepaths on either side him, he sat in the free chair, which moulded around his body and reclined.

The custodian fixed electrodes to his temples, forehead, and cranium. "This is a little uncomfortable for a short time and you may gag a little," the custodian said, before placing an apparatus with tubes trailing from it over Coaliferos' nose and mouth.

Coaliferos winced as the custodian injected tubes into his nostrils, their tentacles plugging into his brain. He gagged as two thicker tubes slid deep down his throat.

"Place your hands in the sockets to commence the connection." The custodian operated a screen at the foot of Coaliferos' reclined chair.

"Once you're in, visualise the directory and it will appear in your periphery. I'll make the first connection to the Edwards residence for you. The father is very influential. We've made a concentrated effort to sway him from his fight against the warming, but he's strong-minded. It will be interesting to see what you come up with, Lord Coaliferos. And remember, subtle connections only, if you alert the humans, they may find a way to restrict our presence."

Coaliferos nodded, placed his hands in the sockets and a sensation like a vacuum sucked him away. Vertigo and nausea racked him. He shrunk and a huge sun swallowed him. He resisted an urge to pull his hands from the sockets when he streaked through a void of flickering light. Infinite waveforms shimmered, then collapsed. Before he'd time to take it in, a dark hole sucked him in. Fear pressed in on his projection.

By focussing on arriving at the Edwards residence, he raised his energetic vibration. A prick of light, as though at the end of a tunnel, pierced the darkness, and then the darkness broke into flickers of purple and red and blue light. The light brightened, awareness spread, his vision, hazy at first, cleared. He was a bodiless entity looking out from a screen at a closed doorway. On a shelf by the door was a small picture of a raptor, and beside it, a portrait of Sam and Russell Edwards.

13

CYBER-ATTACK

I landed smack bang back into my body. My eyes shot open and I gasped. Three girls were staring at me. I was still on the bus. It was as if I'd been on an epic adventure, but when I glanced out the window, I realised we hadn't travelled far at all and the whole ordeal must have taken place in a matter of seconds. The girls kept staring as though I was a freak. The bus stopped at a light and the driver glared at me in the rear-view mirror.

Totally spaced, I smiled and waved. "I'm okay," I said.

The bus turned left, and everyone stared off. Bone-deep tingles vibrated through my whole body. What the heck was it all about? It was as if I'd really gone to America and seen the Statue of Liberty. And that guy in the office tower – he was weirdly familiar. Then those dolphins, the wonderful glow and angelic tones. But it was creepy seeing waves wash over the Tonga Trench, like the screensaver on the home computer. The hair on my neck stood as I remembered the darkness, the seething vent, and that presence. *What was it? What was it all about?*

My mother's ring must have triggered the vibrations that spread through my body. And when that pulse exploded out of me it was as though I was everywhere at once. I gripped the ring and tried to pull it off. But I could only turn it around my finger, not twist it off. It was stuck behind my knuckle.

The bus reached my stop. My bodily vibrations had subsided, but I was a little unsteady, and my face and teeth were numb. Sunlight brightened the grey sky. Flowers in a garden, then a freshly painted fence with raindrops glistening on it held my attention. All the houses in my street looked so fresh and wonderful. Seeing a neighbour walking her dog near my house, I darted through a break in traffic to greet them.

"Good morning, Mrs Everly, and good morning, Jake. Good boy, good boy, Jake." I'd never been that fond of the Corgi but now Jake felt like a long-lost friend.

"Today's my birthday, Mrs Everly, and tomorrow I meet my dad and fly to Rangiroa. I was born in Rangiroa, did you know?"

"No, my dear. Happy birthday. Did you get any nice presents?" Mrs Everly stared at my ring as she asked.

I put my hand in my pocket. "Just the holiday to Rangiroa."

"Well, have a wonderful trip."

"Thank you. Yes, wonderful it will be." I strode to our front gate, skipped up the steps, and the sound of traffic faded as the front door closed behind me.

The hall clock ticked. Thoughts of how strange the home computer had acted on my way out this morning swirled in my head. My pulse quickened. Edging to the study, I twisted the door handle, but hesitated. My imagination created a monster waiting to leap out at me. But what was there to be scared of? I flung the door open. The screen was blank. The room was empty. Everything sat in its place.

I giggled, hurried along the hall, hung my parka, and bounded two steps at a time to my room. After hanging my school shirt and pants in the wardrobe, I slipped into jeans and a long-sleeved t-shirt. Then I plonked my travel bag on the bed. "Tropical sun, here I come."

From the chest of drawers, I took board shorts, t-shirts, and light cotton pants and packed them. "My dad, Russell Edwards, sold out."

I shook my head and chuckled and packed my favourite Hawaiian shirt, wet shirt, and Crocs. When I picked up my laptop, sounds like distant whispers caught my attention.

A truck rattled up the street and the front door shuddered; then everything went quiet. Something was wrong. There it was again: incoherent whispers coming from downstairs. I crept from my room and inched to the banister.

The hall clock ticked. Export solar flashed green on the energy monitor; everything was as it should be. I focused on a black umbrella at the bottom of the stairs and descended, pausing on each step.

When I reached the landing, whispers floated.

I froze. If only Dad was home. "Hello?" I called.

The whispers faded. My heart thumped. I tried another step, crept in silence until the bottom stair creaked. With teeth clenched, I tiptoed to the alcove and grasped the black umbrella.

"Hello." I crept towards the kitchen.

Creepy laughter sounded behind me. I swung around to face the front door. The laughter faded to whispers. It must have come from the study. The front door shuddered. My knuckles whitened on the umbrella's wooden handle, and I ran my thumb over the spiked chrome tip.

Beyond the front door the street rumbled. I'd left the study door open. I flattened against the wall and inched across the floor. When I reached the entrance, I got ready to stab someone with the umbrella, inhaled a deep breath, took a quick step, and gaped into the study.

An image of the Tonga Trench on the computer startled me. I couldn't see behind the door. I shot a glance back to the kitchen, gripped the umbrella, and burst into the room.

Empty. I backed out toward the hall and focused on the screen. I had shut down the computer. The screen was blank when I got home.

Magnificent blue ocean wavered across the contours of the Tonga Trench. Still gripping the brolly, I pulled the chair back from the desk and sat down. The traffic outside sounded distant. The ocean shimmered and the whispers returned: soothing, enthralling. Warmth spread through my body. My eyelids felt heavy.

A black spot surfaced amongst the wavering blue sea. I moved closer. The black spot spored, and acidic fumes filled the air. The chair took on a life of its own and rolled me into the desk.

I tried to push away, but foul haze swirled from the computer and pinned me to the desk. I jittered in the chair. Adrenaline surged through me. Instincts took over. I managed to reach out with my feet and kick the plugs from the wall.

The screen blanked; haze vanished. I thrust away from the desk and rolled out into the hall.

A loud rap startled me. I bounced in the chair. The top of Tom's head shadowed the frosted-glass panel in the front door. Relief washed over me and I rushed to let him in.

"Are you okay?" Tom asked.

I shut the door and sank into the chair. "Dad's computer – a haze swirled out and like, attacked me."

Tom swallowed, walked into the office, sniffed, and stared at me as if I were crazy.

"Seriously, Tom, the home computer attacked me." I gazed into the office. "I shut it down this morning. It switched itself on, made creepy whispering sounds, and this rank haze swirled out and jammed me into the desk. You can still smell it."

Tom stepped into the office, sniffed again, and nodded. "Something burning or overheating." He bent under the desk and inserted a plug into the socket.

"No! Pull it out!" I shouted.

Tom bumped his head and pulled the plug at the same time. "Take it easy," he said, crawled out, picked up the brolly, and stared me in the eye. "Technology sucks sometimes, but don't let it get you down, Sam. What's with the umbrella?"

I took the brolly and wheeled the chair back into the study. "You don't believe me."

"Who would?"

Swathi came to mind, but I bit my lip and shrugged. My mind flashed back to the pulse and the visions on the bus. *Was I losing my mind?*

"Must have been a power surge," Tom said. "How come you took off from school?"

"You should have stayed for the maths test," I said.

Tom shrugged. "And score zero without you?"

"You should study."

"What happened to the photo of Striker's butt?" Tom asked.

I stared at the ceiling and shook my head. "Everything has gone crazy. I woke up this morning; it's my birthday—"

"Hey, I forgot. Happy birthday!" Tom said.

"Thanks. Dad gave me this ring and says my mother asked him to give it to me when I turned sixteen."

"Your mother?" Tom took my hand and studied the ring. "Cool engravings."

"Yeah, but on the bus, the ring …"

Tom raised his eyebrows, waiting.

"It's stuck on my finger and … anyway, this morning Dad tells me he has new funding, and we're going to the South Pacific. He leaves right away. He just walks out and flies to America. I'm meant to meet him in Los Angeles tomorrow." I folded out my phone. "When I got to school, Swathi showed me this."

I gave Tom enough time to read *The Times* headline and see the first paragraph then my blood chilled as I scrolled further. There was the photo of Atlo Trudock. It was *him*, the Xcon boss. In my vision, I'd been in his office this morning.

"Xcon is funding your dad's research on the Tonga Trench? Awesome!" Tom said

My mind was whirring double time. I squinted at Tom. I couldn't believe what he'd just said. It took a couple of seconds to register.

"Xcon are like the evil empire; they murder protesters and re-open old coal mines," I protested.

Tom led the way upstairs. "Your dad says ocean warming is a greater threat to humanity than the sum of all carbon emissions."

I stopped on the landing, still thinking about the fleeting moment that I'd been in Trudock's office. "The global climate agreements were working, but Xcon is sabotaging everything to make trillions."

"Xcon has loads of money. If your dad plays his cards right, you guys are set for life."

I scrunched my nose and shook my head. Surely Tom was joking. But you could never really tell with Tom, and he never came to any Youth Leading the World stuff with me and Swathi.

"Look, your house is the best this side of the bridge." Genuine concern shone in Tom's eyes. "Your dad spent a packet on the H-Verse Pro and alterations to the loft, but he's famous. Where's the yacht and the country estate? I think you've got to trust Dr Edwards on this one."

"That's what Dad said," I replied, shaking my head. It wasn't until that moment that I really understood how important money was to Tom. I used the umbrella as a walking stick, led the way and stopped outside my bedroom. "He wants me to fly by myself to Los Angeles tomorrow morning."

"Miss school. You're so lucky."

"After L.A., he wants me to go Rangiroa, then to Tonga to help research for three weeks."

The twinkle in Tom's eye vanished. "You'll be away Sunday?"

I nodded.

"Hero-G day." Tom's shoulders slumped.

"I don't even want to go." I felt as though I was falling off a cliff. Everything was crazy – the ring, the vision, my dad and Xcon, the home computer, and flying by myself.

Tom took the pole from the wall bracket, hooked the ceiling panel, and unfolded the loft stairs. "Rangiroa is where you were born, right?"

"Yeah, but I haven't been back since." I led the way up into the loft. Old timber rafters reached high enough to swing an energy blade, and the musty air enhanced the atmosphere.

Tom pressed "start" on the H-Verse controller, and the projectors hummed as they warmed up. "I'm jealous, but what a shame you can't leave Monday, after Hero-G day. I could stay here. We could practise for the tournament and maybe invite Sonia and her cute friend over."

I pictured Sonia in a Hero-G outfit. Home sounded wonderful. I rested the black brolly next to the H-Verse console and opened a blackout shutter. Light poured in. I sat on a swivelling chair in a patch of faint sun. We'd trained for this contest all year. It wasn't fair to Tom.

Tom bent over the console. "Hey, Sam, something's wrong with the Wi-Fi."

"I pulled the plug in Dad's study; we can play offline."

"Offline? Are you nuts? Scores won't register. I'll fix it." Tom headed for the hatch.

"No Tom! Something weird is happening with the home computer."

Tom climbed down the stairs. "You're paranoid."

"Don't plug in the computer! Just the Wi-Fi," I called.

"Okay. Okay. Just the Wi-Fi."

I went running after Tom, stopped, and shook my head. *Maybe I was paranoid? Maybe I was going crazy?* How cool it would be for Tom to stay over. We could win the Hero-G tournament together. I was sixteen, an adult, and old enough to leave home. I sat on the swivel chair in the sun, took the phone from my wrist, and called my dad. The line rang. My stomach fluttered.

Tom's footsteps raced back up the stairs.

When the call went to message I exhaled with relief and took a deep breath. "Dad. Sorry, but I can't let Tom down. I can come on Monday, after the tournament. Bye."

"Yeah!" Tom raced over and high-fived me.

My heart thumped. Heat rushed to my face. I couldn't believe I'd left that message. But what would happen with flights? Now I felt guilty about letting my dad down. I was about to call and leave another message, but Tom bear-hugged me. We fell on the sofa and by the time I wrestled myself up – stars twinkled; a comet streaked.

I turned my phone off and put my Hero-G shoes on. I attached thigh armour and slipped chest and back plates over my head. My heart pumped strong and slow as I slung the assault blaster over my shoulder and clipped the energy blade onto my accessories belt. Holographic light beams gave me enough energy to play. I closed the shutter and pulled the mask over my head.

The outside world ceased to exist.

Backlight dimmed. Subwoofers rumbled. Thoughts of my dad, saving the world, the flight, narcolepsy, the ring, missing the goal, and Xcon jettisoned. Cymbals trembled; stars streaked across the night sky; bass drums thundered, and the Hero-G symphony burst to life.

The floor dropped away. We floated in space. Shivers ran up my spine as I burnt through the atmosphere and landed with an explosion of white light on the steps of a stone temple.

A battlecruiser launched into a quick exit.

The Emperor appeared before us: "Vaxion rebels kidnapped Princess Zola. You must rescue the Princess and destroy the rebel base."

"Yes, Emperor!" Tom and I shouted.

The Emperor bowed his head, drums and trumpets resounded, and we launched from the planet. Stars elongated, and my armour vibrated as I thrust into hyperspace.

"Prepare to enter the Adolphus system," piped through our masks. Subwoofers shook the floor as we landed in an arid, rocky landscape.

"Head to the ravine," I said.

A bright sun shone in a blue sky. I held my blaster to my chest, ran on the spot, and my feet crunched over holographic sand.

"Incoming! Behind!' I leapt over a boulder. Blast fire erupted behind me. My heart raced and my whole body tingled.

Two starship fighters swooped overhead.

"Now!" I shouted.

Tom and I rapid blasted. The lead fighter burst into flames; the second streaked through the explosion. A fast tak-tak-tak issued from my gun – white flame burst from the barrel. A fiery explosion burst from the second fighter.

A troop carrier roared overhead. I turned and unloaded into the carrier. Black smoke streamed from the carrier; the bulky craft landed beyond old wreckage. Troops disgorged and opened fire at us.

"Run to the wreckage," I called, telescoped my blaster into a pistol, ignited an energy blade, and ran. Blast fire streaked toward me. My blue blade flashed as I blocked a blast. Reaching the cover of the wreckage, I collapsed my blade and rapid- blasted the rebels.

Six rebels fell, but eight reached the other side of the wreckage. Grey acrid haze drifted. I ignited my blade. For a second everything went quiet; then the rebels attacked.

The first rebel groaned as I slashed his arm, then blasted another clean off his feet. Tom and I fought back-to-back. My blade spat as it sliced the neck of a rebel, sizzled through the heart of another.

The holographic projection flickered. Timber beams and the sofa appeared before the projection retook the loft. A glitch. I frowned. The H-Verse had never done that before. I sliced another rebel and an acid stench hit me.

"To the canyon!" Tom shouted.

"Wait!"

The grey haze darkened. Foul fumes like the ones that had come from the computer in the study wafted. They had to be coming from the controller. The haze thickened and swirled into the form of a Dark Warrior.

I aimed my blaster and unloaded at the aberration. White blasts vanished into its churning dark form.

Tom raised his blade and charged the Dark Warrior.

The Dark Warrior thrust its arm. A midnight-blue blast shot from the heel of its palm, slammed into Tom's chest, lifted him off his feet, and smashed him into the rafters.

I gasped. Without thinking, I turned from the Dark Warrior, focused on the H-Verse plug, and ran.

In my mind's eye, I sensed a blast shooting toward me. Before I could duck, it struck the back of my head. Pain, like the stings of a thousand wasps, stunned me. I face planted into the carpet five paces short of the H-Verse. An intense whine jammed my hearing.

The Dark Warrior came for me.

I dragged my body and crawled to the H-Verse. An acid stench gripped my throat and squeezed. With one hand clasping my neck, the other outstretched, I collapsed.

The Dark Warrior swirled above me. I turned on my side to look up.

Its eyes and its blade glowed midnight blue. It smiled, took the blade in two hands and thrust it into my ribs, through my heart and out the other side, pinning me to the floor.

14

SWATHI

There was no pain. For a second I was calm, then my body convulsed. I strained to fight, to shout, but couldn't raise a whimper and slouched limp on the carpet.

A cold shiver ran through me as the blade was ripped out of my ribs. The Dark Warrior dissolved into a churning cloud and streamed into my nose and mouth then swirled into the H-Verse controller.

I saw Tom and my own body on the floor. Holographic sand blew over us. *Was this the end? Was I already dead?* My life couldn't end like this. I needed to fight. I reached out with my hand, but the dark cloud tightened its paralysing grip.

My awareness drifted. I floated into a dark abyss, a stinging void of nothingness where layer after layer of cryptomesh smothered me. This was real. I was dead. But I couldn't let go yet.

Light pierced the darkness. From a distance someone called my name. I wondered if I was in heaven. I saw a vision: Swathi in the attic; my body on the floor with black tendrils reaching into it. But I wasn't in my body.

Swathi searched the holographic wreckage. "Sam!" she gasped and rushed to kneel by my side then recoiled in horror.

"Pull the plug! Pull the H-Verse plug!" I called. She couldn't hear me, but now she realised what was happening.

"No!" Swathi screamed at the black tendrils that tore a translucent form from my body and streamed into the H-Verse controller. Gripping me by the shoulders, she tried to drag my body away.

"Pull the H-Verse plug! Pull the plug!" I shouted.

"The plug," Swathi said. She must have heard, but it was too late.

Dark tendrils spilt and shot into Swathi's chest. She tried to tear them out. I saw the darkness clamp her heart and squeeze like a python. She collapsed. The swirling tendrils streamed into the H-Verse.

"Fight it! Fight it! Get the plug, Swathi," I sobbed.

Fighting to rise, Swathi poised on one knee like a sprinter and lunged for the controller.

"Go Swathi!" I shouted.

A wave of dark matter rushed from the H-Verse, jolting her back. She spun, powered, and clutched, just short of the plug. Her outstretched fingertips brushed the wooden handle of the brolly. It fell.

"Ahhh!" Swathi bellowed, caught the wooden handle and speared the chrome tip through the H-Verse controller.

Sparks exploded. The dark cloud evaporated, and the rugged desert landscape reverted to the loft. My mind went blank, then I was spinning, unravelling. I gasped to life.

Swathi knelt beside me, tears streaming down her face. "Are you okay?" she sobbed.

"I think so," I said, but I couldn't move. "Could you open the shutter please? And see if Tom's okay."

Movement returned to my arms and legs as Swathi rushed to open the shutter. Tom blinked as dazzling light poured in. Swathi helped him into a sitting position. He rubbed the back of his head and his eyes and mouth widened.

"Oh shit!" Tom scrambled to his feet and rushed to the H-Verse.

Thinking that thing must have come back, I sat bolt upright.

Tom switched the socket off and pulled the H-Verse plug. He shook his head, grasped the wooden handle, pulled the umbrella from the smouldering wreckage, and glared at Swathi.

"Swathi saved us." I stood up and rubbed the spots where the blade pierced my ribcage. "Do you remember that dark swirling figure coming from the canyon?"

Recognition flashed in Tom's eyes.

"That wasn't part of the game," I said

Tom rubbed his head. "I ... just sort of blacked out."

"The dark figure blasted you, hurled you into the ceiling. That's why you're rubbing your head."

"A Hero-G figure physically attacked us. Are you serious?" Tom asked, looking at the blood on his hand.

"We both saw it," Swathi said. "Black tendrils dragged the life from Sam and swirled into the controller. Then it attacked me."

Tom squinted. "Great. Holographic games can kill you. Parents will love that."

"How else do you explain it?" Swathi asked.

"Explain what? A power surge. I bumped my head. A lunatic with an umbrella smashed the H-Verse."

Swathi stepped toward Tom, fists clenched. I moved between them.

Tom scowled at Swathi. "You should go."

"Tom, Swathi saved me! Us. We should all leave."

Swathi made for the stairs. I tore off my boots and armour and followed her.

Tom uncoupled the H-Verse.

"Leave it," I said.

"A friend of my brother's repairs electronics and owes me a favour."

I shook my head and descended. Swathi leaned on the wall by my room. Tears streamed from her eyes.

"You were so brave. Thanks so much," I said.

Swathi covered her eyes with her hands. "I thought it killed you."

I took her in my arms. She hugged me tight, her tears soaking through my shirt.

"Whatever it was, it must have come through the Internet. We should get out of here," I said.

Swathi dried her eyes and followed me into my room. I put the dock for my phone and some toiletries into the small pack, slid my laptop into the bag with wheels and telescopic handle. With my bags packed, I remembered sitting on Dad's shoulders and arranging the stick-on stars on the ceiling. I gazed at the old paperback books Dad had given me – *Blue-Back* and *Jonathan Livingstone Seagull,* on the shelf beside my football trophies and the photo of my mother.

"She's so beautiful," Swathi said.

"Dad gave me her ring this morning," I said, holding my hand out for Swathi to see. Mesmerised by it, Swathi took my hand.

I stared at the photo of my mum. She was tall and slender and stood in a bikini on white sand in front of a palm tree. Her right hand cupped a slight bulge in her midriff, which had to be me. Behind her, the tip of the sun sparkled above the sea.

After all the hours I'd spent gazing at the photo, it wasn't until now that I noticed the ring on her finger. She held her left hand like a presenter. The tip of her ring finger met the sea, in line with the dazzling sun flaring over the horizon. I wondered where the photo had been taken. It seemed so weird that not even Dad knew.

"Uh-hum." Tom cleared his throat at the doorway, the packaged H-Verse in his arms.

I slung the small pack over my shoulder and picked up the other bag. Leading the way downstairs, I remembered sliding down the banister and Dad catching me at the bottom. When I reached the bottom step, I saw myself running in from the kitchen to bowl down the hall, and Dad taking guard with the cricket bat at the front door. Happy memories. I wondered why they made me so sad.

My dad had always seemed invincible, like an iron man. But now, for the first time, I feared for his safety. My heart thumped as I pulled the door shut on the study, then opened the front door and held it open as Tom and Swathi filed outside.

Childhood memories flooded the hall. Chest pounding, I stole one last look and closed the door. Swathi waited on the other side of the white wrought-iron fence. Tom stood on the second step with the H-Verse balanced on his leg.

"You should call your dad," Swathi said.

I swallowed, and blood drained from my face.

15

DECISION

Lightning flashed, raindrops pattered, and thunder rumbled across the heavens. It was warm and cosy in the reclining chair by Aunt Jindhi's window where I sat sipping spicy chai tea.

Footfalls splattered outside. Tom raced along the garden path and knocked at the front door. Swathi rolled her eyes and stood to let him in.

So much had happened yesterday. My mind flitted from the cyber-attack to my dad, the trip, the ring and my mother, the ring and the pulse, to the cyber-attack, that rank acid stench, and my dad again.

"Are you okay, Sam? Have you spoken to your dad?" Tom asked.

I just shrugged and shook my head. Tom sat on the lounge opposite me.

Aunt Jindhi entered the room. "Tom, tell me. Yesterday in the loft, what happened?"

"We were playing Hero-G. A power surge or something struck me and knocked me out. When I came too, Swathi had speared an umbrella through the H-Verse."

Swathi unfolded her arms, inhaled, and her mother lifted a finger.

"Swathi and Sam told me that a dark figure and swirling tendrils projected through a gaming controller and attacked you all. Did you see this Tom?" Aunt Jindhi asked.

"H-Verse graphics are real-life. You can't blame Swathi for panicking and spearing the controller."

"Sam saw it too," Swathi said.

"A dark figure that wasn't part of the game attacked us," I said.

"Now you're not going to get in trouble, but I need you to tell the truth," Aunt Jindhi said. "Did any of you experiment with drugs yesterday?"

"Mum! No," Swathi said. I shook my head, held Aunt Jindhi's gaze then glared at Tom. He hadn't backed us up at all.

"Tom, you saw the dark figure before it blasted you into the rafters and split your head. How could a power surge do that?" I asked.

"I don't know, Sam, but a H-Verse Pro costs thousands of pounds. Swathi should just switch the machine off nex—"

"I tried, but that swirling thing was killing Sam and held me back." Tears welled in Swathi's eyes.

"The good news is the damage isn't as bad as it looks," Tom said. "The repair will cost two hundred … and ninety pounds and be ready this afternoon."

"Give me the bill, Tom." Aunt Jindhi waved Swathi's and my objections away. She didn't believe us. To her, using drugs was the rational answer.

Tom smiled. "If required, my brother's company can check the electrical and Internet connection this afternoon."

"Please, Tom," Aunt Jindhi said. "Now, Sam," she looked into my eyes, "I spoke to the Weston Hotel in Los Angeles. Your father checked in, but no one has seen him since, and he's not in his room. I called the British embassy. No news. I'm sure Russell is fine, but we should consider postponing your flight."

Rain pelted down outside. I stared at the ring from my mother. I'd only just received it yesterday and I was sure it had triggered the weird experience on the bus and the cyber-attack. And now my dad was missing. I'd used soapy water and cooking oil to try to remove it, but there was no way it was coming off.

Swathi's place felt so warm and homey. Staying with Aunt Jindhi sounded terrific, but something was wrong. I thought I should catch the flight and meet my dad. *But what if he wasn't there to meet me?*

"You have narcolepsy," Tom said. "Your dad is missing. You shouldn't travel alone."

I nodded. Maybe Tom was right.

Lightning ripped across the heavens. Everyone flinched. Thunder boomed and windows shuddered.

"I don't want you to go, Sam, but Dr Edwards may need help when he shows up," Swathi said.

I inhaled a sharp breath. Swathi's words took me back to the last time I'd spoken to him – *I could really use a little help right now* – he'd said. I also recalled the message he gave me from my mother – *Follow your heart*.

I looked from Swathi to Aunt Jindhi to Tom, then stared out the window. There was no doubting I wanted to stay, but going to meet my dad seemed like the right thing to do. *Which came from the heart?* I gripped the ring on my finger and turned it in an anti-clockwise direction, then turned it the other way.

From the haze swirling inside my head, a clear thought emerged, and I made my decision.

16

COALIFEROS

Inside the telepath dish, Coaliferos's eyes flickered with rapid eye movement. He fought to repress the fear and dread he experienced but pulled his hands from the sockets and his eyes shot open. The Milky Way shone on his face and settled his heart as he stared at it. Having barely become accustomed to working inside the net, he'd launched an all-out attack and failed. The boy had escaped him.

The encounter with his father had been more successful, but the boy had the ring; Coaliferos had seen it on his finger and couldn't resist the opportunity to take it. And now the boy was offline. But humans depended on the net as if it sustained them. There would be opportunities, but the boy would be wary. How would he find him? He'd have to use the industrialist. Yes, visit the industrialist and be more subtle this time, implant a viral thought, a strong desire into Trudock's mind.

Now that he'd experienced the human net, everything would be so much easier next time. Coaliferos inserted his hands into the sockets, closed his eyes, and focused on the cyber directory – Atlo Trudock, boss of Xcon, Earth's most powerful corporation. Relax and focus on the prize, Coaliferos repeated the words and visualised his wonderful victory, the untold power awaiting him. With waves of positive thoughts circling in his mind, Coaliferos focused on Trudock's connection.

17

ATLO TRUDOCK

First light reflected on Trudock Tower. Behind closed curtains, Atlo stared open-mouthed at a holographic display – tendrils of dark matter slithered out of his nose and mouth as Coaliferos released his grip. Having transferred an overwhelming desire for the boy's ring to the human, Coaliferos's presence evaporated into the holograph, where the rise of Xcon stocks on the London market had frozen.

The hologram flickered. Atlo blinked, and Xcon shares jumped three percent. His eyes widened at the sudden increase, and then he realised an hour had passed. He thought of yesterday's epic Wall Street rally, and wanted to smile, but a strange idea and a rank smell disturbed him. He reached for a glass of water, gulped, and sniffed around for the stench, so thick it caught in his sinuses and throat.

Many prosperous ideas had come from daydreaming in front of his computer, but this one confused him. He massaged his temples and didn't like what he was thinking. The tone of a personal call roused him. He swivelled his chair. The curtains opened. Smog clouded the Great Lady, and sunrise was a sickly, red glow.

With nostrils flared, he right winked and his favourite New York sunrise, that perfect morning when his father had met with an unfortunate accident, projected on his window. Atlo took another sip of water and reclined. "Hi, honey."

"I hear you have enough money to cover the U.S. national debt, congratulations," Atlo's third wife said.

"Thanks, honey. It's amazing what a few words from a farty shock jock and a trumped-up climate scientist can do."

"We should plan a celebration," she said.

"I'll need to stay at the office the next few days. A week, tops. We can get away after that."

"Your son's sixteenth birthday is the weekend after next. How about our island? The Pacific is lovely this time of year."

Atlo thought of Xcon activities in the Pacific and frowned. He rose from his seat and sniffed around the holographic display. "Skiing … let's go skiing, somewhere quiet with no Internet."

"I don't think places like that exist nowadays, and it would devastate Atlo Junior. Leave it with me. And speaking of your son, here he is. I love you and am so very proud, Atlo."

"Thanks, honey, love you too." Atlo focused on the rise of his fossil fuel stocks.

"Hi, Dad," Atlo Junior said.

"Hey, Junior, how ya doing, champ?"

"I'm fine, Dad," Junior answered. "Are you really the world's richest man?"

"I believe so, and that makes you the richest boy."

"You need to give me the money for that," Atlo Junior said.

"Smart answer. It could all be yours one day, Junior. I need to work now, but how about skiing for your birthday?"

"Cool."

"Love you, Junior."

"Love you too, Dad."

Atlo squirmed in his seat and scratched his head. He took another sip of water, winked at the intercom icon, and spoke.

"Bring fresh water – this water tastes like shit. And send someone from maintenance – the air stinks."

From the top draw of his desk, Atlo took his encrypted phone and made a call.

"You're accommodating the climate scientist, but what about his son?" Atlo said.

"The son is aboard a flight from England to Los Angeles," replied the speaker.

"Get me the airport security footage of his departure." Atlo said, and watched his stocks continue to rise as he waited until the phone bleeped. Footage of Sam Edwards at the airport security screener appeared on the screen. Atlo froze the footage and zoomed in on his ring. The maze-like etchings fascinated him.

"Make sure Master Edwards is looked after; deliver the ring he's wearing and I'll triple the bonus."

18

THE ICE-POD

Much farther west of New York, in the dead of night, the wind abated, and the setting moon cast a golden path over the Pacific Ocean. Beneath the moon-licked surface, dolphins clicked, probing the darkness.

"PFFFH." Tali, the Ice-Pod's matriarch, blasted spent air. Her echolocation fixed on the shark. She swam with an exaggerated motion, snapped her jaws, and prepared to ram the attacker.

The shark surged. Tali flicked her tail, closing her eyes an instant before the collision.

The shark veered. Moonlight glimmered from its white underside. The predator disappeared.

"PFFFH." Tali exhaled and drew breath. Beside her, the other dolphins surfaced, replenished oxygen, and clicked sound waves into the liquid darkness.

The frenzy of mako sharks dropped away.

The sharks were starving and had already taken a cow and a bull from the pod. Tali thought it was strange the sharks would just disappear. Smaller sentries took over the flanks, and the pod's enforcers moved inward to rest.

Mist drifted from Tali's breath as she surfaced. It seemed like yesterday the Ice-Pod had fled the Alaskan Gulf with salmon sharks then orcas in pursuit. The warming had triggered a food chain collapse. Life in the ocean had gone crazy. The sudden disappearance of the sharks triggered a deep dread in Tali.

"Report," she chirped.

"Nothing to rear, flanks clear," the sentries chirped in reply.

"Something ahead, at the end of my range," chirped Miki, Tali's baby sister. The dolphins tightened formation.

"Got it too," chirped a forward sentry.

Tali changed tack from southeast to south.

"Something ahead," Miki chirped.

"Closing in from the side, several large—" chirped others.

Tali led the pod, turned 180 degrees. Echolocation showed clear water. They increased speed, but frightening shapes loomed.

A haunting whistle cut the darkness – *Orca!*

The dolphins trembled. Tali tracked east, urged Miki to stay close as her clicks bounced – *Orca surrounded.*

Haunting cries ripped through the water. Tali rallied her pod. "Breathe, stick together, we'll find a path."

Black and white giants surged from the darkness. Dolphins scattered and regrouped. A panicked bull broke ranks, darted low, and disappeared in a cloud of blood.

Tali searched for the weakest link. As the pod surfaced for air, a wave of orcas surged, pushing them down. She whistled and fled toward four smaller orcas on the western flank. Tali and Miki led; nineteen dolphins followed. The younger orca offered a glimmer of hope, but eight huge beasts surged from the watery blackness, cutting their escape.

"Hold course!" whistled Tali. There was nothing else they could do.

Mighty jaws crunched a dolphin. Blood exploded through the water.

Miki and Tali strained for speed, but the black and white giants intercepted. In her periphery, Tali saw Miki dart right.

"No, Miki!" whistled Tali. Her little sister peeled away, charged the lead orca.

The lead orca hesitated; those following hesitated. Miki surged through snapping jaws.

Miki's distraction worked. The pod reached the western flank, jumped, and dived. The young orca struck, but half the Ice-Pod escaped. Tali turned to search for her sister.

Miki dipped a fin and darted left. Orcas converged, surrounding her.

"My sister!" Tali cried.

Blood spread through the water, revealing her ultimate bravery. With a shattered heart, Tali pushed her tail, forcing herself to join the pod.

19

LOS ANGELES

Smog hung in the air above houses with blue pools, and I gazed at the oil platforms just offshore. The undercarriage clunked, buildings grew, and tyres screeched as we touched down in Los Angeles. A hurricane of reverse thrust slowed the hulking aircraft. My heart thumped as the plane taxied to the terminal. I missed my dad and couldn't wait to see him.

The seatbelt sign chimed. Hundreds of people stood – overhead lockers clicked. It took an eternity for the queue to move. A hostess smiled as I exited, enabled my phone, and stomped through the covered ramp. Announcements echoed over the PA. I kept glancing at my phone as I followed the herd of passengers to the snaking queues at immigration.

The phone vibrated. My eyes lit. I'd connected to a carrier, but no missed calls, only a "bon voyage" from Swathi. I bit my lip and waited for Dad's message. A gap grew in the queue – I shuffled to the bend of the taped corridor and rechecked the phone.

The immigration officer flicked through my passport, then glanced at me and the vacant space behind. "Are you travelling alone?" he asked.

"Yes. I have a notarised letter of consent from my father," I said, placing the letter on the counter.

"Is your dad meeting you here at the airport?" the immigration officer asked.

"Yes," I nodded.

With fingerprints and a photo taken, the officer stamped my passport and waved me through to baggage. People with trolleys crowded numbered carousels. Along with the travellers from my flight, I waited for the bags to flow. There was still no message from Dad, so I tried calling him. The line rang. *Yes.* I gazed around the hall with the phone to my ear.

The call was picked up.

"Dad! Dad," I pleaded. The line was quiet. I was sure someone listened, but no one replied, and then the line went dead.

20

SUNGLASSES

The corridor walls and ceiling narrowed. My ears rang as I approached the exit. Near the last duty-free shop, I waited for a family with two young children to pass and then followed them.

My pulse increased as I glimpsed faces beyond the exit. I adjusted the backpack on my shoulder, re-gripped the handle of the bag on wheels, sucked in a deep breath, and strode into the arrivals hall.

Faces stared at me. Heart in my throat, I searched the crowd. Announcements echoed. I paused beyond the tape barrier and my eyes lit – tweed jacket, tan slacks, phone to ear.

"Dad!" I called, overcome with relief. The wheels of my bag skidded as I ran.

The man turned, smiled, looked away and resumed talking.

I stood open-mouthed. Around me travellers hugged family and friends. I scanned the length of the hall to the doors, windows, and traffic beyond. In my periphery, I saw that a man wearing sunglasses and a dark suit was checking me out.

The flow of passengers slowed. The assembly behind the tape dwindled, but the man in sunglasses lingered. I checked my phone, walked to the wall of windows, and stopped at the threshold to the USA.

Yellow taxis and baggage-laden travellers formed queues. A man in a uniform hurried an old car away from the kerb. I couldn't imagine a reason for Dad not meeting me or sending a message. If he were in hospital, the British Embassy or Swathi would have called.

I released the wheelie bag, rubbed my temples, and called him again. It went straight to message. I should have stayed home. I checked the airline ticket. The flight to Papeete with Air Tahiti departed at 11.45 pm that night. A late flight. If I found him, Dad would have to carry me aboard. The return legs were fully flexible, and the flight to Rangiroa left two hours after arriving in Papeete.

I clamped the phone on my wrist. People, cars, and shuttles bustled beyond the glass. It was 3 pm. Sunset was at 6.30 pm. The Weston Hotel was only a ten-minute shuttle ride away. If Dad wasn't there, I'd call Swathi and catch the next flight home. Happy with my decision, I slipped the pack from my back, unzipped the front pocket, and took out an envelope that Dad had left for me with five one-dollar, two five-dollar, and two ten-dollar dollar bills.

Dad had said small notes were handy in America because you needed to tip. I put the notes in my wallet, slung the backpack over my shoulder, surveyed the arrivals hall one last time, and walked through the retracting glass doorway.

Horns beeped. Sound echoed from the overhead roadway. It was cool outside. Exhaust fumes drifted in the air. A Weston shuttle pulled in across the road. I squeezed through the multitudes. My bag's wheels grated as I hurried across the bitumen. The driver hung from the steps, looking over the heads of the passengers.

"Wait!" I called, waving and swerving past luggage and travellers.

The driver smiled, beckoned, and waited on the pavement.

With the handle telescoped, I passed my bag to the driver and climbed up the steps. I slipped the pack from my shoulders and a shiver ran down my spine.

Sunglasses stood on the kerb, staring at the shuttle with a phone to his ear.

21

THE WESTON

A row of tall palm trees divided West Century Boulevard's eight lanes. The shuttle powered past burger joints, a gas and electric vehicle charge station, car hire, and the LAX Hilton. A lot of the cars were bigger than those in the UK. The boulevard was busy, but there were hardly any pedestrians.

The Weston Hotel towered into a cloudless grey sky. Gardens and lush green lawn extended from the hotel to the road. The shuttle took a right, then left into the driveway, and pulled up under the portico near the entrance.

Scents of lavender and citrus sweetened the air as I exited, tipped the driver two dollars, and wondered if it was enough.

"Thank you, young man," the driver said, handing me my bag.

Before I could extend the handle, a porter intervened: "Allow me, sir." The bag was small, and I felt awkward as I trailed the porter through the towering glass entrance across the marble floor to reception.

A receptionist smiled at me. "Welcome to the Weston; my name is Nelda. Are you checking in?"

"I'm meeting my father, Dr Russell Edwards. He checked in yesterday."

"And your name?"

"Sam Edwards."

"Do you have identification, Mr Edwards?"

Expecting her to announce a tragedy or say Dad was missing, I placed my passport on the counter.

"Yes, Russell Edwards, a corner suite and Sam Edwards as his guest. And a message to say he is sleeping, come up to the room."

I exhaled, looked to the heavens, and smiled.

"Here's the key to room 714." The receptionist gazed to the entrance. "I'll call a porter."

I saw all the porters were busy helping arrivals from another shuttle.

"My bags are small. I'm fine to go alone."

After receiving directions, I walked to the elevators. A door opened before I pressed a button, and two adults and a child stepped out. I stepped inside. My hand trembled as I pressed number seven, suddenly wishing I had waited for a porter.

The lift shuddered, whirred to full speed, slowed, and chimed as number seven lit. The door opened onto a deserted hallway. A faint rumble, like being on a plane, sounded. My bag rolled silently over the grey carpet, past silver doors with black numbers. My stomach fluttered as I passed room 713. "I'm meeting Dad, everything will be okay," I whispered and stopped outside room 714.

I released the bag and searched the hallway—no one in sight. I held the key near the sensor, hesitated, rechecked the corridor, and put an ear to the door. My acute hearing detected no movement. I clenched my fist and knocked.

My chest thumped. Why the hell hadn't I waited for a porter? I listened for footsteps, heard none, then shook my head. Inhaling a deep breath, I held the key to the pad. The lock clicked.

"Dad," I called as I pushed the door open.

"Dad," I stood inside the rectangular room holding the door ajar. At the far end, windows and a glass door led to a balcony. A briefcase rested on top of a desk against the wall.

I smiled as I recognised the old brown leather case. I let the door shut. A window rattled as a plane landed so close to the hotel it startled me.

"Dad," I called, quieter now. Apart from the briefcase, there was no sign of him. The sofa and coffee table looked untouched. There were no beds in the room. I gazed at a closed door and slipped the pack from my shoulders. Cool air chilled my neck. I walked to the desk, rested a hand on Dad's briefcase, and stared at the closed door.

My pulse quickened. I crept to the closed door. Blood pulsated through my temples. I noted the position of my bag and the exit and pushed the door open.

"Dad!" I called.

An acid stench poured from the room. Adrenaline triggered the urge to run.

22

LIFELESS

Silver curtains blacked out the room. I readied to run and switched on the light. The bed was made. Dad's laptop lay open on a desk. To my right, the bathroom was empty. The acid stench smelled the same as in the loft back home.

I inched backwards from the room. A shadow under the bed caught my attention. My eyes zoomed in on a hand. The rest of the body lay hidden, but I recognised the watch.

"Dad!" My heart thudded. I should run – call an ambulance – police – reception – run. But maybe he needed immediate attention. I hurried across the floor, ducking before the laptop and crawling past the desk. I lifted the bedspread, and Dad's pale face stared at me.

"Dad," I whispered. Someone had jammed him under the bed. The body looked all wrong. I felt his cold, limp hand and remembered last time we'd spoken he'd said he could really use a little help. I slipped my hands under his shoulders and eased him out. His pale face seemed alien, not like Dad anymore.

I slumped on the floor. I'd arrived too late. Dad's lifeless body blurred through my tears.

"I'm so sorry, Dad." I knew it was no use, but I felt for a pulse.

On the desk, Dad's laptop flickered. Blue Ocean wavered and darkened on the screen. I jolted back, slid up against the wall and stood. Black haze swirled from the laptop. A dark tendril surged at my chest. I leapt sideways, snapped the laptop shut, and cracked it on the desk.

The tendrils evaporated. I smashed the laptop until it broke in two, then flung it against the wall. As the crashing reverberation subsided, a loud knock on the door startled me.

Someone to help. I ran and ripped the door open. The man wearing sunglasses shoved a foot in the jamb.

Sunglasses—shit! I whipped the door against the man's foot.

"I'm Agent Clyde – British Embassy. Are you okay, Sam?"

I shoved harder. Agent Clyde grunted and held his ID into the room. I reduced the pressure and he relaxed.

In one movement I snatched the ID, kicked the man's shin, and slammed the door shut. With the chain lock engaged, I glared through the spyhole.

Agent Clyde removed his sunglasses. His grey eyes made me shiver.

"Sam, I'm here to help. Are you okay?"

The embassy ID appeared official. "Why are you following me?"

"Making sure no one else follows you. You and your father are in grave danger. Call the embassy. I'm here to help."

My lips trembled. I rechecked the ID. I didn't trust Agent Clyde, but with his English accent and the ID, it was as if we were on the same team. Torn by my instincts and desire for help, I unlatched the door and let him enter.

Agent Clyde limped in and took his ID with a thin smile. "Have you seen Russell Edwards?"

"My father is … dead. In the bedroom." The words echoed in my head and the weight of what I'd said crushed me.

"Russell Edwards dead?" Agent Clyde didn't look surprised. He just shut the door and latched the chain lock.

Panic thumped through my chest.

Agent Clyde met my eyes, "So the hotel staff don't enter," he lowered his gaze.

He was looking at my ring. The thought made my head spin. I closed my eyes and Dad's pale face swam before me.

Agent Clyde's hulking frame commanded space. "Lead the way, Sam," he said, ushering me into the bedroom.

The agent was like a giant black spider pushing me into a sticky web. I gazed at my dad, lifeless on the floor. Agent Clyde blocked the exit.

"I feel sick," I said and broke for the bathroom.

The agent moved quickly for a big man and came in behind me.

"Sorry about your dad. I'll call an ambulance. Take it easy, kid." Agent Clyde checked that the window didn't open, stepped out, and pulled the door shut behind him.

I opened the curtain, and sun poured through the window. Grief combined with fear and the acid stench to overcome me. I dry-retched. Agent Clyde didn't even check my dad. I heard the agent talking, spat into the bowl, wiped my mouth with the back of my hand and pushed my ear to the door.

"Russell Edwards is dead, and the boy is in the bathroom."

I visualised the agent's phone and focused my hearing.

"Get the ring and feed the bodies to the pigs," the voice on the other end said.

23

RUN

Agent Clyde opened the bathroom door in time to see me vomit airplane fruit salad into the toilet. He winced. "Are you okay, Sam?" he asked. "An ambulance is coming for Dr Edwards. Best we leave now and get you to the embassy."

Mucus stretched from my mouth to the bowl. A high-pitched whine jammed my mind. Giddiness drained me. I couldn't believe I'd left the bathroom door unlocked. I was afraid I might faint.

Agent Clyde handed me a towel. "Sorry, kid. We best go now. The ladies at the embassy will take care of you."

The power to react had abandoned me. My dad lay dead on the floor. Agent Clyde planned to kill me and feed us both to pigs. Like a zombie, I put on my pack, gripped my bag, and let Agent Clyde steer me out of the suite.

Tears ran down my cheeks. I pictured my dad on the floor. Memories flashed through my mind – practising football together; swimming with humpback whales; Dad on the news; his sharp tongue, imposing presence, cutting wit. I pulled back.

"Sorry, kid. We best get out of here." Agent Clyde gripped the pack on my back and steered me down the grey corridor to the elevator. "My car is in the parking garage under the building."

The light chimed, the door opened, and a couple with no bags stood in the elevator. Agent Clyde put an arm out to restrain me, but I ducked under and dragged my bag inside. Clyde followed, pressed B1, and stood in front of the door as we descended. I could tell that my actions put Agent Clyde on edge. He reached into his jacket, and I was sure he was reaching for a gun.

I stared at the couple, wanting to plead for help. But what could they do? I swallowed, tried to talk, but no words came out. Before I knew it, the lift doors opened at the lobby, and Agent Clyde's hulking body blocked the exit. I struggled to see reception and searched for a porter or security.

"Excuse me, buddy," the man said.

With one hand inside his jacket, Agent Clyde glanced at me and squeezed back against the jam.

I released the wheelie bag. I had to run or shout. Sweat trickled down my neck. I turned the ring on my finger as the male guest sidled out.

"Hey, buddy, give the lady some room." The man took his partner's hand and scowled at the agent.

Agent Clyde squeezed back against the door again. A strip of daylight opened between the woman and the lift.

I launched, hit the gap, and surged like a running back. The woman sprawled against Agent Clyde. I sprang out.

"Sam, wait!" Agent Clyde shouted.

My runners squeaked on the marble floor as I darted past columns and shouldered a trolley-laden porter. Shouts boomed from behind. My energy waned as I bolted through the lobby doors.

A shuttle stopped under the portico. Travellers milled around. I had to tell someone … run … Where … Who?

Time slowed. Agent Clyde ran towards me. Guests, porters, and the doormen stood with stunned expressions and raised their hands as Agent Clyde drew a chunky pistol from his jacket.

Adrenalin jolted me. I sprinted around the shuttle and into the sun, raced across the driveway, leapt over a low hedge and landed on a sidewalk. A solid wall of traffic sped up Century Boulevard. Cars queued at the side street bordering the hotel. I ran to the side street and weaved through waiting cars. From the other side, I turned to look back. A uniformed policeman ran across the hotel lawn with a pistol in hand.

Thank God! Someone to help me. Agent Clyde had vanished. The police must have him. I waved both hands at the policemen.

The policeman stopped, gripped the pistol double-handed, and aimed.

Who was he aiming for? I gaped around. Something fizzed past my ear. I jerked back. There was no one behind me. *Who was the policeman shooting at?* I was the good guy. He couldn't be shooting at me. I froze like a rabbit in a spotlight, holding my hands in the air.

A puff of smoke rose from the policeman's pistol. A bullet tore through my shirtsleeve and a metallic crack rang out. I grabbed my sleeve, gawked at the hole and yelled at the policeman.

"You've got the wrong person."

Another puff of smoke issued from the policeman's gun.

I ducked and ran hunched forward. A metal fence with barbed wire at the top ran the length of a car rental to the left. Four lanes of traffic sped up Century Boulevard to the right. The policeman crossed the side street. Any second he would have a clear shot at me.

There was no time to run the block. I darted behind a silver car. The shuttle following blasted its horn. A red civic in the second lane skidded to a halt; I ran in front. The civic jolted as a big family car cannoned into its rear. Metal crunched. Horns blared. Hands snatched for the non-existent steering wheel of a self-driving SUV.

A bullet hissed past my head into a big, black city car's windscreen in the fourth lane. Slivers of glass exploded. Tyres screamed. The black car locked up, lurched sideways, and skewed right at me. I leapt over the bonnet, pushed off the roof, and hit the asphalt running.

Metal groaned and crumpled. I scurried onto the median strip and crouched behind a cactus at the base of a tall palm.

Horns blared. Burnt rubber wafted. The policeman put one foot on the road, then jumped back as a pickup skidded into a rear-end shunt.

Policemen should help. Why was this happening? I picked a half break in the westbound traffic and took off. A white luxury car locked up. Horns sounded. A driverless e-cruiser made a silent, abrupt halt. To my astonishment, I reached the sidewalk with no westbound pileup.

Sirens whirred. The policeman and Agent Clyde weaved through the wreckage on the eastbound lanes. With no time to think, I ran for my life. Pounding along Century Boulevard, I jumped a wall into a car park, ran past a diner, and hurdled a chest-high block wall. I landed in a gas and battery station and stopped to spy back up the boulevard.

Agent Clyde was out of sight. The policeman stood on the median strip, one hand resting on a palm tree, the other holding a phone to his ear.

I ducked, inhaled five breaths, and spied again. The policeman was weaving back through the pileup. *Why would a policeman and a British agent try to kill me? Was it all about the ring?* If I could just get it off my finger, I'd give it to them. But no, the ring was a gift from my mother and there was magic in it. I was sure of it. They'd killed my dad and they weren't going to get it.

The battery station bordered a six-lane side street and as the lights turned red, traffic stopped, and a yellow bus drove past on Century Boulevard. I sprinted through the battery station, sidled through waiting traffic, and hot-footed past a pedestrian wearing a hoodie. Nobody waited at the next stop, but the bus pulled up. A passenger stepped off. I still had two hundred metres to run.

I concentrated on breathing, ran flat out, and waved at the driver's reflection in the side mirror. The driver nodded, and I slowed at the rear to glance back. The traffic jam in the eastbound lanes was building. There was no sign of the agent or the policeman. I boarded the bus.

24

ESCAPE

Chest heaving, I held an overhead rail and stooped to look back through the windows. There was no one following so I slumped onto a seat. The bus passed the Hilton and continued to the airport. Grief and fear and adrenalin churned through me. *What was I going to do?* I needed to tell someone. *Was that a real policeman?* My eyes welled as images of my father and pigs consumed my mind.

"You're a fast runner," said a woman seated to my right.

I wobbled my head.

"You're a fast runner," repeated the woman.

"I really needed to catch the bus."

"Yeah, but you run real fast. Ever thought of going for the Olympics?"

I wanted to tell her that someone had murdered my dad; that a British agent and an L.A. policeman had tried to kill me.

"I don't run so fast on cloudy days," I said.

The woman burst into fits of stuttered laughter. Her phone rang. To my relief, she answered and then told the caller that she'd met the world's fastest boy.

"He says he don't run so fast on cloudy days," she said and laughed out loud again.

The bus turned right at the Marriott Hotel. Mind spinning, I opened maps on my phone. Who else could I call besides the British embassy and the police? The FBI? Traffic jammed side streets and boulevards. It was 6 pm. The sun would set in half an hour, and then I'd get tired. The flight to Tahiti left at 11.30 pm. I could change my ticket and fly home. But my dad was dead. I had to tell someone … But who?

Turning left at a Burger King, the bus headed along 96th and detoured off the road into the LAX transfer station. The airport looked close on the map. Instinct told me to get off. When the bus stopped at the first bay of a shelter, I stepped off.

A passenger jet thundered into the sky. I scanned the length of the shelter, which ran for 100 metres. Round concrete pillars supported the roof; scattered commuters stood or sat on benches. Trees and shrubs shielded the station from the road, and a shuttle disgorged passengers at the far end.

I hid behind a column near the entryway. Another column diagonally in front gave me a gap to spy through. I unclipped my phone from my wrist, whispered "Swathi," and leaned against the column. An aircraft landed. Another bus pulled into the station. It was three in the morning in England. Sweat trickled down my temples as the line rang.

"Sam! Are you okay?" Swathi asked.

"Yes. No … my dad is dead. I think a cyber-attack killed him. Like in the loft."

"Oh god … Dr Edwards …" Swathi's voice quavered. "I'm so sorry."

I wiped my eyes. "A British agent and an L.A. policeman tried to kill me. I'm on the run."

"Tried to kill you? That's crazy," Swathi said.

"A policeman shot at me outside the hotel. I'm hiding at a bus station near the airport. What should I do?"

"I'll wake mum. No … hang on," Swathi hesitated. "That's strange. A car just pulled into our drive. Have you spoken to Tom?"

"No. Why?"

"I'm sure he's at your place. Two men in a black e-cruiser were parked out front all evening."

"Will call back in five." I hung up, kept my eyes on the entry road and called Tom. It was too strange that a car had pulled into Swathi's in the middle of the night, and while I was talking to her. The evening chilled. Green parrots squawked in a sycamore tree. The sky to the east was orange and grey with storm clouds building.

"Sam! How's L.A.? Is your dad okay?" Tom asked.

Tom sounded bright for the middle of the night, and I heard him grunt.

"Dad's dead. A policeman tried to shoot me," I replied.

"Ha! Say hello to the old tool for me."

I heard more grunting, and "KSHH" as blades clashed. "Are you playing Hero-G?"

"Yes. Shit," Tom replied as explosions signified game over.

"You're at my place."

"Yes. I used the key under the pot. Just testing the H-Verse, it works perfe–"

"Tom, listen! My dad's *dead*. I found him at the hotel, then a policeman and a British agent tried to kill me."

"You're kidding, right?"

"No!" I shook my head. The sky turned pink around the cloud. Another yellow bus pulled into the station and a big guy with long hair and a baseball cap ambled in.

"Seriously – a policeman and a British agent tried to kill you?" Tom said.

"I'm hiding at a bus station near the airport; I don't know what the heck to do," I clutched my head.

"Shit. Get the next flight home, Sam."

I nodded. "I will. Now open the shutter. Is a black e-cruiser parked outside?"

The guy in the hat leaned against the column three metres in front of me while I listened to the shutter opening in my loft.

"Yes, a black e-cruiser … and two men are getting out," Tom said. "How did you know? Wait. Shit. They're coming through the gate."

"Get out, Tom! Go through the window. My dad is dead! Someone is trying to kill me! Get out. Don't go back."

I listened as the window squeaked open and pictured Tom climbing across the roof. Just then, a police car pulled into the transit station.

My heart jumped into my throat. The driver wore a uniform. Glare obscured the passenger. The police car came straight toward me and stopped eight metres from the front column. I edged around and spied between the columns as a door opened and Agent Clyde got out.

Wind blustered and thunder rumbled. I looked to the heavens, flattened against the concrete column and readied to run. The burly agent approached from the front of the station to my right, and the car circled around the rear to my left. I pressed against the column and edged right as the police car approached, but any farther and Agent Clyde could see me.

The black fender rounded the column. Agent Clyde's footfalls crunched on loose gravel. I braced to run. Lightning forked and Agent Clyde glanced up.

I scurried to the front column and flattened against the contour. My heart pounded. I held my breath and dared not peek. After two seconds passed and I hadn't been discovered, I crept around to where the guy with the baseball hat leaned against the column and peered over his shoulder.

Agent Clyde's shoe scuffed the kerb as he mounted the pavement. I ducked behind the column. Baseball Hat concentrated on his phone and provided extra cover. The police car idled up the transit centre. I surveyed the station entry and the busy road.

When they reached halfway along the shelter, I would run. Then another thought made me shiver. When I called Swathi, a car pulled into her place. *At three in the morning.* When I called Tom, two men raided my house. Now Agent Clyde and the policeman searched as if they knew I was here.

I stared at my phone and shook my head.

"Shut down," I said.

"Confirm shut down," replied the phone.

A blue bus marked Santa Monica-Rapid entered the station, and Baseball Hat picked up his pack.

"Cancel shut down," I whispered as the blue bus pulled up right in front of me. Agent Clyde and the police car had travelled thirty metres up the station. I spied a pocket open in Baseball Hat's pack and slipped my phone into it.

Baseball Hat boarded, and the Santa Monica-Rapid pulled out. Twenty seconds later Agent Clyde ran to the police car, tyres screeched, and they took off after the bus.

***

The sun descended into a hazy red set. Lightning flashed out to sea. I boarded an airport shuttle and scratched my wrist where my phone should be. They tracked phones … Police … British Agents … Men at my house. What chance did I have at the airport?

The shuttle pulled into the Tom Bradley terminal. All I wanted to do was collapse into a corner and sleep. I exited the shuttle feeling like my future was hanging over a cliff, a slender thread of will holding me from a dark abyss.

Bustle and activity surrounded. Announcements echoed. A policeman walked toward me. My pulse spiked, but with no energy to run, I could only surrender.

The policeman walked straight past. At least the whole world wasn't against me. I thought of my dad lying on the hotel floor, and the chase and pile-up outside the hotel. My eyes zoomed in on departures – a British Airways flight left for London in two hours. Maybe I could change my booking and catch it. The Tahiti flight left in four hours. I wanted to go home, but my dad was dead. Maybe I could find Dad's friends in Rangiroa. But there was no way I could stay awake to board the Tahiti flight.

The policeman doubled back.

Tell this policeman what happened, that's what I should do. I wished someone would tell me what to do. I fiddled with the ring. Was this what all the trouble was about? I tried to pull it off again. It didn't budge, so I turned it to the right, then to the left, and made up my mind.

25

THE ICE-POD

As lightning pierced the dark skies over Los Angeles, golden light washed a curved expanse over the South Pacific Ocean. On the breath of the evening breeze, an albatross soared over crumbling whitecaps, hunting to nourish her famished body. Movement caught her eye. She dipped into a dive, then levelled as a dolphin surfaced within a rising swell.

"PFFFH," Tali exhaled and drew breath.

The Ice-Pod surfaced around her. Mist from their breaths drifted with the breeze. They swam with empty bellies and sadness in their hearts. Tali didn't like swimming in open ocean; she was a coastal dolphin from the Alaskan Gulf, but the Gulf was now a distant memory.

The albatross circled in the sky above her, then glided in the opposite direction. Tali surveyed the pod and whistled a mournful tune. *I wish Miki were here. I miss my sister.* Orcas and sharks had killed half their number in last night's massacre. Bola swam beside her. He was big and strong and brave. His presence usually settled her, but Miki had given her life for the pod, and grief gnawed at Tali.

To escape the tragedy, her mind wandered to her youth, to the Alaskan Gulf, before the warming. A time of plentiful food, when the salmon migration brought excitement, and abundant life meant they never went hungry. When sharks and orcas rarely threatened them. She drifted and found herself swallowing a tasty squid, so vivid she could taste it and feel the cold, sediment-rich water passing over her skin. When she was young, the Ice-Pod had numbered over one hundred, and Tali had thought they were invincible.

Dwelling in the past brought a moment's respite, but Tali crashed back into the present. Orcas had taken her parents, her children, and now her baby sister. Miki was so young and brave. Tali surveyed her weary family. Only nine white-sided dolphins remained. The once mighty Ice-Pod neared extinction. The dolphins floated, and the albatross glided, searching for a solitary flying fish or a squid to fight starvation.

The hot, acidic ocean pressed in. Tali swept her tail.

"PFFFH." *I love my sister. Miki has gone.*

26

FLIGHT

My chest rose and fell with a deep, relaxed rhythm. Like a falcon, I soared through the blue sky, detached from the world, over an ocean to a green island with a single cloud clinging to its cone-shaped peak.

Dipping a wing, I streamlined and dived into the cloud. The whiteout lasted longer than I expected. When I burst through, I saw myself standing beside a pool nestled into the side of the peak.

Wings became arms. My eyes shot wide open. A panel of gun turrets pointed at me. I lay flat on my back. Nothing made sense, until the gun turrets transformed into reading lights and air vents on the panel above me.

I had made the flight. My panic subsided. I closed my eyes, clutched for my blissful dream, and tried to return. *Dad!* I sat up and stared at the vacant seat beside me. My heart raced.

The cabin was dim. Screens and reading lights glowed, but most passengers slept. Showing my narcolepsy certificate and the notarised letter from Dad at the boarding gate was my last blurred recollection. There was no sign of cabin crew, and the curtain leading back to economy was drawn.

If someone had wanted to kill me and take my ring on the flight, I assumed they would have done so by now. I collapsed on the bed, glad my dad had booked business class for the overnight leg, but a storm rumbled in my head. The stench of death by a cyber-attack, my dad's alien face, the agent, and the policeman shooting at me.

I clutched my arms and squirmed through shuddering troughs. Swathi. Tom. I hoped they were safe. Waves of emotion subsided, only to drag me back and pound me – pigs – bullets – tyres screeching.

My dad had been murdered. I would arrive in Tahiti at sunrise and then take a small plane to Rangiroa. Was I crazy? I didn't even know anyone there. What were Dad's friends called? Matavi and Yoko or something?

Thoughts of my dad stirred frantic emotions and I cried. I tried to keep pigs out of my mind and inclined the seat to a sitting position. What were Swathi and Tom doing? Were they okay? A passenger walked past. The "toilet occupied" sign lit up. I lifted the window shutter.

A burnt orange glow illuminated the edge of the world. Far below, a vast sheet of the Pacific Ocean heaved like a sleeping giant. That first intense glow stirred desire and pulled my face to the window. Rays of hope burnt through my darkness.

Sunrise expanded, softened to apricot, and the sky blued. Cathedral sunrays burst over the horizon. The Pacific glistened. Tropical islands and being alone on an adventure sent tingles up my spine. Then I looked at the empty seat next to me. I rubbed my wrist where my phone should be, and slumped.

Aromas of coffee and croissants filled the cabin. I tapped "flight path," and a holographic image played before my eyes. The plane had crossed the equator into the southern hemisphere. Papeete was two hours and thirty-three minutes away. The aisles became busy as passengers woke. A hostess wearing an aquamarine hat and scarf came to my seat.

"Good morning, Sam. You're a sound sleeper."

"Thanks to whoever helped me to my seat. I can't even remember boarding."

The hostess smiled. "You're welcome, and you must be hungry. Can I get you a snack or refreshment? Tea, coffee, juice?"

"Do you have any mango?" I asked. I craved mango, especially whenever I'm stressed or depressed.

"We have fruit salad with mango, and a pineapple-mango juice blend."

"Fruit salad and juice, please." I wanted to ask for tea as well, but three things seemed greedy. While the hostess went for my refreshments, I found my backpack in the overhead locker. Without a phone, I felt naked, and I wondered about my bag at the hotel, and what went down with Baseball Hat and Agent Clyde.

At least I had a laptop, though I didn't feel game to open it. The hostess returned with juice and two tubs of fruit salad.

"Sure you wouldn't like tea or coffee?" she asked.

"Tea would be lovely. Thank you." With a fork, I speared a mango chunk and savoured the sweet juicy texture. I speared another chunk and scrolled to holographic gaming. Hero-G didn't appeal this morning, or any game, really. I opened the juice. Far below, wisps of cloud floated above the shimmering sea.

Sunlight streamed through the window. I finished the mango chunks, downed the juice, and thought of asking for some more fruit, but if I ate too much – I'd fart a lot.

Angelic clouds and ocean couldn't stop my mind spinning. I opened games and scrolled to Super Mario, the only game that Dad ever won. The holographic display in business was better than flat screen economy. I tapped and blinked, manipulating the tiny figure until breakfast arrived. I chose continental, heaped every bit of mango jam onto a croissant, licked the knife, and played one-handed.

Super Mario is a clunky retro game, but I liked the way the little guy threw blasts and smashed huge bricks with his head. Jam oozed from the croissant and slid beneath the ring. I sucked most of it out, but the sticky residue annoyed me and my gut rumbled – the fruit and the croissant had given me wind. I farted and continued playing, but my stomach rumbled again. I paused the game and went into the tiny restroom. As soon as I'd closed the door, an announcement piped into the cubicle.

"Good morning, this is Captain Martel speaking," he spoke with a thick French accent. "We'll begin our ascent shortly. It's 5.05 am local time. The sky is clear over Papeete, and the temperature is currently 19 degrees celsius. On behalf of the crew, I hope you enjoyed the flight, and we hope to see you in the air again soon."

The toilet roared as it flushed. I left the cubicle as the announcement repeated in French. The cabin crew collected rubbish, and every time I got back into the game, another announcement interrupted. The "fasten seatbelt" sign chimed. I gulped some water, handed the bottle to the hostess, and stared out the window.

Billowing clouds scattered across the heavens. I caught glimpses of water and thought of those dolphins with white sides I'd seen during my out-of-body vision on the bus. The clouds opened. A cone-shaped island rose from the shimmering blue. Low clouds clung to a lush mountain. Fringing reef and blue water surrounded the island. Waves peeled, tiny figures surfed, and boats floated in the harbour. The plane's shadow crossed a village, and the ground loomed close.

Tyres bumped, the engines roared and shook with reverse thrust. Announcements blurred through the cabin. As we taxied to the terminal, an overwhelming thought troubled me. *What the hell was I doing here?* Everyone else smiled, happy to be getting off the aircraft, but I could easily have spent another day lying back and playing games, with meals brought to my seat.

I descended the covered steps to the runway. The humidity hit me. It was already warm for six in the morning. My stomach hollowed as I reached the tarmac. Terror pounded in my chest. *Kidnapped? Killed? Arrested? What would it be?* I'd fled without even reporting my dad's murder. *What could I say? Who would believe me?*

Potted palms lined the access. Two men wearing turquoise shirts sat on a wooden stage – one played the ukulele, and the other a Tahitian banjo – a barefooted lady swayed her hips and danced with graceful hands.

I stopped. My lips trembled as I smiled. Passengers filed past me. The performers seemed so happy. They smiled back. I watched until they finished playing, then realised I was the only one left. I kept glancing back over my shoulder wishing for some of their happiness as I pulled myself away to join the immigration queue.

Guilt, as if I'd done something evil, worked me into a frenzy. I knew for sure that the immigration officer was going arrest me.

"Welcome to Tahiti," the officer said, handing my passport back.

I stared blank-faced for a second. "Thank you."

With no bag to collect, I made customs first and the officer waved me straight through. Only the duty-free shop stood between me and the arrival gate. Although I was terrified, I walked straight through it.

Women, children, and men wearing bright, short sleeved shirts stared at me, then focused back on the gate. Sunlight flooded through huge windows. The scent of flowers refreshed the air. I shuffled out through arrivals, and a big man wearing a black suit and dark glasses approached.

27

DARK GLASSES

"Please. No." I whispered. The man with dark glasses stared at me, then stared at my ring. The other passengers waited for their bags. Only one lady walked behind me. Beyond the crowd at the tape barrier, the vast building was near empty.

I turned back.

The man in the suit came for me.

I jerked away and stumbled.

The man in the suit kept coming, then embraced the lady behind me, and kissed her.

I sucked in deep breaths, wiped my forehead with the back of my hand, and wandered into the bright, airy hall. A few cars, taxis, and shuttles lined the road out front; beyond, an iridescent green mountain rose to the heavens. A sign for inter-island flights pointed to the other end of the terminal. The two musicians I'd seen earlier emerged from customs smiling and laughing as they wandered to a podium. I searched for the dancing lady but couldn't see her. A policeman with a funny peaked hat walked toward me.

Now I'd be arrested. I froze. Guilt washed over me. The idea of being arrested, of ending this misadventure, brought relief.

The policeman strolled past toward the cafe.

Relief, disappointment, and anxiety clashed inside. Chirpy rhythms floated from the musicians. The flight to Rangiroa left in two hours. My mind raced across the Pacific to my dad in Los Angeles, then jumped the Atlantic to Swathi and Tom in England.

I headed to a public phone, wondering about the men at my house. I'd never used a public phone, but the instructions were clear. With no device to pay, I tapped the back-up card Dad had given me and punched in the numbers.

"Tom." Tears welled in my eyes.

"Sam! Shit! Are you okay?"

"Alive," I answered. "You?"

"I'm okay," Tom said. "Did you hear about your house?"

"What do you mean?" I closed my eyes.

"I got out the window and waited on the roof. Those two men ransacked your place, then set it on fire!"

"What?" Anger then despair flared inside me.

"Burnt to the ground. Fire engines. Police, but I got back in and saved the H-Verse just in time. Where are you, Sam?"

Shaking my head seemed to absorb some of the shock. An announcement echoed in French.

"I spoke to Swathi," Tom went on. "The British embassy said Dr Edwards is missing, and you were distressed and ran from their agent."

"That's crap. My dad is DEAD. The agent saw him, I swear. A policeman shot at me when I bolted – I ditched my phone because they tracked me. The embassy is lying."

"I believe you. Where are you? Come home, Sam."

I clutched my forehead. They were probably listening to this call. Just speaking to Tom could put his life in danger. I stared at my ring.

"Are Swathi and Aunt Jindhi okay?"

"They're fine, but worried about you. Where are you?"

"This is serious, Tom. Calling you or Swathi could put your lives in danger. I won't call you again. I'll be away a while. Tell Swathi I'm okay. Look after yourself." I clunked the receiver into place, stared at the ceiling and closed my eyes. My dad, my home, photos, trophies, books … everything … my life – gone. Barely holding it together, I stumbled to a plastic seat, slumped, and pictured Tom running through flames with the H-Verse in his arms. I laughed and snivelled and wiped tears from my eyes until a familiar ukulele rhythm caught my ear.

As the chords repeated, I leaned forward, and with my elbows resting on my knees and my hands covering my eyes, I rocked in time. Then a supernatural voice shocked me.

I'm so glad the sky is blue ... cause that's my favourite colour for a day.

The stout guy with the ukulele lifted the roof and set my body tingling.

A clear blue sky makes me smile.

And all my troubles melt away.

The voice was so true. I wondered how a human could make such a sound. I mouthed the words and sang along.

The sea is like our mother, reflects us like no other.

And there are fishes all the colours of the rainbow.

Sky and sea and sun, dolphins having fun ...

What else could you want in just one day?

Crystal mountain streams, frangipani dreams, coco palms a-swaying.

Coral sand beach, blue lagoon and reef ...

What else could you want in just one day?

The man's voice and the *Blue Sky* song carried me through the Tahiti stopover, and still played in my head as Flight 113 to Rangiroa taxied from the terminal. I stared at the vacant seat next to me. *Blue Sky* was the soundtrack for a South Pacific documentary Dad and I had watched years ago on Sunday evenings. The tune was a favourite, and at the start and end of the show, we'd sing along. The memory made me cry, but at the same time, repeating the words steeled me.

28

RANGIROA

A power surge snapped me into the present. Props whirred. The 19-seat Twin Otter hurtled along the runway and lifted. Waves broke on the fringing reef, and the intense green vegetation faded as we climbed through the cloud.

It took some time to get used to the noisy propellers. I unhitched the tray to receive a small fruit platter and chose traditional French pink lemonade to drink.

Clouds cast shadows like small islands on the sea, and I wondered what it meant to be born on Rangiroa? Neither parent was from the atoll, and since I'd only spent the first week of my life there, I didn't expect it to feel familiar.

Ukulele music stopped playing in my head. The ocean sparkled and heavenly white clouds floated. I chewed my lip and wriggled. What if Dad's friends weren't in Rangiroa? The British Embassy or LAPD could easily track me. *Why had the embassy said that Dad was missing? And why burn our house?*

Scattered green islands gave way to atolls where the old volcanic island sank back into the earth and fringing reefs grew to form new islands around a lagoon. The ukulele music resumed, and I hummed as a blurred outline appeared in the hazy distance.

I sniffed my armpit and detected faint BO through the new-shirt smell. Not bad, considering I hadn't showered since I was at home. Fashion shopping at Papeete airport wasn't exactly my style, but I'd found a plain blue cotton T-shirt and tan cargo shorts, which would have been better if they didn't have so many pockets. Red Crocs, quick-dry board shorts, a blue hibiscus shirt, and two pairs of undies completed my purchases. The clothes I'd just bought, plus the outfit I'd set out in, combined with my laptop, toiletries, and backpack, were my only worldly possessions now.

Rangiroa Atoll took form through scattered clouds. Hundreds of tiny islands stretched like a pearl necklace to the horizon, circling a turquoise and jade-green lagoon. Palms and green vegetation covered most islands. Only two housed permanent settlements, and many smaller islets were just coral sand and a few palms. The magnificent lagoon stretched eighty kilometres into the hazy distance. Swells broke white on the fringing reef, and the sea outside was the deepest blue.

A small town and palm plantations gained definition. I studied the line of over-water bungalows, knowing my dad had booked the second from the end. This island was two metres above sea level and stretched two kilometres, with a pass where boats could enter the lagoon at either end.

Water closed in on both sides. The propellers descended between coconut palms; a tyre screeched, bounced, and settled. The plane taxied to a small terminal. I pulled weird faces stretching my jaw as I waited for the door to open, and I wondered if someone waited there to kill me.

Heatwaves shimmered from the tarmac as I descended the aluminium steps. Sweat beaded on my brow and I positioned myself in the middle of the dozen passengers, scoping the shingle-roofed structure.

Salt breeze ruffled my hair and took the edge off the heat as I neared the terminal. Ukulele music started. Everyone smiled, and a woman wearing a crisp white blouse and turquoise skirt approached.

"*Maeva, manava*. Welcome to Rangiroa," she said. Her gentle brown eyes reached out and she presented me a floral lei. "Mr Sam Edwards?"

I nodded and bent to receive the lei. The aroma of fresh flowers calmed me.

"I am Rani, from the Kia-Ora resort," she searched the tarmac. "Is Dr Russell Edwards with you?"

"He … couldn't make it."

"I hope he's all right," Rani said.

I shrugged and screwed my face.

"As soon as we collect your luggage, I'll take you to the resort. It's beautiful. You'll love it."

I nodded and tried to smile. "I've got no checked luggage."

The gentle breeze evaporated sweat and cooled me as I followed Rani to a minibus decorated with pictures of hibiscus flowers, thatched bungalows, and a blue lagoon. Rani pulled out onto a worn bitumen road. I tried to picture what it would have been like to grow up on Rangiroa as we drove through the shade of an old copra plantation. Tall stems stretched into the sky, allowing glimpses of the ocean to the left and a turquoise lagoon to the right.

The minibus turned right at a stone Kia-Ora sign and drove through the green lawn, past red hibiscus bushes, to a towering thatched roof. A smiling porter came looking for my bag and insisted on taking my tiny backpack. A hostess added another lei around my neck and presented me with a spectacular mocktail garnished with fruit and umbrellas.

All the attention made me blush. The fruit mocktail was cool and refreshing. I tasted a hint of mango. Rani beckoned me to follow her and stopped near reception.

"Will Mr Edwards be joining us another day?"

I shook my head. "I don't think so. I'm meeting two of his friends."

"What are their names?" Rani asked

"Matavai and—"

"Matahi?" Rani asked.

My eyes widened. "That's it. Do you know him?"

"Know him?" Her concerned expression became a mischievous grin. She glanced to the heavens. "Matahi is my grandfather."

Waves of relief rushed through me. I was so happy, I wanted to hug Rani.

"You never know where Matahi will be, but I'll send word. If he is a friend of your father's, he will come." Rani pursed her lips. "I'll make sure he doesn't lead you astray."

It seemed a strange thing to say about her grandfather. Rani spoke to reception, and I was glad I didn't need to lie about my dad again. I showed my passport, swallowed as I presented my credit card, and exhaled when it worked. Rani led me from reception through fragrant gardens.

"The pool, restaurant, and water sports are to the right," Rani said, taking the left-hand path that ran parallel to a white sand beach, to the overwater bungalows.

Colourful fish swam in the shade of the pylons. The curvature of the earth obscured the other side of the lagoon. Transparent water turned light blue and turquoise as it deepened, and was so enticing, I fought an urge to plunge in as I followed Rani along the grey wood pier.

"Tonight, we have sunset drinks with music and fire dancing at the bar," Rani said. "You must come. I'll keep an eye out for you, and maybe Matahi will be there."

We reached the bungalow with its private deck, lounges overlooking the endless sparkling water, and a place to dive into the lagoon. It was a cool bungalow, but when Rani opened the door, it got even better: windows in the floor brought turquoise water right into the wood and thatch hut.

I sensed Rani savouring my bewildered expression.

"This is amazing. Thank you," I said and fumbled for a tip.

Rani held up a hand. "That's not necessary, Sam. *Manava*. See you for sunset drinks."

I flopped on the bed, stared at the ceiling, then rolled and stared through the floor window. The turquoise colour reflected on my face, and a small fish foraged, sucking and blowing out sand. Quick as a flash, a camouflaged flathead swallowed the small fish.

"*Manava*," said a voice outside. No one replied.

I stared as the flathead settled and wriggled back into the sand. I shivered, thinking something wasn't right, but decided the lagoon was whispering my name, and I needed to jump in. The labels from my quick-dry board shorts tore free, and the thin material felt smooth on my skin. I pulled my shirt off and looked in the mirror.

"You made it," I said, acknowledging my handsome self.

The tiny fish occupied my mind as I latched the chain lock, opening the door just enough to see a strip of blue, then farther to see the private deck and the beautiful glistening water. I figured I was being paranoid, unlatched the chain, and stepped outside.

A man stepped into the courtyard and pointed a long-barrelled handgun between my eyes.

29

ASSASSIN

"Do exactly as I say, or I blow your brains out." The man was tall with dark hair and a moustache. He pointed a silenced pistol at me.

I thought of ducking and diving for the lagoon.

"Slowly—back into the room. Reach for the door, and you're dead." The gunman reeked of aftershave, and his legs were as white as his pressed shorts.

With my eyes on the barrel, I took a step backwards towards my room.

A sudden movement sent the pistol catapulting into the air. The gunman thrust his elbow into someone behind him and turned to face his assailant. The pistol splashed into the water.

Fists flew at the gunman. He blocked and struck back. A smaller Asian man ducked left, ducked right, spun, and kicked the gunman's head. The gunman fell but flipped back to his feet and threw left and right punches. The Asian man deflected the blows and slammed his fist into Gunman's throat.

Gunman stumbled.

With a flying sidekick, the Asian man smashed Gunman into the wall. His head bounced with a loud thud, and Gunman collapsed on the deck.

I stared at my attacker lying on the grey timber, then looked at the Asian man standing before me.

"Thank you," I said

An outboard motor started under the bungalow. I jumped.

A hand gripped the railing, and an islander with wavy black and grey hair peeped over the top. The Asian man rolled the attacker's limp body over the edge, and it thudded into the boat.

"Get the gun," the islander said.

The black pistol stood out in the shallow turquoise water.

"We're friends of Russell Edwards. You look ready for a swim, Sam," the Asian man said.

I blinked, walked to the edge of the deck, eyed my attacker and the islander, and turned to the Asian man.

"Quick, Sam. We can talk later," the Asian man said.

I sighted the pistol and dived. As I struck the water, my ring flashed.

Again, just like on the bus, a pulse burst out of my chest. My consciousness scattered as though I was on the leading edge of an explosion. I knew my body was underwater, but it was as if I was everywhere at once. I was in the middle of a pod of dolphins, I was in Trudock's office again, in the depths of darkness of the Tonga Trench, then plunging into the water near an island where a blue star shone from the drop-off wall. The blue star stirred a desire to reach out and grasp it, but I blasted through the stratosphere past nebulas and stars to a dark matter cluster that made me shiver. There on the edge of the dark matter cloud was a weird dish with freaky wasted bodies lying inside it. And in their midst lay a dark warrior. The warrior's eyes blinked open, glowing midnight blue.

"Holy shit." It was the warrior from the cyber-attack in the loft.

30

COALIFEROS

Coaliferos's eyes blinked open. "I see you," he whispered.

To most, the vibration was subtle and abstract, but Coaliferos sensed the guardian's presence. He read the vibration like a secret code. The ring and the pearl would soon be united. And with this knowledge his fears rekindled – fear of failure, fear of not realising his destiny. Fear burned and smouldered, then exploded into raging desire.

He pulled the tubes from his nose and mouth and snatched the sensors from his head. Dizziness struck as he stood, and he almost fell on the telepath next to him. The boy had escaped him. The boy's presence had vanished from the net, but Coaliferos had found the guardian child among billions of humans. Now he'd tasted the boy's essence and was sure he could track him.

The custodian hurried into the telepathic platform. "Lord Coaliferos, if you're finished, you should wait for me to terminate the coupling," he said.

Engrossed in inner dialogue, Coaliferos only nodded. Xcon was on the boy's trail, but now that Coaliferos was patched in to receive the latest progress, there was no point wasting more time in the dish. Trudock's thirst for power had made him very useful. Thinking he could profit from planetary warming, Trudock had mobilised Xcon and unwittingly protected the Zorag by sabotaging research into the heat gushing from Tonga Trench. The boy was headed to the trench, that's where Coaliferos would find him. The guardian child would try to stop the warming. It was in his nature to be the hero.

Now it was time to locate a weakness in the convergence zone and acclimatise to the Milky Way. Coaliferos looked back at the blind telepaths lying limp in the dish and shivered. What a meagre existence. Cyber warfare was interesting, but no place for a real warrior.

"The ring and the pearl will soon be mine." Coaliferos smiled and visualised killing the guardian child and taking the treasures.

31

THE ICE-POD

"AM–AAMM," Tali quivered. The weary Ice-Pod scattered among the swells. The albatross dipped in the sky above them. Nervous energy pumped through Tali's heart.

"What is it?" Bola chirped.

"He's here! I saw him," chirped Tali. With the sea connecting the ring and the pearl, a subtle vibration folded through the Pacific Ocean. Tali's mind flashed back to her youth: monochrome visions of playing with her cousins and racing Bola when they were calves. Her eyes glazed, bringing colour to the past. She remembered the day when a humanoid figure appeared in the blue-green water. When Tali turned to flee to her mother, a voice had sounded in her head.

The figure wasn't human, but had communicated with telepathy, and the most wonderful light radiated from her being. Such a happy memory of joyful times, before the warming, before salmon stopped migrating, before the squid died out, and before salmon sharks and orcas hunted the Ice-Pod from the gulf.

"The Princess from the light planet," chirped Tali. "Her child, the guardian, has come. He can help the ocean. We must find the guardian and protect him."

<h1 style="text-align:center">32</h1>

THE ZORAG

Superheated clouds gushed from the wall of the Tonga Trench, and beneath, where the earth's crust recycled into the mantle, a creature of alien origins awakened. The Zorag stretched, expanded, and pushed through layers of hot rock into an undersea volcano's magma reservoir.

33

ATLO TRUDOCK

"For Christ's sake! He's just a kid! Hold it a second." Trudock held the phone against his chest and swung around, searching his office. It was that damn presence again, but he had no idea what it was. How the kid escaped his men in Los Angeles was ridiculous. Atlo gazed down at the golden foliage of the trees in Battery Park. He knew the British agent didn't like working with the young target, but he had so much dirt on him that this was the agent's only ticket to freedom. That's what Trudock told him anyway. And the L.A. cop was competent. They both were, or they wouldn't be working for him.

Atlo inhaled a deep breath and resumed his conversation. "Okay, so you tell me this guy you sent to Rangiroa is the best. It should be over by now." He gazed from the park to the traffic and pedestrians on the street.

"Let me know as soon as you hear. In the meantime, get a whole goddamn army over there."

34

OKO AND MATAHI

I surfaced in the turquoise water. The pistol was below me on the bottom of the lagoon. It was as though I'd raced around the universe in the time it had taken to glide to the gun. Seeing the dark warrior in that dish freaked me out. I glanced at my ring and then to the blue sky. I sensed a dark intrusion pressing down on me, and visions of the dark warrior were so vivid.

"Quick, Sam," urged the Asian man, climbing into the long narrow boat.

I quivered, shrugged the darkness away, and dived for the pistol. When I swam back to the boat the Asian man took the gun from me.

"Silenced Beretta," he said, and flicked through the assassin's wallet and phone as the islander assisted me aboard the fishing dory.

A blanket covered the unconscious gunman. The Asian man put the gunman's phone, wallet, and gun in a slimline black case and handed me a hessian sheet.

"Lie flat and cover yourself, Sam," he said.

Dripping wet, I lay covered in the bow. The outboard chugged. Smells of fish, salt, and petrol blended. Water trickled and splashed against the hull until the revs increased to a whir and the bow slapped and lifted. Through the hessian weave, I spied the islander and bunga-lows disappearing into the distance. The islander looked too young to be Rani's grandfather, but he must be Matahi, and the Asian man Yoko.

The masts and white hull of a luxury catamaran whisked by as we planed past the anchorage. I was so relieved and grateful. Flying to

Rangiroa was the right decision and escaping with a martial arts expert, exciting. Sea rushed under the hull. I wondered who the gunman was. I guessed he was after my ring. *But why did he want it so much? Why try to kill me and murder my dad?*

After fifteen minutes the whir of the outboard quieted and the bow eased into the water.

"Okay, you sit up now," called the islander.

I pulled the hessian from my head and eased up onto a bench seat. Two hundred metres away was a deserted palm-lined shore with no signs of any buildings. On the other side of the dory, the vivid blue lagoon stretched for as far as I could see. The Asian sat beside me and the gunman still lay covered on the floor.

"Are you sure you tied him well?" the Asian man asked.

The islander nodded; the outboard whirred, and we powered off again.

"Where are we going?" I asked.

The Asian man cupped his ear.

"Where are we going?" I spoke over the motor.

"Matahi Island," he said.

"Is that Matahi driving the boat?"

The Asian man nodded.

"Are you Yoko?"

The Asian man shook his head. "My name is Oko! Matahi Island is not far, we'll talk there."

After everything I'd been through, it felt strange to find myself smiling. But I'd found Dad's friends, my mother's friends. But then my smile faded. Dad should be here to share all of this with me. I wondered if Oko and Matahi even knew Dad was dead. *And what did Matahi and Oko know about my mother? How did they meet? How did they know each other?*

We sped past a coral sand islet covered by patchy grass, a stand of palms, and shrubby vegetation. Oko's hair stayed neat in the breeze, and he wore a pressed collared shirt, slacks, and shiny shoes. Matahi wore faded blue shorts with side pockets, no shoes, no shirt, and a silver neck chain. He looked fierce and not to be messed with.

At the end of the islet, a deep blue passage fed out to the open ocean. Towering coconut palms and thick scrub covered the next island, and at the top of a white sandy beach, nestled amongst palms and casuarinas, stood a thatched hut.

Matahi eased the throttle until the outboard purred. Fish scattered and made tiny wakes as the boat glided through a narrow channel between weed and brown boulders. Ahead, a plastic bottle with a rope attached floated above what looked like an old engine block, with chain snaking along the bottom.

Oko pulled off his shoes and rolled up his trousers in neat folds as we cruised through crystal-clear water – shells and old broken pieces of coral littered the bottom. Matahi cut the outboard and ratcheted the prop from the water. Calm, relieving silence surrounded me as the dory glided until the bow crunched into the sand.

Oko jumped out, beckoning for me to follow. Warm water swished around my calves, and the sand was coarse and lumpy underfoot.

"Sam, come and hold the stern out from the beach," Matahi said.

The prisoner wriggled, and muffled grunts came through the hessian. Oko and Matahi stood on either side of the dory in calf-deep water. Tidal surge lapped against my legs; my chest thumped as Matahi reached into the boat and pulled the hessian covering back.

A black rag covered the gunman's eyes; a gag muffled his shouts as he struggled against his bindings. I stumbled and re-grasped the stern.

Matahi inspected the zip-tie bindings on the prisoner's wrists and ankles. "I leave the prisoner here for a while. When I return, if he answers our questions, I won't feed him to the sharks." Matahi pulled the hessian back over the gunman.

Oko took a shiny, black waterproof pack from the hull and gestured for me to wait. Matahi turned the dory, waded to the floating plastic bottle, retrieved a barnacle-covered rope and looped it over a bollard on the bow. After gathering a tatty shopping bag from the stern, the islander led the way through the shallows.

The swish and splosh of our steps accompanied the distant rumble of breaking waves. Coconuts dotted the top of the beach, and hot sand sent me prancing to the shade of a casuarina tree near Matahi's hut.

The hut was made from bamboo, thatched roof, and woven wall panels – a solitary chair sat by a fireplace out front. Scents of seaweed and husks mixed with a whiff of fermenting fruit. Matahi carried his bag into the hut and reappeared carrying two chairs with faded Kia-Ora resort logos on the backrests. He placed the chairs in a shady spot near the circle of rocks with remains of a fire in its centre.

"Ooheee." Matahi smiled. His fierce expression vanished. Birds chirped, and the whole world brightened.

"*Manava*, Sam. I am Matahi, a friend of Hila and Russell. Welcome to my island."

"Thanks. I'm really pleased to meet you." I glimpsed youth and mischief in the old islander's eyes. We shook hands and Matahi drew me into a firm embrace. The islander's grip was strong, and he smelled of sweat.

Oko stepped forward. "I am Oko Yanzi. I am friend and admirer of Hila and Russell and very glad you are safe." Oko gazed into my eyes.

"Pleased to meet you, Oko." I remembered Oko's wicked martial arts. "Thanks for saving me ... both of you."

Matahi smiled, strode to his hut, and returned with a machete and three green coconuts. "Sit, sit ... What a crazy day. Until yesterday, I had not seen Oko for sixteen years. The same with you, Sam ... and Russell and Hila."

It was kind of comforting to know that Matahi must have seen me as a baby, and my ears pricked when he mentioned my mother. I wanted to ask questions but I waited as Matahi sliced the tops and passed coconuts to me and Oko.

"*Manuia*," Matahi said, raising his coconut.

The sweet-tasting water was refreshing, and I wiped the drips from my chin. I prepared to ask how Matahi knew my mother, but crashing sounds came from the dory. We all stared as the crashing stopped, then escalated into thrashing.

Matahi's fierce expression returned. "We interrogate the assassin."

Assassin? Did that guy really come to kill me? I clenched my teeth and scratched my chest.

Oko turned to me. "Before we proceed, Russell is not here. I fear the worst. Do you know what happened, Sam?"

I don't know why, and I didn't want to, but I kind of smiled. Then I blushed, stared at my feet, and scratched the hessian itch on my arm and chest.

"Matahi, get Sam a shirt," Oko said, and he took sunscreen from his pack and offered it to me.

"I don't burn," I said and tried to push the dumb half-smile from my face.

Matahi returned with a collared checked shirt. It was grubby and smelled of sweat, but I put it on, left the buttons open, and after a few seconds it comforted me.

I closed my eyes. "Yesterday, I flew to Los Angeles to meet Dad. He didn't show at the airport. I went to the hotel and found him dead."

Matahi sucked in a sharp breath then dropped his head. Oko winced and stared at the heavens. He and Matahi glanced at each other before turning to me.

Oko put a hand on my shoulder. "Sorry, Sam. Your dad was very good man. Can you tell me what happened?"

I shook my head. "Murdered."

Thrashing, more violent this time, resumed. Matahi half-stood, then sat. "My sympathy is with you, Sam," he said. "I am here to help. My island is your island. You were born here. Stay for as long as you wish."

I was all teary and nodded. "Thank you."

"What happened when you found Russell? Was anyone else there?" Oko asked.

"A man followed me from the airport, turned up right after I found Dad. He showed a British agent ID, but he made a call, and I overheard a voice tell him to feed our bodies to pigs."

Oko winced. "How did you escape?"

"I ran. A uniformed Los Angeles policeman shot at me outside the hotel."

"Police?" Oko's eyes widened. "No one stopped you at the airport?"

I shook my head. "No. But two men ransacked our house in London and burned it to the ground."

Oko kept firing questions. "How you know this?"

"I spoke to a friend."

"Just one friend?"

I nodded.

"Does your friend know where you are?" Oko asked.

I shook my head.

The sound of feet bashing the hull raised Matahi. "We find out who killed Russell." Matahi clenched his fists and strode to the water.

"I am sorry for you and Russell, and amazed you made it to Rangiroa by yourself," Oko said. "You did good, Sam. Your dad would be very proud," he stood. "Keep your distance while we talk with the assassin."

35

WATER TORTURE

I hurried across the hot sand, then lagged as they waded into the lagoon. Water gurgled as I knelt to splash my face and clear mucus from my nose. Oko and Matahi reached the old timber dory. Seawater dripped from me as I watched, standing five metres from them.

Matahi pulled the hessian back. I stepped forward and to the side to get a better view. The assassin was still blindfolded and gagged; black hair matted his stark white legs.

"Answer my questions or I feed you to the sharks. Do you understand?" Matahi said.

The assassin nodded.

Matahi untied the gag. The prisoner coughed, trying to expel a cloth ball from his mouth.

Oko plucked the cloth out, tossed it in the dory, and swished his hands in the sea.

The assassin flexed his jaw and tried to swallow. "Water," he demanded.

Matahi reached into the hull, withdrew a bottle and unscrewed the lid.

The assassin swallowed two gulps. "More," he said.

Matahi poured three more gulps, replaced the lid, and the bottle thudded as he dropped it in the dory.

The assassin smiled. "All of you are dead."

I took a step back and ran a hand through my hair. If someone hadn't already tried to kill me, I might have laughed.

"Everyone dies," Oko said.

"Fuck off, Chink. You don't know who you're dealing with."

Oko shook his head. "A racist assassin. Your driver's licence says you're Dwain Tilley from Vancouver. Enlighten us, Dwain. Who are we dealing with?"

"You're dead meat." A crooked tooth showed through the assassin's smile, and flaky skin caught in his moustache.

"Who do you work for, Dwain?" Oko dragged the assassin's name out in a mocking way.

"I work for myself," the assassin said.

Matahi jammed the gag back into his mouth. "We feed him to the sharks."

The assassin shook his head and thrashed like a giant tuna. Matahi drew back. The assassin twisted, spat out the gag, snapped his body, and flipped onto his feet.

I gasped and stumbled.

The assassin somersaulted backward, right out of the boat, and landed in waist-deep water. "You can't hide," he shouted, trying to break his hands free.

The words and the way he said it scared me, but blindfolded and with his hands bound, I didn't think there was much he could do.

Matahi stepped forward and slammed the heel of his palm into the assassin's chest. A hollow squeak issued from the man, and he fell back into the water.

"We're not playing Marco Polo," Matahi said. He slammed the assassin again, and this time held him under.

"Oko, bring the gag and more zip ties," Matahi said.

I stood open-mouthed in the shallows. It was like watching a movie.

Oko arrived with huge zip ties. Matahi allowed the assassin one breath and dunked him again. This time, Matahi submerged with the prisoner and surfaced with a rusty mooring chain.

The assassin gasped, and while he caught his breath, Matahi wrapped the chain under his armpits and around his neck, then zip-tied the chain in place. Before the prisoner fully regained his breath, Matahi tripped him, pulled the chain tight, and tied it off, so the assassin knelt, up to his waist in the water. Oko applied the gag with only a minor struggle.

"He will drown with the tide unless the tiger sharks get him first," Matahi said.

At the mention of sharks, the assassin tried to shout through the gag. I thought he was yelling, *I'll tell you. I'll tell you what you want to know,* but the gag muffled his cries and I couldn't tell.

We were only standing in waist-deep water, but I squirmed at the possibility there were tiger sharks in the lagoon, and I eagerly made my way back to the shore with Oko and Matahi.

"I'm starving, let's eat," Matahi said.

"Don't let assassin spoil your lunch," Oko said.

Matahi's chest heaved and his hands trembled, but Oko seemed calm, almost relaxed.

"That's a good old-fashioned Rangiroa water torture you set for our prisoner," Oko said.

Matahi laughed and shook his head.

36

HILA

I sat in an old resort chair in front of Matahi's hut and pictured a fin rising from the lagoon. Glad that I wasn't in the assassin's shoes, I sipped the last of my coconut. Oko and Matahi sat either side of me. Dozens of questions ran through my mind, but one came to the fore.

"How did you meet my mother?" I asked. A pang of guilt jittered because I didn't mention my dad.

"I met Hila first," Oko said.

"No. She booked a trip to the Blue Lagoon with me," Matahi said.

"Well, yes, she booked a trip with you, but I was first to converse with Hila."

"No. We talked when she booked my boat," Matahi said.

"First meaningful conversation," insisted Oko.

Matahi shook his head, laughed, and allowed Oko to continue.

"I was sitting at the Kia-Ora resort bar," Oko's eyes glazed over, "and I see a woman with striking emerald eyes swimming in the lagoon. Our eyes met and she swam to the steps. I took her a towel and introduced myself, told her I am an oceanographer. She joined me for a cocktail and was very knowledgeable about the ocean and the warming."

"Did she say where she was from?" I asked.

"Hila had a way of deflecting questions, and her eyes, her smile, so ..."

"Oko acted like a love-struck idiot, and Russell charmed her away," Matahi said.

Oko inhaled a deep breath, glared at Matahi, then stared at the lagoon.

"Oko and Russell were both attending an international climate and oceanography summit. They chartered my boat for field trips, and we became friends. When they discovered Hila had booked a tour on my boat, Oko and Russell decided to come too. We came here for lunch and ate where we sit now. Hila asked lots of questions but never spoke of herself." Matahi picked up a stick, and the smell of ash wafted as he poked the fireplace.

I tried to picture my mother and father, here, sitting around the open fire pit.

"What did Russell tell you of Hila?" Oko asked, looking at the ring on my finger.

"I don't really know anything about her." I gazed at the blue sky and recalled how Dad never really answered questions about my mother, but gave vague answers. *Your mother was a beauty from a far-off land; your mother loved you; she was the most wonderful person I ever knew.*

"Dad said that my mother was a galactic citizen and worked for a secret United Nations agency. Until three days ago, I didn't even know you guys existed. I last spoke to my dad the day before I left England; he was already in America. He said I needed to know some things about my mother. Now I guess I'll never know. How do you have a child with someone and not even know where they're from?"

Matahi and Oko looked at each other.

"What?" I asked. They were hiding something.

Oko swallowed and swayed his head. "Sam, you must tell us more of Russell."

I hunched over and focused on my sandy toes.

"Sorry Sam, but we need to know who killed Russell – for your safety. Start from the beginning, everything."

If I told them about physical cyber-attacks through computers and games, they would think I was on drugs, or crazy. They didn't say anything, but I wondered if they'd seen the ring flash and the pulse when I dived for the gun. Those real-life visions of Atlo Trudock and the dark warrior freaked me out. *But how could I explain it?*

As if Oko could hear my thoughts, he said, "Leave nothing out."

I inhaled a deep breath. "It all started the morning of my birthday. My dad surprised me with this trip, coming to Rangiroa, then Tonga." I fidgeted with my ring, turned it left, then right. It was a gift from my mother, and the longer I wore it the more attached, the more protective I felt of it.

"Speak freely, Sam. Nothing is impossible since I met your mother."

"Dad's computer freaked me out. It was like someone was watching."

"Russell's research attracted attention from governments and corporations worldwide; many could spy," Oko said.

"Sure, but the morning of my birthday, the computer in the study sucked me in and jammed me to the desk. I had to pull the plug with my feet to get away. You ever hear of physical cyber-attacks?"

Oko shook his head. "Tell me of the cyber-attacks."

Breeze whispered through the palms, and tidal surge lapped the shore.

"Later that morning I played a holographic game called Hero-G with a friend. A dark warrior came to life in the game, knocked my friend out, and tried to suck the life from me." The words echoed in my head as if I were in a bubble as I spoke. Oko concentrated on my every word, but Matahi drifted away.

"I prepare for lunch," Matahi said, and he walked to his hut.

"I think I might be dead if another friend hadn't smashed the game. An acid stench lingered. Whatever it was, it must have come through the net. Dad died near his laptop. The same stench filled his room, and when I tried to help him, a dark fog swirled out and attacked me."

"Describe the attack in more detail – what you see, what you feel, what you smell?"

A great weight lifted from my shoulders as I talked of Swathi and Tom, Hero-G, Dad's computer, and how he had accepted Xcon funding.

Matahi lit a fire. Twigs crackled and leaves smoked, drifting into my face and making my eyes water. Guilt, the idea that I'd done something wrong, vanished as I answered Oko's questions about the hotel and how I'd escaped.

"Until this trip, Dad never let me come with him to the tropics. He said I was safer in a cool climate," I said.

"Safer, why?"

"He never explained it. I thought you might know."

Matahi approached with spears, fins, and masks. "Your mother broke our hearts when she chose Russell," he said. "Come, I show you my reef, and we catch lunch."

I stared at Matahi as if he'd spoken a strange language. "Catch lunch?"

"Yes, spear a fish," Matahi said.

Spearing a fish was the farthest thing from my mind. "I … need to talk."

"A lot of the world's coral is dying. My reef is still healthy." Matahi glared at the assassin. "I'd hoped Oko and Russell could stop the warming, but tomorrow bleaching could start. You were born here, Sam. Experience the reef's magnificence before it's dead and gone."

Surely there was plenty of time to see the reef? Matahi had said I could stay as long as I wanted. Diving and spearing a fish seemed strange with a killer tied up in the lagoon. And what about the tiger sharks Matahi talked about? Matahi held a hand spear, mask and snorkel, and fins out to me.

"Take the opportunity while you can," Oko said.

"I don't use a mask or snorkel," I said.

Matahi and Oko raised their eyebrows and studied me.

"Like your mother," Matahi said. "Do you have clear underwater vision?"

I nodded. I knew it. I *was* like my mother. Coral sand grated beneath my feet as I followed Matahi up the beach toward the passage at the end of the island. I thought about the funny look Oko and Matahi had exchanged when I talked about my mother. I was sure they were hiding something.

"The sea clears the mind and will help you think," Matahi said, waiting for me to catch up.

Coconuts, jellyfish, and shredded vegetation marked the tide line. The casuarina trees became stunted as we neared the passage, and the smell of seaweed wafted as breakers came into view.

"Didn't you mention tiger sharks?" I asked, staring from the protected lagoon to open water.

"Blacktips mostly, but I see tigers sometimes. Have you speared before, Sam?"

My throat tightened. "Free diving, never spearfishing. Isn't it dangerous with sharks around?"

I knew that sharks were like the ocean's immune system, and they rarely bothered humans, but the idea of coming face to face with a big tiger shark terrified me.

"My people have lived in harmony with sharks and shared their ocean for many generations," Matahi said. "Sharks are essential for a healthy ocean. If you are lucky, you will see one today. Respect them, do as I do, and you have nothing to fear. Sharks have a lot more reason to fear humans. People kill tens of millions every year to make soup from their fin."

Matahi had a spear gun with a wooden stock and a trigger. My handspear had four prongs on an aluminium shaft, with a rubber sling. Matahi showed me how to stretch the rubber up the shaft and release to shoot.

The wind strengthened and funnelled as we waded into the water. I stumbled on a sharp rock and regained my footing. On reaching waist-deep water, Matahi plunged into the channel.

When I leaned forward to dive after him, tiger sharks lurked in my mind. I pulled back and straightened. Wind gusted, scoured the channel, blustered my hair and rumbled in my ears.

Matahi stared back through his mask.

I inhaled deep breaths, stared into the water, and dived. With the barbed prongs out front, I finned over weedy rock, almost straight into Matahi.

"Careful with the spear," Matahi said. He turned and kicked across the surface.

At first the reef was rocky, with just a few fish riding ebbs and flows. The water deepened. A small orange and white wrasse swam around the base of a brain-coral boulder. Below the water, the roar of crashing surf and the ruffle of wind hushed. I followed Matahi through the passage toward the open ocean, and my ears tuned into the subtle chime and crackle of living coral reef.

Mauve and yellow corals abounded. A profusion of yellow- and black-striped fish drifted over the drop-off. Thousands of gold-banded fusiliers schooled, and beyond was the big blue.

So much life. I dived to get closer and hovered five metres below the surface with a beaming smile on my face. The abundance of life and the blue abyss stirred a primal longing. No matter how long I stared, I couldn't get enough. The ocean called, and I gazed from the vibrant reef to the big blue.

Matahi swam down, caught my attention, and we ascended through sunrays and schooling fish to the surface.

"There is a cavern at the bottom of the wall," Matahi said. He took several deep breaths and submerged.

I took a normal breath and dived into a mass of vivid-blue tangs that parted and regrouped behind me as I swam. Two butterfly fish took refuge beneath a yellow plate coral. A surgeonfish swam from a purple branch coral. The transparent water felt silky smooth. Down I swam past Matahi, past sea fans reaching from the coral wall. As I approached a ledge, four giant trevallies scattered.

My knuckles whitened on the spear; the trevallies faded into blue. Matahi swam beneath the ledge, circled in a grotto and, using a hand to push down, stood on the sandy bottom.

A dozen red squirrelfish with large round eyes hovered nervously at the back of the grotto as I circled and stood beside Matahi. I had excellent underwater buoyancy control and didn't need to leverage myself to stand on the bottom.

Cathedral sunrays streamed through the water. Silhouettes of hundreds of fish circled. The light, the life, and the colours invigorated me as I gazed into the wonderful deep blue.

Matahi tapped me on the shoulder and stretched out to exhale a bubble that wobbled into a perfect ring, expanding as it ascended.

The abyss drew my attention. I sensed a shadowy presence though I saw nothing but blue. Then yes, a grey shadow, then nothing. Then, clear as day—a shark loomed from the blue.

My pulse spiked. I raised my spear, tensioning the sling.

The blacktip shark swam straight at me, cruised close. But when it became aware of our presence, it flicked its tail, darted well clear, and glided with such grace. I was mesmerized by it. My pulse relaxed, and I wished the shark would come back as it melded into the blue.

Matahi shook my shoulder and pointed to the surface. The colours and light held me with a magnetic attraction. I gazed from the big blue to wallowing dreamy sunlight on the surface, to the squirrelfish in the grotto, and nodded.

Matahi began his ascent and was halfway up before I finned from the shadowy depths, up through glimmering silhouettes of hundreds of fish to wavering brightness. I broke the surface smiling. "That was awesome."

Chest heaving, Matahi smiled and nodded. "We were both born here Sam. The ocean is our mother. That ledge is fifteen metres below. You hold your breath like Hila."

"Did my mother swim to the cavern?"

"She loved the cavern, but Russell didn't have the lungs to free dive it."

I wanted to ask how long my mother could hold her breath, wanted to dive back down to the cavern, but Matahi swam over the top of the coral wall. I followed and drifted over a clam with electric blue-green flesh. A clownfish rested amongst swirling tentacles and, defending its territory, a tiny damselfish darted at me.

Matahi took long breaths, signalled for me to follow, and dived past a green moray eel with sinister eyes and jaws agape. Deeper we swam, past sponges, to where the reef blended into sand. A second blacktip shark cruised past. The tide swept us into the pass, and I stayed close to Matahi as we surfaced.

"Time for spearing. It's good for coral trout in the pass," Matahi said.

I nodded. I could identify most fish and corals from having read so many books on the ocean and marine biology. The small sharks were cool and didn't scare me so much, but I didn't like the idea of spearing a fish while they were cruising nearby. Swimming alongside Matahi, I decided to leave the spearing to the islander.

The coral in the pass wasn't as spectacular as the drop-off. I dived and found a lobster family hiding in a crevice, and a stingray camouflaged on the sandy bottom. Matahi swam ahead. I trained my spear on a small brown cod, with no intention of shooting, when a plump fish caught my attention: fawn with bright blue spots, coral trout.

Matahi snorkelled twenty metres ahead. I thought of swimming after him or calling for his attention. The trout, half a metre long and plump, finned lazily near a weedy boulder. Since the second blacktip encounter, I hadn't seen a shark. Hunting instincts took hold of me.

37

SPEARED

I scanned the water in every direction, took a breath and dived, tensioning the rubber sling as I finned. Brown weed swayed on the boulder. The trout cruised, oblivious of the danger. Half wishing the trout would scoot away, I pointed the spear. My heart thumped as I aimed behind its head, did a quick check for sharks, and released the shaft.

Four barbed prongs slammed through the gills. Blood burst from the wound and swirled in the water. The trout quivered. I pulled the rubber sling and grasped hold of the aluminium shaft.

A blacktip shark charged in, darting in a figure eight in front of me. Sheer terror jolted me. The trout flapped. I tried to fend the shark with the spear and shake the fish off the prongs at the same time.

A second blacktip attacked. Shit. A feeding frenzy! I jerked back and forth, trying to point the spear at both sharks. The spear ripped and thrashed. Bubbles swirled, and went up my nose. I fought the urge to drop the weapon and scarper. Gripping the spear, I floated to the surface.

The thrashing stopped. Both sharks and the fish had vanished.

I surfaced, and my fins slapped the water as I powered for the shallows, standing when it was knee deep.

Matahi surfaced close behind, with a hand over his mouth and shoulders shaking. At first, I thought he was injured or choking.

"Those sharks … that can happen when you try to steal their fish." Matahi's eyes bulged, and he burst out laughing.

I didn't find it funny. But the old islander's belly shook and he laughed so hard that I had to join him.

"Sorry, Sam, you had such a nice trout. While the sharks ate your fish, I got this one." Matahi hoisted his spear as he waded. "A healthy coral trout, but not as big as the one the sharks stole from you."

We walked along the water's edge, Matahi's shoulders shook and his eyes reddened as he kept bursting into laughter. "You did good, Sam. You held onto the spear."

As we rounded the beachhead, the mood became sombre. The water was up to the assassin's chest, and smoke floated from the fire out front of Matahi's hut. Oko waved. Matahi held up the fish, tossed it to the waterline, and continued up to the hut.

"Nice coral trout," Oko said.

"Not as nice as the one the sharks stole from Sam," Matahi said.

"Sharks stole your fish?" Oko asked.

I nodded.

"You scared?" Oko asked.

"Yes," I said, the image of the two sharks attacking the fish still vivid in my mind.

Oko put a stick on the fire. "It's good to face your fears."

"I'm still scared of sharks," I replied.

"He didn't drop the spear," Matahi said.

"To respect a powerful predator is healthy," Oko said.

"He can hold his breath forever, like Hila," Matahi said. "I will clean the fish and make steaks."

"Coral trout is better for fillets," Oko said.

"Either is good," replied Matahi.

"I prefer fillets," Oko said.

"Do you prefer fillets or steaks, Sam?"

"I don't care, I'm not that hungry."

"If you had to choose?" Matahi asked.

"Fillets … or steaks," I said.

"Fillets taste better and no bones," Oko said.

"Okay, I do fillets and steaks." Matahi scaled and gutted the trout at the water's edge. With a thin knife, he sliced along the spine from the head, flayed white fillets from the bones, and used a machete to chop four steaks nearer the tail.

"Steaks and fillets," Matahi said, rinsing the knives at the water's edge. I followed him to the fire and sat beside Oko.

"A good fire." Matahi placed the fillets and steaks on palm leaves, added grated coconut flesh, and wrapped them. He used a stick to dig out embers and expose the rocks. After placing the wraps on the hot rocks, he covered them with the ashes and joined Oko and me sitting around the fire and staring out to the lagoon.

"That's a handsome motor on your boat. Is it new?" Oko asked.

"Yes," Matahi said.

"How did you pay for it … work?"

"Of course, I work. You think I catch one fish, sleep, and play ukulele all day?"

Oko nodded.

Matahi laughed. "Now I have my new motor, I relax more, but I caught many lobsters to buy the motor. My grandson catches lobster for the restaurant now."

The tide pushed in, swallowed the beach, and lapped the assassin's neck. A line of weed, husk, and dead insects stretched across the beach two metres below the fire.

"Matahi, does the tide reach the fire?" I asked.

Matahi nodded. "In three hours, the sea will extinguish this fire, and tomorrow the king tide will inundate my home. This has never happened since my father's father built this hut."

"Do you think people are responsible for melting the ice-caps and flooding your hut?" I asked.

Matahi looked to the sky. "If people even suspect they harm the climate, they must stop. Humanity has lost their connection with nature. Possessions and electricity are more important than the earth and the ocean. Your father said that the Tonga Trench warming is now the greatest threat. Oko, it's time you saved the world. Get those ice caps freezing again."

Burning sticks crackled. Oko stared into the fire and nodded. Matahi walked to his hut and returned with an old camera. "We should take a photo." He moved his chair toward the lagoon so he could set the camera on it. Oko rested his phone against the back of the chair.

They set timers and half-ran, half-waddled to either side of me. The shutters blinked.

"Come, Sam. I have something to show you," Matahi said.

I followed Matahi into the thatch hut. Woven mats covered the sand floor. To the left sat a bed made from bamboo; a driftwood table and shelves with photos occupied the area to the right. The rear door was open and led to an assortment of barrels, nets, a table with scattered spanners, a gas bottle coupled to a single burner, machetes, green coconuts, and an old outboard cover. In the distance, hundreds of coconut palms grew in rows.

From a shelf, Matahi took a framed black-and-white photo of a woman wearing a long skirt and blouse standing in front of the hut. "My wife gave birth to three girls and four boys in this hut. She died giving birth to my fourth son."

The hut hadn't changed, and the fireplace was in the same spot. The photo pulled me back in time. I wondered where all the kids had slept.

Matahi replaced the photo and picked up another. A crowd of faces, some serious, most smiling, crowded in front of the hut. "Here are my children with their families."

I smiled. There must be thirty or forty in Matahi's family. How wonderful it would be to have brothers and sisters.

"When my kids were young, everyone worked on copra plantations. Now my grandchildren work for hotels or black pearl farms, but the bleaching slows tourism, and the oysters struggle. The increasing acidity from all the carbon in the ocean is bad for their shells. Soon, the rising water will force my children and their children away from Rangiroa."

I pictured the fireplace, the hut, and the palms underwater.

Matahi reached for an album on the third shelf and removed a photo.

My eyes widened. "Mum, Dad … you and Oko … Dad looks so young."

My mum stood tallest, and her emerald eyes illuminated the photo. They were gathered around the fireplace with the hut behind, and I recognised the pointy rock at the front of the fireplace.

"That was sixteen years ago, after the trip to the Blue Lagoon," Matahi said.

"Hila gave birth to you three weeks later," Oko said.

I stared at Oko, then at the picture. There wasn't a good view of my mum's stomach, but she didn't look pregnant.

"You said my dad – all of you met Hila the day before you went to the Blue Lagoon. How could I have been born just three weeks later?"

38

FREAKAZOID

Smells of coals and smouldering palm rose as Matahi dug the trout from the fire. He prodded the wraps away from the fire toward his feet. Juice oozed out as he picked up a wrap and scalded his fingers.

"Ah," Matahi said and dropped the wrap at my feet.

I stared blank-faced at the wrap. Inside I smouldered. *Why hadn't Russell told me? And who was my real dad?* I felt like the victim of a cruel joke.

"I'm not hungry," I said and stood and walked from the fire to the water's edge.

"Sam, wait," Oko said.

I half glanced over my shoulder and waved Oko away.

"Sorry, Sam," Oko said.

Not looking back, I walked toward the end of the island. After the cyber-attacks, Dad's death, fleeing Los Angeles and the assassin, I thought nothing could surprise me, but Oko had sure dropped a bomb.

"I'm a freakazoid." I ran for no reason, ran where the sea lapped the sand. *Why hadn't Dad told me?* The water splashed at my feet, and wind streaked tears across my cheeks. Faster I ran. Tears built to sobs and mucus blocked my nose. I ran to the end of the island, staggered into the passage, cupped my hands to my face, and my heart exploded. Dad … No … Dr Russell Edwards, had lied. He betrayed me, and now he was dead … Why?

In the shallows, I fell to my knees and cried. As my sobs subsided, I crawled elbow-deep, cupped water to my red eyes, and blew my nose.

Submerging to cool my face, I crawled until the water covered my head, then pushed away from the sand, floating over rocks and reef.

The tide ran in. I swam against the current and sank onto a sandy patch with branch corals and sponges surrounding. Light rippled as I rested like a giant starfish on the sand.

My heart slowed, pulse relaxed, and I rolled onto my back. Eight metres of transparent water absorbed the cries in my head. Sun waves washed over my body. A pair of iridescent yellow and blue angelfish swam around, as though I were a part of their reef.

Lobster feelers swayed in a crevice, and an octopus slid stealthily over a rock. Warm sensations flooded my chest, spread to my stomach, arms, and head. My gums and forehead numbed. Every molecule in my body vibrated as if I weren't solid but an extension of the lagoon.

Wind tensioned the surface, sun waves tightened. My hands started to ache, then involuntarily closed with the tips of my fingers and thumbs bunched together. The ache became unbearable. I fought to stretch my hands open, but they were cramped shut. I closed my eyes, drew my hands and knees to my chest, and curled on the sandy bottom. As though peering from space, my mother's emerald eyes illuminated my mind.

I floated from the sandy bottom. Weightless and free, I drifted like coral bloom over the reef. A cleaner wrasse nibbled my ear as I floated up over urchins and weed toward the protected lagoon. Extending my arms and legs, I surfaced, and my cramped fingers inched open.

"Oh," I groaned as the ache subsided, and I floated with the most wonderful blue sky above. Bliss flooded my being. A slow bass rhythm thumped in my chest. Tide pushed and nurtured me until my head and shoulders grated into the sandy beach. Gentle surge washed over me at the water's edge. When I sat up, my mind travelled back to Matahi's hut, wondering if they'd spoken to the assassin yet.

As I ambled back along the beach, pressure built inside me. I stared to the heavens and my whole body throbbed. My hands clamped shut again.

An invisible force struck. "Ahh!" I screamed. My hands flung open; fingers stretched out. Visions detonated in my mind – Dad, Mum … special talents. I saw myself running in a circle, Dad at the centre, his awkward expression discussing my birth and my mother. Faster I circled, tearing around more visions—my special talents, hearing, breath, and night vision.

"NO!" I shouted. I ran into the visions and collided into myself. The visions vanished. The heavens glimmered. My hands shot open with such force I fell to one knee.

"Ah!" I bellowed. *How could I never have seen?* Tears streamed down my cheeks. The sky and the lagoon blended and winked at me—a fleeting moment—but I knew I'd seen something wonderful. Warmth flowed through me, ecstatic vibration tingled, and it was as though I'd connected with the vivid sky and the lagoon. I bent down, scooped sparkling water onto my face, and stared at the heavens.

Somehow the lagoon and the sky strengthened me. I'd never felt comfortable in my body before. Russell Edwards wasn't my genetic father. I was different. I could see and hold my breath underwater; my vision and hearing were better than any of my friends. And when it was sunny, I was much faster and stronger than every kid at school. *What the heck was the solar narcolepsy all about? I looked human and wanted to fit in so much, but could my mother have come from another planet?*

"Maybe I'm crazy," I whispered, "but from now on, whatever I am, I accept it. It's okay to be different. I've got to believe in myself, follow my heart and the ring will guide me."

"Sam." A voice dragged me back from a special place. Oko ran up the beach.

I stood, dusted sand from my hands, and wiped my eyes with my arms.

"I heard you shouting. Are you okay, Sam?"

With calm determination, I nodded.

"Sorry, Sam—"

"It's not your fault, Oko. I don't know why Russell kept everything secret, but he was a good father to me."

39

CHOICES

Matahi held the trout carcass and stood at the water's edge as Oko and I rounded the beachhead. Matahi acknowledged us, waded out, and tied the carcass around the assassin's neck.

Seconds later the carcass bobbed. Water splashed. Fish attacked. The assassin swung his head and shoulders. Matahi retreated as something huge broke the lagoon; wake peeled as it surged for the assassin.

Horror-struck, I pictured a tiger shark tearing the assassin's flesh. A massive frame monstered the carcass, ripped and splashed. A high-pitched scream pierced the assassin's gag.

"What kind of fish is that?" I asked.

"Napoleon wrasse," Oko replied.

Veins swelled on the assassin's neck as he writhed and swung his head.

"Get away, shark." Matahi splashed and grunted. The huge wrasse tore the carcass away. Matahi clamped his hand over his mouth to muffle his laugh. Oko shook his head and chuckled. I laughed under my breath and waded out nearer.

"You answer our questions," Oko said.

The assassin grunted and nodded.

Matahi removed the gag and the assassin gasped.

"Get me out of the water," Dwain the assassin said.

"No deal—Talk now or we leave you for the shark," Matahi said.

"I need water." The assassin clenched his teeth; the lagoon lapped against his neck.

"Talk first. Why do you want the boy?" Matahi asked.

"They want his ring."

I covered the ring with my right hand and stared at the assassin's turned-down mouth.

Matahi punched the surface of the lagoon. "And the boy?"

"Kill the boy. Get the ring. Those were my instructions."

I held my breath. Matahi and Oko stared at me, and at my hand covering the ring.

"Who are they?" Oko asked.

"Water," the assassin said.

Oko poured from a plastic bottle. "Who wants the ring and the boy dead?"

The man bared crooked teeth to form an ugly smile. "I'm freelance. I can't tell you, because I don't know."

"You are no use to us then. I feed you to the sharks," Matahi said, hooking the gag over the assassin's head.

The assassin shook like crazy. "Get me out of this water and I'll tell you what I heard."

"Answer our questions, then I take you out of the water," Matahi replied. "Tell me what you heard."

The assassin caught his breath. "Word is Xcon is hiring everyone— Atlo Trudock—you're messing with the world's most powerful man."

I squinted and slapped the water, spraying a wedge with my hand. Xcon must have launched the cyber-attacks. Xcon must have the technology and used that dark warrior to try and kill me through the net. I pictured a mountainous tsunami crushing me.

Matahi and Oko fixed on me. I sensed them questioning whether it was okay to continue. I nodded.

Oko turned to the assassin. "Did Xcon murder Russell Edwards?"

"As far as I know, someone from the agency took care of him."

My knuckles whitened. I trembled, resisting the urge to step forward and punch the killer.

"Xcon hired my dad. Why kill him?" I asked.

"I don't know. Now get me out of the water!"

"How many of you on Rangiroa?" Oko asked.

"Just me, but the cavalry is coming."

Oko nodded, and Matahi secured the gag over the assassin's muffled shouts, released him from the chain, and Oko assisted Matahi in hauling him out of the water and back into the dory. The assassin wriggled and squirmed on the wooden hull. Oko pulled a hessian sheet over to screen him from the sun.

I felt hollow inside. Atlo Trudock, Xcon, the world's most dominant corporation had killed my dad, and were after me. *What the heck?* The worries that had streamed in the background of my thoughts since I'd arrived: my phone, my house, and what Sonia thought of me paled to insignificance. Xcon killed my dad. The agent and the policeman in Los Angeles must have been working for Xcon. The world's most powerful corporation was trying to kill me. I worried that Swathi and Tom were in danger. But Tom said Swathi was okay, and Tom was a survivor. It was best I didn't even contact them.

I turned the ring on my finger. *This was what Xcon was after, but why?* Atlo Trudock wanted to kill me for it. There was some kind of magic in the ring, and it was all tied in with my dad's secrets about my mother. From the fear and anger and anxiety that gripped me, a grim determination built inside. I didn't know what I was going to do, but at least I had my dad's friends to help me. Atlo Trudock could rot in hell. I wasn't giving in to him. If I followed my heart, the ring would guide me. I had to believe that. It was all that I could do.

"Come, Sam." Matahi led us up past the fire and behind the hut.

"Why did Xcon murder my dad?" I asked.

Matahi kicked husks into the scrub.

"Xcon make a lot of money from global warming," Oko said. "Russell must have known something important. That ring is from your mother. When did Russell give it to you?"

"On my birthday." Heat flushed my face. I covered the ring with my right hand.

"Can I see it?"

"It's stuck," I said, holding my hand out briefly, then letting it fall by my side. "Xcon probably just wants it as proof I'm dead."

Oko looked me in the eye. "Can I touch the ring?"

I hesitated. I didn't want anyone touching the ring, but I allowed Oko to take my hand.

"We should take my dory, go to Makatea Island. Hide away," Matahi said. "Fish, swim … teach Sam island life until the trouble settles."

I smiled. The weight of the giant corporation eased from my shoulders. Matahi and Oko were the best people in the world to help me, and they already felt like family.

"I'm in. That sounds like an excellent idea. Thank you, Matahi."

Oko released my hand. "You want to hide on Makatea and learn island life?"

"Yes," I said.

"This is what your heart tells you?" Oko asked.

I shrugged and nodded.

"Then you and Matahi should get ready. You must leave right away."

"You're coming too, right?"

Oko shook his head.

"Why?" My hopes collapsed as quickly as they had risen. "Where will you go?"

"Russell paid to charter a research vessel, the *D-Sea Explorer*, for one month. The Captain is an ex-US Navy commander. I spoke with him this morning. He believes there's a conspiracy to hide what's happening in the Tonga Trench, so we will continue Russell's Tonga program together. If we discover what's causing the heat to gush from the trench, we may be able to stop it. Stop the ice caps melting, stop the ocean rising, even save humanity."

My gaze shifted between Oko and Matahi. Island life brought visions of sunrise over gentle lagoons and cheerful adventures, versus the Tonga Trench: deep and dark and menacing.

"I should come with you to Tonga," I said.

"Why?" Oko asked.

"To help continue Dad's work. I know all about the hot zone in the trench and score 100% on both robot and manned sub simulators."

"One minute you want to learn island life, and Matahi will be an excellent teacher. Now you want to come with me. Is this your path, Sam? What does your heart tell you?"

I swallowed. I just wanted us all to stick together. Staying with Matahi sounded fun; going with Oko, dangerous. I wanted to stay with Matahi but thought I should go with Oko. Which urge came from the heart?

"You will be safer here with me," Matahi said.

Oko nodded. "Either way, we must get moving."

"High tide will flood the runway. Planes can't land. We're safe until morning," Matahi said.

"Xcon don't wait for nature. We need to move now," Oko said.

"Can't we just stick together?" I asked.

"I never leave my islands," Matahi said.

I studied Oko, then Matahi. Right now, I wanted to hide out among the islands for the rest of my life. My chest tightened. After all I'd weathered, it didn't seem fair I had to make another huge spur of the moment decision. I turned the ring to the left, to the right, and left again. I looked Matahi in the eye, then lowered my gaze.

"I want to come with you, Oko."

Oko nodded.

"How do we get there, fly?" I asked.

"Too dangerous. Xcon will track us. We need to find a vessel equipped for ocean passage."

40

THE BAR

Hot rocks hissed and steamed as the tide reached the fireplace in front of Matahi's hut. Even though Russell Edwards was not my biological father, he was still my dad. By continuing his research, I wondered if I could save Matahi's hut, and maybe the whole island. Matahi grasped handfuls of hot sandy ash from the rear of the fire and urged me and Oko to copy him.

"Russell joins Hila in the great sky, and we say farewell with words from the Kumulipo," Matahi said.

Coals sizzled and spat as the lagoon inundated the fire. Matahi cleared his throat, chanted in his native tongue. Oko whispered the translation,

From the slime of the mother, the stock began
Began in the spirit world
Began in the time of gods—in the world of gods
In the far distant past lost in remoteness
Long ago was the coming of the bright one into the world.

I released a handful of ash for my dad, the other for my mum. Some of the ash floated on the lagoon, some sank through the transparent water, and some drifted with the breeze, a little settling back on the dampened fire.

Tidal surge lapped and echoed with rhythmic precision. The smell of wet ash lingered. As I pushed the dory from Matahi Island, I experienced a floating sensation, as if I were watching myself from above.

Tropical water splashed and trickled against the hull as we slipped from the beach. The assassin lay motionless under the hessian sheet.

From the bow, I stared back at Matahi's home. The tide had flooded the fire and was still running in. There were only six metres of gentle sloping beach to the hut. If ocean levels continued to rise, in a year or two the beach and the hut would both be gone.

The outboard clunked into position. I got a whiff of petrol as Matahi squeezed the primer, pulled the zip starter, and the outboard revved to life. Transparent water deepened to turquoise. Matahi turned the throttle; the engine whirred, and the dory skipped across the lagoon.

White water broke beyond the passage between the islands and I thought I was lucky to have dived the grotto with Matahi. Hiding out together sounded perfect. I wished I could relax and clear my head for a month, or a week at least. It sucked I had to leave after a single day. And how would we find a boat to Tonga right away?

Questions crowded my mind and nerves knotted my stomach. I closed my eyes, and a ukulele played in my head. I hummed and harmonised with the whir of the motor and sang.

I'm so glad the sky is blue ...
Cause that's my favourite colour for a day
A clear blue sky makes me smile, and all my troubles melt away.

The whir of the outboard blended with my voice. Sparkling water flashed by.

Matahi pulled into a small islet and, with Oko's assistance, tied the squirming assassin to a coconut palm.

"You stay here for the night; I'll send word in the morning. And don't struggle, or a coconut will fall on your head."

Blue Sky played in my head, and I sang and hummed as dark-based clouds with towering white tops mushroomed behind us.

The sea is like our mother, reflects us like no other
And there are fishes all the colours of the rainbow
Sky and sea and sun, dolphins having fun ...
What else could you want in just one day?

The afternoon breeze backed, and the lagoon glassed off. We drifted while Oko scanned the shore with binoculars and Matahi spoke on the VHF radio. The music in my head faded, and my eyes zoomed in on the Kia-Ora resort.

Matahi finished speaking on the VHF. "No suspicious people in town and no evening flights," he said and started the outboard and cruised to the resort.

A crowd congregated at the bar. Voices, laughter, and music carried across the water. There were seven yachts anchored near the resort. I focused on a slick white catamaran with dagger boards and raked-back hulls, my choice if we had to escape. There were four smaller catamarans, two mono-hulled yachts, and an old wooden schooner that resembled a pirate ship.

Matahi motored slowly past the moorings and pointed at the pirate ship. "This yacht comes here often. It's happy hour. If you want a boat, go to the bar."

Oko nodded.

"I'll drop you at the bungalows, send the twins to guard the wharf, and see you later at the bar," Matahi said.

The dory glided alongside my private deck. I slipped Matahi's checked shirt off and placed it on the bench seat. Oko had the bungalow next door but came into my bungalow first.

"Get changed and packed. Back in five minutes," Oko said.

Aqua light rippled across the ceiling. It seemed impossible I'd only arrived in Rangiroa that morning. A hot spa would be so soothing and relaxing, but I got the shower steaming hot and stood under blasting water for three minutes. I pulled the label from my blue hibiscus shirt; tan shorts and runners completed my look.

Oko knocked right at five minutes. He wore navy shorts and a hibis-cus shirt almost the same as mine, but red. We set off along the bungalow pier. Across the water, the bar was alive with beating drums, and a group of kids bounded after a man in a grass skirt who ran with a flaming torch and stopped to light bamboo lanterns.

Oko spoke with a hefty islander guarding the bungalow access, and distant lightning flared and flickered.

"A storm is brewing," I said, looking to the west, but nobody paid attention.

The sun dipped to the horizon, and bamboo lanterns wavered in the breeze as we walked along the garden path through the resort.

"*Manava*," said two huge smiling twins at the foyer of the bar and restaurant wharf.

"*Manava*," Oko and I replied.

"They are Matahi's grandchildren," Oko said as we entered the bar. "Get me a pineapple juice and something for yourself. I see someone I need to talk to." Oko handed me a fifty Pacific-franc note.

Two islanders entertained the crowd with a guitar and a ukulele. Guests and yachties crowded the bar, loading up with the last of happy hour drinks. Everyone was older, and smells of alcohol, sunscreen, and perfume drifted. A woman sitting at the bar kept smiling at me. I joined the three-deep queue and recognised a face.

"I've been looking for you," Rani said. "Did you find Matahi?"

"Yes. He'll be here soon. Your grandfather is awesome."

"He's a lovable rogue. What did you get up to this afternoon?"

"Just … relaxing," I said.

Rani smiled. "I need to collect glasses. Enjoy, and don't let Matahi lead you astray."

Most of the men wore tropical shirts and propped sunglasses on their foreheads. The ladies wore sarongs or light cotton dresses. The woman near the bar kept smiling at me. I smiled back then turned away, wishing she'd stare off. The bar staff wore floral bands on their heads. It took ages to reach the front.

"One pineapple juice and a mango smoothie, please," I said.

"*Maeva, manava*," the smiling woman said. She had a dark tan, bright red lipstick, and wore a bikini top with a short sarong around her waist.

"*Manava*," I said.

"Your eyes are bluer than the lagoon," the woman said.

She rocked on the stool and slurred a little as she spoke. I blushed and turned to the bar. The next thing I knew the woman squeezed my butt. I jumped and bumped a man carrying cocktails, which dribbled and spilled down my back.

"Sorry," I said, tensing.

The man with the drinks shook his head, and the smiling woman shimmied her shoulders. She must have been forty or something and I couldn't believe she was hitting on me. To my relief, the drinks arrived, and Oko appeared beside the woman.

"Come, Sam, there is someone I want you to meet," Oko said.

Aqua light from floor windows washed the thatched ceiling. A lady danced into me as I squeezed through the crowd to a deck overlooking the lagoon. A man with wiry grey-black hair and dark eyes caught my gaze, held it for a second, then turned to a lady sitting at his side. The man wore a white singlet with a picture of a yacht on the front. I looked out at the old timber schooner anchored behind the catamaran I'd noticed earlier and had liked the look of.

Oko waded through the crowd to the waterfront table. Two islanders, sitting opposite the man in the white singlet, smiled.

"*Manava*," they said, stood, and left. Oko and I shuffled in.

The man in the white singlet reached out to shake my hand.

"G'day. Laurie Piper's the name."

"Sam … Sam Edwards."

"And Madam Estelle," Laurie said.

"*Bonsoir*," the attractive younger lady by his side said. "Please excuse me – I am just leaving. Will you be joining us for dinner?"

"Thank you, but no, we leave tonight," Oko said.

"Well, *au revoir*, gentlemen." Madam Estelle left the table and melded into the crowd.

Oko leaned over the table. "We need to bypass immigration and leave for Tonga as soon as possible."

"What are you carrying?" Laurie asked.

"Ourselves and hand luggage, nothing illegal."

"People smuggling, I lose my yacht if I get caught."

"How much you want?" Oko asked.

A glint sparked in the old captain's eyes. "Half a million US." He stretched back. "I could leave the day after tomorrow."

"We need to leave tonight," Oko said

"I need provisions, and I can't disappoint Madame Estelle."

Lightning flashed, and a *fap-fap-fap* sound caught my attention. I strained my ears and nudged Oko as the sound of a helicopter got louder.

Oko pulled a slim black bag from under his shirt, unzipped the corner, and slid it toward Laurie. "One million US—two hundred thousand in advance, but we leave right away."

"One million!" I shot a glance at the schooner wondering how Oko had so much money to splash around. "That yacht's not even worth that. The catamaran would be much faster."

Captain Laurie took a deep breath, as though inhaling the cash from the table. "*Atlanta* won the class in the Antigua Tall Ships race. If a storm's coming, I know where I'd rather be. I can be ready in fifteen minutes," he said and leaned back with hands behind his head.

"Ten minutes," Oko said, holding the pouch halfway across the table.

"Half in gold bullion when we arrive in Tonga, and the balance in Xspace cryptocurrency," Laurie said.

"Gold is difficult," Oko said.

"I'm sure you can manage," Laurie said, lifting his gaze to the black chopper.

Oko released the black bag, nodded, and they shook hands.

Laurie wiggled his fingers and casually grasped the bag as the chopper disappeared below palms near the airport. "Can you get yourselves to *Atlanta*?"

"Yes, ten minutes—no longer," Oko said.

As we left the bar and marched back to the bungalow, I kept glancing at the old schooner anchored in the lagoon. Anxiety swirled in my chest. I was worried about the black chopper and tried to visualise escaping to the open ocean on *Atlanta*, but all I saw was danger. And why did Oko carry two hundred thousand cash? How would Oko get the gold bullion? By the time I arrived at my bungalow my mind was whirring.

"Okay, Sam. Make sure you have everything in your bags. I'll be back in one minute," Oko said and continued to his bungalow next door.

I entered the luxurious bungalow wishing I could soak in the spa bath then slip between the crisp sheets to fall asleep, then wake in the morning to find my dad was there and that everything had just been a bad dream. I walked into the bathroom and looked in the mirror. Sweat beaded on my forehead, I looked pale, and my pupils were dilated.

"Hold it together. You can do it. Do it for Dad," I whispered.

41

ATLANTA

A gentle tap on the door alerted me it was time to go. An outboard chugged as I stepped from my bungalow. Loud cheers came from the bar as flames twirled and drums beat. Faint orange light reflected on the lagoon, and the storm cell darkened the sky to the west. Matahi cut the motor. Exhaust fumes wafted as he drifted to my swimming platform. Oko handed his bag to Matahi and we slipped quietly into the dory.

"Lie low and cover yourselves," Matahi said. He idled from the wharf until we were behind the sleek catamaran then accelerated to skim over the water.

"Okay," Matahi said. Oko and I slipped our hessian covers. The white hull of *Atlanta* hid us from the resort. There was no sign of Captain Laurie. All was quiet. Two timber masts towered overhead. Oko and I stood and grasped the timber gunnel as we cruised alongside.

A small dog barked and nipped Oko's hands.

Oko let go. A white inflatable dinghy zoomed toward us. Captain Laurie approached at speed and cut the motor.

"It's all right, Wiggols, they're with me," he called. The dog was small and mostly white with black eye patches and grey spots.

Laurie leapt aboard *Atlanta* with a bulging velvet pouch in his hand. He pulled Oko's bag aboard one-handed, assisted me, then Oko aboard the same way, and disappeared below decks with his velvet pouch. Matahi motored away.

Wiggols sniffed my legs. "Hi, boy," I said as I bent to pat him.

Atlanta's decks and coach houses were all timber; the masts had rigging you could climb. The ship smelled of rope and salt, and I felt as though I'd stepped back in time.

"Welcome aboard *Atlanta*, gentlemen," Laurie said.

Wiggols cocked his leg and peed on Oko's shoe.

"Wiggols!" Laurie scolded.

"Oh." Oko's nostrils flared, and he shook his foot.

Quick as a flash, Captain Laurie dashed a bucket on a rope over the side, scooped seawater, tipped a splash on Oko's shoe and the rest over the deck.

"Sorry, Oko. Mr Wiggoly owns you now. He won't do it again."

I tried not to laugh. Oko scowled at the dog and Captain Laurie ushered us to the cockpit with a classic old timber wheel in the centre.

"I'll do a quick tour," Laurie said.

My vision zoomed in two hundred metres over the water, to the bar. Three men in dark suits searched through the crowd. I scanned the resort, seeing another three headed along the walkway to the bungalows. Oko strained to follow my gaze, and I figured he couldn't see the men in the fading light.

"We should leave and do the tour later," I said.

Laurie looked at me, then followed my gaze toward the bar. "Okay," he said and swung our bags through the hatch and dropped them on a long-cushioned seat in the main cabin. "Get the dinghy aboard, raise the anchor, and we're away."

I thought we should just tow the dinghy and leave right away, but before I knew it Laurie had taken a rope from a wooden baton. "Hold that," he said, handing me the halyard, and climbing into the dinghy.

Ashore, three men reached into their jackets and drew guns as they approached my bungalow. "Three armed men at my room, three more in the bar," I whispered.

Oko nodded.

Laurie passed the orange fuel tank to Oko. "The outboard is heavy – the two of you should haul it up."

My blood chilled as my bungalow door flung open. Two men darted inside. The third kept watch on the pier.

Laurie passed Oko a rope attached to the outboard. "Just take the strain. Don't lean hard on the timber rails; grab the rigging for support."

I reached over, grabbed the outboard lift bar, took all the weight one-handed and hauled it aboard. After placing it on deck, I stared back at the bungalow.

"Where did you get your muscles?" Laurie asked. "Pass the halyard."

I passed the halyard and kept my eyes between Laurie and my room. The two men came out and marched for Oko's bungalow.

Steel ropes attached to the dinghy floor and Laurie threaded the halyard through the eyes, tied a knot, then sprang up over the rail. "All right, muscles, you can haul the dinghy up," he said and released the other end of the halyard.

"Take cover," I said, crouching behind the coach house.

Oko ducked, but Laurie hesitated.

"Three men out front of the bungalow, one has binoculars scanning the boats," I said.

"Can't see a bloody thing," Laurie said, squatting with the halyard in hand. "What have you blokes been up to?"

"Nothing illegal," Oko said.

I waited ten seconds and peeked over the coach house. "They're running back to the resort."

Fire sticks twirled, drums beat, and over the top of the festivities, the *fap-fap-fap* of a chopper resounded.

"What the hell have you blokes done?" Laurie asked.

"Nothing," I answered. "My dad was a climate scientist. They killed him."

"Who are 'they'?" Laurie asked.

A sleek black helicopter flew over the resort; a huge spotlight burst to life and shone on the catamaran closest to the bar. We sat with our backs to the coach house, and Wiggols rested his muzzle on my leg.

"These guys are over us like a rash," Laurie said. "There are compartments below for smuggling. I'll hide you and sneak out in the middle of the night."

The *fap-fap-fap* got loud. Ripples fanned across the lagoon, and the spotlight hit the catamaran to port. Oko and I stayed behind the waist-high timber coach house. Laurie crawled to the cockpit and skulked on his haunches to the stairs.

Blinding light turned dusk into day. Turbulence blasted my hair and shirt.

Laurie stood, stretched as though he'd just woken up, shielded his eyes, and waved.

An automatic weapon blazed from the chopper. Splinters exploded from the coach house in front of Laurie.

42

REUNION

East of Rangiroa, the sun descended to the horizon. Tali pushed her weary tail and sensed that three of her cousins were losing their will to live. An albatross glided overhead. The pod hadn't found a single squid or flying fish since they'd escaped the orcas. It seemed there was nothing left to eat.

From way back at the start of the human's industrial revolution, the ocean began to absorb vast amounts of man-made carbon from the atmosphere. The carbon had reacted with the water to form a weak carbonic acid, and now the ocean's increasing acidity had triggered a collapse of the food chain.

Hope, sparked by the vibration they'd felt, strengthened Tali's will and energised Bola, but the rest in the pod were younger; to them stories of telepathic communications with the light planet, and the legend of the princess, were just tales from their youth.

"PFFFH," Tali exhaled and drew breath. She carefully avoided swallowing a deadly plastic bag and sifted white sediment from the water, hoping to ingest a morsel of plankton from the barren, acidic ocean. She needed to find a way to rally the pod, to fuel their will to survive.

A whistle cut the silence.

Tali twitched. *A ghost whistle. Orca, playing tricks.* Others heard it. The nine surviving dolphins tightened formation and swam in silence to avoid detection. Bola patrolled the flank.

The whistle repeated. Tali whistled back.

A small white-sided dolphin, dark grey, almost black on top, skipped across the ocean. Her creamy undersides glistened in the pastel light as she leapt into the air and landed amid the pod.

"Miki! My sister!" chirped Tali.

Overcome with joy, she threw her head back and slapped her tail. The whole world brightened. *But how could it be?* Tali recalled the blood in the water when the orcas attacked her sister.

Miki frolicked, chattered, nodded her head, and rubbed against Tali. No dolphin could believe that Miki had escaped the orca, or how she had found the pod in the middle of the ocean.

Tali quivered with pride as everyone petted her three-year-old sister, youngest of the pod. The bravest of heroes brought joy to hearts and strength to tails.

"You saved us. You're a hero," chirped Tali. "You made the orcas hesitate then drew them away. In the moonlight I saw blood when they surrounded you. If I believed there was a chance that you'd survived, I'd have waited. Please forgive me!"

"You did well to lead the pod away," chirped Miki. "I thought I was dead myself, but slipped through their jaws and swam as fast as I could. They herded me away from you."

"How did you find us?"

"You were heading east, and I followed an albatross." Miki exhaled and drew breath. Her thoughts were drawn back to swimming alone that morning. "Did you notice a weird vibration earlier today?"

Tali looked Miki in the eye. "You sensed that?"

"Yes," chirped Miki.

"The guardian child has come to save the ocean."

"That's just a story," chirped Miki.

"It's true. When I was your age, I saw the princess, the guardian's mother, ignite energy so powerful it inspired nature," Tali replied.

"Inspired nature?" Miki asked.

In fading light, the pod gathered as Tali retold her story: "The princess had a treasure, a pearl that released an energetic pulse. The pulse induced a current that stirred nutrient-rich water from the depths. Phytoplankton bloomed, then zooplankton flourished. Whales came back, and by mixing and fertilising the ocean's surface layers, the whole food chain thrived. At the same time, cold weather and snow slowed the ice-caps melting."

"What happened then? What went wrong? Why did the Ice-Pod have to flee the gulf?"

Tali went silent. The ocean's increasing heat and acidity had a human scent, but a dark presence had slipped into the earth, a presence she couldn't explain.

"Humans turned back to their ignorance when something terrible impregnated our planet," Tali chirped. She sensed it growing stronger. The presence drew her to it, and she had to believe that somehow, she could make a difference and destroy it.

Dusk settled over the ocean. Beneath the surface, the water was dark. The dolphins took time to mourn the loss of their cousins, but with a young hero in their midst, their spirits were strengthened, and a sense of security surrounded them.

"PFFFH." The pod surfaced in unison and pushed onward through the night.

43

ATTACKED

Captain Laurie raised his hands in surrender. Bullets pierced timber panels; shrapnel exploded inside. Fury blazed in Laurie's eyes. He dived through the hatch into the main cabin.

The helicopter hovered over the bow; wind from the rotor buffeted *Atlanta* and the spotlight scanned the deck. Flattened against the coach house, I gaped through a porthole as Laurie landed on our bags and snatched a floor hatch open.

Two ropes uncoiled from the chopper. Silhouettes slid silently down and landed on the bow.

I focused on the water. I could jump in, hold my breath, and escape. Oko crouched, signalled me to stay low, and ran for the bow.

Through the confusion of swirling wind and noise from the chopper, I heard a muffled groan. Grief, fear, and anger exploded inside me.

"Oko!" I shouted, and stood, shielding my eyes from the blinding light as Oko cartwheeled into a somersault. A man in tight black clothing fired a submachine gun. Oko launched high and spun. Flame burst from the barrel tracing Oko's trajectory.

No! I stared in horror.

Oko dipped, pushed the flaming barrel down with his foot, and crashed a knee into the attacker's face.

The attacker fell back over the rail, splashing into the lagoon. A second gunman sprawled on deck, shook his head and reached for his submachine gun.

"Watch out, Oko!" I shouted.

The attacker opened fire. Oko dived behind the forward coach house, and the gunman swung the weapon toward me.

This was is it. Now I die.

Sparks spat from the barrel. I ducked left. Bullets seared past my right ear. A white flash leapt from the forward coach house; Wiggols launched at the attacker's throat. The gunman fell back.

Wiggols ripped and tore, then yelped as the attacker tore him away and slammed him into the forward hatch.

I ran and dived, crashing my fist into the gunman's temple. The gunman crumpled. I grabbed his gun and threw it into the water.

Wiggols growled and barked. The chopper manoeuvred close, its wind sending a bucket crashing across the deck. Oko stood at my side. Two men stood in the open doorway training machine guns on us.

"Down!" Laurie bellowed.

We dived. The *tak-tak-tak* of an automatic weapon raged behind.

Two men fell from the chopper; sparks flew; the windscreen shattered. The chopper veered and jerked away. Laurie ran to the bow with a rifle. "Can you fire a weapon?"

"Type 99 Chinese assault rifle," Oko said, taking the weapon.

Laurie handed me a floodlight. "Scan the water while I get us out of here," he said and ran to the stern.

Smoke streamed from the chopper. A figure swam in the dusky dark. I switched the spotlight on, and a man in a dark outfit froze.

Oko moved the latch from automatic to semiautomatic and fired a single shot. Water kicked up in front of the man and sent him swimming to shore.

I kept an eye on the retreating swimmer and bent over the rail, checking close to the hull. The music at the bar had stopped; only a huddle of startled drinkers remained to watch the battle rage on the lagoon.

"Yeah!" cheered one of the drinkers as the chopper retreated with smoke trailing from it. The chopper disappeared behind trees and an eerie silence fell over the lagoon.

A stuttering whir preceded the chug of *Atlanta's* diesel. Water and smoke pulsed from the exhaust and Laurie ran to amidships. One end of the halyard was still attached to the dinghy, but the other swayed high above our heads.

Laurie grasped the shrouds, climbed the ratlines to halfway up the mast, and jumped. I gasped as the skipper snatched the halyard and fell. The dinghy lifted, and Laurie landed with a thud.

"Follow me," he said as the dinghy flopped on deck. At the bow, he opened a locker, handed me a boat hook and Oko a winch controller.

"Listen carefully. Oko, when I motor forward, press the green button, and the winch will pull the chain in. With your free hand, point in the direction the chain is laying—ahead—to port—below—behind. Pull the anchor right up into the sheaf. Got it?"

Oko nodded.

Laurie bent and beckoned me to the anchor locker.

"Sam, if the chain piles up it can derail and fall back into the water. Your job is to spread the chain with the boat hook."

I nodded. Laurie ran to the cockpit and the engine clunked into forward gear.

Oko pressed the green button and guided Laurie. Chain rattled into the locker; rusty saltwater splashed as I spread the chain, and sandy mud oozed as the anchor clanged into its sheath.

Captain Laurie swung the wheel and put power to the prop. I wiped rusty water from my brow. The smell of gunpowder lingered. Brass shells chinked at my feet. I scanned Kia-Ora village and my lips trembled as I smiled. We'd defended ourselves. Pride and euphoria swelled through me. The bullets and the noise and the violence terrified me, but we'd survived Xcon's attack.

44

DRONES

Twilight sank into darkness. Shore lights reached out and shimmered on the surface of the lagoon. Tiputa Pass was a nautical mile away, and beyond, the Pacific Ocean.

"You did well, Sam," Oko said.

I shrugged. "Thanks, but you were awesome. Where did you learn to fight like that?"

Captain Laurie approached the bow, Wiggols panting at his feet.

"The shore is only fifty metres from the centre of the pass. If they wait there, they can blast us to pieces."

I swallowed and scanned the seaboard.

"Have you ever used an assault rifle, Sam?" Laurie asked.

"Never. Not a real one, but I use a replica for holographic gaming."

Laurie scanned the lagoon and the shore with binoculars and paced to the cockpit. The timber wheel turned as autopilot held course. Laurie disappeared into the cabin and surfaced ten seconds later with a second assault rifle.

"Oko, can you teach Sam to shoot this?"

Wide-eyed, I took the weapon. Adrenalin pumped through me. Blasting holographic figures was the best, but I didn't know if I could shoot a real person. The Type 99 weighed slightly more than my Hero-G rifle and didn't fold into a pistol.

Oko demonstrated how to switch from semi-automatic single shot to rapid fire, replace the magazine, and sight a target.

"Try a single shot. Shoot that buoy," he said.

I switched from safety to semi-automatic, held the butt to my shoulder, sighted the buoy, and squeezed the trigger. Water splashed to the side and just behind it. My second shot fell just short of the target. With my third shot, the buoy jolted instantaneously. The speed of impact surprised me, and the recoil was less than I expected, but the power, the lethal reality of the weapon, chilled me.

"Nice shooting." Oko nodded. "Now try automatic. Sight the buoy and squeeze the trigger for one second."

With the rifle set to automatic, I aimed and squeezed the trigger. Flame spat from the barrel. Water kicked up all around the buoy, and if it hadn't disappeared, I wouldn't know I'd hit it.

"Excellent." Oko handed me another magazine.

"Remember, semi-automatic is more accurate. You have thirty rounds in the magazine, just three seconds on auto and you're empty; practise changing the magazines. I'll position myself behind the foredeck hatch. You stay behind the coach house near Laurie and keep your eyes peeled."

Lights from guesthouses and restaurants reflected on the lagoon. A few tourists peered from balconies, and locals congregated in groups under palms on the beach. I crouched, concealing my weapon, and searched the waterfront leading to the wharf near the pass.

The wet exhaust gurgled and spat. White smoke trailed. The motor sounded like it was working hard, but the resort wasn't far behind, and the lights marking Tiputa Pass were a long way ahead.

"Is this full speed?" I asked.

"Nine knots is quick for a cruising yacht," Laurie said.

I thought I could swim faster. Only one nautical mile to the pass, but at this rate it would take ten minutes. The assassins had plenty of time to set an ambush.

Laurie adjusted the autopilot and, without touching the companion-way ladder, swung from the hatch into the cabin. He reached into the floor hatch and grabbed two more assault rifle magazines and a mini Uzi gun. Laurie laid the Uzi on the seat beside the wheel, gave one magazine to me, and raced to the foredeck with another for Oko.

Lightning forked and flashed the lagoon. I wondered why Laurie had so many guns. Thunder rumbled. Wake spread from *Atlanta*. Ahead, blinking red and green lights marked the channel and behind, the roaring sound of an approaching engine.

The rumble of a V8 engine brought Oko running to the coach house. We all stared into the twilight. A speedboat skimmed across the lagoon toward us. As I watched, the speedboat closed in so fast that *Atlanta* seemed as if she were going backwards.

"Laurie, if you have hyperdrive, now is a good time," I said.

"Hyperdrive is on the blink, but Mr Wiggoly's working on it," Laurie said.

Oko knelt and rested his rifle on the stern rail.

"Sam, bring a spare magazine, and use the stern rail to steady your aim. Find your range with a few single shots; aim for the hull at the waterline. Then wait for my command. When the boat is close, switch to automatic and blast holes in the hull."

Shooting a boat didn't trouble me, but my hands trembled as I knelt as Oko did and aimed. Oko's gun flashed and bullets hit the hull.

"Find your range now, Sam." Oko said. "Don't hold your breath while you aim. You can pause to squeeze the trigger but keep breathing."

I squeezed the trigger and water kicked in front of the speedboat. I squeezed again and water kicked up closer this time. The third shot pierced the hull. A second hole appeared just above the waterline as I fired a fourth time.

The speedboat's orange hull continued to charge across the smooth lagoon towards us.

"Okay, Sam, switch to automatic," Oko said.

"Hold … hold …"

A man stood in the speedboat, aimed a gun, and bullets whizzed through the air above me.

"Fire," Oko said.

I squeezed the trigger. White light spat from the barrel. The stock jolted as I sprayed a one-second, then a two-second burst. The rifle clicked empty. I fumbled to change the magazine. Oko unloaded his second magazine into the hull. The enemy fire stopped; then the speedboat's bow dipped as I unloaded my second magazine.

"Excellent shooting, guys," Laurie said. "Remember, Sam, semi-automatic is more accurate."

I trembled with nervous energy. My ears rang and my shoulder throbbed. I couldn't believe how easily the rifle blasted holes in the speedboat. A yawn interrupted my smile as I swapped the magazine. The sun had gone down, but even with all the adrenaline in my system, I was running out of energy.

Atlanta chugged over the lagoon. Laurie searched with night vision binoculars. All was quiet and still on either side of the pass. Sunset faded. The moon hadn't yet risen. Apart from the flashing channel markers, the lagoon was dark. The rocky shoreline offered countless places for gunmen to hide.

Movement, close behind in the water, startled me. I turned to fire.

"It's Matahi! Don't shoot! I bring supplies," Matahi's outboard zipped to life.

Laurie eased the throttle and Matahi motored alongside.

"My grandkids barricaded the road, and there are no assassins at the pass." Matahi passed three bulging sacks. One smelled of mango. "You starting World War Three?"

"We didn't start it," Oko said.

The flashing green light of the channel marker illuminated Matahi's face, and he caught my eye. "Goodbye, my friend, you're welcome to stay with me anytime. If you ever need to find me, search for a message in a jar amongst the rock pile above my place."

"I will. Thanks for everything." I hadn't seen the rock pile, but it must be easy to find.

"Live slow—fly fast, Sam," Matahi said.

I froze for a second as I considered Matahi's strange farewell, then waved as Laurie accelerated and the old islander faded into the night.

"Live slow—fly fast. I like it," Laurie said. *Atlanta's* hull rose and ploughed through the swell. I crouched ready with my rifle, but Matahi was right – we chugged through the narrow pass into the Pacific Ocean unchallenged.

I walked to the bow. The sound of water splashing against the hull was comforting. I yawned, *Atlanta's* rise and fall making me even sleepier. The lights of Rangiroa twinkled, but I sensed the battle wasn't yet over.

I yawned again, my head drooping with thoughts of blissful sleep. Thunder rumbled and sporadic raindrops fell.

My eyes flew open. I stared into the night. "Something is coming."

"What is it?" Laurie searched with binoculars.

"There! A small plane, an arrowhead, coming for us. No—two of them." I switched my rifle to semi-automatic.

"Where?" Laurie yelled.

"Can't see a thing," Oko said.

Two drones, two metres across with no vertical surface, attacked. Bullets exploded through *Atlanta's* hull. Laurie and Oko dived for cover. I squeezed the trigger, but the drones were too small and fast. A storm of bullets smashed into the hull. I dived onto the cabin roof, rolled, and fell between Oko and Laurie.

As the drones rocketed overhead, I stood. White flame blazed from the barrel as I fired into darkness. The deck rose and fell, but even if it had been steady, this was nothing like Hero-G, and ten times harder than the lagoon.

The drones banked and circled back.

"To the other side," I shouted.

"I can't see them," Oko said, running around the coach house.

I sighted the nearest drone and fired single shots, one after another. I had no idea if my shots were even close. Hitting the zooming arrow-like drones seemed impossible. Bullets splashed beside *Atlanta*, then thudded into the hull. Bilge alarms sounded.

"We're taking water!" Laurie ran for the forward hatch. "Those damn drones are going to sink us."

The look of helpless rage in Laurie's eyes triggered my instinct to run. I ran for the hatch, ran to shelter in the hull. As I reached the hatch, the drones scorched overhead. Oko fired random shots into the darkness; his fearless determination stopped me. Xcon had killed my dad, destroyed my house, and now they were going to kill us all. Oko couldn't even see the drones. I was our only chance of destroying them.

For a second I closed my eyes and inhaled a deep breath. As the drones circled back, I took position behind the coach house at Oko's side. *They killed my dad.* I needed to use my talents. As the drones attacked, I focused my telescopic night vision on the lead drone and let my body move with the deck, but kept the rifle still and fired single shots, one after another.

The first drone burst into orange and red flame. The second scorched through the explosion.

"Yeah, Sam!" Oko cheered.

The second drone circled fast and attacked. Bullets smashed portholes on either side of my legs as I aimed and fired.

Oko rolled over the coach house. "Take cover, Sam!"

After two shots, my rifle clicked empty. "Ammo!" I shouted.

Oko threw his rifle.

Flame spat from the drone's guns. Timber splintered. It rocketed, kamikaze, at the hull.

I dropped my rifle, caught Oko's, and blasted. White light blazed. Shells sprayed. My shoulder jolted, my eardrums quaked. Red sparks spat from the drone. Collision was inevitable. My rifle clicked empty.

A second before impact a red flash engulfed the drone. Flaming debris torpedoed into *Atlanta*.

Belowdecks, bilge alarms rang out. Lightning flashed as the storm cell dumped rain on the palm-lined shore. I yawned and slumped onto the smouldering deck. Random raindrops splattered my face. Stars twinkled in the sky ahead. Helpless to avoid it, I closed my eyes and fell asleep.

45

BACKGAMMON

A loud slap, then a sound like driving rain, startled me. I experienced a falling sensation and clutched at the darkness. Something moved and yelped. "Wiggols … sorry."

Wiggols jumped from beside me. The terrier stretched and glanced back, before scampering up the ladder out into the night.

I couldn't remember falling asleep, or how I'd come to lie on the bunk at the bottom of the cockpit ladder. I hated being put to bed like this, but at least we hadn't sunk. The last drone exploding was a blur of sparks and flame. It was hard to believe that yesterday even happened. Stars twinkled through the hatch above me and swung with the yacht's motion. I sensed first light nearing and spotted my pack leaning against the bulkhead at my feet.

I craved my bed, my pillow, the sound of Dad's footsteps on the stairs, the smell of Swathi's fruity shampoo, her laugh, and the sound of traffic as we walked up our road. But everything around me was foreign and strange.

Behind my head a pencil rolled on a chart table, and red lights glowed from navigation equipment and switches. The scent of old wood mixed with salty sweat, diesel, and a hint of garlic. A gimballed two-burner gas stove swung idly in the galley opposite the chart table, and something stirred behind the bench top.

I rose on my elbows and craned my neck. Oko slept on a double berth alongside a long wooden table in the saloon. At least we survived. *Atlanta* rocked and I lay back, closed my eyes, and listened to the swish and splash of the ocean.

A pronounced rise preceded a juddering fall. My eyes shot open. Cutlery clinked, and spray drove against the hull. Autopilot grated behind the bulkhead at my feet, and the gentle swish resumed.

The splintered ceiling stared down at me and, as if I hadn't had enough of them, a terrible thought occurred. I reached for my pack. There was a hole in the centre. My heart skipped a beat. I fumbled with the zip and pulled my laptop out. The hole pierced the cover; I flipped it open.

"Shit!" A lump of shrapnel had smashed the screen and embedded between the G and H keys.

Laurie's head poked through the hatch. "What's wrong?"

"A chunk of shrapnel smashed my computer."

"Is that all?" Laurie withdrew.

My nostrils flared. *Was that all?* Everything was gone. The computer had my photos, games … My dad was dead—my house incinerated. It was my last link to home. I folded the laptop shut. Now glass fell on the bunk and jammed the device open. "No. No," I groaned.

Oko propped on his bed. "Are you okay, Sam?"

"I'm okay. Shrapnel smashed my computer." I grabbed a towel from the bunk opposite, tipped the loose glass onto it, and crunched the laptop shut. I shook my head and slouched back into the bunk, but no matter which way I lay, I couldn't get comfortable. Visions of my dad's pale face on the floor of the hotel brought tears to my eyes. Somehow *Atlanta* hadn't sunk and we were alive, but everything seemed grainy and sullied. I couldn't imagine life ever being good again.

The faintest hint of sunrise filtered through the hatch. I pushed my legs over the side of the bed, reached for the grab rail, and climbed the ladder.

Stars filled the sky. Autopilot turned the old wooden wheel. A faint orange glow illuminated the edge of the world, and water surrounded me three hundred sixty degrees to the horizon. A ruffling sound made me turn to look. Towering white sails luffed, then *thoomped* as they stiffened. Near the top of the taller rear mast, Captain Laurie kept lookout.

The main and foresail were almost square but angled up where they were lashed to wooden booms and attached to the mast with rattan hoops. A smaller triangular sail ran from the foremast to the bowsprit. A dozen round bullet holes pierced the coach house. I thought how much bigger the blowouts were inside. Scratched-up Perspex covered the two smashed portholes, and the timber was blackened where I'd stood and blasted the last drone.

A dull thud announced Laurie's return. The skipper ambled to the coach house, rubbed his fingers over the bullet holes, and cursed. "I built her myself, you know."

I didn't know but nodded.

"Designed her, sourced the timber." Laurie shook his head.

"Sorry … we didn't think they would attack like that."

Laurie huffed. "Should have let you charter that catamaran."

I avoided eye contact and studied the orange glow to the east. I'd lost everything. He was getting paid and could fix his boat.

"Tea," Laurie said.

"Huh?" I replied.

"You want tea?"

"Huh?" I knew he was offering me a cup of tea, but the sun was yet to rise, and I didn't like the way he spoke to me.

"Do you want a cup of tea?" Laurie emphasised every word as he spoke.

"Yes … thank you," I said, satisfied that I'd annoyed him a little.

"How do ya have it?"

"White, no sugar, please," I thought about the million dollars the skipper was getting and was glad when he climbed below. With Laurie gone, the endless sky and smooth rolling sea calmed me.

A larger wave approached. *Atlanta* surfed the face, then rounded into the wind. The wheel turned as the autopilot made a correction, and the schooner sailed with the breeze.

The motion seemed stiller and less tilted outside. Fresh sea air tingled my skin. I walked forward to where the round wooden bowsprit reached three metres out over the water and anchored stays for the three foresails. It looked like a cool place to sit. Carved railings surrounded the first two metres of the bowsprit and I edged out over the ocean to sit on the rail with my feet resting on the sturdy round column. The bow rose and fell, parting the deep blue sea, and from within the motion came the faintest glimmer of hope. Hope that I could still have a life.

Atlanta surged on a wave. The bow reared, then dipped, and cool spray wet my feet. Smooth swells rolled from behind and across the hull.

The sky above the orange sunrise was the lightest blue and deepened to black in the west.

"Ahoy," Laurie called from the cockpit. He raised a cup then disappeared. A large wave loomed. It was nice up here and I wished the skipper would have taken longer. *Atlanta* surged as I slid back along the bowsprit. When I reached the cockpit, Wiggols was lapping tea from a cup. I laughed.

"You like tea too, Wiggols," I said.

Behind the wheel, burgundy cushions had been placed to form a huge sunbed. Laurie came back to the stairs, handed me my tea, threw four smaller cushions onto the sunbed, then emerged with his own cup and a brown leather case.

"You play backgammon?" Laurie asked.

I shook my head and headed for the bow.

"Sit. I'll teach you." Laurie pointed to where I should sit.

I just wanted to be alone, but it would be rude to ignore him. Laurie organised a cushion behind his back and opened the case. The felt-lined board had twelve brown or white triangular spurs alternating on each side. Four dice rested in a slot, and Laurie arranged black and white disks in groups on the spurs.

"Black or white, Sam?"

"White." I stared at the sunrise, sipped tea, and wished I had my phone or that my laptop worked. I could've played a game or looked through photos. And not being able to check Swathi and Tom's social media was disturbing. Wiggols finished his tea and sat on a cushion beside me. I scratched his neck.

"The idea is to move all your white disks to my end of the board, throw off, and the first person with none left wins. It's easy." Laurie gave me two dice. "Playing is the best way to learn. You throw first and I'll help you."

I jiggled the dice and tossed one-handed.

"Five and a four," Laurie said.

"You can move two pieces, or one piece nine spaces. Try and keep two discs on a spur, because I can knock single pieces back to the start."

I bit my lip and moved two discs to single positions on two spurs.

"Okay, you didn't double up, you're exposed." Laurie's eyes took on a fiery intensity. With both hands, he shook the dice close to his chest and threw.

"Double fours!" Laurie shouted.

I flinched and spilled hot tea on my leg.

"Ship's rules are that if you throw doubles, you move four times the number and roll again." Laurie moved his pieces and *Atlanta* rounded on a towering swell. The black and white discs slid. Laurie arranged them back into place, levelled the board with a small cushion at one end, and threw again.

Old tattoos with thick outlines adorned his arms – a devil with a trident and a mermaid on his dark-tanned skin and below the knuckles, *love* and *hate* were scratched in faded blue ink.

"A misspent youth," Laurie said, and I tried to stop staring at the tattoos.

The tip of the sun flared above the blue Pacific. I stood and held a backstay for support. A tunnel of millions of orange and yellow circles rushed toward me. The flood of dazzling solar radiation invigorated me. I focused on absorbing the sun's energy until a chinking noise caught my attention.

"Your throw," Laurie said, shaking the dice.

The game sucked, but with the sun blazing, my spirits soared.

"Was Wiggols drinking tea?" I asked, scattering the dice and moving my pieces.

Laurie nodded, rolled, and lifted his eyebrows as he knocked one of my pieces off the board.

"What breed is he?"

"Tenterfield Terrier. Australian breed."

I rolled a four and a six, got my piece back on the board and created a block.

Laurie threw the dice. "Double fives!"

His deep, loud shout made me flinch and I spilled more tea on my shorts.

Oko's face popped up at the hatch. "Everything okay?"

"Just teaching young Sam backgammon," Laurie said. "Kettle's boiled. Tea, sugar, and milk are out."

Oko disappeared back into the saloon, and Laurie smiled as he moved into what looked like a dominant position. "Where did you learn to shoot in the dark?"

"Holographic gaming. I use a Type 99 replica, the new folding version, to blast drones." I shook the dice carefully with two hands and threw: still no double. The game was boring, but at least now I knew how to play.

Oko stepped out with a shiny metal teapot and a small cup.

"Brought your own pot," Laurie said.

"Chinese tea. Do you want to try?"

"Yes, please," I nodded, my cup already empty. The brown tea, served without milk or sugar, tasted refreshing, and I sipped while Laurie moved into my in-zone and began throwing off.

"Looks like poor little Sammy gets thrashed first game," Laurie said.

I scrunched my nose and squinted at Laurie. The skipper was meant to be helping me learn the game. It seemed weird that he was acting so competitive. Holding the dice to my lips, I blew, shook them, and rolled double sixes. Warmth flowed through my chest.

"Good throw, but too little too late." Laurie jiggled his dice as I removed pieces from the board and rolled double threes on my free throw. I moved four more pieces off. I'd caught up. The skipper cleared his throat. If I threw doubles on my free throw, I could win the match. I concentrated on the dice and rolled.

"Yes!" Laurie cheered when they settled on two and one. The skipper threw a five and a four and took two more discs off the board, leaving a single black piece.

I stared at the board. A swell slapped the hull, and droplets of spray landed on my neck. Laurie would win – unless I threw double fours or better.

46

OKO AND LAURIE

I jiggled the dice, flared my nostrils, stared at Laurie, visualised double sixes … and threw.

The dice clunked and rattled against the board. I held my breath as they spun impossibly long. One settled on five. The second teetered on one, but at the last second flipped onto five.

"Double fives," I shouted.

"Beginner's bloody luck!" Laurie looked angry and dejected.

The skipper's reaction set my shoulders shaking. I couldn't restrain a laugh and gazed at the heavens. Above the sails, the sky was a strange fuzzy-blue colour.

"What's that blue haze above the masts?" I asked when I'd settled down.

Oko and Laurie looked up.

Laurie smiled. "You can see that?"

Oko squinted. "See what?"

"The stealth screen projection at the top of the masts," Laurie said. "Satellites can't pick us up. Turns out you guys got a real bargain; that catamaran you liked would be on the bottom of the lagoon. *Atlanta* is as stealthy as they come. Timber hull and Kevlar rigging barely register on radar, and with the stealth screen, even spotter planes struggle to see her."

Black and white disks clicked as Laurie packed the game and folded the board shut. "I wouldn't have taken you two for all the tea in China if I'd known I was walking into World War Three. Who are you people? Who's after you? And why do they want you dead?"

"Where did you buy the Chinese military weapons and stealth gear?" countered Oko. "You smuggle black pearls – do you smuggle weapons too?"

"Are you a Chinese spy?" Laurie asked.

"We're on a mission to stop the warming in the Tonga Trench. I pay one million US for passage. You accepted the cash, the Xspace crypto transaction has been completed and the gold bullion will be in Tonga. That is all you need to know. I will add an extra gold bar for the damage."

Captain Laurie stared down at a cushion. I could almost hear him doing maths in his head. *Atlanta* dipped and rolled with the swells, and a blue-footed booby flew overhead. Laurie was risking his life for us, and I thought he had a right to know that Xcon was responsible for the attack.

"Well, if you want to save the world, best get some more sail up – get there quicker. Follow me. I'll do a tour of the ship." Laurie descended into the main cabin. "Life jackets are under that bunk," he said, pointing to where I'd slept.

My heart sank as I glanced at my bag; it seemed the last of my old life had been smashed with the computer. I followed Laurie past the galley, into the saloon.

"The library and theatre," Laurie said, leaning on a long wooden table with Oko's double berth on the other side. The library comprised two shelves about a metre and a half long, and the theatre a small TV above the bunk.

"The sacks of mangoes, coconuts, and eggs your friend brought are under this bunk," Laurie said. "You may as well sleep here, Sam. It's more comfortable and quieter amidships."

I liked the idea of being near the mangoes, and the bunk had cosy appeal with the books and shelves, perfect for lying back and gaming.

"Do you have any games?" I asked.

Laurie looked at Oko before speaking. "Chess, draughts, cards, and backgammon," he said, then stared at the bullet-torn ceiling. Light and blue sky peeked through a dozen holes, and the skipper swore under his breath. "There's plenty of rice, porridge, and tins in the galley cupboards, and I still have a few onions and a cabbage."

With a sack of mangoes under my new bunk, the limited menu didn't concern me. Xcon, Atlo Trudock, the world's most powerful man, had murdered my father and wanted me dead, too. If only I had my computer, I could immerse myself in a game and escape my brutal reality.

Laurie stepped through a doorway with round ends. "The captain's quarters," he said.

A double bed with shelves and a cupboard opposite occupied the rear. Packages, boxes, clothes, rags, and tools littered the floor. There were two long narrow bags in the middle of the mess.

"What's in these two bags?" I asked.

"Birds," Laurie said.

I scrunched my nose. "… Birds?"

A noble expression, like he knew something I could never know, shone through Laurie's eyes. His voice deepened.

"Birds, hang gliders … I like to fly."

My pulse increased. "Can you teach me?"

"That would be another million," Laurie said.

Breath caught in my throat. I so wanted to fly and that was a mean thing to say.

"There were no more attacks after you fell asleep," continued Laurie. "Bilge pumps worked overtime, and I spent most of the night stopping holes with these plugs." Laurie threw a conical wood plug to me.

The floor steepened at the bow, and Laurie opened another rounded door at the front of his quarters. "The throne," he said.

High on a pedestal sat a porcelain toilet bowl with a shower nozzle and a small sink to the side. Space was tight, and it looked as though you needed to sit on the toilet to shower.

"What if you're asleep and we need the toilet?" Oko asked.

"If you need to shit, just come through. Take a leak over the side. To use the toilet, push this lever and pump with the handle to bring saltwater in, do the business, close the intake lever and pump till it's gone. Don't leave the intake open, or you could cause a flood. Got that?"

I nodded. "How come there's only one tap for the shower?"

"Cold water only, and I didn't have time to fill the tanks. No freshwater showers unless we get rain."

Oko frowned. "How do we shower?"

"Don't you have a water maker?" I asked.

"Saltwater deck shower. The water maker is for drinking water."

Oko grimaced.

Laurie rummaged through the sail bags. "Sam, help me with these topsails, and maybe Oko can get some porridge together for breakfast."

"I don't cook," Oko said.

Laurie passed me a drawstring bag. "I didn't have time to hire a cook before we left. Under the circumstances, I think it's only fair we share the chores."

Porridge was easy to make, but I didn't like it. My dad was rarely home at mealtimes, so I'd learned to cook at an early age. "I can cook a few dishes. Why don't we just have mango for breakfast?"

"Sails up first, then we'll think of breakfast." Laurie ignored Oko and spoke directly to me. The only natural light in Laurie's quarters came from the hatch. I shouldered the sail bag up the ladder and climbed through the swept-back cover into bright morning light. No land. No boats. Just sparkling blue for as far as I could see.

"Take this." Laurie held another bag to the hatch, and I hauled the second, larger sail. "These are the topsails," Laurie said, emptying the smaller sail out of the bag. Six coils of rope hung from a pin rail attached to the rigging. "These are the halyards and sheets. Do you know how to tie a bowline?"

I nodded. I'd learned knots from boating with my dad. Laurie released one halyard and tied a bowline through an eye in the sail's head. He attached a second halyard halfway down the sail, tied a sheet that looked the same as a halyard to a corner he called the clew, then told me that the downhall was already attached to the sail's foot.

"I can help with the sails," Oko said.

"You just relax, take it easy, Oko." Laurie gave him a sarcastic smirk.

Oko inhaled a deep breath and frowned.

With halyards and sheets and downhalls, I wondered how Laurie knew which did what. The skipper handed me the free end of one halyard and kept a halyard and a sheet himself. "Pull," he said.

Stiff Dacron brushed against my arms as the sail lifted. We hauled hand over hand until the small triangular sail took shape above the foresail. Laurie tensioned and secured the sail.

The creamy white topsail soared fresh against the blue sky and combined with the foresail to make a tall majestic shape. Water whooshed a fraction louder against the hull. Laurie threw the empty sail bag down the hatch and carried the larger bag to the rear mast. I tied a bowline and hauled the peak halyard. When the main topsail took shape, *Atlanta* heeled an extra two degrees and rode the sea with a more defined motion.

While Laurie put a pot of porridge on the stove, I sliced the mangoes into cheeks and peeled the seeds.

Through the hatch, Laurie handed Oko three bowls of porridge, and I surfaced with a larger bowl of mango pieces. While Oko and I arranged breakfast in the cockpit, Laurie disappeared down the forward hatch and surfaced from his quarters with a length of nylon rope and two fishing rods. He tied one end of the rope to the stern bollard and cast the eight-metre length into the water. "The lifeline, gentlemen. If you fall off, swim around and grab it."

"No personal GPS?" Oko asked.

"Nope," Laurie said, taking a seat.

Wake peeled and frothed from the stern and I imagined falling overboard and floating in the middle of the Pacific with *Atlanta* sailing into the distance. I poked the porridge with the spoon, wondering how I could dispose of it without being seen, and reached for a mango cheek.

Juice trickled down my wrist, and Oko turned away as I licked it off. Sweet flesh melted in my mouth. I scraped the skin clean with my teeth and reached for a fleshy seed.

"Juicy mangoes your friend gave us," Laurie said. "I should probably freeze half of them."

The taste and texture of the mango took me to a special place. With no computer, the wonderful taste was the only thing that slowed my whirring brain. I calculated how many pieces for each person in the bowl and took another cheek.

"How long to Tonga?" Oko asked.

"Tonga's about eighteen hundred miles. A little farther if we head south and give Tahiti a wide berth. Two, maybe three weeks, depending on the weather."

As soon as I'd finished my last piece of mango, I thought of my dad and my computer, and stared at the last piece on the plate.

Laurie grinned. "Go on, take it."

"I have had enough," Oko said as I glanced at him, then took the last piece and with dreamy eyes gorged and scraped every last bit.

Laurie stood and picked up a fishing rod, then handed one to me. A long dangly lure resembling a colourful squid hung from heavy-duty line. Working with sticky hands, I copied Laurie in releasing the drag. Taking care to avoid the lifeline, I let the lure run thirty metres behind the boat and placed the rod in a holder.

"Ten years ago, I could fill the freezer sailing across the Pacific. These days you're lucky to catch a single mahi-mahi or tuna." Laurie cast a bucket with a rope overboard and scooped some water to wash his hands and face. He rinsed his cup and bowl, then scooped a fresh bucket for me and Oko. "I need to patch more holes. Can you gentlemen help keep watch?"

We both nodded.

"A tanker can appear from nowhere and run you down in twenty minutes. You need to scan the horizon every ten minutes. You can relax on deck or take time out below, but make sure you scan the horizon at least every ten minutes. Sam, you're first watch."

My stomach rumbled. With all this sun, I didn't need to eat, and when I didn't need to eat, food, especially mango, made me fart. Laurie and Oko went downstairs. A wonderful sense of freedom abounded – just sun and wind and a blue-footed booby gliding over the heaving Pacific. I threw my porridge overboard and rinsed the bowl.

A dark patch rippled, racing across the water, and wind ruffled my hair as *Atlanta* surged with the gust. Laurie emerged wearing stained grey shorts and an old maroon Atlanta T-shirt. He carried a tool tray and began sanding holes in the high side of the teak deck. I headed around the low side. Laurie didn't look up from his work. The mango made my stomach rumble again, so I continued well downwind to the foredeck.

The breeze strengthened and white caps littered the ocean. Spray burst from the hull and rained over the deck. Laurie's brow knotted – he studied the sails and the sea, put his wooden plugs and sander in a tool tray, strode to the cockpit and eased the mainsail.

Atlanta levelled a few degrees, sailing with a steadier motion, and Laurie returned to his work. A speck on the horizon caught my attention. My vision zoomed in and my pulse raced.

"A ship to starboard," I shouted, pointing.

Laurie squinted, put his tools down, and fetched binoculars. "Fair dinkum, you can see that?"

I nodded.

"Keep an eye on that ship and keep me posted." Laurie resumed work and dropped two wooden plugs.

I scooped them up.

"Thanks, kid … and hey, you saved our butts last night. Excellent shooting, and sorry about your dad and your computer."

"Thanks. Sorry about getting you into all this." I focused on the ship, smiled, and scratched my shoulder.

"Was that pearls in the velvet bag yesterday?"

"The finest black pearls in the Pacific," Laurie said.

"Will you sell them?" I asked.

"Sell some and along with the gold bars from this charter, add to my hidden treasure. Can't trust banks and paper money these days."

"You have a buried treasure?"

The skipper's voice deepened. "Buried under the sea."

Warmth swelled through my chest and a smile lit my face. How cool was that? *Atlanta* sailed as a pirate ship, and I pictured Captain Laurie's gold and pearls and other treasures in a chest beneath the sea.

47

MANGO

Captain Laurie resumed sanding the bullet holes with a cork block and fine paper.

"Can I help patch the holes?" I asked.

"You just keep an eye on that ship," Laurie said.

"I could do both," I whispered and clambered forward, gripping a stay and edging out to sit over the bowsprit. *Atlanta* rose to conquer a crest. As she ploughed into the trough, transparent water sheeted from the bow and disintegrated into spray and mist. Wind ruffled and blustered; whitecaps crumbled across the sea.

The schooner crashed into a pit. Blue ocean swallowed my feet. I gasped and stood as the sails luffed then snapped taught. Spray swept from the bowsprit as it reared. The wind strengthened and the hull plunged deeper. The ship I'd spotted disappeared over the horizon, and I stood on the bowsprit, charging into the future.

Two powerful swells rolled *Atlanta,* and she lurched into a crest. My knuckles whitened around a forestay as the Pacific engulfed my knees. For a moment, I thought I was going underwater, but the bow lifted, and spray drenched me.

Now seemed like a good time to make an exit. There was a lull after the big swells so I climbed back to where Laurie was working.

"Hey, Laurie. That ship has disappeared. I'm saturated. Is it okay to go below and get changed?

"No need to ask, Sam. Just make sure you keep a sharp eye out every ten minutes."

I wondered how Laurie kept working as I held grab rails and manoeuvred back to the safety of the cockpit where Wiggols raised his head from a cosy nook and tapped his tail against the coach house.

When I'd first boarded, *Atlanta* seemed huge. Now she sailed under a vast blue sky, a speck at the mercy of the windswept ocean. Even though it was sunny, the salt and wind and constant motion made me drowsy, and after scanning three hundred sixty degrees, I took refuge belowdecks.

At the bottom of the ladder, I exhaled and ran fingers through my damp, salty hair. My cheeks tingled from spray and sun and wind. A wave swept over the hull and sounded distant in the shadowy cocoon. Beyond the galley, Oko sat cross-legged on his bunk.

A single drip fell from the ceiling and landed on the saloon table in front of Oko. Bullets had pierced the exterior with small precise holes, but then had sure made a mess as they exploded inside. I crept to the galley. A towel lay on my bunk, and I ran a hand over my wet shirt and shorts.

Oko sat with eyes closed, swaying and absorbing motion. He looked so peaceful that I didn't want to disturb him.

"You must have lots of questions?" Oko spoke without opening his eyes.

"I got wet and wanted to change." I did have many questions, but Oko took me by surprise.

The captain's quarters provided the only private space, so I took my board shorts, the new blue cotton T-shirt, and boxers from my pack and slipped forward to change. Clean cotton felt nice on my skin, and I returned dry and refreshed.

Oko opened his eyes. "Would you like talk, Sam?"

Another drip fell, hit the table. I wiped it with my towel. "Where do you get all the money and gold to pay Laurie?"

"A Chinese government agency."

"So you are a spy?"

"I seek truth to help the Earth and humanity. After your mother passed away, I was disillusioned with the world. The People's Liberation Army was recruiting people with science degrees. I joined the army and progressed to the Ministry for State Security, specialising in environmental counterintelligence."

Atlanta crashed over a rogue swell. Oko glanced over his shoulder as pots clanged and cups clinked in the galley.

I sat on my bunk with my legs dangling. "How come my dad never told me about you? When did you become involved in his Tonga Trench research?"

Oko gazed into my eyes. "Russell said you were a very talented boy, but he has always been very secretive about you and Hila. He contacted me three months ago after yet another potential source of funding pulled out of the Trench program. Xcon was his only option. I was suspicious that British and American intelligence were involved."

"Why doesn't the Chinese government go to Tonga and do research themselves?" I asked.

"That's not so easy. America and China fight over the Pacific. Xcon exerts much influence in American politics, and Russell said they were hiding something. He agreed to accept funding from Xcon to get close to them."

Guilt swirled in my gut for ever doubting Dad. "So my dad was like a spy too?"

"No Sam. Russell worked through the university to preserve nature and help humanity. He didn't work for any secret agencies. He never took money from corporations for himself. Russell was a good man – very stubborn, but a good man. He accepted Xcon funding on the condition he could hire his own team for Tonga. That's where I and the captain of the *D-Sea Explorer* came into the picture."

I nodded, then flinched as my tummy rumbled. "I'm on watch, be right back." I regretted eating so much mango and scrambled up on deck. Laurie was using a scraper to apply epoxy resin. He inserted a wooden plug into a hole. With no ships in sight, I farted and traced the fishing lines. A lure broke a crest, skimmed, and disappeared into the messy sea. I headed back to Oko and leaned on the saloon table.

"Who's my genetic father, and why didn't Russell … Dad … tell me?"

Oko shook his head. "I hoped you could tell me more of Russell and Hila's history."

"Why don't I have any energy when it's cloudy? Why do I fall asleep at sundown?"

Oko shrugged. "As far as I am aware, Hila experienced no such difficulty."

"Why … I can see in the dark and underwater. I'm stronger and faster than anyone at school. Maths and science are so easy for me. Do you think I'm an alien or something?"

"Only you can answer that question, Sam. What do you think?"

I shrugged. If Oko didn't have anything to say about it, I didn't want to go there. I sat back on the bunk wishing I hadn't asked.

"Why does Xcon want to kill me?"

"Russell said Xcon was hiding something in Tonga Trench. They make trillions from the effects of global warming with their floating cities and space colonies. They must think Russell shared something with you, Sam. Can you think of any important detail or secret?"

"Undersea eruptions, rapid warming. I know a lot about his research, but nothing secret." I thought I should tell Oko how the ring had slipped over my knuckle but now it wouldn't slide off, and about the strange pulses and visions. And I wondered again if Oko had witnessed the flash when I dived for the gun. I trusted Oko … but not the Chinese government. I didn't even trust my own government. Not wanting to attract attention to my prized possession, I stopped myself from turning the ring.

"Do you know anything about physical cyber-attack technology?" I asked.

Oko shook his head. "My department is investigating, but your report is the first of such capability."

A shadow moved across a porthole, and Laurie's tool tray clunked overhead. Scratchy sanding sounded and dust fell onto the table.

"What happens if we make it to Tonga and discover why the ocean is warming? What happens to me? Where will I live?" I asked.

"Paths will open. You must listen to your inner voice and decide for yourself."

I exhaled, scratched my chest, and stared at the ceiling. There never seemed to be answers to the big questions.

"Something strange is happening in the Tonga Trench. By continuing Russell's research, we can prevent suffering, even save humanity," Oko said.

Avenge Russell's death, continue his work, and save the world. I smiled. Waves of energy tingled through my shoulders, skull, and thighs. My arms goosebumped, and warmth radiated through my chest.

"I best head up and keep watch," I said, headed for the ladder and stopped at the chart table. "Do you have a computer or phone?"

Oko nodded.

"Are there games on them?"

Oko shook his head.

"Is there Internet out here?"

"Satellite, but we should only use it for emergencies."

No gaming. Just white-capped ocean. Wake built from the stern to form waves, which collapsed under constant challenge from the rolling messy sea. I searched for the lures in the swells, wishing I could stretch out on my bunk, play a game, and switch off for a while. *What did Laurie say? Two, maybe three weeks to Tonga! Even then, I'd have to buy or borrow a device.*

Laurie stripped naked on deck. I turned away in surprise, and then back as he cast a bucket over the side, scooped saltwater, and tipped it over his head. Soaping his armpits and butt preceded a two-bucket rinse, then Laurie descended through the forward hatch. A short time later, exotic spices and the smell of ginger floated from the galley.

I entered the saloon through the main cabin, and found Laurie working in the galley. He was wearing green Thai-fisherman pants and a white Atlanta t-shirt.

"That smells delicious," Oko said, as Laurie spooned rice from a wok into bowls.

Oko's berth doubled as the seat, and the three of us sat at the long wooden table. I wondered how rice, egg, cabbage, and onions could taste so good, but mindful of my stomach, I didn't eat much.

"This is very tasty. You're a good cook, Laurie," Oko said.

"Dig in," Laurie said, staring at the ceiling. "The exterior patches blend, but inside's a mess. I'll have to paint the interior, lose the natural wood finish. I built her myself, you know."

"You are very talented," Oko said. I swallowed another mouthful and nodded.

"I used the keel from an old Tasmanian pearl lugger and built her up from that."

Atlanta rolled, and Oko and I nodded as Laurie told how he designed and built his ship. When he finished the story, he put his plate in a plastic tub beside the sink.

"Now, gentlemen, I haven't slept. Can you two share the watch while I take a nap? Hang onto something when you move around up top. Remember the rope if you fall off. We're on a 270-degree heading. If we wander off course or you see a boat, a plane, anything—wake me. And if you have any essential washing, just a few things, throw it on a bunk in the main cabin. I'll do a small load before I go for a kip."

Relieved to get some clothes cleaned, I dumped my travel jeans, shirt, socks, boxers, and tan shorts on the bunk. Sifting through the pile, Laurie took the tan shorts, boxers, and socks and put them into a string bag with some of his own washing.

"The jeans are too big for this load, I'll do them later," Laurie said, then ascended to the cockpit and a minute later, I saw him walking forward.

After piling the dishes in a plastic tub, I climbed up on deck. Loading a dishwasher sucked but using saltwater in a bucket outside on a tilted moving deck was the worst. As I washed, rinsed, and transferred clean dishes into a second tub, I noticed something dragging behind the boat.

What the heck was it? At first I thought it was a fish, but it bulged through swells and was attached to the lifeline. It looked vaguely familiar, and I trotted to the forward hatch and ducked my head into the captain's quarters.

"Laurie, there's something dragging at the end of the lifeline."

"Washing," Laurie said.

"Washing?"

"Yeah, you drag it a few miles. Hang it up and shake the salt out when it's dry."

Now that I knew, it seemed obvious, and I felt silly for asking. By the time I dried up and put the dishes away, I felt a little queasy and yawned. Glad that Oko had offered to take over watch, I retired to my bunk, still wishing I had my phone or that my laptop worked.

With no distractions, my mind wandered back home to Swathi. I wished I could speak to her and make sure she was okay. I wondered what happened after the men showed up at her house when I'd called her from Los Angeles. Tom had said Swathi and Aunty Jindhi were fine during the call from Tahiti. Xcon must have bugged them so it was probably safer not to contact them for a while. And what about Tom risking his life to save the H-Verse? I shook my head and chuckled at the thought. I didn't worry about Tom so much as Swathi. I remembered Dad saying that only cockroaches and Tom would survive a nuclear disaster. If only my dad were here with me, everything would be okay. I thought about the policeman, secret service, and Xcon trying to kill me and get my ring. Well they weren't going to get it. I turned the ring on my finger and wondered what would Swathi and Tom be doing now, wondered how often they thought about me.

"Something's dragging behind," Oko called through the hatch.

"The washing," I said.

I flopped on my bunk and read the titles of books on the shelf, *Landfalls of Paradise*, *Pillars of the Earth*, and *Treasure Island*, but just reading the titles made me queasier.

Atlanta pitched and rolled. I shut my eyes and drifted.

Afternoon naps never happened on sunny days, and my pulse raced as I woke. Something had changed. I sat up and stared along the companionway to the hatch. *Atlanta* tilted with a gentle heel. The Pacific trickled and gurgled against the hull.

Autopilot grated, and the old wheel turned as I clambered outside. White sails towered into the sky. Oko sat on the foredeck, gazing out at the lumpy sea with an occasional white cap crumbling. A blue-footed booby glided overhead, and I wondered if it was the same bird from the morning.

The brass compass swung back and forth over the 270-degree heading. Energy-sapping wind abated. *Atlanta* relaxed into a calm rolling motion. I sauntered to the foredeck where only yesterday an assassin had tried to kill me and the kamikaze drone had exploded.

"You fought well in hand-to-hand combat yesterday," Oko said.

"Thanks." Golden light shone on my face as I sat on the railing. "But you were amazing. Did you learn to fight in the army?"

"Shaolin monks raised my father and taught him Kung Fu. My father taught me, and I continued training in the army. You ever do martial arts?" Oko asked.

"No, but I'd like to."

"You want to learn Kung Fu?"

My eyes lit up. "Yes, please."

"The first thing you need to know is power comes from the mind. We start with Tai Chi."

A peach tinge illuminated the sky to the west. I followed Oko's instructions to focus on my breath and copied his sweeping hand movements. The sun melded with the world. Water gurgled from the bow, and the horizon smouldered burnt orange. The booby landed on the rigging, breeze slid over the sails, and the jaws of the timber booms creaked against the mast.

"That's enough for today. Sunset over the water is spectacular," Oko said.

I smiled in agreement.

"You want leftover rice and preserved tuna for dinner?"

"No thanks. I don't get so hungry on sunny days," I finished the sentence and the thought of a fat, juicy mango tantalised me.

As I resisted the lure of a mango, thoughts of my dad and the urge to play a game gnawed at me. The evening on deck had been so cool, and I wanted to stay with that wonderful feeling.

"I need to use the toilet. Hope I don't wake Laurie," Oko said, and he disappeared into the forward quarters.

I crept into the saloon, opened the hatch beneath my mattress, selected a mango, then something made me grab a second mango, and I tiptoed back out to the cockpit.

The sunset wrapped around the world. Rolling swells reflected orange light, and the first stars sparkled. A sooty tern skimmed over the surface. The ocean relaxed. The mangoes were golden and orange like the sunset, and my mouth watered as I peeled one. Juices drenched my hands and chin, yellow flesh stuck to my nose and lips.

Oko's smiling face popped through the hatch.

I jumped.

Oko glared at my sticky dripping face. His smile soured, and he backed into the cabin.

48

SIXTH SENSE

A dolphin with white sides swam beside me. An enormous shark charged, vanished into blackness, and burning red eyes came for me. I flinched and shuddered but didn't wake. Now I stood on *Atlanta's* foredeck. Sails towered above, the sun shone, and there was no one else, not even a bird in sight. A gentle breeze ruffled my hair and felt cool on my face. I spread my arms. The breeze caught under my chest, lifting me into the air.

Wow! This was super cool. Higher and higher I soared. Flying was awesome. I wondered why I'd never done this before. A white superyacht appeared, vanished into the distance beneath me, and I soared to an island with a resplendent peak and where dolphins swam in a sparkling lagoon. So wonderful—so vivid—amazing! *Why had I never flown before?*

Now I noticed a silver cord running from my chest to the sea far below. That was strange. I was flying like a kite. *But how could I fly at all?* I plunged from the sky, fell toward *Atlanta* and through the teak planking to my bunk.

Water splashed against the hull. I opened my eyes, remembered flying, and stared at the ceiling. Flying was awesome. I was so sure I'd done it but felt silly for thinking I could. Glasses clinked as *Atlanta* ploughed through a larger swell, and Oko turned in his sleep.

I lay back on the pillow. The flying dream felt so real, and the cord was strange. What was the cord about? The sun's first glow was half an hour away. My stomach rumbled and guilt gripped my chest as I remembered sneaking the mangoes. I farted. It went on longer and was louder than I expected.

"Oh!" gasped Oko.

I flinched.

"Sam, you have been farting the whole night, I got no sleep."

"Sorry." Heat rushed to my face.

"No more mango dinner!"

"No, I won't. I'm really sorry." I slid my feet over the side of the bunk and thudded onto the wooden floor.

Overcome with embarrassment, I slipped my hoodie over my shoulders and lumbered along the companionway. I knew I shouldn't have eaten that second mango. I'd made a grub of myself in front of a man who had saved my life.

Outside, the most awesome sky jolted my regret aside. Countless stars – Orion, Pleiades, the Southern Cross and, I couldn't believe my eyes, the Andromeda Galaxy glowed faintly amongst the brilliant starry sky.

Captain Laurie slept on a bed of cushions behind the wheel. Wiggols wagged his tail beside him. Stars reflected on the black Pacific. A meteor burned bright and disappeared just above the ocean.

I crept around the coach house, lay on the foredeck with my hands behind my head, and my vision zoomed in on the Andromeda Galaxy. It was hard to see from England. Narcolepsy ruined rare opportunities, and I'd never seen it so crisply. Warmth flooded my chest. I wondered what kinds of life forms lived in Andromeda, and I wished humanity would soon develop the technology to travel millions of light years to another galaxy.

I thought about my mum and dad and death from cyber-attacks. If I was going to avenge Dad and survive a corporate army, I needed to aim up. I remembered Dad telling me that this trip would be the making of me. To make the most of my situation, I needed to get over my cravings for gaming and mangoes and learn from Oko and Laurie.

A subtle glow crept over the horizon, illuminating a band of cloud. Andromeda faded, and I remembered my flying dream. Weird, but I really believed that I could fly. The gentle breeze tingled over my skin. I stood, faced the breeze, raised my arms, and cupped my chest. With eyes closed, I visualised rising and soaring high above the world. I smiled. My whole body felt light. I experienced a floating sensation and opened my eyes. My feet were planted firmly on the deck. I laughed. *Why would I even think I could fly?*

The burnt orange sunrise made me think of mangoes. I shook my head and pushed thoughts of the sweet texture from my mind. I crept back to the cockpit. Laurie snored, and Wiggols wagged his tail.

"Great watch-keeping," I whispered.

I descended to my bunk and returned on deck with clean boxers and a towel. Beneath the fading stars I undressed, tossing my shirt and shorts on the coach house, I stood naked under the stars and cast the bucket overboard. The rim skimmed, and the rope nearly jerked from my hand when it dug into the sea. I snatched and hauled, plucked half a bucket and tipped it over my head.

Cool water splashed over my shoulders and chilled my back. I caught a full bucket the second time, used soap for my armpits, crotch, and butt, and rinsed. The eastern sky blued, and I tipped another bucket over my head, towelled dry, and ambled back to the cockpit.

Laurie sat and surveyed the new day dawning. "Morning, Sam."

"Good morning." I bent to pat Wiggols. Grey and pink clouds glowed right across the east horizon.

Laurie yawned and stretched. "Must have dozed off, but I have a sixth sense for danger. I wake up if danger approaches."

I descended to the galley. The foot pump squeaked as I worked it and the kettle amplified the sound of squirting water. A blue flame burst to life. I put the kettle on to boil and returned to stand at the top of the cockpit steps. "How do you and Wiggols like your tea?"

"White, no sugar, Wiggols likes a lot of milk." Laurie scanned the horizon, ambled to the bow and climbed down the forward hatch.

Cups chinked as I placed mugs of steaming tea on deck. Wiggols waited for his tea to cool, and I wondered if I'd added enough milk. Early morning light reflected on smooth organised peaks. *Atlanta* cruised and creaked with an easy rhythmic motion, until a set of swells rolled into the stern. She rounded into the wind, autopilot grated into action, the wheel rotated as if a ghost was steering, and the quiet rhythmic motion resumed.

The brightest point on the horizon held my attention. I smiled when I heard the backgammon board rattle as Laurie emerged.

"I'm not going so easy on you this time," he said.

A sooty tern skimmed the glassy water, a booby glided overhead. I figured they must be the same birds from yesterday. Low clouds shone brilliant white with a golden lining, and rays streamed as the tip of the sun blazed over the horizon.

I closed my eyes and smiled. For the first time in ages my mind had found a happy space. Laurie threw dice and shouted as though life depended on the contest. I laughed as I threw my way to a second narrow victory.

"Beginner's bloody luck," Laurie said. And he looked like he'd been mortally wounded when I won a second game that morning.

Oko slept well into the morning and woke grumpy.

"I couldn't sleep because of your farting. I went on deck and Laurie was sleeping. I woke him up. He says he has sixth sense for danger, but he must stay awake for watch. And you farted so much the smell wafted outside."

"Sorry, I won't eat mango for dinner again," I said, and meant it, but I had to bite my lip to stop from laughing.

"Was Laurie awake when you went up this morning?"

I nodded, but then decided I shouldn't lie about Laurie. "No. He was just kind of waking up."

Laurie patched blowouts inside the main cabin. Whitecaps formed as morning progressed, just ocean, sky, and a blue- footed booby gliding over the sea. I made fried rice with a little mango and cashew nuts for lunch, and we ate in the saloon.

"Nice lunch," Laurie said.

"Yes, very … creative," Oko said.

It was kind of tasty, but the rice was gluggy, and I knew they both said it to encourage me.

"I sailed *Atlanta* around the world twice, and am the only person to design, build, and skipper a yacht to victory in the Antigua Tall Ships race," Laurie said.

"You are very talented, Laurie," Oko said.

"Two movies were made aboard *Atlanta*."

"Movies?" I said.

"*Islands of Fire and Magic* had a fancy opening night at the Sydney Opera House, and *Atlanta's Child*, a documentary on my daughter growing up aboard *Atlanta*."

I didn't expect pirates to have daughters and movies made on their boats.

"I'll put *Islands of Fire and Magic* on," Laurie said.

When we finished lunch, we slouched back on Oko's double berth with our feet resting on the saloon table.

"*Atlanta* looks amazing," I said.

"She was new, and her hull was coated with clear varnish," Laurie said.

"Why did you paint it white?"

"Varnish looks the part, but it's hard to maintain on the hull."

The documentary about sea kayaking in New Guinea was cool, and it was funny seeing Laurie looking younger and acting with his daughter. After the movie, Laurie got to work patching blowouts inside the hull. Oko tried to sleep, and I volunteered to clean the dishes.

The Pacific Ocean surrounded us, and with no one else on deck, it was as though I was alone on a stage in the centre of a great wilderness with the universe as my audience. When the dishes were done, I imagined being captain of my own pirate ship as I strutted up front, slid out on the bowsprit rail, and dangled my feet. Bubbles formed at the tip of the bow and streamed away with constant frothy collisions.

An hour passed and Oko appeared, more cheerful after his sleep. I retreated to my bunk, wished for a miracle, just an hour of games, and opened my laptop. The smashed screen tore at my heart and I ran my fingers over the keys, depressing the start button five times.

I packed the laptop in a plastic shopping bag, slipped it behind the books on the shelf, and selected a tatty old hardback copy of *Treasure Island*. I read with the rise and falling motion, teetered on yesterday's queasy feeling, but the book absorbed me, and when the sun dipped, I headed up onto the foredeck, hoping for a Kung Fu lesson with Oko.

"Your opponent may be bigger, stronger, and possess superior technique, but when mind and soul synchronise, the universe conspires to protect you. We do more Tai Chi," Oko said.

"When do we start Kung Fu?" I asked.

Oko smiled. "When you learn Tai Chi."

And so began a routine I grew fond of – a mango sunrise with Wiggols, beating Laurie at backgammon, training, keeping watch, lunch and a movie, washing up, reading, and Tai Chi.

Captain Laurie worked long hours getting *Atlanta* back into shape, but the interior still looked a mess after patching all the blowouts. Laurie used white hull paint on the interior. The old wood finish was lost, but the white paint brightened the inside of the yacht.

Breathtaking sunrise after sunrise eased my urge for gaming. Days blended into a week. The throbbing weight of death and uncertainty relented for hours at a time. Oko began my Kung Fu training. Southeast trade winds blew. I treasured each morning and grew to appreciate the desolate windswept afternoons. Evenings on the foredeck practising Kung Fu with Oko were the best, especially when the ocean calmed, and the wind backed.

Life with a spy, a pirate, and a Tenterfield Terrier kept my troubles at bay. But that was never going to last.

49

TUNA

The witching hour cloaked *Atlanta*. Rigging creaked. The old Huon pine hull groaned and settled in harmony with the sea. In the early hours of my eleventh night aboard, I tossed in my bunk. I remembered how dumb I'd acted the last two times I'd met Sonia; hoped Tom and Swathi were okay; and wished I'd spoken up more often for Swathi. A maths test where I only got 90% nagged me. I rolled left.

Dad's pale face haunted me – cyber-attacks, the acid stench, Xcon, the dark warrior, assassins. My heart thumped, and I tossed onto my right side. I imagined descending into the depths of darkness in a mini-sub, and Xcon attacking me. I flipped onto my back, but the gentle rock and gurgle brought no comfort this morning. Tonga was only two days away. My nerves fluttered. I swung my feet and thudded onto the floor.

Sleep provided little energy; I shuffled through the companionway and climbed one step at a time into the night. Laurie slept on the cushions behind the wheel; Wiggols stretched and wagged his way over for a pat. Sails billowed, stars twinkled, and *Atlanta* held her 270-degree heading.

"Good boy, Wiggols," I said.

The terrier scratched as I made my way to the foredeck, sat in my favourite position, and focused on breathing. Oko's training helped keep me in the present, and I tried to centre my mind.

Water splashed. A sheet snapped taut. This morning, even the rise and falling motion annoyed me. For the last two days I hadn't even craved my computer, but now I craved something out of reach: sun through the loft window, a fresh-painted iron gate, Swathi's smiling face, the sound of passing traffic, Dad's footsteps on the stairs.

Sunrays streamed over the Pacific. Practising Kung-Fu, I stood in the cat-stance with my eyes closed, and sensed Laurie's approach.

"Crouching like that on a moving deck must be excellent for balance," Laurie said.

"Huh?" I replied.

"I'm heading for the throne. Can you take over watch?" Laurie climbed down the forward hatch without waiting for an answer.

Annoyed that he'd disturbed me, I stood and trudged amidships. When I reached the cockpit, the fishing rod twitched. After ten days without a bite, I'd given up on fishing. The rod twitched again. I crept close.

"ZZZZZZZZZZZZ!" The rod bent and line spooled out.

I jumped, then froze.

"ZZZZZZZZZZZZ." Line kept spooling out.

I spun toward the bow. "Laurie," I called and took the rod from the holder.

"ZZZZZZZZZZZZ," sang the reel. The line tugged and surged.

"Laurie!" I called again, gawking at the line racing from the reel. I gripped the rod and engaged the drag.

The rod jerked. Sunlight flashed as the fish leapt from the water.

Laurie ran to the stern. "Tuna! Ease the drag."

I eased the drag and waited for Laurie to take the rod, but the skipper came up behind me and strapped a rod holder around my waist. Line continued to spool from the reel as I placed the butt of the rod in the holder.

"Soon as the line stops spooling out, wind." Laurie reeled in the second rod, then eased the main and foresails to shed speed.

The moment the line stopped spooling out, I pulled the rod above my head, reeled in as I lowered it, and repeated the cycle, but the tuna fought and pulled the line out again.

With the lifeline hauled aboard, Laurie stood with the gaff in hand and a glint in his eyes. "That's it, nice and steady," he said.

The deep-blue water suddenly appeared transparent as the tuna swept past. Sun sparkled on its silver belly, and it thrashed and tugged when it saw the boat. Fighting back, I hauled the tuna alongside. Laurie lunged with the gaff and ripped the fish from the water. Magnificent silver and dark blue scales sparkled. The tuna twisted from the gaff and thrashed around the cockpit.

Laurie grabbed a wooden baton, cracked the fish on the head, and wrangled it into a plastic tub. "A fifteen-pound bluefin," he said.

Oko's eyes shone through the hatch. "I will prepare sashimi."

"Thought you didn't cook," Laurie said.

"Sashimi is raw," Oko said. "The flesh behind the head is best."

The tuna flapped. Laurie took a knife and made an incision behind its pectoral fin. Blood gushed into the tub. Laurie sluiced the deck with a few buckets of water, then rummaged under the bunk at the foot of the stairs and returned with a chunky wooden cutting board, cleaver, and filleting knife.

"May as well make the best of it," Laurie said, "the ocean's getting so hot and acidic we may not catch one again. Oko can make sashimi from the flesh behind the head, and I'll make steaks from the rest."

"I prefer fillets," Oko said.

"Okay. And you, Sam, fillets or steaks?"

I shrugged. "I don't mind." We didn't have much food aboard, but with so few tuna left, I wondered whether we should be eating one.

"Okay, I'll do fillets and preserve some in jars."

"You have wasabi?" Oko asked.

"Only the best for my passengers."

Oko grinned and rubbed his hands together.

Laurie filleted the tuna so no flesh remained on the skeleton, then called Oko and me over. "Look here. You get fresh water from the backbone. If you're stranded at sea, this could save your life." Laurie snapped the head off, leant back, and water ran into his mouth.

I scrunched my nose and wondered how many fish you would need for a decent drink.

The sashimi was melt-in-the-mouth delicious, and Laurie's barbecued fillets made a superb dinner. I went to bed with a contented mind, but as the night progressed, an alien presence slithered into my unconsciousness.

50

COALIFEROS

At the edge of the Milky Way, the convergence zone hummed a deadly warning. Its power to isolate intruders diminished as the galaxy matured and spiralled into the age of Aquarius. But the zone was still potent. Its vibration still wrecked electronics, crushed the strongest shields, and imploded spaceships.

Having located a weakness in the zone, Coaliferos engaged conventional flight and launched headlong into the galaxy's protective vibration.

"Ah!" he bellowed. A paralysing sting bit into him. He clenched his teeth until he could bear no more, then laughed.

Coaliferos embraced the pain as he floated amongst the toxic vibration to acclimatise, then entered the galaxy. Having touched the boy through the net, his consciousness reached out and searched for the boy's essence. From Trudock's intel, he knew the boy was aboard a vessel somewhere on the South Pacific Ocean. Trudock was useful, and might even catch the boy, but Coaliferos couldn't rely on him. And he was sure the boy was headed for the Tonga Trench.

While Coaliferos acclimatised, his astral projection scoured the Pacific. Over dark troughs and moon-licked troughs he searched, scanning container ships and yachts. When he approached an old timber sailing vessel, his projection sparked metallic blue.

Back at the convergence zone, Coaliferos shuddered. On earth, his projection travelled through the deck and he couldn't believe what he was seeing. There was the boy. There was the ring. The urge to launch into full-bodied astral flight overwhelmed him. But no! His destiny depended on it. He needed to acclimatise, make sure he was ready. Now he had a trace on the boy, he could take the boy at his leisure; enjoy killing him. Excitement exploded within Coaliferos. "Haha!" he cackled, and sent his projection colliding into Sam.

51

JUMP

My eyes shot open. It was my thirteenth day at sea. The hair on my neck stood. A faint and familiar acid-whiff terrified me. The boom creaked against the mast. I sat bolt upright, pushing remnants of a dark intrusion away. Memories of the dark figure attacking me in the game, then my dad's pale face replayed in my mind. *Had Xcon found a way to track us?*

I stared at Oko, sleeping in his bunk. Oko had his own secret coms gear, but he only switched it on when necessary. To avoid detection, Laurie relied on a sextant, the sun, and the stars for navigation and sailed with all communications systems, including GPS switched off. I was sure there was no path to *Atlanta* via the net.

Wanting to believe it was just a bad dream, I lay back on the bunk and turned the ring on my finger. Xcon and Trudock were after me, after my ring, but why? There had to be more to the story, something I was missing, something to do with my mother.

Sounds of sails flapping stole my attention, and the schooner's motion felt wrong. Heart thumping, I threw my feet off the bunk and clambered up the ladder.

Laurie leaned on the coach house with binoculars hanging around his neck. The mainsail hung limp.

"What's wrong?" I asked.

"Becalmed. How about putting on the kettle?"

Clouds bloomed to the east. The glassy water reflected the sky and *Atlanta* like a mirror. I descended into the galley. Water echoed into the kettle, the gas flame *floomped* to life, and I hurried back outside and helped Laurie drop the jib. The kettle whistled, dragging me belowdecks, and two minutes later, I placed Wiggols's cup on deck and spotted Laurie up the mast.

The air was still, the ocean so smooth and silent it felt as if no one else inhabited the planet. Suddenly, Laurie leapt from the mast. My eyes boggled. Laurie fell through the air and smashed the glassy water.

Oko came running to the hatch.

"Laurie just jumped from the mast," I said.

Oko nodded and returned to his bunk to contact his man in Tonga. Laurie stroked to the stern and climbed the rope ladder.

"Can I jump?" I asked.

Laurie grabbed a towel and nodded. "Keep your eyes sharp while you're up there."

Hand over hand, I climbed up the ratlines. Cathedral rays burst from behind the clouds. Perfect glassy water surrounded me, three hundred sixty degrees. Alone at the top of the mast, the vista was so perfect and pure, but it seemed much higher peering down. I knew sharks liked to feed early. Jumping into the middle of the Pacific Ocean had lost its appeal. I wished Laurie was still in the water and considered climbing back down.

"Keep your feet together when you hit the water," called Laurie.

I bent my knees as if to jump, trembled a little, straightened, stared into the glassy water—and leapt. My stomach hollowed. I plunged wide-eyed, surprised I had time to panic before my feet slapped the water and bubbles engulfed me as I speared beneath the blue.

Oko ran out again. Wiggols barked. Oko and Laurie frowned at each other and Oko retired below.

The water felt warm, almost hot. Panic shot like electricity through my butt. With the ocean floor five kilometres below, anything could ascend and eat me. My chest thumped as I swam for the ladder, and something bumped into my shoulder.

I gasped, swung around. A stripy yellow and black fish the size of my thumbnail bumped against my chest. I smiled and, weird as it seemed, the little guy relaxed me. I might never have this chance to swim in the middle of the ocean again, so I swallowed my fear, submerged, and swam under *Atlanta*.

Stripy fish followed. Sunrays streamed forever. The big blue beckoned. I descended, drew eight strokes, exhaled and sank as if falling through space. Stripy fish finned around my shoulders. At fifteen metres below, I rolled on my back and sank.

A patch of brilliant sunlight shimmered on the surface. *Atlanta* appeared distant, and stripy fish bumped into my nose. The blue depths whispered. Shivers jittered through me. I swirled around, then swam for the surface. The closer I got, the faster I stroked. I burst from the water, scrambled for the ladder, and climbed.

Dripping over the stern, I gazed back into the water. Stripy fish finned back and forth; beneath, the ocean darkened.

"Shit." I drew back.

Laurie leaned over the stern rail as a huge shadow passed under the yacht.

My pulse throbbed. "Shark?"

Laurie shook his head. "Too big. Must be a whale."

The shadow melded into the depths and Oko appeared again. "What's the matter now?" he asked.

"A whale or whale shark swam under *Atlanta*," Laurie said.

Oko shook his head and didn't even bother to look. "I contacted my man in Tonga—"

"If the wind doesn't pick up in the next hour, I start the motor," Laurie said. "Either way, we reach Tonga tomorrow."

Oko walked to the stern, held a backstay, and stared to the heavens. "Shit has hit the fan in Tonga. Xcon navy are everywhere, four crew disappeared from the *D-Sea Explorer*; the captain postponed our rendez-vous."

"Xcon navy … what the …" Laurie's demeanour went icy. "I kept my part of the bargain. I want my gold and you two off *Atlanta* tomorrow. No offence, but you want to play heroes with Xcon? Do it on another boat."

I clutched my chest and swallowed.

Oko glared into Laurie's eyes. "You will have your gold … the day after tomorrow."

52

KOTA

Tali's fin cut the surface, "PFFFH," she exhaled and drew breath.

As the new day dawned, a subtle vibration pulsed through the glassy Pacific Ocean. An image of the warrior child swimming in the ocean entered her mind. The vibration was so strong and close, and she tried to reach out with telepathy, but the connection stopped after two minutes.

Pushing her tail, Miki circled as though searching for the source of the vibration, then settled to swim beside Tali and Bola. The farther they swam, the hotter the ocean became, and a nagging fear, dark and destructive, grew. But the vibration carried hope. Hope, that from within the darkness, they swam for something good.

Sadness filled Tali's heart as she watched her sister; her life was an endless fight for survival. Since Miki's birth, orcas and sharks had killed all the pod's calves. With only nine surviving members, the once mighty Ice-Pod faced extinction.

Swimming over the vast ocean sapped the coastal pod's strength. The energy sparked by Miki's return was long gone. They hadn't eaten for days, and Tali feared the weakest would not survive another night. *Was she leading the pod to their death?* She prayed for the universe to guide her and deliver the pod to safety.

Onward they struggled through hot acidic ocean, but as morning progressed, they swam through patches of cooler water. There it was again, cooler, fresher. Their skin tingled, eyes brightened. A gentle current swept them.

Miki's echolocation bounced. Visions of islands formed in her mind; distant whistles and chatter cut through endless blue.

"Dolphins," chirped Miki.

"Many," answered Tali.

"Do you think I will find someone my age?"

"Hope so," Tali replied, but she feared the resident pods might shun or attack them.

With energy beyond the others, Miki chatted, veered, and darted. Tali's mind wandered back to the Alaskan Gulf when the pods combined to find new mates, share experiences, and play.

"PFFFH!" The Ice-Pod surfaced in unison; nervous energy livened weary tails. Masses of whistling and chirping excited Miki, and her sonar detected more dolphins than she could imagine. Sound waves bounced, revealing the ocean floor rising. A sea mountain loomed, and twelve shadows charged from the blue.

Bola surged forward. The Ice-Pod tensed.

A dozen large bulls, bottlenose greys, glided across their path. Sweeping back, the greys whistled, breached, and chattered.

Excitement tingled within the Ice-Pod. They returned the chatter.

"PFHFF," Tali exhaled with relief. The Ice-Pod had been accepted.

"They are so sleek and graceful," chirped Miki.

"Not as graceful as you," chirped Tali.

Bottlenose greys cruised everywhere, hundreds of them, sun waves rippling over their sleek grey forms. Most of the greys had never seen a white-sided dolphin and surrounded the Ice-Pod with curiosity.

Compared to the greys, Miki thought herself stumpy and ugly. She swam glued to Tali. No younglings cruised with the greys, and Miki became the centre of attention. She wished they would stare off, and finned through the luxurious cooler water, butting against Tali like a newborn calf.

As she searched for someone her age, Miki's embarrassment ebbed, and sadness welled in her heart. Many greys carried scars and shark wounds. Of the hundreds of dolphins gliding, most had dull, patchy skin, and their welcoming eyes bore strain. Miki realised they were in poor condition, though not so bad as most of her own pod, and then she spotted a smaller dolphin with bright polished skin.

Her body quivered with excitement.

"Tali … over there," she squeaked.

The young bottlenose grey saw Miki and swam to her.

Miki's heart quickened. She bobbed to the surface, forgot to exhale, sucked in water and choked and spluttered. The young bull darted to the rescue.

Seeing him approach, Miki tried to hide her embarrassment. She dived, flicked her tail, and launched into the air.

The young grey waited for her splashdown, but it took much longer than he expected.

Miki jumped high, and just before she hit the water, the young grey dolphin surfaced. She fell belly-first to lessen the impact and struck the young bull with a loud slap.

Through a confusion of splashing and bubbles, Miki recovered. The young grey tried to swim, but his tail flukes hung limp. What had she done? The injured dolphin swam toward Miki, using his pectoral fins for propulsion. She gasped in horror—*I crippled him.*

Swak! The injured dolphin clipped Miki with his tail. Confused and bewildered, she froze. The young grey flicked his tail, launched, and splashed down beside Miki.

"Hi, I am Kota," he chirped, swimming freely and appearing quite pleased with himself.

He isn't injured. Anger exploded within Miki. She flicked her tail and charged Kota. The young grey darted left. Miki darted after him.

Kota thrust his tail and launched skyward with tremendous velocity, with Miki right behind. They splashed down, and Kota weaved through the pod with Miki in pursuit. Dozens gawked in amazement as Kota and Miki flashed through canyons, veered left and darted right.

The reason these two younglings survived was on show for the hoards to see. As the fastest amongst his pod, Kota thought it strange the smaller white-sided youngling stayed with him. He dived deep, screeched left, flashed into a swim-through, and out the other side. Miki stayed right behind.

Kota rocketed from the bottom. Miki gained on him. He swam harder. Hundreds of dolphins chirped and whistled and chattered.

Kota sensed Miki catching him. His nose broke the surface. One last flick, and he launched skyward.

Miki clipped Kota's tail just above the water, sending him tumbling through the air and flopping down amongst a mass of bubbles.

By the time Kota recovered, Miki had vanished.

53

BAIT BALL

The crowd of grey dolphins parted, clearing a path for their matriarch. Seeing the sleek and powerful grey approaching, Miki swam nearer Tali.

"My name is Shakala," chirped the powerful grey. "The nine pods welcome you to the super-pod congregation."

"I am Tali and this is my sister, Miki. The Ice-Pod is honoured by your welcome."

Bola led the Ice-Pod to mingle with the greys, but Miki stayed glued to Tali. With Shakala swimming with Tali, the super-pod spread out and gave them clear water.

"Miki, you gave Kota a good lesson. Please forgive my son's insolence," chirped Shakala.

"Sorry. It was my fault." Miki couldn't believe that she'd chased the matriarch's son, and remnants of her anger slipped away. The super-pod settled to float and drift in the windless glassy Pacific. Emotion subsided and left Miki drained. Her empty belly ached. She finned as if joined to Tali and listened to the matriarchs' discussion.

"At this time of year, shoals of thousands of fish pass the sea mountain," chirped Shakala, "but the shoals have dwindled. Last year everyone went hungry. The cool current upwells around the sea-mountain, but heat and darkness spreads from the trench. There are still a few places where we can seek refuge, but our oasis is crumbling."

"PFFFH." Dolphin after dolphin exhaled and drew a lazy breath. A tail splashed here, a pectoral fin there; water gurgled, and sun waves rippled over the slick of basking dolphins. Consciousness joined, and security of numbers allowed the congregation to relax, switch off, and drift with the pinnacle of the sea mountain at the centre.

Tali told of her pod's escape from the gulf and how she'd travelled east to find the guardian child and confront the darkness.

"Beyond the sea-mountain lies the trench. Death lives in the trench," warned Shakala.

"PFFFH." Sick of bleak depressing chatter, Miki exhaled, drew breath, and her mind wandered to Kota. *Acting injured, how was that funny?* She sank into the faintest gentle swell, and visions of schooling fish swirled into her head. The idea that she had bested the matriarch's son amused her. A few minutes later, she was sure she could smell fish, and whistles swept through the blue.

Dolphin after dolphin twitched, focused echolocation, and whistled. Scouts located schooling fish. Masses of clicks pulsed all around Miki. The sea erupted like a breaking wave as two hundred and eighty dolphins charged across the ocean.

Adrenalin surged as Miki swam amongst masses of excited bulls and cows. She thrust her tail eight times before breaching, then thrust eight times again. Her dynamic rhythm rushed her through the big blue. She arrived in the first wave and stopped just short of a massive shoal of bigeye scad.

Thousands of fish, more than she ever imagined, tightened into a writhing massive bait ball. Miki snapped a small scad and joined those keeping the bait ball in motion, while others swept into feed.

A dozen cows attacked from beneath, pushing the bait ball to the surface, and the albatross dived for a fish. Organised chaos ensued as hundreds of dolphins rocketed, bigeye scad swirled, and petrels speared into the water. Reef sharks darted around the outskirts – a tiger shark launched through the centre.

The bait ball shimmied and flashed. Miki found Tali – they gorged on tasty scad and swam to keep the ball in motion. Kota appeared a little way off and followed them. Miki tried to ignore him for a time, but she couldn't stop looking at his powerful form. Soon they were darting through the schooling scad together.

Relieved and overjoyed to see Miki playing with Kota, Tali eased to the edge of the action.

"Am, Am." Miki chirped with joy in her heart.

The tone of Miki's chirp transported Tali to when she was just two years old, when the princess from the light planet had swum alongside Tali and her mother. Tali dipped a pectoral fin, pushed her tail and, still watching Miki, drifted beyond the group.

"AM, AM," Miki chirped again.

The sound described the vibration of the Princess so perfectly. Masses of motion swirled and through milky-blue water, Tali spotted her white-sided family feeding, the last of thousands of generations. This feast would sustain them for a week or more, but what then? Without a miraculous change, they would all perish.

Up from the depths surged the billowing mouth of a humpback whale, swallowing hundreds of fish. The bait ball thinned. Sharks charged in, their number growing. With bellies full, the dolphins took the sharks as a sign to snare a last scad and meander back to the mountain.

Tali inspected her weary pod, contented for the first time in ages. At last Miki had found a friend her own age, and after such a long journey, her pod needed to rest. But the pulses and intermittent vibrations meant the guardian child was near. *What else could it be?* Even now tingles urged Tali to follow the vibration. At the back of her mind she knew the vibration would take her on a collision course with the dark presence.

"AM, AM," chirped Bola.

"AM, AM," replied Tali. Bola sensed the vibration, and he would never leave her. She needed to leave the pod and travel with Bola.

The albatross circled overhead and glided east. Tali pictured the guardian child igniting light energy to inspire the ocean. *But could the child defeat the darkness?* The sky above seemed to flicker. In her heart, she knew she must answer the call to save her pod, to save all dolphins, or the ocean and the planet would suffer the consequence of her inaction.

In the gentle afternoon light, Miki and Kota bobbed and played near Kota's pod. Tali spent time with Shakala and Kota's aunts, and told them of her and Bola's plan.

"Travelling east over the trench is too dangerous," warned Kota's mother. "The darkness presses in on us. Sharks followed the school of fish. Many are still hungry and will soon attack. There is nothing a thousand dolphins can do to stop the darkness in the trench. This oasis is lost. Come with us, we know of others."

"Please take Miki and the rest of the Ice-Pod with you," Tali replied. "I have to find the guardian child and confront the darkness."

As the sun descended to the horizon, the Ice-Pod whistled mournful tunes and wanted to follow Tali. But the darkness chilled their blood, and they knew the endless journey was beyond them. Miki thought differently.

"Kota's pod knows the territory," pleaded Tali, "there's food, you have a friend; stay until Bola and I return."

"I'm coming with you," replied Miki. Determination radiated through her eyes.

****

Sharks circled beyond the mountain shelf. Many had either missed or caught the end of the bait ball and were very hungry. As night fell over the Pacific, Tali, Bola, and Miki farewelled the super-pod and their family. The rest of the Ice-Pod would disperse with the greys before sunrise. With sadness in her heart, Miki chirped goodbye and left her new friend behind.

Predators cruised back and forth in the inky darkness. Tali clicked soundwaves ahead and detected a yawning gap. Bola, Miki, and Tali cut communication and swam in a tight triangular formation. Miki swam bottom left, the turbulence from Bola sweeping over her.

With zero visibility, they finned in silence, hugged the bottom contour, and swam into the darkness.

54

MAKOMAILE

Atlanta charged over the Pacific on the breath of a pre-dawn breeze. Through the hull, the vast chasm of ocean drew my thoughts to the depths. I clutched my chest and sensed we were sailing over the Tonga Trench. I wished I could sail forever, but tomorrow would be my last day aboard *Atlanta*. Continuing Dad's work sounded noble, but how could I save the world, or even make a difference? With Xcon navy patrolling, just thinking about diving the trench sent my pulse racing.

With my eyes closed, I concentrated on breathing and tried to stop my mind spinning. As I relaxed, I felt a presence—something distant, calling. I slung my legs over the bunk and eased onto the floor. Three steps later I stopped and pumped water into the kettle.

Yesterday was the first day Laurie and I hadn't played backgammon. Tea would cheer Laurie up, and I smiled as I pictured adding to my undefeated run.

A blue and orange flame burned under the kettle. Mugs clinked. So as not to disturb Oko, I turned the gas off before the whistle gained momentum, poured steaming water into the mugs, and braced as *Atlanta* rode a set of swells. Having learned not to overfill the cups, only a little tea spilled, which I mopped up with a cloth. I jiggled the teabags and added extra milk for Mr Wiggoly.

"Nice cup of tea. Morning, Sam." Laurie sounded cheerier today, but I sensed his tension, and when I returned with my own tea, Laurie stood amidships, sipping and staring into darkness.

I followed his gaze—"Lights!" I froze. Green and white lights pierced the darkness.

Laurie nodded. "A green starboard light and two white lights means a power vessel over fifty metres is approaching. Unless I change course, we cross paths midway across the Tonga Trench."

I stared at the lights. Since Rangiroa, a dozen vessels had passed in the distance, but never this close. I glanced into the dark ocean, then at the depth sounder, but the display was in error. "The depth sounder's not working."

"It's nine kilometres to bottom. Too deep for the sounder to register." Laurie gulped his tea.

"They're gaining fast. It's first light in an hour. We can't hide. I'm turning the navigation lights on."

"But they'll see us."

"They'll see us when it gets light. Best not appear to be hiding."

"I agree." Oko's voice startled me.

For the first time during the voyage, *Atlanta's* red and green side-lights and white stern light glowed in the night. Fusty odours of diesel, stale saltwater, and oil wafted as Laurie lifted the bilge trapdoor inside the main cabin. A battery powered screwdriver whirred as he removed timber panels either side of the engine.

"Better prepare for the worst." Laurie placed two assault rifles, the Uzi, and metal ammunition boxes on the bunk.

"Time to reacquaint yourselves with the assault rifles, gentlemen."

Visions of the helicopter, wood splintering, spotlights, and drones flashed through my mind, and my chest thudded as I checked the Type 99 assault rifle. Guns were fun for gaming, but they were cold killing machines in real life. I hoped there was no need to use one again.

Laurie disappeared into his quarters and returned wearing a loose unbuttoned Hawaiian shirt and holding a black pistol in each hand. He tucked the Colt 1911s into his belt and placed the Uzi on the shelf inside the hatch.

"You gentlemen stay below," he said and climbed outside.

I paced from the main cabin to the saloon and back again, peered through a porthole, and repeated the process. Stars vanished into blue sky. A cloud band screened the sunrise. Eerie pastel light washed the Pacific, and an albatross glided over the approaching vessel: navy-blue hull, eighty metres long, white topsides three levels above deck with tinted windows.

"It's called *Makomaile* and flies a flag with a coat-of-arms. It doesn't look sinister," I said.

The assault rifles rested on the bunk, and the superyacht sliced through the ocean. Laurie's footfalls patted on the deck, and the pistols in his belt looked menacing as he backed down the ladder.

"I'll hail them on the VHF," Laurie said

"Why? Someone else might pick up our transmission," Oko said.

"Boldness has power and magic in it. VHF radio is line of sight. I'll use low power. Being bold will divert suspicion."

Oko studied Laurie for a second and nodded.

Boldness has power and magic circled in my mind as I stared through a porthole: two people in white uniforms stood outside the bridge on the second level of the superstructure. Rules of navigation gave *Atlanta* right of way. The *Makomaile* should pass well ahead, but the vessel altered course, closer to us. I focused on a figure behind a tinted glass window on the bridge.

Laurie stepped beside the chart table, grasped the handpiece, adjusted the squelch, and took a deep breath. "*Makomaile, Makomaile, this is Atlanta, Atlanta.*"

The VHF crackled. Everyone stared at the radio.

"*Makomaile, Makomaile*, this is *Atlanta, Atlanta*, the sailing vessel off your port bow," Laurie repeated.

"*Atlanta, Atlanta*, this is *Makomaile*, go to channel seven-four, over," replied a man's voice.

"*Atlanta* going to seven-four." The VHF blipped as Laurie scrolled from 16 to 74.

"*Atlanta, Atlanta*, this is *Makomaile*," said a male voice.

"*Makomaile*, this is *Atlanta*. We're an Australian vessel on our way to Nukualofa. I called to say good morning, and can you tell me what your coat-of-arms signifies? Over."

"Good morning, *Atlanta*, and welcome to Tongan waters. The coat-of-arms belongs to the Kirangan royal family."

The superyacht's engines droned as she powered right alongside. A tinted window on the bridge slid open and a girl with long black hair and a heavenly smile gazed over us.

I froze, then a smile broke over my face.

"*Atlanta*, we have a young princess aboard who wishes to ask you a question. Over."

"*Atlanta* standing by." Laurie's eyes lit up and he nodded with his mouth wide open.

I spied through the porthole as the girl took the transceiver in one hand. Swells splashed against the hull and the VHF crackled.

"*Atlanta*, this is Princess Lani."

Her voice sounded like sunrise. I shivered and my whole body tingled. I climbed up the ladder and stopped on the top step as her dreamy voice continued.

"I love your yacht. She has so much character. Where was she built? Over."

Music chimed with her every word. My heart pounded. I stepped outside, and my eyes zoomed in on the princess. Joy and happiness glowed around her.

"A real princess," I whispered.

She raised binoculars, and I waved.

"Get down, Sam!" Oko called.

I dropped my arm and stared into the cabin.

Laurie held a palm up. "Too late; stay there—wave."

I felt the princess's gaze fix on me. I smiled and waved and listened to Laurie speaking.

"Thank you, Your Highness, I designed and built *Atlanta* myself."

With telescopic vision, I watched the princess as she lowered the binoculars, smiled, and raised the handset.

"You are very talented. Congratulations for building such a magnificent yacht. I will hand you back to the captain," she said, and disappeared from the window.

I gaped and my arm slumped to the side. Makomaile's captain bid us a safe passage.

"*Atlanta* out." Laurie hung the transceiver on the clip, pulled the pistols from his belt, and put them under the chart table.

"Always nice to get a royal welcome," he grinned, and bounded up on deck and waved.

Oko stayed inside and peered through the porthole.

"You may as well come up," Laurie called.

Oko emerged wearing a hat and sunglasses and joined Laurie and me waving as the superyacht crossed ahead. I waited for the princess to emerge again. Thinking I could see her behind a tinted window, I walked forward and slid out onto the bowsprit as *Atlanta* hobby horsed over *Makomaile*'s wake.

Oko strolled to the bow.

"A real-life princess," he said, "but there could be a spy aboard that ship. News travels fast. Be more careful next time."

"Huh." I stared at Oko, then back to the ship motoring into the distance. "I had a good feeling about that ship."

Oko shook his head, turned abruptly and returned to the cockpit.

I started to apologise, but hesitated, closed my eyes, and imagined stepping aboard *Makomaile* to meet Princess Lani. Her dreamy voice replayed in my head. My heart thumped double time in my chest. I experienced a floating sensation, as if I were dissolving into the air.

Upon opening my eyes, my teeth, jaw, and forehead were numb. I expected the royal yacht to be way off in the distance, but *Makomaile* had changed course. She lay beam-on into the wind, adrift. I squinted, slid from the bowsprit, paced to the cockpit, and Laurie emerged with a smile on his face.

"The Captain has invited us aboard the royal yacht."

55

THE TRENCH

First light reflected on the Pacific. Beneath the surface, the water was still dark. Eerie tremors radiated from the ocean floor eight kilometres below.

"PFFFH." Miki, Tali, and Bola exhaled and drew breath. To the south a dirty cloud blanketed the ocean.

"The cloud rises from the dark presence, the source of the heat," chirped Tali, leading the pod away from the cloud in a northerly direction across the Tonga Trench. She hoped it was the chasm of unknown that spooked them, hoped there wasn't an alien creature rising from the depths to swallow them. But if only the alien presence were all she had to worry about …

"Clear ahead," chirped Bola.

Miki circled, her echolocation bouncing. "Something following," she chirped. Had starving sharks tracked them through the night – or was it something else?

Dawn neared. The three dolphins travelled in tight formation, their every muscle aching. The presence that followed them disappeared, but Miki continued to sense it now and then.

The sun blazed over the horizon. To the north, the albatross glided in a crisp blue sky. Tali drew comfort from following the majestic bird away from the dark cloud, away from the heat. But then at the end of her range, Tali sensed the presence that haunted them throughout the morning.

"It seems close, then suddenly far away," chirped Tali. Sound travelled farther in the hot acidic ocean that saturated her organs and irritated her eyes. Confusion clouded Tali's brain, disrupting her perception and navigation.

The creature following them picked up its pace. The dolphin's hearts raced. Something surged towards them. They couldn't sense whether it was coming from behind or below.

"Scatter!" Tali chirped.

Tali, Bola, and Miki darted in different directions. A whistle startled them, and as they regrouped, Kota surfaced looking very coy.

56

PRINCESS LANI

Sweat dripped from my nose and beaded on the topsail as I folded it. *Atlanta* looked elegant with six sails up but dropping them was hard work. I stowed the last topsail in Laurie's quarters and ambled to the cockpit.

Oko paced to the stern, held a stay, and shook his head. "What will we tell them? We need to get our stories straight."

Laurie threw a burgundy cover over the mainsail. "Don't worry, Oko, it's good to make friends in high places. Tell the truth; just don't mention Rangiroa or the shootout. Have you guys been to Tahiti?"

"Yes," Oko said. I'd only flown over it and been to the airport, but I nodded.

"Say we met in Papeete instead of Rangiroa," Laurie said.

Oko gazed at the *Makomaile* with a furrowed brow. "Why sail covers? We're not stopping long."

"Got to look your best for royalty," Laurie said.

I helped with the sail covers and with *Atlanta* looking shipshape, Laurie deactivated autopilot. "Sam, take the helm while I have a quick shower," he said.

Nervous energy fluttered in my stomach as we closed to within half a mile of the royal yacht. At first, I stood at attention behind the wheel, wondering if the princess watched. Next, I stood to the side and guided *Atlanta* with a casual one-handed grip. Really, she was just another person, but I was so nervous and excited to meet a princess.

Atlanta's motor chugged along and she looked sharp with burgundy sail covers and halyards neatly coiled. I surveyed the patched holes, and my eyes glazed with the memory of bullets smashing through the decks. Earth's most dominant corporation had murdered my dad, wanted me dead, and now I motored toward a royal yacht to meet a princess. She seemed young, maybe about my age. I wondered how old she was, and what kind of stuff a princess would do all day.

Aftershave wafted as Laurie surfaced clean-shaven and looking kind of dashing in navy-blue slacks, brown leather shoes, and a long-sleeved white cotton shirt. "Snap to it, Sam, got to look your best for royalty," he said.

I had my first freshwater shower on *Atlanta*, put on my blue hibiscus shirt and tan shorts, and was back on deck in three minutes. Oko's tan slacks and red shirt looked freshly ironed. I considered changing into jeans, but it was hot, and the denim felt slimy after Laurie's saltwater wash.

A huge door opened on the port side of *Makomaile*, revealing a centre-console tender and four jet skis. *Atlanta* chugged as Laurie eased alongside the stern. I stood on the foredeck, ready to throw a mooring line when the princess emerged on the second level.

I smiled and Princess Lani smiled back at me.

I looked away for second and when I looked back, she was leaning on a rail, talking to a man with wild curly grey hair. Four crew wearing white sailors' uniforms with epaulettes on the shoulders manned the stern dock.

Atlanta's diesel clunked into neutral, then reverse. My heart throbbed as I smiled at the princess again. Our eyes met and she waved.

"Throw the forward line," Laurie called.

I smiled and waved and threw the line at the same time. The deckhand stretched, but the line splashed into the water.

My cheeks burned red. I sensed Laurie's frustration as I snatched the wet line from the water. We were so close now I handed it to the deckhand. Fenders squashed and squeaked as *Atlanta* pushed alongside. Princess Lani turned from the railing and vanished.

Laurie strode forward, checking the mooring lines and fenders. I followed him to the cockpit, and the man with the wild grey hair appeared.

Deep wrinkles lined his face. He wore a brown sarong, white T-shirt, no shoes, and his eyes sparkled.

"I am Chief Alyseyu. On behalf of Princess Lani, welcome."

"Pleased to meet you, Chief Alyseyu. Laurie Piper, captain of the good ship *Atlanta*, at your service. This is Oko Yanzi and Sam Edwards."

Water sloshed between the hulls and *Atlanta* bobbed with lively motion compared to *Makomaile*. Two crewmembers assisted us aboard. After weeks at sea, the luxury yacht was like standing on solid ground, and I rocked and stumbled as though I could still feel *Atlanta* riding the waves as I adjusted to the sturdy platform.

Chief Alyseyu regarded Laurie and Oko, then focused on me. His eyes looked peaceful, but his gaze penetrated deep. "So, you're the one who stopped our boat," he said.

I shot a glance at Oko and Laurie and shrugged.

The chief's face crinkled into a smile. "Be careful what you wish for, Sam Edwards. Come," he said.

A stairway led to a huge sparkling pool with a diving board and sun lounges. Everything shone and smelled of polish. The chief continued around the pool and paused at another stairwell.

"Do you have engine trouble, Chief Alyseyu?" Laurie asked.

"Yes, both our engines mysteriously stopped after we passed you," replied Chief Alyseyu.

"If you need help, I'm happy to assist."

"Thank you, Laurie, but you are my guest, and I trust our engineers will find the problem. Now tell me, Laurie, *Atlanta* is an Australian vessel. Are you also from Australia?"

"Yes, Chief Alyseyu, but I spend most of my time cruising abroad on *Atlanta*."

Chief Alyseyu nodded. "Oko, may I ask where you are from and your occupation?"

"I am from China and I am an oceanographer."

"A worthy profession," Chief Alyseyu said. "And you, Sam?"

"I … live in England and I'm a student." I thought of saying I was born in Rangiroa, but that could lead to uncomfortable questions.

The chief's eyes bored into me. "What year are you in? And what brings you all together, Sam?"

"I'm in Year Ten." My heart thumped. I looked to my feet, willing Oko or Laurie to jump in and answer, but after a short silence, I met the chief's eyes.

"My father is a climate scientist, I came to meet him, but he … disappeared. Oko is Dad's colleague, and Laurie is bringing us to Tonga to continue his research on the Tonga Trench."

"Your father is Russell Edwards?" the chief asked.

"Yes." My pulse raced.

"Please accept my sympathies, and I pray for your father's safe return."

"You knew … know my father?" I wondered how the chief had learned of Dad's disappearance and what else he knew.

"I have not had the privilege of meeting your father, but his work has been invaluable to our kingdom. We relocated a small village to higher ground based on Dr Edwards's forecasts. The ocean has risen and inundated our archipelago, as he predicted. In your father's absence, I thank you for his work."

"Thank you, Chief Alyseyu." Warmth flowed through my chest. It was so nice to hear how my dad had helped people.

"Please let me know if I can assist you in any way, Sam."

Chief Alyseyu led us up the stairs to an expansive teak deck with white lounges, and a spa overlooking the spectacular shimmering Pacific. Two women worked behind the bar, and a man dressed in white smiled as he set a table. Every table, chair, and rail sparkled. Oko and I grinned, but Laurie didn't look so impressed.

A waiter advanced with a tray of glasses, garnished with pineapple and palm-leaf figurines. The chief gestured for us to sit on shaded lounges, and I sipped on a delicious cool fruit cocktail and searched for the princess.

"An elegant ship, Chief Alyseyu," Oko said.

"Yes, but for me … I am more comfortable on a sailing canoe," Chief Alyseyu said.

Laurie nodded.

"The boat belonged to my brother. We planned to sell her when he died, but Princess Lani loves her, so we charter her twice a year to contribute to her upkeep."

"I do the same sort of thing with *Atlanta*, a couple of charters a year," Laurie said, "and excuse my ignorance, Chief Alyseyu, but I'm not familiar with Kiranga."

"Few are. Kiranga is a group of twelve small islands to the north," Chief Alyseyu said, pointing.

I traced the chief's arm to bumps on the horizon and it was as though the distant islands were calling out to me.

"Okay, I'm familiar with the group, but not as a separate kingdom," Laurie said.

"There is a tendency to associate us with Tonga, but we follow in the tradition of our ancestors and the Tongan royal family tolerate us."

My heart thumped. I sensed her coming. I turned to the bar and stared at a door as the princess stepped out. Her dazzling emerald eyes held me. Silky dark hair fell to her shoulders. She wore a cream dress and her skin was smooth and brown.

"Princess Lani of Kiranga," announced the chief. His face glowed as he met her halfway and escorted her to the table. I was the last to rise and join Oko and Laurie, standing like soldiers at attention.

"This is Laurie Piper, Captain of *Atlanta*," the chief said.

"I am honoured to meet such a talented yacht designer and builder."

"At your service, Princess Lani," Laurie said, and he bowed with a wave of his hand, as if he were in an old movie.

"And Sam Edwards is a Year Ten student and son of Russell Edwards, the oceanographer and climate scientist who helped our kingdom."

Alarm and distress tensioned Princess Lani's beautiful face.

"Is there news of your father?"

I shook my head and heat rushed to my face.

"I am so sorry, Sam. I pray your father returns in good health."

I wanted to say, *My dad is dead, murdered by Xcon*; I wanted to say, *I miss him, life is tough, thanks for your sympathy*, but I nodded and more heat rushed to my face. An uncomfortable silence ensued, and everyone stared at me.

"Our last guest is Oko Yanzi, oceanographer and colleague of Dr Russell Edwards. Mr Yanzi and Sam are continuing Dr Edwards' work."

"A pleasure to meet you, Mr Yanzi," the Princess said.

"The pleasure is mine, and please call me Oko," he bowed with a precise graceful movement.

Princess Lani sat beside the chief. A waiter served her a fruit cocktail and her emerald eyes reached out to me.

"Dr Edwards' work is so valuable to our people. It's tremendous you continue the research, Sam, and it must be difficult without your father. But I have a question on the statement he made about the warming in the Tonga Trench being a greater threat to humanity than the sum of all carbon emissions. In the new year, I will address the Youth Leading the World congress and the United Nations to voice my concerns over the re-introduction of coal power stations. Does Dr Edwards still believe in the fight against carbon emissions? No doubt you have heard the coal lobby is blaming green militants for your father's disappearance."

"It wasn't green militants—" I cut myself short from mentioning Xcon. Princess Lani and Chief Alyseyu stared, waiting for me to resume speaking. I wanted to tell my story but Oko cut in.

"Dr Edwards is as committed as ever to fighting man-made climate change," Oko said. "The attack must be two-pronged. Reduce carbon emissions and find out what is happening in the Tonga Trench. Tomorrow Sam and I will board the *D-Sea Explorer*, the research vessel Dr Edwards chartered. Sam is an accomplished mini and robot sub operator and very knowledgeable about his father's work. Finding the cause of the warming is the first step to stopping it. If the ocean continues to heat at its current rate, catastrophic climate change is inevitable."

"Good luck. The whole world may be depending on you," Lani said. "And Sam, it must be so hard with your dad missing, but Atlo Trudock is using your father's statement to justify Xcon opening old coalmines. Could you make a statement on your father's behalf to emphasise the importance of continuing to reduce carbon emissions?"

"Yes, I'd like to." I nodded. I was a Youth Leading the World member, but I'd always been in Dad's shadow. It was time I spoke out.

Princess Lani took the phone from her wrist. "We can do it right now. This will go viral."

My jaw dropped, and my chest tightened as I tried to speak. A viral clip of me on the net could put everyone in danger.

"Please, Princess Lani," Oko said, "this is a very difficult time for Sam. Right now, he is not comfortable to speak about his father. When we return from the Tonga Trench, Sam will make a statement."

"Please, accept my apologies, Sam. I shouldn't have been so insensitive," Princess Lani said and replaced the phone.

The tightness in my chest released, but I saw the disappointment in her eyes. I itched to speak up. My gut churned at the thought of how pathetic I must look.

"I am very worried the press will hound Sam if they find him," Oko said, "Princess Lani, may I ask where you and Chief Alyseyu heard of Russell's disappearance? Was Sam mentioned?"

Blood pulsed through my temples. This conversation was like walking through a mine field.

"I heard the sad news on the Radley Jones program. There was no mention of Sam," Princess Lani said.

I exhaled with relief.

"It's most important we keep our plans discreet until after the dive," Oko said.

"Understood," the chief said, and he kept glancing into my eyes as waiters placed fruit and seafood platters on the table. Although not hungry, I spotted mango on the fruit platter. The sweet flesh relieved my tension, and I helped myself to a second, then third serving.

"Do you like seafood, Sam?" Princess Lani asked.

"Yes, thank you," I said, surprised that she even bothered to speak to me again. I selected a prawn, took a bite, and tried to think of something to say to redeem myself. She looked older than me, spoke so beautifully, and I felt so inadequate in her presence. I finished the prawn and picked up another slice of mango, completely unaware that I'd eaten all the mango on the platter.

"Take it easy on the mango," whispered Oko.

Princess Lani heard him. "No, help yourself, we have plenty of mangoes," she called on a waiter to bring another plate of sliced mango.

The chief caught my attention. "Sam, your eyes are the most the magnificent blue."

I tried to smile and reached for another slice of mango.

"I must say Princess Lani's eyes are like exquisite emeralds," Laurie said.

"That is true," the chief said.

The princess smiled, and I recognised the flicker of discomfort in her eyes.

"Tell us of building your yacht, Laurie," the chief said.

"I used the keel from an old Tasmanian pearl lugger and built her up from there. I'm the only person to design, build, and skipper a yacht to victory in the Antigua Tall Ships race."

I zoned out as Laurie spoke. I couldn't believe how I'd blown my chance to make a good impression. Hearing firsthand how Dad's work helped people steeled me a little, but refusing to speak up on climate change made me feel weak and stupid. I took another slice of mango while Chief Alyseyu and Laurie discussed sailing. The chief and Laurie laughed, and Oko smiled in distant agreement.

"Would you like a tour of the ship, Sam?" Princess Lani asked.

My eyes widened. I wasn't sure I heard right, and blushed.

"Can I give you a tour of the ship, Sam?" Lani repeated.

I felt myself go even redder. "Yes, please."

"Uncle Aly, I thought I would give Sam a tour of *Makomaile*."

"Excellent idea."

"Please excuse us, gentlemen," she said.

Laurie snuck me a cheeky wink. Oko looked worried.

I felt as though I was floating above my body as I followed the princess past the bar, through a short passage, and up a flight of stairs to the bridge. Four plush swivel seats sat before screens and gauges. The window where I first saw Princess Lani remained open.

"I love it in here," she said. "The captain lets me steer. Look, the joystick steers and these levers control the engines."

"*Atlanta* has a big wooden wheel. It's amazing you can steer such a big ship with a tiny joystick," I said, relieved to put a few words together.

Princess Lani nodded and led me to an outdoor passage. The sweet scent of frangipani trailed behind her, breeze flowed through her hair, and I loved the way she walked with shoulders back, hips swivelling, and arms swinging loosely at her sides.

"The top deck is my favourite," she said and pressed a pad beside an entrance. The door retracted, and I followed her up a spiral staircase made with fine oak joinery.

"You can see forever from up here," she said as we strolled into a most exquisite space. Windows wrapped around the cabin. A plunge pool and spa occupied the forward deck. Islands floated in the distance, and the glimmering Pacific stretched to the curved horizon.

Princess Lani slipped off her shoes. I copied, wiggled my toes in the soft cream carpet, and gawked at the massive bed.

"There are bathrooms and walk-in robes either side of the bed, and a holographic theatre projects from the ceiling."

My eyes blanked as I imagined holographic gaming with Princess Lani in the cabin. I'd never experienced such opulent surroundings. The smell of coconut oil and hibiscus flowers drifted. A carving of a humpback whale with a calf decorated one wall, a framed bark painting of a turtle another. Behind the bed, a huge painting of sun waves washing over dolphins energised the cabin.

"The dolphin painting is amazing," I said.

Princess Lani smiled, and I detected a hint of a blush. "I painted it myself. Thank you."

"Really?" I studied the painting, and a stomach cramp bent me forward.

"Are you okay?"

I nodded, wishing I hadn't eaten so much mango. I held my stomach as I followed the princess to the stern deck, where a sleek white helicopter was parked.

The breeze blew steadily. Sweat beaded on my brow. I walked downwind and breathed a sigh of relief as my stomach cramp subsided.

"Have you flown in the helicopter?" I asked.

"Yes, but I don't like helicopters much anymore."

I focussed on a dirty grey smudge to the south, "That cloud. It's the hot zone in the trench, isn't it?"

Princess Lani nodded.

"Have you been there?" I asked

"We've been close, but the smell and the heat, it was so creepy we turned away. You're very brave, Sam. And I hope you find something, but I wish you wouldn't go."

Lani's words brought a smile to my face, and I gazed at the grey smudge questioning whether I was stupid or brave.

"Let's check on the engines," Lani said.

As we descended the spiral staircase, my bowels rumbled again. *Why didn't I listen to Oko?* I followed Lani through a rounded steel hatch to stand on an aluminium grating above the engine room.

Oil and grease thickened the air. Machinery and ducts absorbed light and cast shadows over the captain and two engineers inspecting a huge engine. Seeing Princess Lani, the captain shrugged.

Stomach cramps returning, I thought of asking directions to the toilet, but followed Princess Lani from the engine room to the water-level garage.

Both sides of the ship were open. A tender and four jet skis occupied one side, a speedboat the other, with scuba tanks, kite surfers, and paddle boards in the centre.

I imagined skimming across the sea with Princess Lani's arms around my waist, and my bowels twisted. I strode to the far jet ski, bent over, pretended to study the engine, farted, and stood to walk away, but the princess walked right up to me.

"Jet skis are fun," she said, scrunched her nose, and looked around the garage.

I blushed and nodded.

"We should go back now," she said.

I walked behind Princess Lani and punched myself in the jaw. I fought the urge to punch myself repeatedly, and we arrived on the dining level at the same time as *Makomaile*'s captain.

"May I speak with you, Chief Alyseyu?" the captain asked.

"Go ahead."

"Our engineers are still working on the engines. If you wish, we can launch the speedboat and you can be home in two hours."

"Well, I guess we should launch the speedboat—unless our new friends wish to sail to Kiranga."

57

GASPED

Amazed she had even come aboard *Atlanta*, I helped untie the sail covers, wishing I could stop acting the dumb idiot.

"You need to impress ladies," Laurie said. "If you struggle for conversation, tell her how good you are at martial arts, or how you want to be a famous scientist like your dad."

I paused, considered Laurie's advice, continued pulling cord from the eyes of the sail cover and admired an albatross gliding in the sky. I wanted to be a space explorer, but hadn't said anything intelligent since we'd met. Trying to impress Princess Lani sounded ridiculous.

After only a short time on the *Makomaile, Atlanta* felt kind of clunky as she pushed through smooth swells. A hint of morning breeze ruffled the ocean. Oko tidied below.

"Raise the mainsail," Laurie called.

I hauled both halyards at once.

"Raising the gaffed mainsail is normally a two-man job," Laurie said, "but Sam is so strong, good at navigation too."

Princess Lani and Chief Alyseyu stood leaning against the coach house. I re-gripped the halyards and hauled. Timber jaws and rattan hoops slid up the mast and the creamy white mainsail took shape.

Oko emerged from the forward hatch as I prepared to raise the foresail.

"Tidy, except for Laurie's cabin. I'll help with the sails," he said.

We took a halyard each and hauled. The boom slid up the mast, and we reached again to grip.

"If you struggle for words around a lady, speak of something you love," Oko whispered. "Talk of sunrise or the ocean."

We hauled until the sail took shape, turned the halyards over the belaying pins, and tensioned the foresail.

"I go blank and smile like a dumb idiot."

"Your smile is charming. And relax, you are very intelligent. Asking questions is good for conversation. Ask how many islands in Kiranga. Which island is her favourite?"

I slid out on the bowsprit and released the jib sail-cover.

"I told Laurie the sail covers were a waste of time. Now he enjoys talking while million-dollar passengers do the work," Oko said.

I laughed, and Oko joined me.

As I raised the topsails, my eyes met with Princess Lani's three times. With five sails catching breeze, I returned to the cockpit, determined to at least say something.

"The sails look amazing, but that must be hard work," Princess Lani said.

I smiled and nodded. "It keeps you fit."

Laurie switched to autopilot. "I'll get a chart so we can look at your islands."

He descended into his quarters and returned with a large-scale chart, which he unrolled on the coach house. Everyone crowded around.

Princess Lani pointed with her nail. "This is where we live, the island of Kiranga. Motupu and Lakua are the second and third most populated islands."

"The names on the chart are different," I said.

"Yes, the names on the charts are Tongan. I call them by the traditional names," Princess Lani said. "My favourite island is Mokua," she continued, pointing with the tip of her clear-polished nail, "it's uninhabited and has a protected lagoon and a waterfall where you can swim."

"That sounds awesome," I said, relieved that finally some words had come naturally.

"You can see Mokua's peak in the distance," the chief said, pointing.

When my vision zoomed in on the island, I shivered.

"We could visit Mokua," Princess Lani said.

"Yes," I said. The peak held my gaze with a magnetic attraction.

Princess Lani stared at me, and we both turned to Laurie and Oko.

"Is there an anchorage?" Laurie asked.

"The anchorage is excellent, but you must enter and leave on high tide," the chief said. "If you go to Mokua, you can stay overnight. There's no internet or mobile reception, but I can arrange a transfer to Kiranga for Princess Lani and myself on *Atlanta's* radio."

"Mokua is heavenly, you'll never want to leave," Princess Lani said.

Laurie raised his eyebrows. Oko nodded.

"Mokua it is," Laurie said.

Princess Lani's enthusiasm lifted our spirits. Everyone smiled, but I sensed something in the water below us. I turned to the stern. A massive shadow blended into the depths.

"Did you see something, Sam?" Princess Lani stood beside me and stared into the water.

"It's gone, but I thought I saw a whale or something," I said.

"Okay, now we're friends, I suggest we dispense with formalities," Chief Alyseyu said.

"Away from the public eye, Princess Lani prefers Lani, and I prefer Chief or Chief Aly."

"Excellent, Chief Aly," Oko said. "Captain Laurie, now would be a good time for you to fix some refreshments for our guests."

Laurie shot Oko a deadpan look before climbing belowdecks; shortly after, chirpy island music piped through the speakers. Lani swayed with the rhythm.

"Sam, help me with drinks," called Laurie.

Lani smiled and swayed, and I took my time descending.

Laurie chuckled as he added ice to soda and juice cocktails, made from the gourmet fresh provisions. "I asked to buy provisions from *Makomaile*, but the Chief wouldn't hear of it. His staff loaded us up with everything at no cost. I cleaned out their kitchen. And Sam, I've seen the way Princess Lani looks at you. Be cool, she likes you. Head up the steps and I'll pass the drinks."

I passed the drinks to Lani, Chief Aly, and Oko, then took one myself.

"*Atlanta* sails with a strong steady motion," Chief Aly said.

Laurie's chest puffed. "She won her class in the Antigua Tall Ships race," he said.

"Really," replied the chief.

"Yes. I'm the only person to design, build, and skipper ..."

I smiled at Lani. "Do you like to snorkel?"

"I love snorkelling. Most coral reefs south of Mokua are dying or dead, but the coral surrounding Mokua lagoon is spectacular. I have a favourite pair of angelfish, and they live near a giant clam we call Elvis."

"Mokua sounds wonderful," I said.

A light wind and a gentle swell angled across the beam. I imagined exploring the colourful reef with Princess Lani, and an idea entered my head.

"Would you like to go up to the foredeck?" I stammered forcing myself to speak.

"Yes, thank you, Sam."

White sails towered fresh against the perfect blue sky. We ambled forward with water splashing and gurgling around us. Laughter between Laurie and the chief sounded distant.

"It's cool sitting out on the bowsprit rail. Try it if you like," I said.

Lani smiled and looked at her glass.

"Let me take your glass, if you're finished."

I took Lani's glass, strode to the cockpit, and handed both glasses to Oko.

Oko shook his head and smiled. "Now you think I'm your servant," he whispered.

I slid out on the rail. Lani followed, and her wavy black hair streamed in the breeze.

"If you dangle your feet, your toes get wet on bigger swells," I said.

Lani smiled, and we dangled our feet as we dipped into a trough.

"Be awesome if dolphins raced the bow," I said.

Lani nodded with a hint of sadness in her eyes. "We used to see dolphins every day, but with the warming, they're rare these days. I hope you and Oko can find the source hend stop it."

The idea of helping dolphins sent tingles up my back and shoulders. With my confidence increasing, I ached to ask a question. "Do you live in a palace?"

Lani laughed and swished her hair. "I live in a bigger modern version of our traditional thatched huts."

It was so cool sitting beside Lani. I was conscious of how close she was to me. As the bow rose and fell our legs touched and neither of us moved them. I watched an albatross gliding in the distance, and the ocean swished over our feet as *Atlanta* pushed through a wave.

"Are your mum and dad the King and Queen?"

Lani's smile vanished. She moved a little away from me and gazed ahead. "My parents died in a helicopter crash."

"Oh, I'm sorry."

"I miss them," she said.

We sat in silence. The ocean ruffled as the morning breeze strengthened, until whitecaps toppled the peaks. I stared into the inky water, and a vibration drew my consciousness to the depths. I shivered and stared south. The dirty cloud faded over the horizon, but even from this distance the hot zone gave me the creeps.

Atlanta raced across the sea and crashed into a powerful swell. Spray sheeted and burst from the bow. Lani and I laughed as our legs dunked past their knees, but I sensed Chief Aly and Oko's concern.

"We'd better head back," I said.

Laurie eased off the wind, and we clambered back to the cockpit. The deep purple water became blue as we crossed the eastern wall of the trench, and the lump on the horizon grew to a towering cone with a solitary cloud clinging to the peak.

"That peak is the shape of a volcano," I said.

Chief Aly nodded. "It last erupted two thousand years ago."

Broad-leafed vegetation clung to steep rugged cliffs and swayed in the breeze as we approached. Princess Lani pointed to the sky. "Photius is there."

A bird soared the summit. I stared, then shut my eyes, and for a moment I soared as the bird. "Is Photius a falcon?"

"A peregrine falcon, the fastest animal on Earth," Lani said.

As we sailed close around the southern tip of the island, waves surged into cliffs and bounced. Spray burst from sea caves and salty mist drifted.

"Spearfishing around the caves is excellent when the sea is calm," the chief said.

I eyeballed the deep blue, thought of the sharks from Matahi Island, and was sure I'd never spearfish again.

"The mountain has potential for hang-gliding," Laurie said. My ears pricked.

Wind and swell abated as we sailed into the lee of the island. Sheer volcanic cliffs plunged to a boulder-strewn ridge that tapered to the water. I glimpsed fringing reef and a magnificent lagoon.

Princess Lani raised her hand. "Look, the waterfall."

Water cascaded from high on the peak. Rainbows glistened as sheets plummeted hundreds of metres to crash onto a rocky ledge and tumble a second stage into thick green forest.

I gazed at the waterfall, the falcon, the lagoon, and then Laurie and Oko. They both stood open-mouthed. Princess Lani and Chief Aly were enjoying our expressions.

"This island feels so alive," I said.

As we sailed around a rocky point, I decided I'd arrived at the most wonderful place on Earth. The lagoon was big and blue and calm. Coral sand ran up to the foreshore, where three open shelters with thatched roofs nestled amongst coconut palms that merged into tropical forest.

"See those two shallow reef sections near the channel through the reef?" Chief Aly asked.

"We call them bomboras in Australia," Laurie said.

Chief Aly nodded. "The tide is still rising. How much does *Atlanta* draw?"

Cylindrical waves peeled along the reef beyond the bomboras.

"Seven feet," replied Laurie, "and surfers would love those barrels."

"We need to wait until the swell stops breaking over the second bombora. The current is not strong. We can drift for half an hour, then go in," Chief Aly said.

Sails fluttered in the shifting breeze. Laurie and Oko dropped the mainsail. Lani and I took the foredeck, and I was surprised at how neatly she coiled the halyards.

With the sails dropped, Oko and I left Laurie with the covers. We drifted along a drop-off. The sea on one side of the yacht was almost purple and the other light blue, fading to turquoise at the fringing reef. Everything was shiny and smooth. Sun-waves rippled over tropical fish teaming around the stern.

Lani and I leaned over the rail. The crystal water offered views of corals and larger fish on the bottom. Lani just looked at me and I nodded.

"Can we go for a swim, Uncle Aly?" Lani asked.

Chief Aly looked at Laurie.

"Sure," the skipper said.

Oko apologised for Laurie's mess, and showed Princess Lani to the captain's quarters to get changed.

"Laurie, can I jump from the mast?" I asked.

"No worries," Laurie replied.

I ambled to the stays, took my time climbing the ratlines, and reached the spreader as Lani emerged, wearing an emerald wet shirt and black stretch swimming shorts.

"Wow. That's high, are you going to jump?" Lani asked.

I nodded and jumped. My board shorts ballooned, and fish scattered as I speared feet first into the blue, then followed my bubbles to Princess Lani's smiling face on the surface.

Lani clapped and cheered and before I knew it, she'd climbed the ratlines with Laurie's guidance. From the spreader, she peered into the depths, smiled at me, and dived.

Panic shot through me when I saw her dive, but she clasped her hands out front and pierced the water with a tiny splash. Bubbles streamed behind her as she arched into a turn and kicked with pointed toes.

"That was a perfect dive," I said.

Lani smiled and backstroked away. I followed out to where the ocean turned purple. Suddenly, my pulse raced. I stared into the water.

"What is it?" Lani asked.

An urge to dive overwhelmed me. I submerged my face and gazed into the blue. A coral wall teeming with life dropped into the depths, and sunrays went forever.

"What is it? Are you okay?" Lani called.

My ring tingled, and something compelled me to dive.

"Wait here. I'm going down," I said.

I pulled ten strokes, descending close to the coral wall. Lani followed and stayed with me. Eight rapid strokes later, I was sure Lani would give up, but she swam harder, grabbed my leg and signalled to ascend.

My body craved something in the depths, but I couldn't believe Lani had held her breath this long, and I worried she would black out. I turned to ascend by her side. Sunlight swallowed us at the surface.

"Look!" Oko shouted.

Lani and I gasped.

58

ENOUGH MARINE LIFE

Adrenalin pumped through my arteries. I swam for the ladder. Chief Aly assisted Lani aboard while I dangled in the sea. Bewildered that no one stayed to help, I climbed the rope ladder.

Everyone stood cheering. A dolphin launched from the water in a huge arc. Another broke the surface, then two in quick succession. They charged so fast. The lead dolphin swam straight for me on the ladder. An instant before collision, I braced.

The dolphin launched skyward. Water dripped from her fins, splashing my face as she soared right over the stern. I pulled myself up, ran across the deck. The black and white dolphin splashed down and darted back alongside.

"AAMM! AAMM!" the dolphin chirped, and leapt up level with my eyes. The others joined in. Four dolphins jumped and splashed and chirped. Three black and white dolphins, plus a single grey. They were so beautiful. Overjoyed, I lay on the deck and hung over the side.

"Great dolphin show you arranged for us, Chief Aly," Oko said.

"I think Sam arranged the dolphin show," Chief Aly said. "They are calling his name."

"AAMM," Oko mimicked. "Close, but not quite."

"You of all people should know dolphins cannot sound the letter S," Chief Aly said.

Oko squinted as he looked at Chief Aly, then laughed.

"AAMM! AAMM!" the dolphins chirped with heads above water, and the grey dolphin flicked water at me.

"I've never seen black dolphins in these waters," the chief said.

"They're white-sided dolphins, usually found in the North Pacific, Japan, and Alaska," Oko said.

The smaller white-sided and the grey dolphin had the smoothest shiny skin, bobbing and chattering, exuding energy. The larger dolphins hung back, and one smiled at me with her eyes. I glimpsed something I couldn't explain, a soul as deep as the ocean, and thoughts of my mother entered my mind.

"These two look younger," Princess Lani said, lying beside me. As though we read each other's minds, we turned to Oko and Chief Aly.

"Can we swim with them?" Lani asked.

"Of course," the chief said.

"Just let them come to you, don't chase them," Oko said.

Chest pounding, I went to dive over the rail, but hesitated. I saw the same fear and excitement in Princess Lani's eyes as she prepared to dive.

I leapt first. Bubbles cleared. The dolphins chirped. They seemed much bigger in the water. A moment of panic subsided as Lani plunged beside me. The grey dolphin swam so close, she reached out and we touched.

The smaller white-sided dolphin chirped and chattered close to me. Another swam below on her side, looking up with smiling eyes. *Tali*, the name, sounded clearly in my mind.

Sun waves rippled over the dolphins' smooth bodies. I submerged, drew two strokes, and the smaller white-sided dolphin swam right up to me. I reached out, and her skin felt like smooth rubber. And there again in my mind, *Miki*.

"Hello, Miki and Tali, my name is Sam," I said in my mind.

Bizarre as it seemed, I was sure they understood me. And it was as if I could hear them talking, the bottlenose grey was called Kota and the biggest of them all was Bola.

"AAMM," chirped Miki. She pushed her tail and rubbed alongside, until I grasped her fin.

Miki arched, flicked, and towed me through the silky warm water. This was a dream come true. I turned to see the smaller grey towing Lani. Her wide-eyed gleam captured this perfect moment.

Tali watched Miki and me from below and suddenly it was as if I could see my mother in the water with Tali, but Tali was young with an older dolphin, who must have been her mother, looking on. Tali whistled sounds of joy, and I'm sure she was saying that she wished their mother were alive to see them now. Miki and Tali must be sisters. I was sure they were.

"PFFFH." Miki with me, and Kota with Lani, surfaced in unison. Joy flooded through me. Miki dived and swam side by side with Kota and Lani, out over the drop-off.

That sensation hit me again. My ring tingled, and I stared into the blue. Endless sunrays streamed. I wondered if Miki could tow me deep. But hearing a loud shout, I released Miki's fin and ascended beside Lani.

"Lani and Sam! Breaststroke back to the boat—slow and calm!" the chief called.

Alarm bells rang. Chief Aly's tone demanded immediate action. I calculated *Atlanta* was forty metres away.

"Sam!" Oko shouted.

A fin cut the surface near *Atlanta*.

"Please be a dolphin," I said.

Oko shaped to dive in, but the chief grabbed his shoulder.

Miki, Kota, and Bola shot away. Tali stayed with Lani and me.

"Lani and Sam, stop! Stay still, be calm," the chief called.

Wake peeled from a fin. It was far too big for a dolphin.

"I'll get a gun—" Laurie turned for the cabin.

"No," the chief said, "it's not an aggressive shark. If you make it angry, it has the power to destroy this boat."

Lani and I treaded water. The fin kept rising and came straight for us.

I dipped my eyes into the water. A massive blunt head with gaping jaws slid through the water. Miki flashed in front, but the giant came straight for me.

Kota glanced past, charged back. The shark's jaws flashed. Kota swerved, making a narrow escape.

Water splashed as Bola thrust, circled behind the massive jaws, and charged for the gills. The giant shark swung its head and butted him.

Tali slapped her tail.

The shark's eyes were darker than black. Huge teeth in massive jaws formed a brutal smile that came for me. I pulled Lani behind me.

Miki darted. Kota dashed. Tali fin-slapped and the monster shark veered.

I eyeballed the gliding giant, the subtle stripes on its back, and shot a glance to *Atlanta.*

Oko stood on deck clutching his hair.

"Keep still—doing well, Lani, doing well, Sam," the chief said in a low, measured tone.

Oko stared into the water and nodded to Chief Aly.

"Breaststroke—slowly—" directed the chief.

The dolphins circled. Lani and I drew panicked strokes to within twenty metres of the yacht. Heart thumping triple time, I fought the urge to overarm sprint.

"Stop!" Chief Aly called.

Lani and I gasped. We wanted to keep swimming but obeyed the chief.

"God save us," sobbed Lani.

Laurie appeared with an assault rifle.

"Do not use that gun," Chief Aly said. A fin, rounded at the top, sliced the water between me and the boat. Dolphins charged. Jaws snapped. The fin towered a metre out of the water.

Tali, Bola, Miki, and Kota darted in front of me, but the massive tiger shark surged.

I pushed Lani away. The giant shark struck.

Light flashed in my head. Sounds blurred. This was it, life over. I pictured blood leaking from my savaged body. My ears rang. The ocean thrashed. I broke the surface, glimpsed sky and *Atlanta*, and bounced on the shark's back. An enormous tail broke the water and thrust. I slid on the shark's sandpaper skin. The giant dorsal fin smashed my hands into my face and knocked me into the water.

Bubbles swirled. I didn't know which way was up and reached for the surface, amazed to still live.

"Go!" Oko shouted.

"Go!" The chief yelled.

My arms swung; my legs kicked. Ahead, Chief Aly and Oko yanked Princess Lani from the water. I pictured the shark coming for my legs.

"Sam!" Lani screamed as I reached for the ladder. Oko and the chief ripped me out of the water, and we fell in a heap onto the deck.

Laurie stood with the assault rifle, and the shark swam under *Atlanta*. Princess Lani sobbed. The pod rushed away. The massive tiger disappeared beyond the drop-off. For a full minute, no one said a word.

"That's enough marine life for today," Chief Alyseyu said. "Shall we go into the lagoon?"

I stared at the island, then into the sea.

"Did you feel that?" I said, thinking of the creepy feeling I had during my visions in the Tonga Trench.

"Feel what?" Oko asked. Everyone stared at me.

"An earth tremor," Lani said.

59

THE ZORAG

Superheated clouds gushed from the wall of the Tonga Trench. The ocean carried a vibration, and the Zorag's head jammed in a side vent as it tried to push into the sea. In seventeen years, the creature had grown from an element of gas to the mass of a thousand whales.

Based on a dependence on carbon and heat, a symbiotic relationship with the Coaliferite Nation had developed and thrived. Without the Zorag, the Coaliferite would still be a minority, scratching an existence from tortured, discarded planets. But through the unlikely alliance with the Zorag, the Coaliferite had risen to rule Andromeda.

The Zorag probed, thinned, and thrust, but the vent was too narrow. The alien serpent-like creature recoiled and struck. The ocean floor shook. A side vent exploded. Dark clouds gushed and magma balls spat, glowing orange and red in the darkness.

Eyes of fire emerged from the trench wall and a black tongue flickered, tasting the vibration.

60

RAMBALA

Laurie steered *Atlanta* between the bomboras and through the narrow channel. Chain rattled from the locker as the anchor fell through eight metres of water and wedged into the sandy bottom. I helped Laurie roll out an awning to shelter the cockpit. Oko served water, corn chips, and guacamole. We sat around the sunbed and crunched and dipped. Words couldn't express what had taken place, and I felt comfortable with the silence as I scanned the lagoon.

To the southeast, a sand spit formed an edge; beyond was the drop-off where we'd met the pod and the attack had taken place. I remembered that sensation pulling me to the depths and prayed for the dolphins to come back. The palm on the sand spit in front of the drop-off triggered thoughts of my mother.

"I didn't think tiger sharks grew that big," Oko said.

Chief Aly nodded. "Rambala in the body of a shark."

"Rambala?" Laurie said.

"Spirit of the ocean, protector of our people," Lani said.

Laurie raised his eyebrows, pursed his lips, and nodded.

"It didn't act protective," Oko said.

"For a shark, it wasn't aggressive. It could have taken Sam and Lani," Chief Aly said.

I rubbed the side of my head where the shark's enormous fin had struck me, shivering as I relived the jaws and those dark eyes.

"And those dolphins—three white-sided and a grey." Chief Aly looked to the sky. "Spirits are at work here today."

"You think it's the work of the gods?" Laurie asked.

"You don't believe in spirits?" the chief said.

"I believe in karma and nature," Laurie stood, "Sam, can you help me get the dinghy ready to go ashore?"

Patches covered bullet holes in the inflatable sides and fibreglass bottom. Laurie attached a halyard, I hauled, and the skipper guided the dinghy up over the rails, then down into the lagoon.

"Jump in and inflate the pontoons until they're firm, Sam."

I gazed into the water. "Do you think it's safe to go in the lagoon?"

"That shark is too big to come in here." Laurie waited for me to climb into the dinghy then handed me the fuel tank and outboard. I worked the foot pump until the bow and side pontoons firmed.

Having changed into a shirt and sarong, Princess Lani climbed up on deck and stood with Chief Aly watching me work.

"Do you think the lagoon is safe from the shark?" I asked the chief.

Chief Aly nodded. "The shark is too big to enter this lagoon."

While everyone converged on deck, I peered into the water around the dinghy and under *Atlanta*.

Laurie passed an ice box, and I assisted the chief and Lani aboard the dinghy. Lani and I sat at the bow and Laurie idled to shore. White sand ran up to three bamboo shelters with thatched roofs set amongst coconut palms at the top of the beach.

"What are the huts for?" I asked.

"That's our camp," Lani said. "Uncle Aly keeps stuff for camping in a cave behind the trees."

The last ten metres shallowed, so we got out and pulled the dinghy. Princess Lani waded ahead, reached the beach, and ran.

I waited for Oko's approving nod and took off after her. Sand crunched under my feet, and crabs scattered as I ran up the beach. As Lani ran toward the shelters, a presence attracted my attention to the sky. Way up high, a falcon flapped its wings, tucked into a stoop, and plunged like a space fighter.

"Look!" I said.

The falcon came at us fast. Wings unfolded, talons stretched, and with a flurry of movement, it landed on the bamboo hut in front of us.

"Whoa." I stared in awe.

The falcon had bandit patches around the eyes, grey wings, and mottled slate bars shaded his white chest. A knowing look in the raptor's eyes captivated me.

"Photius never comes this close," Lani glanced at me, "you seem to attract wild animals, Sam."

I smiled, my chest expanding as I pictured myself prince of wild animals. It had been hell-scary, but since my encounter with Rambala my confidence had grown. And I noticed how Lani's eyes and her whole demeanour had changed towards me.

Chief Aly led Laurie and Oko up the beach. Photius vanished with a snap of wings as they neared.

"Can I show Sam the waterfall?" Lani asked.

"Everyone should go," the chief said.

"Count me in," Oko said, arriving with the ice box and a bag.

I stared at the entrance to the lagoon, to the palm tree on the sand spit, and to where the water darkened.

"Are you okay, Sam?" Oko asked.

I blinked from my daydream, nodded, and felt another tremor, but not even Lani noticed it this time.

"Race you to the rocks," Lani said, turning to run. With a grin, I charged after her.

The end of the beach was two hundred metres away. Lani glanced over her shoulder and sped up when she saw me coming. She ran with fluid grace and surprised me with her speed. I drew level with fifty metres to run. She sprinted hard, finishing just ahead.

"You're fast," I said, barely puffing.

"You let me win." Lani didn't look tired either.

I shrugged and shook my head.

Lani led the way up the rocky point. When we reached the top, a boulder cove with a narrow pebble beach lay before us. The cove led out to the drop-off where we'd swum with the dolphins and the shark.

"It's called Shark Cove. Really," Lani said, and we laughed.

"Rambala is a cool name for that shark," I said.

With no sign of the giant tiger or dolphins, I focused on where the sea turned deep blue. The drop-off called me like sirens whispering in a dream. My urge to run across the rocks and dive through the breakers ended abruptly with a vision of Rambala. The ocean, the rocks, and the sky vibrated as if alive.

"I hope we see the dolphins again," Lani said.

"The dolphins without Rambala," I said.

"I'm with you on that." Lani led the way up the rocks into fleshy green scrub. The trail smelled of decaying leaves. Thick canopy crowded overhead. Small birds flittered, and the sound of pummelling water vibrated through the forest.

As we progressed, I glimpsed the waterfall through the trees. The path dampened. Lani picked up the pace, then slowed as we emerged onto a rock ledge.

Water glistened, teemed from the heavens, plunging into the pool at our feet. Fine mist floated, and deep green jungle opened to the magnificent blue sea. Smiling and words just couldn't explain. I laughed and Lani joined me.

Princess Lani removed her sarong. She wore black swimming shorts underneath, kept her T-shirt on, and dived into the pool. I dived after her. The crystal-cool water excited my skin. I swam behind Lani to where plummeting water formed a wall.

Lani submerged and swam under it. Water drilled my head as I floated through the fall.

"Hello," Lani shouted. Her voice bounced between the smooth rock face and the wall of water. Light pulsed. Sheets of water warped jungle, ocean, and the pool into an ever-changing blue and green collage.

"This is amazing," I yelled and laughed at how different I sounded.

With a hand, Lani cut through the sheet of water. The rumble of the fall changed pitch. I copied her, then followed as she dived through the fall and swam to the far side of the pool. Lani climbed out and sat where the water overflowed and cascaded over smooth rock.

"This is Cove Pool. From here the water drops to beach pools." She eased herself onto her back, lay on a wet slippery chute, and watched water plunging from high on the peak. She beckoned me beside her. "If you relax your eyes and unfocus, the water will appear to go up."

I worried that Lani was too close to the plummeting torrent, but figured she must do this all the time, and lay beside her. Sheets of water teemed, some spread into droplets, and after fifteen seconds I saw the illusion; I traced water rising to the top of the fall, and my ring tingled.

"Can we climb to the top?" I asked.

"Island Pool is at the top. From there you can see the Earth's curvat—"

Lani's eyes widened. She reached for me in a panic, then slipped into the torrent. Water gushed over her legs. I grabbed her wrist, but the force of the fall dragged her. I clutched at the smooth rock, straining to pull her to safety.

We slipped an inch.

Like a starfish, I clamped to the rock, but Lani slipped farther, wrenching me into the torrent. I fell headfirst and slid. Lani slipped her wrist and sped away.

I skated out of control. Raging water blinded me. I turned feet first, twisted onto my back, rode a bend, and fell through a vertical section, pleading for Lani's safety.

The rock ramped. I shot from the torrent, tumbling through the air. My vision blurred from trees to rock to ocean. A loud slap announced my back-flop entry into the water.

As I surfaced, Princess Lani clenched her teeth. "Sorry. That was a mean trick."

"Oh," I groaned, arching my shoulders and shrugging the sting from my back. I stared at Lani and the fall and shook my head. "That was … kind of awesome, but now I'm going to have to pay you back."

"Oh, really?" Lani smiled. "What are you going to do?" She swam slowly toward me, enticing me to try something.

"I'll surprise you when you least expect it," I said.

"I like surprises," she said, swimming closer.

Voices filtered through the forest. Unable to hide my disappointment, I screwed my face, Lani rolled her eyes, and a minute later Chief Aly led Laurie and Oko out from the forest.

"Paradise," Oko said.

Lani softened her eyes, looking helpless and innocent.

"Uncle Aly, may we camp on the island tonight?"

61

CAMPING

"Camping is a good idea," Chief Aly said. The words were music to my ears.

I bathed in bliss, but then my stomach fluttered. *What about dinner and sleep?* I'd have to explain my narcolepsy. Memories of farting in front of Lani, and my dad dead in the hotel dragged me down. I thought Lani was warming to me. But she was a beautiful princess. I was probably dreaming. And if we did get close, I could be putting her in danger. It was bad enough worrying about Swathi and Tom. The future closed in: Xcon; Laurie leaving us. Whenever I got my hopes up, the world collapsed around me.

Laurie, Oko, and the chief plunged into the pool.

"Can we slide down the waterfall again?" Lani asked.

"Sunset is near. We need to set up camp," Chief Aly said.

After a quick swim, Lani led the group along a trail following the fall. Cool clear water flowed across rock pools past a Pandanus palm, through a sandy gully where the tangerine flowers of a beach hibiscus sweetened the air. A sandy waist-deep pool formed at the head of Shark Cove, and then the fresh water rippled over swathes of pebbles into the ocean.

The sun dipped low as we climbed the rocky point and descended onto Lagoon Beach. Water glimmered golden at the drop-off. *Atlanta* rested like an old-world postcard, and the palm on the sand spit had me thinking about the photo of my mother.

"I need help with the camp boxes," the chief said when we arrived back at the shelters.

"If Sam and Oko help with the boxes, I'll head out to *Atlanta* for some of the lovely food provided by your kitchen," Laurie said. "Mahi-mahi fillets or steaks are on the menu tonight."

"Fillet for me, please," Oko said.

"Fillets are fine, but I prefer steaks," Chief Aly said.

"Steak for me, please," Lani said.

I dreamt my computer miraculously repaired itself so I could check the photo of my mother standing by a palm, then realised everyone was looking at me.

"Either is fine," I said, then trudged behind Lani and the chief to the cave.

"Look how high the tide comes," Chief Aly said, pointing to the line of debris deposited by the recent king tide.

"If the warming continues, we will have no beach and the cave will flood."

The cave was three metres across. I reached up and touched the highest point with the tips of my fingers. Two long wooden trunks with brass handles sat on the sand floor. Four long nylon bags lay on top.

The chief passed me one of the long nylon bags.

"Take these grass mats, then come back for the trunks."

The mats were light, but awkward to carry through the scrub. By the time we came back, the sun had set, and I yawned as I carried one end of a heavy wooden trunk. The chief took white canvas walls from the trunk. Lani helped hang the canvas on the huts, and I couldn't stop yawning as I unrolled grass mats for the floor.

"Are you okay, Sam?" Chief Aly asked.

"I get tired quickly after sunset."

"I'm not surprised after such an eventful day. Will you tend the fire while I organise our hut?"

The smoke kept changing direction, stinging my eyes. I placed extra sticks where the flames burnt most. The fire crackled, and after a while the smoke diminished.

Lani and Chief Aly prepared plantains and coconut, fresh from the island. Laurie wrapped the mahi-mahi in palm leaves, and Oko put water for the rice over the fire to boil.

Darkness fell on Mokua.

Tired and not hungry, I sat by the fire and yawned, determined to stay awake until after dinner.

"Is that all you're eating?" Princess Lani asked, looking at the portion Oko served me.

"I don't eat much after sunny days," I said.

Lani and Chief Aly glanced at each other.

"Uncle Aly, will you please tell a story after dinner?" Lani asked.

"If it pleases our guests."

I yawned. "Sorry, but I'll probably fall asleep."

"No one falls asleep during Uncle Aly's stories," Lani said.

Those were the last words I remembered hearing that night.

62

SO PERFECT

Tidal surge collapsed on the beach. Shells and coral fragments jangled as the waves drew back. I dozed semi-conscious in the darkness before dawn. Wave after wave lapped the shore. Laurie inhaled a snore and I opened my eyes.

Someone had put me to bed. I lifted myself onto my elbows, recalling Lani saying, "No one falls asleep during Uncle Aly's stories." At least I fell asleep before the story. Oko and Laurie shared the hut. I yawned and stretched, a little freaked that Lani and her uncle must have seen me carried like a child to bed.

I wiggled my toes, swung one leg after the other from the stretcher, and sat up. After another stretch, I stood on the grass mat and crept through the canvas flap. Stars ruled the sky – first light was an hour away.

I sensed Lani breathing in her hut, but Chief Aly wasn't near. I searched the beach, found it deserted, and scanned the mountain; a quarter of the way up, my night vision picked up bodily warmth. My vision zoomed in; the chief sat on a ledge with his eyes shut, as if he was praying or meditating.

High on the mountain, I detected another hint of warmth. The vision of Photius staring back startled me. I focused on the falcon until Photius closed his eyes. There was no sign of the dolphins, but I sensed them near, and I pictured Rambala gliding through fluid darkness.

Cool sand massaged my feet as I wandered to the water's edge and strolled along the beach to the solitary palm. I remembered the photo of my mother standing under a palm, pointing to the tip of the sun as it peeped above the horizon.

What were the chances that I'd stumbled onto the same island? I gripped the ring. Something lay in the depths beyond the drop-off, something from my mother. But after Rambala, even thinking about swimming in the protected lagoon was terrifying.

The palm tree was much bigger now, but as in the photo, there was a distinct kink in the trunk. I wished for my phone or computer to compare the image. Falling to my knees, I rested my forehead in the sand. What a crazy journey. I pictured my mother standing by the palm with me inside her. *Who was she? Who was my father?* I flopped belly-first onto the sand. Visions of the dolphins and of Princess Lani drifted with the rhythmic wash of the waves.

As the edge of the world brightened, I absorbed faint reflected energy and sat up. Brushing grit from my face, I focused on a flat rock at the water's edge. Sand fell from my shorts and shirt as I stood and trundled to the rock to sit and dangle my feet in the water.

An orange strip intensified over the horizon. Stars faded. I sensed Princess Lani stirring in her hut and wished with all my might that she'd come and sit beside me. The sky blued and my body tingled with anticipation as I listened to her feet scrunch over the sand. Mesmerised by her beautiful form, I stood to greet her.

"Good morning, Sam. Did you sleep well?"

"Yes. Good morning … sorry I fell asleep at dinner."

"That's okay. Oko explained your narcolepsy."

Narcolepsy sounded so freaky. I hated the word, waited for the usual questions, but Lani stood so close and smiled and gazed into my eyes.

"I never thanked you yesterday. When Rambala came for us, you shielded me."

"Anyone would have done it," I said.

"No, you're very brave," Lani took a step closer and put her hand on my shoulder. Her touch was electric, and I trembled with the realisation that she might be about to kiss me. Before I knew it, she kissed me on the cheek.

The sweet scent of frangipani filled my lungs. We gazed into each other's eyes. Everything went quiet as though I'd ducked underwater.

Our lips pressed together and fireworks exploded in my mind. Waves crashed and peeled along the reef. Gulls chirped, and parrots squawked in the forest.

"You're my hero, Sam," Lani said, drawing away.

"No … not really." I blushed and couldn't wipe the smile from my face.

Lani giggled at my reaction. We sat quietly together on the rock, our feet dangling in the water. A small fish splashed near our feet. Lani raised a foot and drips fell from her heel. The intense orange glow faded to apricot. I used my big toe to stroke and splash the glassy water.

"I'm guessing if we line that palm tree with the tip of the sun when it peeps over the ocean, it will intersect where we met the dolphins and Rambala yesterday," I said.

Princess Lani tipped her head and squinted. I stood, and Lani followed me to the palm. Cathedral light brightened the sky and the radiant tip of the sun flashed over the sea.

An imaginary line from the edge of the palm to the sun intersected where we'd swum yesterday. The drop-off beckoned, drawing me to the deep.

Lani moved close. "I don't know what made you think of that, but it's …"

"Kind of weird, like me."

"I was thinking … amazing."

I smiled, held her gaze for a second, then stared out to sea. Way out beyond the breakers, two fins disappeared. Lani followed my gaze. Fins breached and two puffs of mist suspended in the stillness.

"The dolphins!" Lani said. Sunlight sparkled on their backs as they arced above the surface near an unbroken swell. The swell steepened. Sunrise dazzled through the curling lip, and two shadows criss-crossed the barrelling wave.

"They're surfing," she said.

"Wow!" I cheered. "Imagine if they surfed and swam right into the lagoon."

I led Lani from the palm to the rock. The dolphins disappeared behind a wave and didn't breach again.

Lani's brow furrowed. "They must have gone."

I shook my head. Two shadows darted over the white sand bottom at the lagoon entrance. "They're coming right in."

The shadows gathered form. Lani and I laughed and cheered as the two younglings surfaced right near us. "AAMM," they chirped, raised their heads, and splashed.

"The white-sided one is Miki, and the grey's name is Kota," I said without thinking.

Lani gave me a quizzical look, then laughed. "Okay … Miki is cute, but Kota is my favourite."

The sun blazed over the Pacific, supercharging the morning. Chief Aly and Laurie strode across the beach, Oko followed, and Photius soared above the summit.

"Can we swim with the dolphins?" Princess Lani asked.

"Of course," the chief said.

I stared at the lagoon entrance, my smile fading. Lani slipped her sarong, stepped from the rock into thigh-deep water and waded. Miki and Kota swam close. Lani squealed with delight. "Come on, Sam!"

I pulled my shirt over my head and stared at a big dark shadow entering the lagoon.

"La–" I cut myself short as the shadow divided. "Two more dolphins coming."

"I'll keep an eye on the entrance," Oko said, now standing beside me.

I made a shallow dive from the rock. A dark form swam straight to me, and Miki rolled on her side. Her eyes and smile took my breath away. Kota slapped his tail near Lani. Tali brushed against me as she arrived with Bola by her side. Dolphins surrounded us and sun waves rippled through the crystal water.

I dived and swam underwater with Miki and Tali by my side. Bola chirped and chattered. Kota flicked his tail, launched into the sky, splashed down and circled back to Lani.

Miki nudged up to me. I took her fin, and she swished her tail with an exaggerated motion; I streamlined as we surged past a coral head out to deeper water. Miki slowed to a glide as we neared *Atlanta*. Lani arrived with Kota straining to pull her faster and faster.

After stealing a glance toward the lagoon entrance, I released Miki's fin and sank to stand on the sandy bottom with six metres of water overhead. Tali cruised close and chirped and clicked, as though talking to me. I was sure Tali must have swum with my mother.

Lani treaded water at the surface. Kota dived and scooted and launched skyward. I traced the shadowy silhouette in the sky until Kota speared into the water. Pushing from the sand, I surfaced beside Lani, and Miki leapt right over the rising sun.

On shore, Chief Aly, Laurie, and Oko smiled and laughed with delight.

"Come on in," Lani shouted, and soon everyone bathed in the fun.

I gazed around the lagoon, at Princess Lani, the dolphins, Chief Alyseyu, Oko and Laurie, the sky, and the island peak. I'd never dreamed that life could be so perfect, and I wished the moment could last forever.

The tide turned, drifted out, and it was still early morning when Tali and Bola exited the lagoon. Miki chattered and floated beside me, and my chest fluttered as I sensed her readying to leave.

"The best morning ever," Lani said as Miki and Kota cruised out past the bomboras.

I bit my lip and nodded. *Atlanta's* engine chugged, and I wondered what Laurie was doing. Everyone except Laurie had retired to the grass mats in front of the huts for breakfast. I restricted myself to one mango cheek. Nervous energy churned my stomach as the anchor chain grated and clanged aboard the old wooden schooner.

"Our boat will arrive at midday," the chief said. Lani's shoulders slumped.

Leaving Mokua seemed crazy. I needed to convince Oko and Laurie to stay longer.

"The *D-Sea 2* will pick us up at one o'clock," Oko said.

"We can't leave now," I said.

"Laurie is anchoring outside the lagoon so he can leave when the *D-Sea 2* arrives."

"Can we talk for a minute?" I asked and motioned for Oko to walk with me along the beach. When we were several yards away from the others, I said, "Yesterday, before the dolphins, I sensed a presence … dragging me to the depths. I'm sure my mother hid something near the drop-off."

"Hila?"

"Yes. I have a picture of her, standing in front of that palm tree, pointing to the tip of the sun at sunrise. It lines up with where the shark attacked."

Scepticism flickered in Oko's eyes. I wished again for my phone or laptop.

"We need to explore here first. Those dolphins are looking after us, we can't leave. I'm sure Tali, the bigger white-sided female, swam with my mother."

Oko exhaled and shook his head. "I spoke with Captain Wilkes this morning. An explosion sank the *D-Sea Explorer* in harbour last night. We presume Xcon is behind it. Captain Wilkes saved the *D-Sea 2*, a fast tender with a mini-sub. He agreed to take us to the hot zone to dive this evening. Then he's out of here."

"Xcon blew up our research ship and you want to dive the Trench this evening?"

"This is our only chance, and, if we discover the source of the warming, most important for humanity."

I scrunched my face. "It sounds crazy. We should use the sub to dive here."

"Come with me today, help with the sub, and we come back to Mokua."

White diesel smoke floated on the water as *Atlanta* chugged from the lagoon. Anxiety gripped my chest. I turned the ring on my finger. "It's too dangerous. This isn't my path. We should stay here."

"The world needs to know what Xcon is hiding. I will go by myself."

I knew Oko hadn't piloted a sub or practised on the simulator in years. I turned the ring on my finger to the left, then right, my whole being screaming not to go. I could stay on the island, camp out by myself, and stay with the dolphins. The thought of staying by myself both unnerved and excited me, but what about Oko—what if the dolphins left?

"Can we come straight back to Mokua tonight?" I asked.

"Tonight or tomorrow. The hot zone is sixty nautical miles south of here."

I closed my eyes and nodded, wondering if I would ever see Miki and Tali again, wondering what had happened to Oko's earlier advice: *Follow your own path, do what your heart tells you.* With paradise shattered, I concentrated on breathing and tried to stay calm as I trudged back over hot sand, the whole way wanting to change my mind.

Chief Aly folded a canvas wall. Lani caught my eye as I approached, then turned to the chief. "Uncle Aly, can I show Sam Island Pool before we leave?"

"You have little time for Island Pool; see how quickly you finish your chores," Chief Aly stared into my eyes, penetrating my soul.

63

ISLAND POOL

To my surprise, princesses had chores and washed up. As I shook sand from the grass mats, Chief Aly pulled me aside. "I trust you to escort Princess Lani. Climb with care, and you must be back by midday."

"Yes, Chief Aly," my chest expanded, and elation fizzed through my body. Lani and I would have some time alone. Now that I had something to look forward to, thoughts of doom relented.

"You only have two hours. Make sure you are back by noon," the chief said.

Sweat trickled down my temples as we jogged along the beach and clambered over hot boulders. Lani led the way up a different trail. Forest shaded the path, and the cool sweet air carried a hint of mildew. I slipped on a steep clay patch then, copying Lani in lowering my centre of gravity, we climbed up past Cove Pool. Thoughts of our sunrise kiss made me smile and I longed to kiss her again. *But what if we got too close?* Maybe I should tell her about Xcon and my dad. Tell her why I couldn't speak out. Lani could be a great ally, but I needed to protect her from danger.

"If we walk quickly, we can spend more time at the top," Lani said, powering ahead.

The trees got smaller, and the undergrowth thinned with altitude. I caught glimpses of ocean as the canopy gave way to blue sky. Thin-leaved dry vegetation clung to the steep slope, which flattened, and we emerged to the most amazing setting.

A rock basin formed an idyllic pool; on the far side, rugged cliffs towered to the old volcanic cone. Princess Lani stood on the northern edge of the basin and surveyed her kingdom. Scattered islands and sparkling sea stretched to the curved horizon. I stood beside her, and for the first time, felt as though I could feel that the planet beneath my feet was spinning in space.

"It's breathtaking," I said.

The breeze lifted Lani's hair. She smiled and nodded. Nature had created a perfect sparkling pool with water plummeting from an infinity edge. Lani led me to where the basin climbed to the summit and sheer cliffs fell to the ocean.

"Those are the cliffs with the sea caves we sailed around yesterday," she said.

I peered over the ledge. Whitewater surged far below. I experienced vertigo, drew back a second, then held the edge and peeked over the sheer drop.

An updraft ruffled my hair and evaporated sweat. I shut my eyes and imagined plunging from the ledge with Laurie's hang-glider. How amazing it would be to fly.

Lani strolled away with her shoulders back and hips twisting. She removed her sandals and slipped her cotton pants. She wore her black swimming shorts underneath. She looked toward me but not quite at me, removed her T-shirt and swimming shorts, placed them on a rock shelf, and walked to the edge of the pool wearing an emerald bikini.

My eyes bulged. I focused on her thighs, then breasts, gawking as though Lani couldn't see me. When our eyes met, I blushed. Lani smiled and dived into the pool.

I pulled my T-shirt off and plunged in behind her. Luxurious fresh water cooled my face and a compelling sensation struck, not as intense as the drop-off, but similar. Lani swam toward the infinity edge. I took a breath, submerged, and swam in the opposite direction beneath a rocky shelf.

A shadowy depression beckoned. I squeezed into a dark tunnel not much wider than my shoulders, pulled myself through four metres of an underwater shaft, and surfaced in an air pocket. A green glow issued from the pool and barely illuminated the meter-round pocket. Reaching up, I pushed off from the jagged ceiling, submerged, and studied a hint of light ahead.

The vibration of Lani's voice travelled through the water. I looked back to the pool, then focused on the hint of light ahead. I half-pulled, half-swam through ten metres of dark aquatic tunnel, and my splash echoed as I surfaced in the floor of a dome-shaped cavern.

Shafts of light illuminated a mandala, some kind of spiritual symbol, etched into the stone ceiling. My eyes bulged at the sight of it. A shiver ran down my spine and goose bumps popped up all over me. Paintings decorated the walls, and I sensed both familiar and alien energy in the cave. Desperate shouts filtered through the water. I fought the urge to explore farther and pulled myself back through the dark tunnel.

"Where did you go?" Lani glared with icy eyes, then submerged below the shelf. I scratched my shoulder and waited for her to surface.

"I found an underwater cave with paintings and a mandala," I said.

"I've seen that opening before, but it's so dark and narrow. I didn't think it led anywhere."

"You can pull yourself through the first section to a breathing space, and then take a longer underwater swim to the cave."

"You lead the way. Let's go," Lani said.

Worry about Lani holding her breath in the tunnel made me hesitate, but I remembered her amazing ability when we'd dived at the drop-off. I pulled myself through and took Lani's hand, leading her to the pocket. We pressed together in the tight space. Her breath sounded loud and her smooth skin sent tingles quivering through my body.

"I saw the light ahead," Lani said.

"It's a ten-metre swim to the cavern entrance."

Lani inhaled four breaths and swam. Sediment stirred and muddied the water as I followed on her heels to surface in the floor beside her.

The cavern was ten metres across and three metres high in the centre. Four shafts of light penetrated the walls at ground level. As Lani's eyes adjusted, she climbed from the pool and proceeded straight to the wall paintings: unusual patterns, pictures of people in canoes, dolphins, and a humongous shark.

"The shark resembles Rambala," she said, "and the patterns are in the style of our tribal art."

I nodded and stared at the mandala in the centre of the ceiling. This looked very different from the other paintings. From a large round stone platform beneath the mandala, I studied the dark etchings, maze-like patterns similar to my ring, that appeared to have been burnt into the stone.

Suddenly a blue spark jumped from the centre of the mandala to my forehead. Warmth flowed through my body.

"Sam! You're glowing!"

I stared at my arms and legs. A blue aura shone around me.

Princess Lani stepped onto the platform. A green spark jumped to her forehead. She shivered. Her eyes shot wide open. An emerald glow radiated around her. A dreamy smile crept over her face.

"I feel woozy," she said, bending.

"Lightheaded," I replied, kneeling.

We lay on the rock platform beneath the mandala, and consciousness drifted from us.

64

PRINCESS

"Wake up, Sam—Sam!" Lani shook me, "it's ten to twelve."

I pulled myself back through the dark aquatic tunnel in a state of panic. Lani gasped as she broke the surface. Photius peered from a rocky perch and launched into the wind. The sun beamed overhead. A cabin cruiser headed for the lagoon.

"Promise you'll tell no one of the cave. It's our secret," Lani said, scrambling to put her clothes on while still dripping wet.

"I promise, but what about the chief?" I thought I should tell Oko.

"Leave Uncle Aly to me."

Two small rocks dislodged as I negotiated a section of the trail where the path was very steep.

"Look out … sorry," I called as a rock tumbled across Lani's path. The descent was more difficult than the climb. Visions of the mandala and the spark clashed with anxiety about being late, anxiety about Xcon and Russell's death, and what would Chief Aly say to me? I shuddered.

Plummeting water greeted us at Cove Pool. Princess Lani scooped handfuls of water to drink and stared into my eyes.

"Uncle Ally will be angry when we return, but don't worry, I'll handle him. Everyone will be rushing. We may not get another chance to talk before I leave."

I nodded. Lani stepped toward me. My heart thudded with the anticipation that she wanted to kiss me again. I prepared to embrace her, but she stopped short.

"Sam, I think you're very brave to continue your dad's research and dive the Tonga Trench, but corporations are turning back to fossil fuel. They're using your father's words to justify the damage they're doing. If you and I don't stop them, who will?" Lani took the phone from her wrist.

"I know it's hard for you, Sam, but if you do a short video, I can use social media to rally young people all around the world. Can you just say a few words, what your father would have said?"

My throat tightened. "… I'm sorry. I just can't do it right now. I'll do everything to help later." I knew that if I did as she asked, her life could be in danger.

Lani bit her bottom lip, half nodded, half shook her head and slid down the slide. I followed, water swirling as I rounded the bend and snaked to the ramp. This time I landed feet-first in the water, but the anguish of letting Lani down stole the fun. I exited the pool and ran behind Lani, wishing I could explain why I couldn't do the video.

As we crested Rocky Point, Chief Aly and Oko marched up Lagoon Beach. Oko threw his hands in the air. The chief's steely gaze froze me.

Lani continued descending the rocks. The chief turned for camp.

Oko waited, and Lani walked past him as if he didn't exist.

"What happened?" Oko scowled at me.

"We lost track of time."

"You have insulted the chief, Princess Lani, Laurie … and yourself."

I scratched my head and rubbed my chest.

"We …" I began, then stopped.

The chief waited for Princess Lani, who walked with her head high, gazed above him as she drew level, and continued walking like a fashion model. Chief Aly fell in beside and glared at her while he spoke. I couldn't hear what she said, but Lani didn't even look at her uncle as she spoke to him. Chief Alyseyu shook his head, threw his hands in the air, and stared back at Oko and me.

The cabin cruiser waited at anchor. Princess Lani strolled, seemingly unflustered. Tension built in the chief's shoulders. Lani headed for her hut where white canvas walls swayed in the breeze; a young lady held the flap open and followed the princess inside.

Chief Aly glared at me, then waded to the cruiser where two crew-members dressed in white stood holding the stern to shore. I walked to the hut I'd slept in; the walls and mats were packed away. My shirt was wet, but there didn't seem to be any point in changing.

Laurie's outboard whirred to life, and he motored from *Atlanta* to shore. I stood in the shade under the thatched roof and searched for the dolphins, thinking how well Lani played the princess when it suited her.

"Change into your nice shirt and shorts," Oko said.

I slung my pack over my shoulder and swung around, not sure where to change. Leaves crunched and a branch snapped as I walked through the scrub to a sheltered spot. Princess Lani was going, and somehow I needed to keep in touch. I hung my board shorts and shirt on a branch, changed into my tan shorts and blue hibiscus shirt, and clambered back through the undergrowth.

Oko glared, and Laurie winked and grinned as I joined them halfway between the huts and the water's edge.

Princess Lani emerged from her hut wearing a cream silk dress. I needed her email, or something. I stepped toward her, but Oko clamped a hand on my shoulder and held me back. Lani's long silky hair glistened in the sun. She looked stunning and older with makeup.

A bulky crewmember marched up the beach, almost broke into a run, and bowed his head before Princess Lani. The maid stepped from the hut. The crewmember ducked inside, emerged with two bags, and Princess Lani led the procession down the beach.

I stared into Lani's eyes. She acknowledged me, but only for a second, and my heart sank as she walked past, nodded at Oko and Laurie, and continued to the water's edge. She raised her dress and waded through the shallows. Refusing assistance from Chief Aly and the second crewmember, Princess Lani of Kiranga boarded her cruiser. Her maid and bags followed, and she disappeared inside the cabin.

Chief Alyseyu approached me with cold eyes. "Sam, if you ever have the privilege to escort a princess again—keep time. Do I make myself clear?"

I swallowed and nodded, "Sorry, Chief Alyseyu."

The chief's gaze bored into me. "This has been a most remarkable meeting—be careful of the trench. Strange things are happening there. Follow your intuition."

"Yes, Chief Alyseyu," I said.

"Now," the chief exhaled and glanced to the heavens, "Princess Lani wishes to celebrate her sixteenth birthday here on Mokua tomorrow."

My heart thudded. The future, my whole world, brightened. And, I couldn't believe I was older than Lani.

"After this morning's effort, you are very lucky to receive an invitation."

"Thank you, Chief Alyseyu," I said, almost bowing.

"Laurie and Oko, Princess Lani will be delighted if you can attend."

"I am honoured, Chief Aly, but please give my apologies to Princess Lani," Laurie said, "I'm late for a prior engagement and set sail this afternoon."

Oko nodded at me, "We will be honoured to attend, Chief Alyseyu," he said.

I glimpsed something in Oko's eyes that worried me.

Chief Aly waded aboard, and the sandy shallows churned as the cruiser powered across the lagoon.

65

GOODBYE

Atlanta bobbed over a sand patch beyond the reef. I stood on deck gazing out to the drop-off, praying the *D-Sea 2* wouldn't come for us.

"Join me for meditation on the foredeck if you wish," Oko said.

I knew that meditation would centre my mind, but Oko's calm manner annoyed me. I felt like I was being dragged away, and my mentor was going against what he'd taught me.

"How about a last game of backgammon?" Laurie asked. "See who finishes ship's champion?"

"You've never even beaten me," I said.

"I must have won a few games." Laurie smiled, opened the board, and set up the pieces.

I didn't agree to play. I searched for the dolphins and stared at Mokua's peak. Thoughts of the cave and the mandala made me pace toward the bow.

"Okay, Sam, roll to see who goes first," Laurie called.

Backgammon was the last thing on my mind. I didn't want to play, but flopped onto a cockpit cushion, picked up a die, and rolled a one.

Laurie threw a five to win the start. He shook the dice, and the killer glint in the skipper's eyes made me smile.

"Double sixes!" Laurie shouted.

I stared at my pack resting against the coach house: a few clothes, toiletries, and a smashed computer, the extent of my worldly possessions.

"Why aren't you staying for Princess Lani's party?" I asked and threw a three and a one.

Laurie threw the dice with intense concentration, "You can pass on my best wishes to the princess and chief."

"What if we need you? Can I contact you if we need help?" I threw a two and a one.

"As soon as I receive my gold, I set sail for an island where no one will find me for a long time."

I glared at Laurie, then out to sea. I wished I'd joined Oko in meditation. It was as if Laurie was deserting us. He'd done it for the money, but Laurie had risked his life and *Atlanta* to bring us here. For Laurie, disappearing was the most sensible thing to do.

The skipper moved his pieces with such concentration I thought it strange he'd never won a single game. With a smile on my face, I rolled the dice and moved two pieces into vulnerable positions.

Laurie's face lit up when he saw the opening. He rolled the dice.

"Double fours! Well, well, little Sammy Edwards is in trouble." Laurie knocked one of my white pieces off and moved the last of his black pieces home.

"Sorry about that, Sammy. Seems like Captain Laurie will finish ship's champion."

"Yeah, you're so good at backgammon, Laurie."

"Oh, did you hear that, Wiggols? I think little Sammy is a sore loser."

I threw the dice but couldn't move back onto the board.

With great delight Laurie kept me trapped and began throwing his pieces off the board. But he couldn't help leaving his last two pieces exposed.

I picked up the dice. If I threw a two or a three, I could knock Laurie off and there was a slim possibility that I could still win. I jiggled, visualised losing the match, let the dice go, and they settled on five and four.

"Yes!" Laurie pumped a fist as though he'd conquered the world. He rolled the dice, removed his last pieces and stood.

"Whoo!" He hooted long and loud. Wiggols raised his head and howled. Laurie laughed out loud, and I joined him.

"Put it here, brother," Laurie offered me his hand. "Thanks for letting me win, what, one of ten games?"

"Closer to twenty," I said, and then I heard something I dreaded—the sound of a motor approaching.

In the distance, a sleek vessel pierced rolling swells. My chest fluttered as my eyes zoomed in on the grey, black, and blue camouflage paintwork, then the name, *D-Sea 2*, on the hull.

"Here she comes," I muttered.

Laurie stood, strained his eyes, and reached inside for the binoculars. Having surveyed the approaching vessel, he rubbed his hands together.

I gazed at my backpack and squatted to stroke Wiggols.

"Nice bit of gear," Laurie said, as the *D-Sea 2* slowed and the bow sank into the water. It was thirty feet long with a sharp bow. The engine throbbed like a muscle car, and a dome hatch retracted. Dressed in a combat uniform, Captain Wilkes stood at the helm. A spherical mini submarine occupied the rear deck near a crane.

I pictured Rambala's dark eyes circling the mini-sub, and shivered.

The captain regarded *Atlanta* with interest as he manoeuvred alongside and tossed mooring lines to me and Laurie. With the tender secure, the captain cut his engines.

"Captain Wilkes, this is Laurie Piper and Sam Edwards," Oko said.

"Pleased to meet you, gentlemen." Captain Wilkes had dark skin and spoke with an American accent.

He listened to the return greetings, as if to be polite, but I sensed him analysing Laurie. Wiggols growled and barked. Invisible tension sparked between Captain Wilkes and Laurie.

"Come aboard?" Oko said.

Laurie glared at Oko.

"I need a hand to unload, then we leave," Captain Wilkes said.

"Why, what's happening?" Oko asked.

"We can talk underway," replied Captain Wilkes.

Oko stepped over *Atlanta's* rail onto the *D-Sea 2* and tapped the hull.

"What is she made of?"

"Acrylic composite. Wait there a minute, Sam." Captain Wilkes urged Oko forward and they spoke for a minute before Wilkes hoisted a metal ammunition box onto *Atlanta's* railing.

Laurie and I took a handle each and lowered the box to the deck.

Laurie opened the box. Gold reflected on his face. He ran his fingers over the shiny surface.

"It's all there, weigh it if you want," Captain Wilkes said. The *D-Sea's* engines roared to life.

Laurie removed two bars and examined his treasure. "Job's right."

Oko climbed back onto *Atlanta*, handed his bag to Captain Wilkes, and turned to Laurie.

"Thank you for everything, Laurie. Can we call on you again if needed?"

"I'm sailing somewhere no one can find or contact me. Good luck to you and Sam."

Oko shook hands with Laurie, and Laurie held out his hand to me. *Had the last two weeks just been a business transaction?* Laurie had risked his life for us, but I couldn't help feeling cheated by the skipper cutting our connection. Wiggols whimpered. I bent and stroked him.

"Goodbye, Wiggols," I said, and when I straightened, Laurie handed me a small black velvet drawstring bag.

I loosened the drawstring and tipped a silver neck chain into my hand. Three black pearls tapered on either side of a delicate white carving of two dolphins.

"I carved the dolphins from fossilised whalebone, and the pearls are Rangiroa's finest. Keep it for yourself, or it could make a fine birthday gift for a princess."

"It's beautiful." I stared at the neck chain. "You made this?"

Laurie nodded.

I gazed along *Atlanta*'s deck, at the patched holes where I'd stood and blasted drones, at the foredeck where I'd practised meditation, and the towering mast from which I'd plunged into the ocean. My eyes welled.

Laurie shook my hand and pulled me into an embrace. "Don't worry, kid. You'll be right. You've got the hero gene ... but you're a survivor."

Captain Wilkes cast the stern line and waited with the engine rumbling.

I slipped the neck chain into my pocket, wiped my eyes, and stepped aboard the *D-Sea 2*.

Wiggols barked. Captain Wilkes reversed from *Atlanta* and engaged forward thrust.

"Live slow—fly fast!" Laurie shouted, giving a double thumbs-up salute.

66

CAPTAIN WILKES

The *D-Sea 2* powered around Rocky Point. My world crumbled as *Atlanta* faded from view. The engines made a throaty roar. Jets of water propelled the vessel, and the exhaust smelled like kerosene. From the bench seat at the stern, I searched for the dolphins. I should have been strong and stayed behind on Mokua.

Just thinking about diving the trench freaked me out. Oko's mantra was, *Listen to your inner voice.* Chief Aly had said, *Follow your instincts.* My mother's last words were, *Follow your heart and the ring will guide you.* My temples throbbed. The sky and the ocean screamed: *Don't go—stay on Mokua.*

Fins broke the surface and my eyes shot wide open. "The dolphins! Stop. Please stop."

Captain Wilkes glared at me as though I were a dumb child.

Miki and Kota skimmed over the water, then leapt high.

Wilkes eased the throttle. "You don't find white-sided dolphins around here," he said as Bola and Tali joined Miki and Kota in racing the bow.

"This pod has formed a special relationship with Sam," Oko said.

Kota leapt over the stern. Captain Wilkes cut the engines, and the *D-Sea 2* drifted forty metres from Mokua's sheer cliffs. With the sun behind the peak, the waterfall seemed to plummet from the sky. I stretched over the gunnels. Miki and Tali chirped and chattered and reached up to me.

My fear seemed to reflect in Tali's eyes, and I was sure it was her voice sounding in my mind: *You're not ready. Don't go to the darkness. You need to stay, find the pearl and ignite the treasure.*

Captain Wilkes stood. "I had a lot of respect for your father, Sam. His passing is a great loss."

Bewildered by the voice in my mind, I had to tear myself away from the dolphins to face Captain Wilkes. "Thanks ... and I'm sorry about your boat and crew."

"PFFFH." Miki and Tali exhaled and drew breath.

"My research team are on their way to New Zealand. I strongly recommend you follow suit. Get the hell out of here while you can."

I glanced up at the waterfall. Arriving aboard *Atlanta* already seemed like another lifetime. I needed to stay here on Mokua with the dolphins.

"You have a sub, and the hot zone is only sixty miles from here," Oko said.

"I want to find out what the hell Xcon is up to as much as you, Oko, but they sank my ship. My old colleagues in the Navy are telling me to keep away. It's coming from the top, the White House. There's a standoff between the Chinese and US navies in the Pacific, and I don't know why or how Trudock did it, but Xcon's corporate destroyers are patrolling the trench."

The hair bristled on the back of my neck at the mention of Trudock.

"We should just dive the drop-off here," I said.

Captain Wilkes stared at me as though I spoke in a foreign language.

"Mankind needs to know what's happening at the hot zone. We can motor there in two hours," Oko said.

Captain Wilkes stared at Oko, then to the open sea. "When did you last pilot a sub, Oko?"

"Testing last year in the Philippines," Oko lied.

"This is a new sub. You need familiarisation."

"Sam gets 100% on the simulator every time. He has been over this dive 100 times with Russell."

"With Russell gone, I don't want to be responsible for Sam's death," Captain Wilkes said.

My heart thumped. This was the perfect opportunity to draw back. I gripped my ring, turned it left, then right. My heart, my head, and even the dolphins told me to stay, but Oko believed this dive could save humanity. Without Oko, the assassin would have murdered me on Rangiroa.

The dolphins circled. I swallowed and shook my head.

"They murdered my dad, I don't want him to have died for nothing. Let's do it."

Oko and Captain Wilkes nodded with respect.

"But after the dive, I need to get straight back here to Mokua, right?" I said.

Captain Wilkes nodded.

Immediate regret knotted my stomach. I'd gone against my instincts because Oko was older and supposedly wiser. But it was adults who were responsible for global warming, and even Oko lied when it suited him.

"Wait here, I'll be back!" I called to the dolphins. The pod gave chase, but the *D-Sea 2* left them in its wake, skimming across the sea at thirty knots. Nothing about this mission felt right. I tried to picture arriving back at Mokua after the dive then having a great time at Lani's party, but I couldn't see it happening.

"Everything will be okay. I'll be back by morning," I whispered, but a hollow yearning told a different story. Mokua shrank into the golden afternoon light. In the distance, *Atlanta's* main, then foresail, took shape and I longed for Wiggols and Laurie's company.

"Single-handed sailing must be hard for Laurie," Oko said.

"He said he usually sails with the main, foresail, and one jib when he's by himself," I said.

The sky and sea were blue, and the sun was shining, but compared to the morning of swimming with Lani and the dolphins, it was as if I was on another planet. *What about the cavern? Did my mother make the mandala? And that spark, how did it make us glow and fall asleep?*

The *D-Sea 2* skipped over a wave, pierced the next. Jet engines thundered, ocean flashed by, and I noted the 150-degree heading. The ride was almost exciting at first, but the irregular pounding and jolting scattered my thoughts, and the motor roared too loud for conversation. And I wanted to say something. *Stop! Take me back to Mokua.* But with every second, the opportunity slipped farther from me.

The dive would be good. I'd trained for this. We might discover something that could stop the warming. Save Matahi Island. Save the dolphins. Avenge my dad. But no matter how hard I tried to keep positive, nervous energy swirled from the pit of my stomach up into my chest. An overwhelming thought that I'd betrayed my heart repeated.

"Are you okay?" Oko called.

I blinked and nodded.

"I am nervous too," Oko passed a blue booklet to me.

"For onward travel, I arranged for Captain Wilkes to bring a passport to conceal your identity when it's time to leave."

I opened the Hong Kong passport and squinted when I saw the picture of me and the name *Sam Yanzi*. Using Oko's second name was creepy. I realised how little I knew of Oko. Noise from the motors made communication difficult. "Do you have any kids?" I had to shout to be heard.

"A son. He's in the Chinese Navy," Oko said.

"Does he know about me?" I asked.

Oko nodded.

Flying fish flicked from the ocean, spread their pectoral wings and thudded into the hull. I turned to the sub, pictured myself and Oko submerging into the depths, and wanted to throw up.

The colour of the water turned the deepest purple as the *D-Sea 2* powered over the wall of the Tonga Trench. I closed my eyes and sensed something I couldn't explain radiating from the depths. Adrenalin pumped through my body. Wind whipped whitecaps from ragged swells as we raced across the deserted ocean toward the dirty cloud on the horizon.

The sea darkened, turned steely grey. Sweat soaked my shirt. A stench of rotten eggs poisoned the air. Oko reached for a towel and wiped his face. Brown haze swept across the deck. Captain Wilkes backed the throttle, and the hull eased into the water. My pulse raced. This patch of brine sucked my consciousness to the depths. There was something horrific down there. A shiver ran down my spine. The hair stood on my neck.

"Open the hatch, power up, conduct a systems check and call me on the radio," Captain Wilkes said.

Swells merged from opposite directions, confusing the sea. Oko hung on as I disengaged the lock and opened the weighty hatch. I descended to waist level, then folded myself into the primary pilot's seat. Oko followed, stepping on my leg as he crammed into position.

The hatch clanged shut. I flipped four switches. Oxygen flowed, and the computer initiated a systems check.

"*D-Sea 2, D-Sea 2*, this is *Sub-Rover*," I called.

"Roger, *Sub-Rover*, are you hearing me? Over."

"Hearing you. Systems checked okay."

"Not much different from the Mark One," Oko said.

Sweat trickled down my temples. I stared through a small porthole. Alarm bells rang. *Get the hell out of here*, the voice in my head screamed.

Captain Wilkes's voice sounded over the radio and echoed in my mind. "Fasten seat belts."

The capsule pressed in on me. I struggled to breathe.

"Breathe deep and slow," Oko said.

The stern gate groaned open, and muffled footsteps climbed up the sub. At this moment, I realised I wasn't getting out. This was it. I was going to dive the Tonga Trench, the hot zone—my dad's obsession.

A tie-down clanged loose.

I should have spoken earlier, but there was something I needed to say. "Oko, something terrible will happen if we go down. We have to abort."

The crane motor whirred; the sub jerked and slid back.

"Deep breaths, I'm nervous too," Oko said. "We dive, record the temperature, take water samples, film everything and head back to Mokua."

A swell slapped the spherical sub, clanging as it collided with the *D-Sea 2*. Under normal circumstances, divers steadied the sub. I peered through a porthole as Captain Wilkes lowered the sub. The blood-red sun neared the horizon. Water splashed, bubbles gushed, and I sucked in deep breaths. I was doing this for humanity. Everything would be okay.

Ten metres below, I shook my head and hit three keys in sequence. The computer checked hull integrity, oxygen, and battery levels. I gripped the joystick and checked the electric motors, wishing something would fail. But everything proved okay. I shut my eyes, swallowed, and depressed Speak on the transceiver.

"*D-Sea 2*, this is *Sub-Rover*, all systems go—Ready to drop."

"Roger, *Sub-Rover*, dropping in five, four, three, two, one."

Vertigo gripped me. We fell through 100 metres. Light from the sunset faded. Dusk swallowed us by 200 metres. My light-headedness and nausea subsided. I held my stomach and stared through a porthole. Maybe Oko was right. Maybe I was just nervous.

"Welcome to inner space," Oko said.

"*D-Sea 2*, this is *Sub-Rover*, we're approaching 1000 metres," I said.

"*D-Sea 2*, copy loud and clear," Captain Wilkes replied.

Bioluminescent creatures glowed in the pitch black. Only Oko's breathing disturbed the silence. The wall of the trench displayed on sonar, and we fell through multitudes of tiny glowing creatures.

I switched on the spotlights as we fell through 1500 metres. Thousands of tiny shrimp swarmed around the lights. At 2000 metres the swarm thinned, and at 3000 I flinched as the trench wall loomed in the spotlight, then blended back into blackness.

Water temperature climbed with depth. I felt a slight tremor, but Oko didn't react. At 4000 metres, water temperature peaked at 75 degrees Celsius, then decreased. Beyond all hope of rescue, falling through total blackness, I checked batteries, cameras, comms, and navigation. Oko sat beside me, but I felt alone.

Seven kilometres below, the temperature dropped to two degrees. Sonar displayed the bottom. I flicked a toggle; lead shot expelled from an exterior chute, slowing the descent. I focused a spotlight down. A moonscape materialised before my eyes.

Thrusters whirred and sediment clouded as the sub gently touched, then hovered a meter above the bottom. A body of water higher than Mount Kilimanjaro weighed above the flat featureless landscape: eerie, peaceful, and quiet. For a moment, my worries vanished into the alien world. Sediment whirled behind as I headed north, following small tracks on the trench floor.

"What are we looking for?" I asked, but I knew the answer: direct descent, five minutes on the bottom, look for anything unusual, ascend and study the western wall, during which time I would probably fall asleep.

"Anything unusual. The cameras will film everything," Oko said.

The tracks in the sediment thickened. There was something to the side of the tracks.

"Oh my god," I gasped. A plastic drink bottle lay on the bottom. "Human pollution down here."

Oko shook his head. "Disgusting isn't it."

I focused a spotlight on some turbulence in the distance. The forward thrust whirred. Black smoke and superheated bubbles gushed from a vent; a mass of prawn-like amphipods swarmed around the base. A creature like a giant centipede crawled toward the vent. We were strangers in the depths of darkness, seven kilometres deep, and I knew I should never have climbed into the sub.

The vent exploded. Black cloud spored. Magma glowed. Masses of bubbles churned.

I backed away and up.

"*D-Sea 2* to *Sub-Rover*—abort," crackled over the radio.

"*Sub-Rover* to *D-Sea 2*, what is the problem?" Oko asked.

I gawked at Oko as though he was crazy.

"Seismic activity—abort—begin your ascent," crackled over the radio.

"*Sub-Rover* to base, ascending," Oko said.

The orange glow of lava faded as we ascended amongst a mass of smoke and bubbles. Oko reached for the joystick, pushed my hand.

"Ascend near the wall," Oko said.

"We should go straight up."

Oko took control of the sub. "Just a little closer, view the wall, the source of the warming. We will never get this chance again."

The wall of the trench trembled. Rocks fell. I cursed Oko for his judgement and taking control. Infinite wisdom evaporated from my mentor. A reckless adult sat beside me. As we approached four kilometres, the hottest layer of water, the tremors subsided. I saw the heat as red. A massive cloud of dense black smoke billowed from the wall above. "Back away from the black cloud!" I urged.

But something moved within the cloud, and Oko manoeuvred closer. I focused the spotlight on a crater the size of an ocean liner.

"Move away from the wall!" I reached for the joystick, pulled Oko's hand.

Black smoke gushed from the crater. Lava cooled black on a ledge. Something moved. Two red lights the size of our capsule blazed through the smoke. The lights transformed to eyes. A giant tongue flicked.

"Ah!" Oko shouted.

"Ah!" I yelled.

The serpent-like predator recoiled to strike.

I jerked the joystick back, hit emergency ascent, and stared into the serpent's eye.

As if it acknowledged me, the enormous beast hesitated for a second then lids closed over its eyes. Enormous jaws opened. The serpent struck. Giant fangs clanged into the sub.

An alarm rang. Jets of hot water blasted me. The sub's lights went out.

67

EXPLODED

It was 1:30 am when Atlo left his desk and entered the situation room adjoining his office. There on the top left screen, in the fading light, he saw billowing murk cloud up from the Tonga Trench. Then the sea erupted.

"Zoom in on Wilkes," Atlo said.

The camera zoomed in on Captain Wilkes who turned from the heat and shielded his face. On the top left screen, the sub spat from the churning sea 200 metres away from the *D-Sea 2*. Atlo watched as Wilkes powered toward the sub. A white light flashed. The *D-Sea 2* exploded.

"Nice shot." Atlo clapped his hands.

Two inflatables and a line of jet skis shot from the stern of his destroyer and bounced over the seething water to the mini-sub. Three men boarded the sub and the top left screen beamed from the boarding commander's cam as they wrestled with the hatch.

"Pass the oxy torch," called one of his men.

The inflatables held the sub steady as the oxy torch flared and cut through the twisted hinge. When the hatch opened, the kid's face stared up and he reached to pull himself out of the hatch. Atlo glimpsed the ring on his finger before two of his men arm-locked the kid and a third tried to twist the ring from his finger. It looked as if it was stuck. Atlo winced as he saw one of his soldiers draw a knife.

"Commander, take the kid back to the destroyer," Atlo thought about Atlo Junior as he gave the order. "Get the ring and kill the kid humanely. Leave the Asian in the sub. Make sure you get the data pack."

Atlo cut the South Pacific feed and returned to his office. Now that he possessed the ring and had put an end to Russell Edwards' plans, it was time to implement a strategy that would surprise everyone.

68

JOLT

Someone stomped their heel into my hand. Excruciating pain shot though me. Bodies crowded everywhere, pinning me down. They grabbed my ring and pulled and twisted so hard I thought they would tear my finger from my hand. The pull relented and the next thing I knew I was falling and crashed onto the floor of an inflatable.

Men with guns surrounded me. I fought to my knees. Dinghies and jet skis crowded around us. The boiling sea reeked of sulphur. Flames leapt from a nearby vessel.

"Where's Captain Wilkes?" I asked.

No one answered. A ship with a sharp bow and dome top, like a massive version of the *D-Sea 2* with cannons, loomed close.

"Get my friend! Oko's still in there!" I said.

A man shoved his boot into my chest, pushing me back-first onto the floor. Another man climbed from the sub and jumped into the inflatable with the sub's data pack.

"Your friend's dead," he said.

"No! Get Oko. He's just unconscious." I spied the empty slot in the data pack and tucked the video card deeper into my pocket.

"We'll look after your friend," said a man in a flack vest holding a rifle.

The inflatable pulled away.

In desperation I struggled to my feet, but a man rammed his rifle into my ribs. Air gushed from my lungs. I collapsed. Five armed men in flak jackets sat on inflatable pontoons above me.

"Who are you? Do you work for Xcon?" I asked. Nobody answered, but it had to be Xcon. I eased up to see what in hell was happening.

"That's as far as you go." The man beside me shoved a pistol into my head.

Flames subsided as the burning vessel sank. It dawned that it was the *D-Sea 2* burning. "Where is Captain Wilkes?" I asked, but they ignored me.

A dozen jet skis surrounded the inflatable I was in; others raced ahead and charged toward the high-tech destroyer.

"Did you get Oko—have you got my friend?" I pleaded. I wanted to jump overboard, but with no sun I didn't have much energy, and there was a gun pointed at my head.

"Your friend is dead," the man with the gun said.

"No. He's still alive," I pleaded, "You've got to save him or you'll pay, all of you. Atlo Trudock killed my dad. I'm going to bring Trudock—and the whole of Xcon down."

The gunmen laughed. "Trudock will eat you for breakfast, kid," one of them said.

The lead inflatable sped up a ramp into the stern of the destroyer. The jet skis followed. A cannon on the destroyer's stern flashed.

Flames burst from the mini-sub. Spouts of water shot into the air. The sub sank into the depths.

"No!" I chopped the pistol away from my head, bounced to my feet and crashed my foot into the driver's chest, kicking him off the boat. A sudden jolt shot the dinghy up out of the water. I fell to the floor. The violent impact sent the four gunmen sitting on the pontoons tumbling backwards, legs kicking up as they toppled backwards overboard.

I grabbed the ropes around the pontoons as the dinghy shot skyward like a roller coaster. *How was this possible?* Higher and higher I surged, the destroyer now below me. *What was lifting me?* I dragged myself up and saw armour-like scales.

The dinghy balanced on the serpent's head, its massive body thrusting from the water. Petrified of alerting the creature to my presence, I swallowed a scream. I thought to jump, but the giant creature surged up over the destroyer, higher and higher.

Cannons flashed, exploding over the serpent and blinding me. My ears screeched. Air caught under the inflatable. My knuckles whitened around the ropes on either side of the pontoons.

The monster lunged for the destroyer. The inflatable flipped.

I swung beneath the upturned craft. Below me, the serpent's enormous body dwarfed the destroyer. The creature bellowed a mournful cry and plunged, smashing into the centre of the destroyer. Only the bow and stern remained above water, pointing straight up.

The inflatable swung and twisted, slowing my free-fall, but the serpent's scaly body still arched above the ocean beneath me. I leaned, gliding the inflatable away. I thought I'd cleared the monster, but I fell quicker than expected. The inflatable clipped the serpent's body and swung, smashing me into the armoured scales.

Light flashed in my head. The ropes tore from my hands. Darkness closed in. I tumbled limp-bodied through the air and plunged into the raging ocean.

69

TERROR

Energy blades clashed. I fought with Tom guarding my back. My dad and Swathi climbed into the loft carrying scones with clotted cream and mango jam. A wonderful, loving warm sensation made me smile, but something out of my control annoyed me. I frowned, blasted a drone. But there again, disturbing my bliss, a splash, something warm lapping my neck. For some reason, Tom and Swathi didn't even react when I floated away. The annoying lapping persisted. I opened my eyes and gasped.

Steam surrounded me. I floated on my back. Something propped beneath me, holding me up. I turned my head, sank into the smelly hot water, and leaned back. The sea stank of rotten eggs and fog cut visibility to a few metres.

Whatever lay beneath me was unstable and barely kept me afloat. I closed my eyes, wishing I could go back to the dream. Images of Oko and that giant serpent overwhelmed me, and I needed to find out what was underneath me. I craned my neck, and a section of ribbed flotation slid from beneath.

My legs sank. Shark and serpent alarms sounded. I clutched for the ribbed flotation, but it sank, and a bloated white face with bulging eyes stared up from just below the surface.

"Awr," I whimpered, pushing the corpse away. "Help—Laurie, Miki, Kota!"

Visions of sharks and the serpent reaching for my legs made me panic.

"Help!" I screamed, not caring if gunmen found me.

"Help," I sobbed. Anything to escape this terror.

Silence throbbed through the stinking fog. Seconds ticked. Sheer panic was impossible to sustain, and shards of rational thought returned. I could take the flotation jacket from the corpse, but it wasn't drowning that worried me.

I breast stroked through the ocean from hell, looking for something else to latch onto and get me out of the water. My mind jumped from the serpent, to sharks, to the sub exploding. The ocean was seven kilometres deep. Thick rotten-egg smog blinded me. I glimpsed something dark, but it vanished into fog.

Treading water, I peered into the murky brine. I couldn't even see my legs. Seconds passed. No shark attacked. There it was again, black and bobbing, but not coming towards me.

Heart palpitating, I stroked through the hot, stinky water. With five metres to cover, I broke into an overarm sprint, trembled as I mounted the jet ski, and stood over the seat.

"Thank you," I shouted, throwing fists to the heavens.

I rested my arms on the handlebars and inhaled relief. My heart slowed and I caught my breath. I wondered if Captain Wilkes had survived, and torrents of memories battered me: Oko, the sub, the *D-Sea 2,* and that humongous serpent. No wonder I was so freaked out by the trench. No flag or name stood out on the destroyer, but it must have been Xcon. I nodded. Xcon had murdered my dad and now Oko and probably Captain Wilkes. I clenched my teeth and struggled through my wet pocket to check for the video card from the sub. The cameras must have caught footage of the creature, and with luck, some shots of the destroyer and the inflatables on the surface.

"Xcon is not getting away with this," I shoved the card deep into my left pocket and remembered Laurie's gift. From my right pocket, I took the black pouch, loosened the drawstring and tipped the silver chain into my palm. Laurie had spaced the six black pearls with tubular white shell, and the delicate carving of two dolphins looked magnificent in the centre, a gift to impress the richest princess.

Just above the east horizon, a round orb pierced the fog with an eerie glow. It was morning, and the jet ski didn't look damaged. If it started, I could still make Princess Lani's party. Chief Aly and Lani would help me.

I pictured myself describing the serpent: armoured scales, blazing eyes, and me riding on the monster's head. *Who would believe me?* But oh, how it had crushed that destroyer. The serpent must be the source of the warming, but if Xcon were hiding the creature, why did it sink their boat? I was missing a piece to the puzzle, something to do with the ring and my mother. And if Trudock was willingly heating the earth for profit or even just letting it happen, he should be jailed for crimes against humanity.

The jet ski key was in the ignition and turned to the on position. I pressed the start button, but nothing happened. I opened the fuel cap, gripped the handlebars and shook. Not full, but more than half. No ignition lights lit when I turned the key off, then on. I pressed the start button and shook my head; it was probably a flat battery or water in the electrics.

At least I was out of the water. I wondered if others had survived. I searched for a way to access the battery and slid a lever to unlatch the seat. In the compartment below I found a water bottle, a tool pouch, and a small anchor on a rope.

The sight of the bottle made me realise how thirsty I was. I unscrewed the stainless steel bottle, sniffed the contents, and drank. Beneath the seat, a cover unclipped to access the battery, but everything looked dry; the connections felt tight and the fuses seemed okay. I replaced the cover and the water bottle, closed the seat, and wondered how long I could survive drifting on the jet ski.

"Find a way," I whispered.

The corpse had drifted close. I screwed up my face, swallowed a dry retch, and in my periphery spied a red-spiralled cord attached to the corpse's wrist.

My heart skipped a beat.

"The dead man's switch!" I studied the ignition panel and located the pin with the missing circlip.

That was it! I lifted the seat and removed the small anchor. The lead claw splashed into the water, then hooked the corpse as I pulled the cord. My hands trembled as I removed the red cord, then using my foot, I pushed the corpse gently away.

The grommet slid into the slot. The pin lifted—the dashboard lit.

"Please … please," I closed my eyes and pressed the start button. The motor choked, and spluttered, then whirred to life.

I stood and pumped a fist to the sky.

"Yes!" I bellowed long and loud, beat my chest, and sat ready to take on the world.

I glanced at the corpse, eased the throttle, and the jet ski purred away. Cruising at eight knots, I swerved around debris. The fog seemed to go on forever. I resisted the urge to speed away and concentrated on dodging semi-submerged panels that must have been part of the destroyer. Gradually the fog thinned.

The bow lifted as I squeezed the throttle and the ski settled at fifteen knots. Patches of blue water began to appear. The rotten-egg stink eased. When the sky turned brilliant blue, I squeezed the throttle to full and burst from the fog into the glittering Pacific.

"Woo!" I hooted, getting air from a rising swell. Spray erupted as I landed and freshened my face. The coast was clear, no islands or boats anywhere. Glad I'd kept note of the course on the way to the dive, I locked onto to a 330-degree reciprocal heading, wondering how far a jet ski travelled with two-thirds of a tank.

Racing used more fuel, so I tried cruising at different speeds and found that at 25 knots the engine hummed and the ski skimmed over swells. At this rate, I would reach Mokua in two and a half hours, in time to meet Princess Lani.

The current swept the hot trench water south to the pole. The foggy cloud faded into the distance and the ocean cooled as I raced in a northwest direction. I stood to power over a wave and thought of Oko, and the giant creature venting superheated water. If I'd dug my heels in when I'd sensed danger, Oko might still be alive. I shook my head. Oko and Dad had not died in vain. Xcon and Trudock would pay. But from now on, I had to follow my heart and never again go against my instincts. When I snapped back to the present, I searched for the dolphins. Something told me they were near, and I hoped I hadn't missed them. The sun shone from a pale blue sky. I angled over a crest and shot into the air. Spray exploded as I landed.

After an hour, a bump appeared on the horizon. Nervous energy stirred as Mokua Peak gathered form. The fuel gauge dipped under half, and a line of cloud formed behind the distant island.

A gusty wind ruffled swells. The engine pitch rose as I accelerated, worried the weather might turn nasty. I stood to absorb hard landings on crumbling waves. The hand that the Xcon crony stomped on ached. But my spirits lifted as Mokua grew before my eyes. I pictured racing into the lagoon, stepping from the jet ski, and marching up the beach to Lani: "Princess Lani, please accept my humble gift." *What would she say? How would she receive me?* Lani had almost ignored me when she left Mokua. But we were in trouble for being late. I remembered the kiss, her scent, the softness of her lips, and I longed to be alone with her again.

Mokua became more defined: the peak, palms, green jungle, Rocky Point. Behind the island, clouds darkened. The wind backed, calmed for ten minutes, then came straight at me.

I launched from a crest. The wind held me in the air. I landed hard in a trough; the stern dug in, and I turned my head as blinding water drilled my face.

The wind strengthened, and the sea turned short and lumpy. My progress slowed, but Mokua grew as I smashed through waves and spray. The sky behind the island blackened, but the sun shone on the lagoon. I looked at the fuel gauge and swallowed: less than an eighth of a tank left.

The wind strengthened to a forty-knot gale and chilled me to a shiver. My eyes stung, hand and back ached. I slowed, stood high on the ski, and in the distance Lani's cruiser and another larger vessel bobbed in the lagoon. The fuel gauge read empty, zero, nothing left.

I gazed to the heavens, closed my eyes to pray and powered into the wind. One minute later the engine slowed, sped up, spluttered, and the revs faded to nothing. The engine stopped.

"No … No!" I clenched the handgrips, stood, and stared at the calm water along the lee cliffs. I was still a long way out—too far to swim. With telescopic vision, I studied the boats in the lagoon. Even with binoculars, there was little chance of anyone spotting me.

Wind blustered loud in my ears, buffeted my wet clothes. I sank forward over the petrol tank, resting my head on my hands.

"Find a way," I tapped the fuel tank, stared at the cap, took the key from the ignition, and opened it. Petrol fumes wafted, but I couldn't see any fuel. The jet ski rolled, and the tank made a hollow splash. My eyes adjusted and spied fuel at the bottom. I replaced the cap, searched beneath the tank and found the fuel tap pointing to ON, with OFF ninety degrees below, and the letter R on the other side.

Reserve! I turned the tap to R, took a deep breath, and pressed start. The engine whirred but didn't start. Swells lapped over my feet, the ski pointed beam on into the wind, pushing from the island. I hit start again. The engine spluttered, and I released the start button as the battery struggled. I imagined the engine starting and the fabulous sensation of speeding into the safety of the lagoon. After fifteen seconds, I hit start again. The engine sparked and revved to life.

Goosebumps stood on my arms and neck. The jet ski whirred, and I charged to Mokua. With only a trickle of fuel, I streamlined and beat steadily into the wind. As I neared, the island came to life. Another cruiser pulled into the sheltered lagoon. Guests congregated on the beach, and I tried to spot Lani. The wind stayed strong, but the swell died and chop abated as I neared the cliffs. Dark clouds framed the peak where I'd stood with Lani just yesterday morning.

The island was within reach, and at the end of the lagoon I spotted a solitary figure wearing a white dress. My heart stuttered. Lani stood on Dolphin Rock and stared straight at me.

"Lani!" I shouted and waved but she looked away.

I accelerated. Ocean flashed past, swell abated, and except for bulleting gusts, the wind eased. Sheer cliffs loomed. Chief Aly and Lani would ask about Oko as soon as I arrived. My lips trembled. What would I tell them? I didn't want to ruin the party. Just give Lani the present, say Oko couldn't make it … apologise for Oko and wait for the right moment. I needed to view the video card before mentioning the serpent, and I shivered as I recalled how Chief Aly saw right through me.

The motor sputtered. I gasped and revved, but the motor died.

70

OUT OF JUICE

I gripped handfuls of my hair. Wind funnelled from the cliffs. A patch of dark water raced toward me. I smelled tropical forest as the wind hit and pushed the Jet Ski from Mokua. Where was the pod? I could easily swim now, but where were the dolphins? The closest point to the sheer cliffs, with no trails or climbing rocks, was a one-kilometre swim. A point where I could climb was much farther, maybe two kilometres. The distance didn't worry me so much as fear of Rambala.

Another bullet of wind swept the ocean, blasting me farther away. My eyes zoomed in on the lagoon and the sand spit. People milled under a marquee, some in suits and others in bright tropical colours. Must be three kilometres to the lagoon, I guessed. My t-shirt dripped, and I shivered as another gust struck, then two in succession.

The safest thing to do was wait on the jet ski. I would be easier to spot. Surely someone would see me, or Miki and Tali would come. A strong wind blasted. The jet ski heeled, and wake formed as it surged from Mokua. *But what if I drifted for days? What if Xcon captured me?*

In the sparkling distance, Princess Lani walked to the end of the sand spit, to Dolphin Rock. She was looking for me. I stood, took my shirt off, and waved it above my head.

"Lani!" I shouted, but she didn't look my way. I sat back on the seat, shook the jet ski and pressed the start button again. The motor whirred to life. My eyes widened, but the motor coughed and stopped.

What the heck was I going to do? I turned the ring on my finger to the left and to the right. At least I'd made it this close. Standing to lift the seat, I took the water bottle and drank until it was empty. Wind swooped again, pushing me even farther away. I opened the mini-tool pouch, removed the biggest screwdriver, inserted it into my back pocket and clicked the seat back into position.

Shorts, T-shirt, runners, a video card, wallet, soggy passport, and the necklace for Lani were all I had left. A sharp bullet of wind struck. I raised my arm to shelter my face. As the wind subsided, I patted the tank and assessed the cliffs and the lagoon. Lightning flashed behind the island and I dived into the blue.

My pulse raced as I hit the sea, exposed in deep water. I controlled the urge to panic by concentrating on my hands cutting the surface. Out of the wind, the water felt warm, and I settled into a rhythm when something dark loomed before me.

Just seaweed. I swam past it then stopped to tread water. The jet ski bobbed on a crest two hundred metres away. Fear of Rambala and the serpent made me want to swim back to the ski.

The memory of swimming away from the corpse, and how panic eventually subsided, gave me the strength to turn and swim for the island. But thoughts of the serpent and Rambala returned.

"When mind and soul synchronise, the universe conspires to protect you," I said, and, as fear returned, I repeated the words that Oko had told me over and over in my mind. My hands pierced wallowing pearly sheets. Bubbles streamed from my fingertips. White dust-like particles floated all around, and sunrays streamed through the infinite blue. The heavens flickered and I swam faster.

A jut in the cliff gave me a reference to gauge how far I'd swum. After stroking for half an hour, the jut passed well behind me, and I was much closer to the island and the lagoon. I resisted looking back for the jet ski and headed more directly for the island. This meant a longer swim to where I could climb the cliffs, but instincts guided me closer to Mokua. My progress inspired me, and generated energy. As I neared Mokua, the current swept me along the cliffs toward the lagoon.

A bouncing swell elevated me. I glimpsed waves breaking along the lagoons outer reef. With less than a kilometre to go, all I could do to keep my mind from murder and death was to picture myself striding from the lagoon and Princess Lani running to the water's edge to meet me.

The sun was past overhead. Probably two o'clock, six hundred metres to swim. Lightning flashed. Mokua Peak obscured the clouds. Thunder crackled and boomed. The invitation had said from 11 am. A fleeting shadow passed over as a white helicopter beat overhead.

Thinking guests might start leaving, I swam harder. The current strengthened, sweeping me toward the lagoon. The helicopter disappeared near the sand spit, but soon took off and skirted around the island. I didn't think Lani would leave in a chopper. Dark clouds swirled over the island.

The entrance to the lagoon was in sight, less than 400 metres away. I drew rapid strokes and surged with the current. Raindrops tumbled and dark clouds covered the sun. A wave barrelled along the reef to my right. With energy spent, I focused on the lagoon entrance and let the current sweep me: one hundred metres to go.

Thunder racked the heavens. Tropical rain pelted and blanketed a cruiser leaving the lagoon. From the depths of my being, I summoned remnants of energy and swam, but the cruiser vanished into sheets of rain. Impossible as it seemed, the rain got harder and the shadow of another boat left the lagoon.

"No," I moaned and tried to swim faster. My arms and legs couldn't respond. I floated to within thirty metres of the bombora. Rain pelted and bounced on the water. A throb pierced the torrential batter.

"Help," I yelled, but rain and thunder drowned my cry.

Two boats gone, one left in the lagoon. The shadow of the third boat loomed through the downpour. The current swept me toward it. Lightning flashed, illuminating Princess Lani peering from the boat.

"Lani! Lani!" I screamed, as thunder ripped across the heavens.

71

WORST FEAR

A curtain of rain swallowed the boat. Heavy drops splattered against my face. I shut my eyes and floated, lost to the sound of my breath and pelting rain. When I turned to swim for the lagoon, current rushed me past the second bombora.

I drew weak breaststrokes, strained for the fringing reef, but the current dragged me toward Rocky Point. Shark Cove lay beyond. Thoughts of Rambala gliding below my feet lurched into mind.

The torrential rain eased to pouring. Swimming diagonally across the current, I fought for the tip of Rocky Point, clutched for submerged rocks, desperate to avoid Shark Cove.

Dark clouds blotted the sun. "Tali, Miki," I whimpered. The current whipped me around Rocky Point to the drop-off at Shark Cove. A sudden jolt forced my attention to the depths. Currents eddied and swirled and no longer controlled me. Mist floated over green water. The depths radiated with a magnetic attraction. The shore was a hundred-metre swim.

I pulled steady strokes, swam for the pebble beach, trying to convince myself that sharks roamed over thousands of miles, that Rambala had probably left long ago. The rain eased to a shower. Sunlight fought through thinning clouds. Fat, irregular raindrops bounced, distorting the reflection of the sky and the island on the green water. A fishy smell wafted.

The edge of the drop-off loomed ten metres ahead, the shore seventy. My heart thumped. I pulled fast breaststrokes and didn't dare look beneath the water. The fin appeared in my mind a second before I saw it.

The rounded fin barely cut the surface, then disappeared. "Please be a dolphin." I knew that it wasn't and shot a glance to the shore. The sun had given me some energy, but sharks swam fast. I glanced out to sea: "Miki, Tali, please save me!" Not seeing the fin was even more terrifying.

I submerged my eyes and lifted my legs. The water darkened. Rambala cruised beneath me.

I hit the afterburners, swam like an Olympic champion, but as I approached the drop-off wall, the rounded fin cut the surface—and kept on coming.

Was this the end? I stopped and drew the screwdriver from my pocket.

The massive tiger shark cruised with jaws agape, flicked its tail, and surged.

Its sudden acceleration stunned me. My knuckles whitened around the screwdriver. The shark's pink gums and triangular teeth formed a savage smile.

My mind blanked. Reflexes kicked in. I rolled right, stabbed for the shark's eye. Its massive jaw rammed me, striking my head and shoulder.

Light flashed in my head. My ears rang. A pectoral fin sent me tumbling. Bubbles gurgled. Blood seeped from my shoulder. I floated face-down, clutching the screwdriver.

Rambala had vanished.

I raced for shore, but the shark charged up under me.

In a wave of froth, I broke the surface on the shark's head. I bounced on its striped back. The dorsal fin smashed into my stomach, doubling me over it.

The shark thrashed its tail.

I held on to the fin.

Rambala dived.

I clamped onto the dorsal fin like a remora.

Rambala descended.

I searched for the screwdriver, couldn't remember dropping it. *What did it matter?* The screwdriver was a measly weapon. The shark would soon flick me off. I would soon be dead.

The shark continued to dive, and I equalised my ears. Dense muscle propelled the tiger shark in a steady sweeping motion. Surprised to be alive, I equalised again, and crazy as it seemed, I admired the subtle striping on the shark's back.

The drop-off wall blurred. The ocean darkened. A shimmering patch of surface light shrank and faded to a distant flicker. Deeper and deeper the shark descended, until depth swallowed light.

Suddenly the shark twisted, flicking me loose. I hovered in the dusky darkness, an alien in the deep, waiting for jaws to rip and thrash me about.

Seconds passed. Even with excellent night vision, I struggled to see shapes. I wondered why Rambala hadn't attacked, finished the job. I ascended, knowing each moment should be my last when a hum—a subtle vibration—caught my attention.

I turned to the drop-off wall. A hint of light beckoned me through the dusky darkness and my ring vibrated like crazy. As I stroked toward the light, the call grew stronger, pulling me. Faint light became a glow and strengthened to illuminate a cavity in the volcanic wall.

I gripped jagged rocks on either side of the entrance and pulled myself in. A whispering soprano chorus led me along a narrow tunnel to a radiant blue-green glow. Ecstasy pulsed through my heart as the tunnel opened into a cavern.

Before me lay a giant clam, its waves of emerald and electric-blue flesh glowing in the crystal-clear water. I searched the craggy ceiling for an air pocket, somewhere to take a breath. There were no air pockets, but a chorus of angels rejuvenated every cell in my body and relaxed me.

I knelt on the sand and bowed before the creature. Instinctively, I reached forward with the back of my hand and my ring chinked against the shell.

The clam juddered, its colossal jaws inching farther open and casting a wavering light on shadowy nooks. The jaws extended to reveal a tubular siphon, like a black hole, in the centre of its flesh. Inside the black hole, deep within the clam, something twinkled.

Wary of the massive serrated jaws, I moved closer. The flesh shivered. Radiant light shone on my face. With water so clear, I forgot I was 400 metres beneath the surface. The twinkle inside the clam intensified. I craned my neck and, through the siphon, beheld electric blue and green colours swirling inside a pearl. I gasped, choked on water, and coughed.

Bubbles domed on the rocks overhead. I closed my eyes to steady myself. When I recovered, the pearl shone like a star. Angelic tones resounded through the deep-sea cavern. The pearl enthralled me, demanded I grasp the treasure. The siphon was easily big enough to reach through, but what if the clam closed?

I turned the ring on my finger and stared in awe at the magical creature. My hand shook. I hesitated, then reached through the tubular siphon. Tingles fluttered through my body as I withdrew my arm.

Blue and emerald waves swirled within the pearl. It was about the size of a large cherry and shone like a blue star in my palm. The clam shuddered, inched closed. I became conscious of how long I'd been underwater, without a sip of air. I'd never stayed under this long. I gazed at my treasure five seconds longer, thanked the clam, and pulled myself through the tunnel into dark open water.

With the pearl grasped firmly in my hand, I ascended. Its glow shone through my fingers. I couldn't wait to study the treasure on the surface. Up and up I swam until distant light swelled, expanding to a shimmering patch.

Rambala cruised above me, his white belly blending with the surface. I clenched my teeth and ascended toward the imposing creature. At thirty metres below the surface, I drew level.

The enormous shark swam toward me. All this time, Rambala had been trying to guide me to the pearl. He was the most powerful, majestic creature that I've ever seen. Although I knew that he was protecting me, my pulse raced, and I had to fight the urge to panic as his giant head brushed against me.

Thank you! I said with my heart, hoping that somehow he heard me. Pushing off his jaw, I continued my ascent. Rambala circled back, below this time, and sun waves rippled across his striped back as the giant merged with the silent depths.

72

MOTHER

Gentle swells trundled and collapsed in the shallows. I kept my centre of gravity low and clambered up Shark Cove's boulder-lined shore. On a sandy patch I stopped to watch Rambala disappear beyond the drop-off.

I opened my hand and stared in wonder. Electric blue and green colour swirled through the pearl. It vibrated like crazy, shone brilliant white, and heated my hand. I held the treasure at arm's length as translucent shockwaves exploded from it.

My hair and clothes were buffeted as if hit by a tornado. My hand clamped shut. Blinding white light streamed through my grasp. I shielded my face with my free arm, expecting to collapse. Three seconds later my hand glowed red with light beams slipping through my fingers.

Thunder rumbled across the seas, and the light beams retracted into my hand. I dropped the arm shielding my eyes. My fingers twitched open, millimetres at a time. I knew the pearl was from my mother, but what the heck was the explosion about?

The sun burst from behind the storm cell. Wet boulders glistened. Rich bass tones vibrated in my ears. The sky, the sea, and the island combined with my consciousness as a single resonating entity. The ring from my mother, the insane voyage to Mokua, all the crazy events, made sense.

In a way, Oko had been right. Humanity needed to know about the serpent in the trench, but I wished that Oko had listened. We could have found it another way, and both survived.

Facing Rambala, discovering the pearl, and then the blinding explosion left me in a supercharged euphoric state. Photius circled the summit of the peak. The dolphins were sure to return, and it occurred to me that someone could still be at Lagoon Beach. I checked the video card and the necklace, pushed the pearl into my wet pocket, and jumped from boulder to boulder up the rise.

Loose stones clanged as I crested Rocky Point. Below, the rain had smoothed thousands of footprints on Lagoon Beach.

"Hello!" I shouted.

Wonderful golden-brown light filtered through the anvil storm. Lightning flickered out to sea.

"Hello," I shouted again.

Distant thunder rumbled, and the glassy lagoon mirrored the storm. I gazed at the shelters and remembered the gear in the cave. I could survive on the island for years. Plenty of coconuts, plantain trees, and breadfruit; I could spear fish and collect the best fresh water. The only thing missing was a mango tree. And the dolphins … but the pod would return.

I scanned the lagoon and the waters beyond, turned to the summit, and my eyes zoomed onto Photius gliding updrafts of wind. The falcon streamlined into a dive and swooped.

A blur of talons and wings shot towards my face. I raised my arms to absorb the collision, but Photius slowed to a hover right in front of me.

A breeze ruffled the falcon's mottled feathers. I lowered my hands. Our eyes locked, and visions—like memories, but not my own—lifted me.

As if I were in the falcon's body, I flew up over the sand. My mother stood before the palm as the sun peeped over the edge of the world. I beat my wings, soared into a perfect blue sky to glide above the peak. On the ledge at Island Pool, there again, my mother gazing up at me. The vision faded into darkness, and her emerald eyes shone in the cave beneath the mandala.

With a snap of wings, Photius launched into the heavens. I shivered with the mandala etched into my mind.

I strode up Rocky Point. Finches flittered in the fleshy scrub, and water from the storm cascaded down the greasy path. The waterfall echoed through the forest. Wet leaves and trunks glistened, and torrents of sheeting water thundered as I emerged at Cove Pool. I smiled as I recalled Lani's fake surprise when she'd slipped down the chute.

From the fall, I ran and scrambled up to the lookout where I'd spotted the chief at dawn. I scoured the ocean, but still no dolphins. Returning to the trail, I continued the final ascent.

The air smelled of steaming rock and earth, and the atmosphere vibrated as I strode from the trail onto the ledge surrounding the island pool. Grey and brown rock, forming the volcanic cone, deepened in colour and glistened with moisture. Brown light filtered through the towering thunderstorm, the bottom of the cell now floating at eye level.

A vision of Princess Lani walking around the pool in her bikini brought a smile to my face. I imagined living on Mokua with Lani and the dolphins, living from the island without a worry in the world. What an awesome adventure that would be. And I thought how my mother must have stood right here on this ledge, and the freak sequence of events that had led me to this point.

From the infinity edge, I dived into the crisp fresh water and swam to the shadowy tunnel. Without stopping at the breathing space, I continued through liquid darkness to the cavern. Splashes and drips echoed as I pulled myself out of the watery entrance. Soft brown light penetrated the floor-level vents. The pearl glowed in my hand, and water dripped down my legs as I crept toward the centre of the cavern.

My whole body tingled as I edged nearer, stepped up onto the stone platform, and stood under the circular mandala. As I held it near, the pearl illuminated the maze-like grooves burnt into the stone. A gentle "chuck-chuck-chuck" issued from a gecko clutching to the underside of the cavern.

I reached up and traced the grooves with my finger. The pattern matched those on my ring. In slow motion, a blue spark jumped from the mandala to my forehead and my body started glowing.

Distant whispers called out to me. My eyelids felt heavy. I yawned, crouched, and lay on the stone platform. Emerald haze drifted from the mandala. I held the pearl and the ring to my heart. A soothing hum buzzed in my ears. My consciousness drifted.

* * *

A vast night sky twinkled. I floated in space, safe and snug in an impenetrable cocoon. Magnificent stars sparkled white, except one that twinkled green, then blue. This star came closer and transformed into an angel.

Her emerald eyes glowed with love as she leaned over, reached behind my head and chest and drew a translucent form from my body. I snuggled as the angel clutched me to her bosom and her heavenly voice called my name.

With one hand under my head and the pearl clutched to my heart, I lay on my side under the mandala. I rubbed my chin against my shoulder, and again someone called me.

As though in a dream, I opened my eyes and beheld the most beautiful image I'd ever seen. Emerald eyes, silky black hair, and a smile that ignited joy and bliss.

"Mother," I said.

My mother reached forward, touched my lips, and nodded.

I hovered in a vast sky with my mother. Warmth filled my heart. The Milky Way whirled around us, then faded, and I faced another spiralling galaxy.

It was as though the universe shrank, and I cruised with my mother as a peripheral presence. Billions of stars swirled in stunning radial arms. It was the Andromeda Galaxy opening before me.

I wanted to slow down, gaze at my mother's smile, ask questions and talk, but as though set on a predetermined course, I drifted to a solar system orbiting two suns. An enormous blue planet loomed. The universe expanded and I became minuscule.

I stood in bright sunshine on the peak of a snow-capped mountain. One side of the mountain plummeted to the sea; the other towered above a rugged range that formed a protective rim around the lowlands. The sheer rocky faces of the mountains dropped to hills covered by dense jungle. Towards the coast, the jungle gave way to rolling grasslands and a river delta, where unspoiled rivers flowed through coastal valleys to meet the sparkling ocean by a white stone city.

"This is Megasis. Altus City lies in the distance," my mother said.

I inhaled fresh alpine air. A cloud swirled over the peak, and I brushed snowflakes from my shoulder.

"Your forefathers carved our palace into the base of this mountain, 18000 metres below us."

I shuffled forward and peered over the icy ledge. Vertical cliffs plummeted to the sea. Two suns shone in the sky above. *Did it ever get dark on this planet? Was this the reason behind my solar narcolepsy?* Questions flowed, but try as I might, I couldn't ask them.

"Four millennia ago Batavian, your direct ancestor, discovered the Cintamani Pearl embedded in the peak of this volcano."

An ancient wooden door opened behind me, revealing a cavern much bigger than Mokua's, with intricate paintings and a mandala, larger but otherwise identical to the one my body lay under.

"Megasis was the centre of a noble empire that ruled Andromeda until the Coaliferite invasion." The mountain dropped away. I hovered in the stratosphere above Megasis,

"The astral warriors of Megasis were the galaxy's most powerful force." Mother's voice sounded in my head, but I couldn't see her and swung around. Wide-eyed, I hovered amongst tens of thousands of grey-battle-suit-clad astral warriors with wrist armour and luminous medallions in the centres of their chests.

"The carbon breathing Coaliferite Nation attacked Megasis."

A massive dark cloud dominated the sky above me.

"Mother!" I called.

No one seemed to notice I was there. Above me, Dark Matter swirled and threatened; shadows moved within the darkness. The shadows grouped into a solid mass, and the Dark Matter flashed.

Red blast-fire rained down. A wall of blood-red warriors catapulted toward me.

I swung my arms, backstroked behind the front line. The astral warriors recoiled their arms and thrust; white blasts shot from the heels of their palms. From nowhere, green- and blue-edged blades ignited in their hands.

"Help! Mother!" I shouted.

The Coaliferite troops clashed into the astral warriors with sickening velocity. Blasts exploded. Energy blades clashed. The front line seethed in close-quarters combat. Crushed and severed bodies floated. The acrid odours of spent weaponry and burnt flesh were thick.

Now hovering shoulder to shoulder with the second line of astral warriors, I saw the Coaliferite troops used blasters to shoot and fought with rounded glowing energy blades rather than the astral-edged blades the astral warriors weilded.

A squad of Coaliferites broke through the first line and charged toward me.

I was alone. No one tried to help as three Coaliferites speared right at me.

"Mother!" I shouted and instinctively thrust my arm.

A first, then second white-hot blast seared from my palm, exploding on two of the attackers an instant before the bone-jarring sensation of high-speed collision demolished me.

I plummeted backwards behind the second line with a Coaliferite squeezing my throat. Of all the terror I experienced at that moment, the acidic stench of my attacker scared me most. I wrenched free, pushed from the attacker, and somersaulted in the zero gravity. As if by magic, an electric-blue-edged blade ignited in my hand.

The Coaliferite surged at me with a red energy blade. Sparks flew as I parried, then stabbed low in attack.

My enemy blocked the blow, but quick as a flash I focused my energy and swung. My blade's electric-blue edge intensified as it cut through my attacker's rounded beam and sliced right through him.

Battle raged in the darkness of space. I hovered open-mouthed, staring from my blade to my attacker's lifeless body floating away.

On the rock in the cave, I felt my pulse spike, and my eyes flicker with rapid eye movement. My consciousness zoomed back.

But I needed more … needed to see my mother again. I had to go back. I concentrated on my breath and tried to relax back into that more than vivid dream. Photius peeked at me through a floor vent. My breath slowed and my pulse relaxed. Deep tones resonated around me. Soulful silky vibrations brought peace.

I yawned, opened my eyes, and blinked. I lay nestled on a bed of swirling white cloud with a magnificent blue sky and golden sunlight above. My mother floated beside me. Her smile bringing pure joy to my heart.

"You are the son of the Duke of Megasis, an astral warrior prince and guardian of the Cintamani Pear," my mother said.

I smiled and rubbed my jaw against my shoulder.

"I don't know if your father or any of our family survived. But you will find your citizens one day. Now show me the Cintamani Pearl."

I wanted to ask questions but couldn't. In the cave on Mokua I took the shining pearl from my pocket, illuminating both the cave and the hand of my astral projection.

"The Cintamani Pearl has the power to alter nature and inspire positive thought. When exposed to the atmosphere and carried by the purest of hearts, the pearl ignites light energy throughout the universe. Beware. Light energy attracts darkness and envy. Too much exposure will invite dark forces. Colours will stabilise within the pearl when the time comes for her to rest beneath a body of water."

I absorbed this information that generated so many more questions.

In the cave, the gecko bobbed its head, sprang from the ceiling, and climbed onto the stone platform beside me. It was as though I was in two places at once.

"If a dark heart controls the Cintamani Pearl, the light within nature and sentient beings will fade. The Coaliferite breathe carbon dioxide and thrive on hot tortured planets. They have killed or enslaved your citizens and taken control of Andromeda. Your purpose is to guard the pearl, grow strong, return to Andromeda, and find the resistance."

White clouds swirled around me. A million questions circled, but I couldn't ask them.

"If Earth's temperature and carbon levels rise, beware. A hideous creature may grow in the core, and a Coaliferite invasion will be imminent. Remember the Coaliferite scent. And be careful; they will infiltrate the human net."

Every hair on my body stood. A deep vibration heightened my projection. I stood in the cloud and tried to say that this was already happening.

"If the Coaliferites invade Earth, keep the Cintamani Pearl at least ten atmospheres beneath water. Wait until you are strong enough to journey to Andromeda."

How would I reach Andromeda? How would I know when I was strong enough? I begged to ask.

"The ring has a cellular memory and will release information when you are ready. Your astral powers are developing. Using visualisation, you will soon have the ability to launch a blast, maintain a blade, and fly. A battle suit will assist in the mastery of both conventional and astral flight," Hila added.

Battle suit? Fly?

A second gecko entered the cavern through a floor vent.

"Beware of the one who betrayed us. He goes by the name of Coaliferos and his eyes are midnight blue. I hope he is dead, but if you ever see him—flee!"

The dark warrior's eyes from the game and the vision were midnight blue. The thought chilled me. *Did Trudock use the dark warrior as his cyber weapon?*

"Your eyes are the blue of the Batavia Tribe. You will be a mighty astral warrior. Know this to be true, my son. Follow your heart and the ring will guide you. And remember an astral warrior needs to laugh and to dance and to love. You may help Earth if the planet is threatened, but most important, you must guard the pearl. Your citizens in Andromeda need you more than you can imagine."

Would I have energy at night now? Questions filled my brain and my mind spun.

"I trust Russell has been a good father to you. Give him my love, and if you see Tali, give her a hug for me."

Tali? My mother knew about the dolphins, but she didn't seem to know Dad was dead. Bliss radiated from her smile and emptied my head of questions. She took me in her arms and squeezed me tight.

"I love you, Sam. Live slow—fly fast, my son."

Although I yearned for her to stay, ecstasy enthralled me as my mother drifted away.

"Look for a present beneath the rock where you lie," she whispered, and merged into the heavens.

73

MORE TREASURE

Two triangular heads with bulging eyes stared at me and nodded. I blinked and propped on my elbows. A shadow moved from a floor vent. The two geckos scurried in short bursts from the stone platform. I raised myself to sit and gazed at the mandala, then at the pearl.

"Me, an astral warrior prince, guardian of the Cintamani Pearl." My voice echoed in the cave. That was too real, too extreme to be a dream. Energy palpitated through my chest, shoulders, forehead, and gums. I smiled and transfixed on the blue and green swirls within the pearl. *Was my heart pure? Was the explosion the light energy? What would the light energy do?*

Seconds passed, and details of my out-of-body experience fragmented like a dream. My mother's warmth and striking emerald eyes came to the fore, and that battle, flying—blasts—energy blades, and that acid smell. And I remembered Matahi saying, "Live slow—fly fast." He must have got it from my mother.

Wind whistled and gusted through the floor vents. The geckos sheltered in a crevice. I stood, strained my ears, and sniffed. My mind flashed back to the loft, Dad's hotel, the battle, and my mother: *If you see the one with midnight blue eyes—flee.*

Thunder rumbled. I froze, my senses reaching. The sun would set in an hour; I thought I should head out to the pool. When I stared at the mandala, I remembered something my mother said: a present, something under a rock.

A dozen small rocks lay scattered. I lifted the largest, but found nothing, and now her words seemed so distant. As I walked to the next rock, too small to conceal much, a faded scuff beside the stone platform snatched my attention.

The platform appeared to be part of the floor. I blew around the base and discovered a crack and two indents I could grip. With legs bent, I pulled and lifted. The stone moved an inch. I shuffled my feet, re-gripped, pulled again, and the slab grated across the floor.

On all fours, I reached into a hole, and felt something cool and smooth. As I lifted the grey micro-octagon material, I caught the faintest scent of my mother.

I marvelled at the weightless grey material. It must have been her battle suit. Shame it was so long and the hips so broad. I stared back into the hole.

"Yes!" I shouted, and my hands trembled as I withdrew wrist armour, and a medallion that glowed blue and emerald like the pearl.

A shadow flickered over a floor vent. "Hello … Photius," I called.

Time to swim outside, catch the last of the sun, and check the gear in better light. I snapped the armour onto my wrist and smiled at the perfect fit. The medallion was round and flat and fitted in my cargo shorts' button-up pocket where I kept the necklace and the data card. I could carry the suit, but then an idea sparked.

Fresh scratches scarred the stone as I dragged the slab back into position. I scuffed over the scratches with my runners, unzipped the one-piece battle suit and inserted a foot, shoe and all, through one leg. With both feet in the suit, I removed the wrist armour and slipped my arms and shoulders inside. Discovering a zip chest pocket, I secured the pearl in it. The suit was all baggy as I zipped up the front. Maybe wearing it wasn't such a good idea, but then my eyes bulged. The material shrank, moulding firmly around my body.

I clicked the wrist armour on, and the medallion fitted into a socket over my heart. Waves of anticipation pulsed as I took to the aquatic tunnel. Water shed from the suit, and pink light glinted on the micro-material as I climbed from the pool.

Lightning flashed through the anvil storm. Steam drifted from the rocky platform, and a leaf floated on a puddle where the dirt trail met the ledge.

Etchings in the wrist armour matched the maze pattern of the ring, and the medallion glowed blue on my chest. On the ledge by the pool, I smiled, shimmied to the side, rolled my hands, leapt into a spin and landed with a sassy clap. Birds chirped and squawked in the forest. I twirled, swung my hips, and wound up to a whip. The glorious Pacific lay before me. I wished Tom and Swathi could see me as I practised a block and punch combination with a side kick finish.

A finch fluttered, bending the branch of a shrub as it landed. I recoiled my arm, visualised a searing blast, and thrust; nothing happened, and I wondered how I'd launched blasts in the dream. The sun sank beneath the storm. It was too real to be a dream.

Returning to the camp seemed the sensible thing to do, but pink and grey clouds stretched across the horizon and lightning flashed in the distant storm. It would be cool to sleep by the pool. Altitude could make the night chilly, but the suit felt so warm and safe and snug. I searched the sky for Photius and scanned the ocean for dolphins and Rambala.

Laughter floated in the breeze.

"Photius," I called, swinging around.

Forked lightning flared. Leaves scattered across the ledge into the pool. I sensed a presence and the faintest acid scent wafted in the breeze.

Thunder ripped and echoed through the heavens. I focused on the rock marking the trail on the other side of the basin. Instincts sparked me into action. Adrenalin injected into my blood. My wet shoes squelched on the rocky ledge as I ran. I prepared to leap over the puddle to the gravelly start of the trail. But from nowhere a dark figure appeared and blocked me.

I gasped and hit the brakes. My feet slid in the puddle, right out from under me. I landed on my back. Air thrust from my lungs and my head whipped against the stone with a loud crack.

74

COALIFEROS

Surprised by the kid slipping and cracking his head, Coaliferos froze. The kid had all the kit, but the battle suit would offer little protection until he depressed and turned the medallion an extra notch.

Coaliferos stared at the ring on the kid's finger, sensed the pearl in the battle suit's chest pocket, and smiled. Planet Earth's oxygen-rich air left him lightheaded, and he inhaled deep breaths. All these years and he'd finally done it. He'd conquered the convergence zone and found the Guardian's Ring and the Cintamani Pearl. Now all he had to do was kill the boy and take the treasures. Destiny restored. *But after all these years, why hurry? Why not take his time and enjoy it?*

The effects of crossing the convergence zone might have weakened him, but the boy posed no threat. Coaliferos gazed at the kid and chuckled. Even without the medallion, if the kid knew how to use the suit it would have projected a shield to protect his head.

The air and the enormity of the occasion left him in a strange euphoric state. He could instruct the kid to lock his medallion into place and make the game interesting.

"Ha, ha," Coaliferos laughed as the kid skittered on his backside away from him.

75

MIDNIGHT BLUE

A high-pitched screech jammed my hearing. I scooted backwards on my butt. My head stung. White blotches blurred my vision.

The dark figure stepped over the puddle.

I scrambled to my feet, turned to run, but staggered. One foot slipped over the edge. I glimpsed sheer cliffs and ocean. My arms skittered as I regained my footing and scrambled.

"Ha-ha." The dark figure ambled toward me. "Nice outfit—with correct visualisation a shield extends from the suit to protect the head."

I backed away, holding my head. The dark figure stood half a meter above me, looked almost human, and laboured for breath. He wore a dark battle suit with wrist armour, and a dark medallion on the chest. I couldn't make out the warrior's eyes, but charred lines marked his ashen face.

"Who are you? What do you want?" I asked.

"I'm your Uncle Coaliferos, and you have two of my possessions." He stared at my ring, then at my battle suit's chest pocket. "I've waited a long time for this moment," he said.

As Coaliferos spoke, my vision cleared. I met his eyes—midnight blue. An acid smell wafted from his breath. I backed to where the volcanic cone rose from the cliffs. That stench, the source of the cyber-attacks and my dad's death stood there threatening me. After all I'd been through, I wasn't surrendering anything. If he kept following, I decided to scoot around the basin, jump the infinity edge, and run for the trail. My heart thudded. Three more paces and I'd run: two, one.

The dark warrior turned, walked in the opposite direction.

Vertical stone cliffs tapered to the middle of the pool on either side of me. If I ran to the left and jumped before the infinity edge, I dropped two hundred metres to dense jungle, and the pool at the bottom of the fall was only two metres deep. To the right, cliffs fell one thousand metres to the sea.

I smelled evil. I was sure Coaliferos had killed my dad, but where did Xcon and the giant serpent fit in? The pearl, the ring, and the battle suit belonged to me. Backing away, I glanced over the edge and wondered if the trees would break my fall.

The dark warrior changed direction and seemed to enjoy herding me.

I shuffled away and felt a sticky mass of hair at the back of my head. I glanced at the blood on my hand and realised I'd gashed my head when I fell. Keeping my distance, I peered over the ledge to the ocean. *If I dived, would I clear the cliffs? Survive the impact with the water?*

Coaliferos strolled a long way around the ledge and jumped the infinity edge, leaving the trail wide open. He was playing games with me.

My temples throbbed. Adrenaline surged through me.

The dark warrior stopped. "You want to go that way? Be my guest," he said, sweeping a hand toward the trail.

As lightning flashed, I feigned to run, but hesitated.

"Ha!" Coaliferos laughed and jumped back over the streaming water. "The ring and the pearl are mine. The suit and the wrist armour belonged to your whore mother."

I gritted my teeth. My attachment to the ring and the pearl strengthened.

"Are you a Coaliferite?" I asked, stepping toward the fall.

"I am an astral warrior," Coaliferos replied.

"How come your skin is so pale and your breath stinks so bad?"

Coaliferos froze. His smirk vanished. He recoiled his arm and thrust. A dark-blue blast rocketed from his palm.

I threw my right arm up and ducked.

The blast exploded on my wrist armour. Sparks spat. My arm flopped limp. A white-hot ache paralysed my shoulder.

"Ha-ha," Coaliferos laughed.

Acrid smoke drifted. I held my dead arm to my chest.

Coaliferos changed direction and jumped the watercourse, daring me to run.

"Deflecting a blast is easier." Coaliferos smirked. I'm sure he was about to tell me something else, but he cut himself short. There was something about him that made me think he was a little drunk or something. He smiled and chuckled and thrust a second blast.

The blast shot straight at my chest. I stepped away and clipped it with the wrist armour on my left arm. The blast deflected and exploded on the rock behind me. Sparks scorched the raw wound on the back of my head. My left arm turned to jelly. I smelled burning, fought to swallow the pain, and my whole body trembled as I struggled to extinguish my smouldering hair.

The dark warrior sauntered farther, leaving an escape path wide open. A blade ignited in his hand. Sunset reflected on the shiny metallic flat of the blade, and a thin midnight-blue strip pulsated around the edges.

The blade set my pulse thumping triple time. I sucked in breath and tried to stop shaking. Escape from blades and blast fire seemed impossible. I had to buy time.

"Do you work for Xcon?" I asked.

"Work for humans?" Coaliferos laughed. "I control idiots like Trudock."

I didn't know whether to believe him. But maybe this was the missing piece of the puzzle.

"Do you know about the giant serpent?"

Coaliferos changed direction, smirked, and strutted around the pool so that he had twice the distance to reach the trail as me.

"The Zorag warms the planet for the Coaliferite invasion. When temperature and carbon levels reach a tipping point, the Coaliferite will attack Earth and set all the forests ablaze. Humans will become slaves. All your friends will die a slow, carbon-poisoned death."

I shook my head. The Coaliferite planned to invade Earth and kill my friends. I had to stop them. Coaliferos must be working with Trudock to accelerate global warming. I wanted to lash out at Coaliferos, but how could I fight an alien warrior?

"How do you travel through the net and kill people?" I asked.

"Masters of the astral arts have great powers. You were lucky to escape, but I had the pleasure of sucking the life from Russell Edwards." Coaliferos dashed his blade into the pool, splashing sizzling water.

Rage erupted inside me. I shielded my face and ran.

Coaliferos darted, impossibly fast, blocked the escape and dashed more sizzling water.

I backed against the towering stone cliffs. Strength returned to my left arm, but my right arm remained numb.

A second blade ignited in Coaliferos's free hand.

I sensed a fatal collision and swayed left, then right. I needed to run, do something.

Faster than I believed possible, Coaliferos cleared the pool in a lightning leap. Blades exploded into the stone at either side of my neck, crossing my throat.

Unable to move in any direction, I closed my eyes. I couldn't escape. Coaliferos was too fast, too powerful. All I could do was surrender, give him what he wanted, and hope to survive.

Just as I gave up hope, Oko appeared in my head: *Power comes from the mind. Your opponent may be bigger, stronger, and possess superior technique, but when mind and soul synchronise, the universe will conspire to protect you.*

Heat from the blades blistered my neck. I lifted my chin and Captain Laurie's voice whispered, *Boldness has power and magic.*

I stared into my attacker's midnight-blue eyes. Seeing my gaze steel, Coaliferos sneered and crossed his blades tighter until the flesh on my neck burned.

I ignored the sting, the smell, my imminent death. I clenched my teeth and glimpsed failure in my attacker's eyes.

"You're just a scared bully," I said.

The dark warrior's forehead wrinkled. With a swish and flurry, talons collided into his ashen face. The blades loosened on my neck. I ducked, ran a step, but a humming blade stopped me.

Photius beat his wings to escape. A second blade streaked through the air and sliced through feathers.

"Photius!" I cried.

The falcon flopped and tumbled over the ledge. I couldn't tell if Photius had survived. Anger and determination gushed from my heart.

Coaliferos held one injured eye shut; blood ran from gashes around the other.

"The time for games is over," he said and levelled the blue edge of his humming blade to my throat.

"Wait! Have the ring, the pearl—anything," I held the ring up to Coaliferos.

The dark warrior hesitated.

My arm trembled as I pretended to twist the ring from my finger. I turned it to the left and to the right.

Coaliferos stared at the turning ring and his eyes glazed as though he'd remembered something.

I thrust the ball of my foot into his groin and shoved. Coaliferos gasped and fell back. His blades extinguished as he splashed into the pool.

My runners squelched as I bolted to escape. The trail was ten metres ahead. Sheer cliffs dropped one thousand metres to the ocean beside me.

Dark fury erupted from the water. The speed at which Coaliferos recovered stunned me. He flew through the air, blades igniting to end my life.

I turned to face the dark warrior. To avoid certain death, I leapt backwards over the cliff.

Coaliferos stared over the ledge as I plummeted, back first. Barely registering what had happened, I bounced on a rocky jut. Air shot from my lungs. I somersaulted into a ragged tumble. Clutching my hands to my chest, I depressed the medallion, which turned and clicked into place. Energy surged through my body. I arched my back and flipped to fall on my stomach.

Jagged rocks flashed close. With arms tucked against my sides, I tracked away from the cliff. Sensing danger, I glanced up. Coaliferos rocketed toward me.

I braced for collision. Right before impact, I flinched and darted as though jet propelled. Coaliferos streaked past, clutching for traction.

I plummeted for the ocean. Coaliferos recoiled his palm and thrust.

I tried to dart, but nothing happened. The dark blue blast rocketed straight at me. At the last instant, I surged left, dodged the blast, charged past Coaliferos, and streamlined for the water. The memory of busting my back in the beach pool flickered as I torpedoed into the sea.

Elongated bubbles streamed from my fingertips as I speared deep. The suit protected my head. As quick as the magical power came, jet propulsion deserted me. Eerie brown light wallowed on the surface, and I couldn't see Coaliferos. I hovered and, sensing a tremor, swung around. The tremor intensified into a quake. Mokua Island and the sea floor shook.

76

THE ZORAG

The Zorag snaked through the lava reservoir and blasted through the wall of the Tonga Trench. Its fiery eyes smouldered and its tongue flickered, tasting the vibrations. Its body extended through the Earth's mantle, and the vibrations it sensed triggered a longing. The longing built to frustration. Frustration vented as anger.

The Zorag bellowed a thunderous roar and its massive body expanded. Planet Earth shook. Faults splintered. Cracks formed. A kilometre section of the Tonga Trench wall slipped and crumbled into the depths.

77

DEATH

I hovered at thirty metres below. A terrifying rumbling boomed through the water. I searched below, left, right, above.

Fading light wallowed on the surface. From beneath the sea, I thought the sky was falling. Boulders splashed. Masses of bubbles streaked from slabs. A rock the size of a coconut struck my head. A car-sized slab crashed down towards me; I pushed away, swimming hard from the island. Rocks and boulders rained down. A whole section of cliff must have plummeted from Mokua.

As the quake eased, the boulder storm abated. Sediment dirtied the water. The ocean fell quiet. Only the faintest light glimmered on the surface.

I hoped a boulder had killed Coaliferos, but I sensed his evil presence. I jerked to my left: nothing. I swung in the opposite direction. Sediment reduced my vision. With a shiver, I stroked for the surface. Kicking, reaching, faster I swam. Just before I breached, a dark blue blast streaked from the murk and torpedoed me.

I experienced no pain and surfaced. A field sparked around me. A second, then third blast slammed into my gut. Around me, a translucent shield became semi-visible and stuttered.

Coaliferos came up under me, grabbed me by the throat and testicles, held me above his head, and hovered a metre above the sea.

I kicked and punched. The grip on my testicles tightened. I screamed. Crushing pressure throttled my throat, cutting my scream and the blood flow to my brain. I swung feeble round-arm blows. The stench of his breath wafted as Coaliferos tightened his grip.

In one last effort, I gritted my teeth and tried to kick, but my body fell limp. Unable to fight back, I thought of my dad, Oko, the pearl. Life couldn't end. Not like this.

Coaliferos released my testicles. Impossible as it seemed, the release hurt more than the grip. It was as if he'd ripped the heart out of me as he took the pearl from my battle suit pocket. A distant voice repeated in my head: *The pearl, save Andromeda, save Earth, the dolphins, Matahi Island, life can't end like this.*

I didn't have a shred of energy to react as Coaliferos pulled and twisted my ring. It jammed behind my knuckle. The Dark Warrior released my throat, gripped me by the wrist, and ignited a blade.

I couldn't draw breath. My vision blurred. I dangled with my feet just above the surface. My consciousness drifted. As though watching from above, I could see Coaliferos preparing to cut my finger off. Beneath the water, Tali circled. She was searching for a weakness to attack. I heard her transmit her thoughts to Bola: The eyes, head, and neck look vulnerable.

"No Tali, save yourself, save the pod," I tried to say.

Thrusting their tails, Tali and Bola launched from the ocean in unison. Black and white streaks shot from the water, slamming into Coaliferos' neck and the side of his head.

I fell and splashed into the ocean. Miki rushed to me.

Coaliferos swung his blade in a glowing arc aimed at my head. Bola leapt from the water between us. The dark warrior's blade cut Bola in two.

"No," I groaned, too weak to move.

Miki tried to tow me away.

Coaliferos raised his blade and focused his bloodthirsty rage on me.

"Go. Save yourself, Miki," I pleaded. This was my battle. I was ready to die.

As though looking through a remote eye I could see Tali eyeballing my attacker. Time Slowed. Visions of Tali's life flashed before me: when she was young, swimming in cool slate-blue water with Bola.

Tali swimming with my mother. And I heard her last thoughts: *I can save myself or fight for the ocean, fight for Miki, and for future generations.*

I gasped back into my body. Sound distorted to slow-motion wailing. Blue-edged blades sizzled and spat amongst masses of splashing. Breath wheezed into my lungs. Blood pumped through my brain. Miki's fin pressed into my armpit, towing me away. Coaliferos came for me. His astral blade humming and spitting dark energy.

Tali erupted from the water, speared at Coaliferos's eyes.

Coaliferos' blade spat as he severed Tali in two.

"No!" I shouted. Miki wailed. Kota's fin cut through the water as he darted back and forth.

Blood dripped from Coaliferos. He hovered, staring into the water. Massacred dolphin parts bobbed. The water was blood red. The dark warrior's blade smouldered midnight blue. He held the pearl between his thumb and forefinger and gloated.

Every molecule of my being vibrated.

Coaliferos gripped the Cintamani Pearl in his fist and attacked me with his blade.

Miki flicked from me, readied to intercept.

I drew my arm back. "Leave my friends alone!" I shouted—and thrust. A pure white blast shot from the heel of my palm and cannoned into Coaliferos' chest.

The dark warrior's blade collapsed. His eyes boggled; his jaw dropped. A field stuttered and sparked around him, then stabilised.

I recoiled my arm and thrust again, but nothing happened. I thrust again—no blast … nothing.

Coaliferos' stunned look turned to anger. His face contorted into a smirk. He ignited a blade.

Wind ruffled the ocean. Lightning flashed in the stormy sky. I pushed Miki and Kota aside. "Go! Save yourselves," I pleaded.

The pearl glowed dark blue through Coaliferos' left hand.

Kota charged. Coaliferos swung.

Kota veered, but the blade sliced the tip of his fin.

"No!" I bellowed and tried to blast him again.

Miki launched. The blue edge flashed as Coaliferos struck Miki above the eye, then he thrust the blade at me.

I swept my arms up, tried to duck below the water. I was too slow. The blue tip speared towards my eyes.

Water erupted. The blue blade jolted. Bone crunching sounds made me shiver. The blade extinguished. An almighty thrashing whipped Coaliferos about.

"Rambala!" I shouted.

Bloodied water sprayed. The Cintamani Pearl flew from the dark warrior's grasp as Rambala monstered Coaliferos and ripped and tore his body in two.

I traced the pearl through the air, ducked my head below water. The blue and emerald glow sank through turbid sea. I dived and swam with all the strength that remained in me.

The glow faded into the murky depths. In blind pursuit, I drew jerky strokes. Kota pushed up under me, and with no energy to resist, I surfaced.

Kota's raw fin butted under my arm, and the dolphin swam me away from the island.

"Where's Miki? Oh God. Miki," I sobbed.

Kota pushed me beyond the island shelf, and then I saw it.

"Oh shit," I gasped.

Dark and smooth, ready to swallow everything in its path. Up I floated. Energy from the depths surged up under me, then sucked me toward the island. The tsunami steepened, thundered into the cliffs, and bounced.

Raging ocean filled the sky.

A mountain of water extinguished my light.

78

POWER OF THE PEARL

s darkness enveloped Mokua, a fresh breeze fanned across the Pacific. The breeze swept smog from Beijing, leaving the air fresh and jasmine fragrant. Temperatures cooled in the Middle East and Africa. Populations throughout Europe inhaled sweet air and smiled at the wonderful blue sky.

Clouds swirled into thick blankets over the poles, and snow fell as blizzards set in. In Asia, South America, and Australia, forests seeded clouds; raindrops sizzled and spat as they teemed over raging wildfires and dampened the dust of once fertile plains.

At the foot of London Bridge, the bells of St Magnus-the-Martyr chimed. Beneath the lofty steeple, a public service began to pray for the safe return of Russell and Sam Edwards. The side doors thrust open, throwing light on the pew where Swathi and Tom sat, and a breeze, so energetic and fresh, filled the church.

"He's here, I can feel him," whispered Swathi.

A new day dawned over New York, and with finger-feathers reaching, a red-tailed hawk glided high above the city. Sunrise sparkled over the Atlantic, and the Statue of Liberty shone with a golden aura. From amongst the dry tan leaves of a white oak, a squirrel stood on its hind legs, twitched, and inhaled a breeze that was fresh and full of vitality. A walker passing under the oak stared into the magnificent clear blue sky and marvelled at the hawk gliding above the towers.

Dazzling light reflected from the chrome fuselage of a chopper beating through the air. The walker shielded her eyes. The hawk dipped, blinking to recover from temporary blindness, and the chopper's rotor sliced through a flock of pigeons before landing on Trudock Tower.

Atlo sprang from the door with his briefcase in hand. Wind from the rotor ruffled his hair, a grin lit his face, and he stared at the wonderful sky. He saluted the Statue of Liberty. Not even the loss of his favourite destroyer troubled him this morning. He sensed it coming. His great fossil fuel sell-off and switch to renewables had taken all and sundry by surprise. This sparkling morning confirmed it; he could smell his latest interests preparing to rocket, and he would invest the profits in space warfare, his latest hobby.

"Today is perfect," he shouted, and with arms and bag outstretched, he twirled in two complete circles.

The guards at the entrance raised their eyebrows, glanced at each other, and stiffened as Atlo approached and stopped before them with a beaming smile.

"Is young Jackson playing ball again this summer?" Atlo asked.

"Yes, sir," one guard said.

"Good," Atlo said, and he addressed the second guard. "Are the twins enjoying their first year of school?"

"Yes, sir," the second guard said, surprised that Atlo remembered he even had children.

"Good, and are your wives well?"

"Yes, sir," they answered, smiled, and nodded.

"You guys do such a fantastic job," Atlo took two folds of new thousand-dollar bills from his jacket pocket.

"Take the day off, treat your families. If we have visitors, I'll let them in myself."

Atlo moonwalked between the waterfalls of his aquatic entrance. He took coffee at his desk, clicked his fingers to open the curtain, reclined in his chair, and imagined the Great Lady coming alive and speaking to him. The day was crisper and clearer than he believed possible. Even better than the day his daddy had died and left him the inheritance.

"Archive the footage of today and update the perfect-day window hologram … and let's hear what that raving old shock jock has to say," Atlo said.

"Yes, Sir," his secretary replied through the intercom.

Without a care in the world, Atlo sat back and listened as drums and trumpets sounded and the song *El Presidente*, a 1964 South of the Border classic, introduced the radio program.

"Good morning, universe, this is Radley Jones, welcome to breakfast in New York."

Atlo shook his head. "That man is so full of himself."

"And what a stunning morning," Radley enthused, "there has never been a better day to be alive. I bear news that will both delight and shock you. First, blizzards dumped unprecedented snow on the South and North Poles overnight. The blizzards appear set in, and later in the show we explore the question: Can these blizzards restore the ice caps?

Remarkable news from China: The President of the People's Republic will soon meet with the Dalai Lama to discuss reconciliation. And peace in the Middle East—heard that one before, I hear you say … well, Radley Jones speaking—believe it."

"So up on himself," Atlo said.

"But the most astounding news comes from right here in New York. To my compatriots waking to this perfect fall morning in New York, this will stun you. For the first time in a century, NYPD reported no murders in our great city overnight—no murders! Why didn't anybody kill somebody last night?"

79

PRINCESS LANI

Planet Earth turned the Pacific toward the sun. East of the Tonga Trench, a soft glow caressed the curved horizon. A white helicopter circled Mokua. With her hands clutching her heart, Princess Lani searched the island. *Where was Sam? Why didn't he come to her party? Did he survive the tsunami?*

The sand spit had vanished, the rocky point diminished, a whole section of the cliffs obliterated. The beach was a mass of uprooted trees and mud. Lani wiped a tear from her eye. Her favourite island was a mess, but at least island and cove pools had survived.

"Photius," Lani called.

The sight of the falcon gliding from the peak made her smile, but then she saw that half his tail feathers were missing. He was flying okay and she wondered what had happened to him. Photius glided close to the chopper and as she gazed at the magnificent raptor it was as though she sensed Sam's essence.

"I'm going to find him," she whispered. "We'll meet again someday."

She thought how shy Sam was, but that was kind of cute, and he wasn't great at conversation, but he'd started to come out of his shell. She still couldn't believe how he'd farted and tried to hide it when they first met. That solar narcolepsy stuff was weird. And he acted as if he was guarding a deep secret. It seemed as if he struggled to be himself. But beneath the confused exterior, his warmth and strength enthralled her. She'd never met anyone like him.

Lani smiled as she imagined camping alone on the island with Sam, swimming with the dolphins, exploring the cave and the Mandala, and who knows what else they could find.

"Princess Lani, shall we turn back now?" the pilot asked.

"No, circle the island once more please, and hover close by island pools this time."

80

THE PUREST HEART

Sixty miles southeast of Mokua, flying fish scattered. A blue-footed booby launched from *Atlanta's* mast, swooped, and plucked a tasty fish for breakfast. Behind the wheel, Captain Laurie snored on a bed of cushions with Wiggols curled in his armpit. Beneath the timber deck, the slap of waves set cups chinking. Scents of old wood mixed with fresh paint and autopilot grated into action.

My eyes blinked open, the lapping and the motion so familiar. I thought I must be dreaming, and my eyes blinked shut, then open again. I was aboard *Atlanta. How was it possible?* I turned to the empty bunk where Oko used to sleep.

I sat up and inspected my battle suit, wrist armour, and medallion. The ring, I still had the ring. Cutlery clinked in the galley as *Atlanta* rolled with a swell. *But what happened to the pearl? To Miki and Kota?*

"Shit!" My stomach twisted. My pulse quickened. I relived the battle with Coaliferos, the wave, Tali, Bola, Kota and Miki—my fallen friends.

How did I end up on *Atlanta*? Tali, Miki and Kota—shit. The pearl—shit. I pictured Rambala slamming Coaliferos, the pearl flying from his grasp, and the blue-green glow sinking into the depths. My mother's image: *Your purpose is to guard the pearl.*

My whole body ached. I ran my hands over bandages covering my head and neck. I prized my wrist armour free and unzipped the battle suit. My right arm and shoulder were black and blue. I struggled to slip from the suit, and my tan shorts and blue t-shirt were dry underneath.

How did Laurie find me? I slid my legs over the bunk, and a sharp pain stabbed my groin. I undid the button and zip of my shorts, lifted the elastic of the boxers, and winced at the sight of my swollen testicles.

A swell slapped against the hull and autopilot grated into action. Using my hands to support my weight, I limped into the main cabin. Tears welled in my eyes as I thought of Miki and Tali and Oko. I climbed the first step on the ladder and stared through the hatch.

The sky was light blue, and sunrise was just minutes away. Wiggols's tail thumped the deck. I eased up onto the second step. Wiggols trotted over and his tongue felt smooth as he licked my face.

Laurie inhaled a raspy snore. I gripped the coach house, climbed into the cockpit, and leaned back on the panel beside the stairs. Wiggols jumped up on the coach house; I massaged his neck and scoured the ocean. Laurie sucked another snore, the sun peeped over the horizon, and a breeze so fresh and pure swept *Atlanta*.

The sea sparkled. The sky vibrated blue. Wiggols gave a muffled woof. I followed the dog's eyes, and my heart jumped out of my chest.

"Miki! Kota!" I shouted.

Sun glistened on their backs as they launched and leapt.

I cried. Staggered to the rail, fell to my knees.

"AAMM, AAMM," they chirped.

All my pain vanished. I hung over the side.

"Thank you so much," I sobbed.

The tip of Kota's dorsal fin was blunt and raw. A blistered wound swelled and bulged around Miki's eye and she held her jaw open awkwardly, as though it was broken.

I wept. "I'm so sorry, I'm so sorry."

My fingertips skimmed over Miki's skin.

"Welcome to the land of the living."

I looked up, and Laurie was smiling at me.

"How did you know? Why did you come back?"

"I have a sixth sense for danger," Laurie said.

I grinned, almost laughed.

"Yeah—no one believes me," Laurie shook his head, "and thank your friends … they brought you alongside. I wouldn't have found you without them."

"Thank you, Laurie," I said.

Laurie stared at Miki and Kota. "Oko?"

"He didn't survive diving the trench."

Laurie's head dropped.

I nodded and sat up as Laurie turned for the steps.

"I'll make some tea and we can debrief over backgammon," Laurie said.

"Tea sounds good, but I don't want to play backgammon right now."

"Okay, maybe later."

"Yes, later." I gazed out to sea. "Where are we headed?"

"Australia." Laurie descended onto the first rung of the ladder. "I still have some frozen mahi-mahi from the *Makomaile*, might thaw some steaks for lunch."

"Do you have fillets?" I asked.

"I thought you liked steaks."

"I prefer fillets."

Laurie nodded and descended another step. "Oh, yeah—what's with the outfit? I couldn't get it off you."

"I missed Princess Lani's party. Someone left their fancy-dress gear behind, and I tried on the suit before the tsunami struck."

Laurie raised his eyebrows. "Nice bit of gear." He half concealed a smile. "I tuned in to a local news broadcast last night. The tsunami caused widespread destruction, but Princess Lani made a good speech to unite her people," he said and backed below.

It was a relief to hear Lani was safe, and I wondered what she was doing now. *Was she angry I'd missed her party? Was she thinking about me? And what was Mokua like after the quake and the Tsunami?* Somehow, I'd get back to Mokua one day. I still had the necklace for Lani, and I smiled as I imagined giving it to her.

Miki and Kota streaked through the water beside *Atlanta*. I hung over the side and watched them, wondering about the giant serpent heating the ocean. My heart was heavy with grief when I remembered Tali and Bola's death. I shivered as I relived the moment Rambala thrashed Coaliferos about. Miki and Kota had survived, so Rambala should be okay. That shark and the dolphins had saved me. They were helping me to save the Earth. And surely Coaliferos must be dead.

"PFFFH." Miki surfaced, mist floated, and Kota breached beside her. *Atlanta* rode a swell and my hand brushed the water. At least Miki and Kota lived. Coaliferos had sliced the tip of Kota's fin, but time should heal it. The blistered skin above Miki's eye should recover too, but her jaw, that bulge, she didn't seem able to shut her mouth. She might not be able to eat.

Tears flooded my eyes. Miki had the purest of hearts, and it was entirely my fault.

Miki swam on her side, staring at me through the water. Her mouth looked all wrong, but her eyes smiled at me.

"AAMM," she mumbled, swished her tail and came right alongside.

I reached out to her.

On a rising swell, she lifted her head and tossed the Cintamani Pearl into my hands.

The End

ACKNOWLEDGEMENTS

A huge thanks to Emma and Abi for their patience and to Mali for being my beta reader, to Mum and Dad for their feedback and help with editing, to Tom Flood for his guidance and encouragement, to Scarlett for helping to whip an early version into shape, to Leslie Dahl for polishing the manuscript, and to Peta for perfecting the written sound of a dolphin exhaling.

If you enjoyed *The Hero Gene*, please leave a review!
Goodreads: https://www.goodreads.com/stevenjdoyle
Facebook: @stevenjdoylebooks

If you'd like to join the tribe and be the first to receive a sneak preview
of Book 2 *Solar Active Man*, I invite you to subscribe to *The Hero Gene
News*: https://theherogene.com

Live slow—Fly fast
Steven J Doyle

ABOUT THE AUTHOR

Steven lives with his wife, two children, and two dogs on Australia's East Coast. An off-grid micro-hydro and solar power system produce his household energy. His wonder of space and passion for nature and the ocean fuels his writing. His favourite place to write is at the desk in the back of his kombi, overlooking a local surf break.

While working with renewable energy has been the focus of Steven's career, his thirst for adventure has led him to sail across oceans and work as a scuba instructor on the Great Barrier Reef. He sold the renewable energy company he founded to begin a live-aboard sailing adventure with his family and finish writing, *The Hero Gene*. He's also a director on OzGREEN's board and supports their flagship program, Youth Leading the World.

Despite the ever-increasing demands placed upon the environment, Steven remains positive that humanity will rise to the challenge of minimising global warming and conserving nature for future generations. He's inspired by today's young activists and their fight to bring about positive change

COMPETITION

Win a limited-edition Hero Gene organic cotton T-shirt!

Two real-life figures provided a little inspiration for one of *The Hero Gene's* characters. By combining parts of their names, I came up with one surname.

One is a very high-profile US citizen, the other a powerful Australian born businessman now living in the US.

Who are the real-life figures behind the name?

For a chance to win one of the monthly draws through to Dec 2021—join the tribe @ theherogene.com and email your answer.